The Coming Woman

A Novel

Based on the Life of the Infamous Feminist, Victoria C. Woodhull

KAREN J. HICKS

SARTORIS
LITERARY
GROUP

A traditional publisher with a non-traditional approach to publishing

SARTORIS LITERARY GROUP
P.O. Box 4185
Brandon, MS 39047
www.sartorisliterary.com

Thank you to Twyla Lambert Clark, who first made me aware of Victoria Woodhull and encouraged me to tell her story

Chapter 1

The early spring drizzle on Great Jones Street doesn't deter newsboys from hawking the April 2, 1870 headlines up and down the thoroughfare between the beer gardens and dance halls of the Bowery and the opulent emporiums of Broadway.

"Petticoat Politician Victoria C. Woodhull to run for President!"

"Indian raids in Wyoming!"

"Sergeant Patrick Gass of Lewis and Clark expedition dies at ninety-eight!"

The heavy, mahogany front door at No. 17 flies open. Victoria Woodhull, lithe and fair at thirty, skips lightly down the steps of the elegant four-story brownstone. Her bobbed and curled brown hair bounces gently against her high forehead. A diamond ring glitters on her right thumb.

"Queen of Finance takes on Government!" yells a newsboy.

Victoria smiles as she hails him. He hands her a *New York Herald*.

"So Mrs. Woodhull is to run for President, is she?" she asks. "What do you think of that?"

"No offense or nuthin' to you as a woman, Ma'am, but it's plum crazy." The boy looks down and shuffles his feet.

Another newsboy waves and calls out, "Mornin', Mrs. Woodhull! You're stirrin' things up for sure today!" He runs on yelling: "Bewitching Broker in dash to the White House!"

The mortified boy on the steps turns as red as the fresh rose pinned to the black velvet band at Victoria's throat. She pats his cheek; her laughter is soft and melodic.

"Don't be embarrassed, son. I'm sure you won't be the only one of your opinion. And I shouldn't have tricked you. Here's an extra penny to apologize."

"Thank you, Ma'am!" The boy scoots away, calling out: "Asa Brainard pitches fifteenth straight win for Cincinnati Red Stockings! New York Knickerbockers can't stop 'em!"

Victoria skips back up the steps, flipping through the newspaper. Glancing up as she opens the door, she spies tall, scarecrow-looking Stephen Pearl Andrews skirting puddles, hurrying toward her. His bony nose, bushy gray hair, and grizzled beard glisten with droplets of rain. His calf-length black coat flaps wildly in the breeze. Victoria grins and goes to meet him, blue eyes sparkling like sunlit waves. She takes his arm and Andrews' wildness softens at her touch. He pats her hand.

"So did the *Herald* print your announcement?" he asks.

"The entire thing! And Ashley Cole wrote the perfect headline and introduction!"

"You are on your way to your destiny, *la mia stella.*"

Inside the house, Victoria walks past tall vases of fragrant flowers and a staircase that curls upward to the second floor. She stops at a marble statue of the famous Greek orator Demosthenes—classic tunic, laced sandals, laurel wreath on his head.

"Demosthenes' promise to me as a child—that I would live in a mansion in a city surrounded by ships and rule my people—It's all coming true! How do you say thank you in Greek, Pearl?"

"*Efharisto.*"

"*Efharisto*, Demosthenes! I will fight for freedom for our people as you did for the Greeks." She pecks Andrews on the cheek. "Demosthenes' prophecy has driven my entire life, Pearl, but you are his corporeal representation and have given me the courage to act on it. So thank you, too."

"Yes, yes. Let's look at this announcement now."

Victoria opens the *Herald* to page eight, and Andrews reads the headline aloud.

"'The Coming Woman, Victoria C. Woodhull, to race for the White House: What she will and what she won't do . . . New ideas on government.'" He beams proudly. "Victoria, a Golden Age is upon us, and you are going to lead it!"

"Come, Pearl, we must tell the family!" She takes Andrews' arm and hurries down the hallway, a spring in her step. Andrews reluctantly allows himself to be dragged along. The cacophony of voices increases as they near the kitchen, and Andrews slows his stride even more. Victoria chuckles. "Come now, you're not going to the gallows."

"I think I would rather," Andrews mutters.

They enter the kitchen, where Victoria's mother Roxanna Claflin, a short, stern woman with tightly curled gray hair, sits at the foot of the table, carping with a heavy German accent. She glares at Andrews through round, wire-rimmed glasses. Victoria's quarrelsome father Buck, whose sharp features are made more ominous by a black patch over his left eye, is at the table's head. The long, wooden benches along each side hold over a dozen sisters, husbands, and children.

Victoria's youngest sister Tennessee looks up excitedly. Tennie is twenty-five, shorter than Victoria, and fashionably plump. Her dark hair is an unruly mop of short, tousled curls, and her eyes resemble deep wells of melted chocolate.

"Did they print it?" she asks.

"Every word!" Victoria says.

Colonel James Blood, Victoria's dark and dashing Civil War hero husband, walks over and kisses his wife. She kisses him back, and then hugs her daughter Zulu Maud. The girl's eyes light up with adoration, looking like a sunny, summer sky. Victoria tries to hug her son Byron as well, but he jerks away, spilling his milk. Byron is physically large for his fifteen years, but mentally he is still a five-year-old. He grins a toothless grin as Zulu Maud sops up the milk. The family begins to bicker.

"My god, people!" Tennie yells, clapping for attention. "Shut up for five minutes and let Victoria read the paper! History is being made here."

"Well, whoop-dee-do and hullabaloo. Who gives a hoot." Victoria's sister Utica stands. Wobbles. She's only twenty-nine years old, but alcohol and drugs have stolen her beauty and zest. She staggers out.

Roxanna pushes back from the table, her face blotched with anger. She glares at the Colonel. "It's you, Mr. Hellbound Blood!" She turns her fury on Andrews next. "And you and your passel of Free-lovers!

You've led my baby onto this path that will destroy her and all of us along with her!"

"Oh for heaven's sakes," sister Polly snaps. "Victoria is not going to the White House. What party will support her? We're just poor people from Ohio."

"Mr. Lincoln was a poor boy from Illinois," Pearl counters. "And look what a fine president he turned out to be."

"Yeah, he was so fine someone shot him," Polly says.

"That's what I mean! You want someone to shoot you, Victoria?" Roxanna rushes out, wailing hysterically in German.

"My god, Sis, you better read before somebody else has a hissy fit."

"I can't. Not with Mama so upset."

She hands the paper to Tennie, who skims the page.

"My god, look at the end! 'Victory for Victoria in 1872!' Whatta brick ol' Ashley is!"

"Miss Claflin, it's unladylike to use such slang," Pearl scolds. "But a fine prediction nonetheless. You must tell your friend I applaud him. I couldn't have written a better introduction to Victoria's announcement."

"At least not in so few words," Tennie teases. She hands the paper to Colonel Blood.

"Ashley probably should have left out this part about Victoria winning if women are allowed to vote. The male zeitgeist will bury a suffrage amendment for sure now," Blood says.

"I agree," Andrews says. "I'm sure he meant it as a vote of confidence, but politicos are threatened by anyone with an intelligent thought and the courage to voice it. Especially if that person is a woman."

"Well, they're just going to have to get used to it," Victoria says. "I'm going to pursue this to the end and with the Spirits' blessing I will win."

Chapter 2

The same morning, inside the redbrick mansion at 10 Washington Street, one of the few remaining homes of wealth in this once fashionable neighborhood near Wall Street, Commodore Cornelius Vanderbilt breakfasts with his dutiful son William. Each has his head buried in a section of the *Herald*. The shipping and railroad tycoon is the richest, most powerful man in America, and his appearance reflects it. At seventy-eight, he is six-foot-one and still slender and handsome. His receding white hair is carefully groomed, and sideburns feather down his jaw line. His black suit is elegantly tailored, and the white ascot at his throat sets off piercing black eyes.

Portly William Vanderbilt scratches his bushy, mutton-chop sideburns as he reads. He frowns when his father gooses the pretty, young Irish maid who pours tea.

"Father, act your age!"

"I'll act any way I mad-dog want to, Billy Boy."

At forty-nine, William is a shrewd businessman who runs Vanderbilt's railroads, but he wilts under his father's gaze and goes back to reading. Suddenly he whistles.

"Well, well, did you know about this, Father?"

"What's that, Billy Boy?"

"Your little friend's sister— Listen to this: 'I therefore claim the right to speak for the un-enfranchised women of the country, and believing that the prejudices that still exist against women in public life will soon disappear, I announce myself candidate for the Presidency.'"

The Commodore laughs uproariously.

"I wouldn't laugh too hard. She wants to redistribute the country's wealth by nationalizing the railroads. Talk about biting the hand that feeds you."

"It's mighty fortunate you made the wise decision to marry me last year instead of that tramp sister of hers, Cornele," Mrs. Frank Vanderbilt says, walking over. She is a tall woman and looks more feminine than her name implies. "You'd be right in the middle of the ridicule."

"For once we agree, Mrs. Vanderbilt," William says. "It's bad enough he sponsors their banking firm."

"Billy, yer a goddamn blatherskite!"

"I don't want them coming here anymore!" Frank straightens into a queenly pose and faces her husband with bravado. "Talking to spirits is evil. Let the dead rest."

"Confound it all, Mrs. Woodhull brought money into this house consulting those Spirits! We might have become paupers last September if she and Tennessee hadn't warned me that Fisk, Gould, and the President were plotting to corner the gold."

"Mr. Grant wasn't involved—"

"Don't be a blockhead, Billy! You think his own brother-in-law would act without the General's knowledge for god's sake?"

"I'm not going to argue with you, Father, but how long are those hussies going to make you pay for that fluke of advice?"

"Them gals don't make me do nuthin'! I gave 'em a start, but they've made their own way. Got more sense than all my sons put together!" He yanks the napkin from his collar, throws it on the table, and strides out.

~ ~ ~

The pandemonium of trading—mostly of Erie, Harlem, and Northern Pacific railroad stocks—stops when Cornelius Vanderbilt strides into the New York Stock Exchange. A flick of his hand resumes the frenzy. Since the day is gloomy, the wide front doors are propped open to let in light and fresh air. Square columns rise to arches above the mezzanine, where full-length, domed windows provide additional light. The elegant fleurs-de-lis décor seems at odds with the raucous business being conducted by some six hundred traders who mill about the vast open floor. Vanderbilt maneuvers his way through the frenzy, stopping to shake Blood's hand.

"Tell Victoria she pumped my blood up good this morning," he tells Blood. "The reaction of my wife and son to her announcement added considerable spice to my breakfast."

"I'll let her know. She's serious about this, you know, and as Cole said in his article, she has the merits of novelty, enterprise, courage, and determination."

"That she does. And I'm sure she'll tackle this competition with the same gusto she brought to Wall Street. I'm right proud to know the three of you."

"Thank you, Sir. Are you coming to the reception?"

"Nah, can't make it. Got me a race in the park and game of whist. But tell the gals I'll be cheerin' 'em on."

"I'll do that, Sir. Your support means a lot to them."

The Commodore pats Blood's shoulder and continues toward the ticker station that clacks noisily at the end of the room. Jim Fisk, partner in Erie Railroad and at thirty-five already one of Wall Street's power players, maneuvers toward him. Fisk's roly-poly physique matches his jolly personality. His short, wavy red hair and walrus mustache accent his ruddy complexion. As Vanderbilt stops at the ticker station, Fisk slaps him on the back.

"Capital day for the market, Commodore!"

"Thanks for the review, Jimbo." Vanderbilt shrugs the pudgy hand off his shoulder and studies the ticker. "You hain't been paintin' the tape, have you?"

"Nah, they did great by themselves today." Fisk says, not the least offended by the insinuation that he has manipulated stock. He laughs heartily and fires up a cigar.

"You gonna smoke that mad-dog thing in here, Jimbo, pay up." Vanderbilt points a thumb toward a large box labeled FINES.

Fisk's crystal blue eyes sparkle with impish exuberance as he drops five dollars in the fine box.

The clock strikes noon. Trading stops. With a final wave to his "subjects," Vanderbilt is gone.

15

~ ~ ~

Morning showers explode into an afternoon downpour as brokers, bankers, businessmen, and reporters flock to the offices of Woodhull, Claflin and Company at 44 Broad in the Wall Street district. A black marble countertop separates the reception area from several wood-and-glass cubicles where business is conducted. A sign on the counter reads: ALL GENTLEMEN WILL STATE THEIR BUSINESS AND THEN RETIRE AT ONCE. The scent from urns filled with red roses removes any trace of mustiness the rain has brought. Exquisite crystal chandeliers dispel the day's damp gloom.

In her private office at the rear, Victoria replaces the wilted red rose at her throat with a fresh one from a vase. Smiling, she strolls to the luxurious reception area where men lounge on dark leather sofas and gold-and-green upholstered chairs set on plush forest-green velvet carpet. A portrait of Cornelius Vanderbilt hangs over the mantle, along with a framed needlepoint tapestry that reads: "Simply To Thy Cross I Cling." The other walls hold original oil paintings, including Frederick Church's ethereal *Aurora Borealis*. Silver buckets are set up around the room, each holding an iced bottle of champagne.

Stephen Pearl Andrews circulates, clearly in his element as he works the crowd. Colonel Blood talks with a group of bankers. Jolly Jim Fisk has his showgirl mistress draped on his arm. His partner at Erie, Jay Gould, stands nearby, funereal-looking even in a stylish gray suit. In sharp contrast to his friend, Gould is rail-thin and reserved. He consults his gold pocket watch as Fisk joins several reporters—including Ashley Cole of the *Herald*, Jim McDermott of the *Sunday Press,* and Johnnie Green, City Editor of the *Sun*—who congregate around Tennie. Luther Challis, a handsome banker with unruly black hair, rubs Tennie's leg suggestively with his black silk umbrella.

"Mr. Challis, you are wetting my ankles!" Tennie scolds. She lifts her tailored navy skirt to show the wet top of her short boot. The men's surprise at her immodesty gives way to admiring whistles. Grinning,

Tennie drops the skirt, adjusts the bright red ascot at her throat, and holds out a cigar for the flustered Challis to light.

"Lemme ask you gentlemen somethin'," she says. "Why is a free man a noble being but a free woman a contemptible one? And why do females fawn upon their male masters, when they might instead lead them by the nose wherever they please?"

"You can lead me anywhere, Miss Claflin," Johnnie Green flirts. He is a smoothly shaven Portuguese man, just turned thirty. Tennie returns his ogle, but Victoria's appearance interrupts the banter. Tennie jumps to her feet, sweeps an arm toward her sister.

"Gentlemen, the next President of the United States, my sister and partner, Victoria Claflin Woodhull!"

The room erupts in cheers, applause, and one or two whistles and catcalls. Reporters scribble their impressions.

"Mrs. Woodhull," Jim Fisk calls out. "Some people think you must be a homely, man-eating spinster because only that type of woman would make such a spectacle of herself."

"That's funny," Luther Challis counters. "I heard she must be a beautiful courtesan because only *that* type of woman would welcome such attention."

"And yet here I am, gentlemen, just a hard-working businesswoman."

"Do you really think you can win the White House, Mrs. Woodhull?" *Tribune* reporter Whitelaw Reid asks.

Victoria glances at the slender man who looks much older than his thirty years. His hair flips up at the top of his ears and on his nape, and his walrus mustache droops below the corners of his thin mouth. Although some consider Whitelaw handsome, his long, pointed nose, sharp-edged jaw, and narrow eyes are disconcerting to Victoria.

"Of course I do, Mr. Reid. Why else would I run? As the physical and spiritual worlds become one, it is time for political action guided by Higher Powers. With Ralph Waldo Emerson's eminence, I say our country is ready for a transcendentalist at its head."

"So you will lead us with Spirits?" Reid probes.

17

"Mr. Lincoln did, so why shouldn't I? But I also have an agile mind and have studied all the philosophies of government so that I might mold my own doctrine from those portions that make sense to me. In politics, like with religion, it behooves us to be aware of credos but not follow them in toto. We must create our own truth as we apprehend it. I assure you that I will spend my fortune advocating my views on equal and just government." She smiles mysteriously. "And I may soon have a surprise—"

The reporters immediately shout over each other for details. Victoria's eyes twinkle, but she refuses to comment. The newsmen turn to Tennie . . . Blood . . . Andrews. But they are as much in the dark as the rest of them. Victoria gestures toward a table filled with fruit, cheeses, and pastries.

"Delmonico's fabulous Chef Ranhofer has prepared a most bountiful spread for us, so everyone please enjoy."

~ ~ ~

The rain has left New York City by dusk, although the streets still glisten as Victoria's white horses pull her white closed carriage majestically around ruts and puddles. They stop at the rain-slicked corner of Beaver and William Streets, where the brick building at No. 56 is home to the elegant Delmonico's restaurant. Delmonico's, the first U.S. restaurant to offer an ala carté menu, is famous for its succulent steak. It is also the favorite of the Wall Street crowd due to its convenient location and its installation of a stock market ticker tape.

Victoria and Tennie alight from the carriage and climb the few steps between columns imported from the ruins of Pompeii. They inhale the mouth-watering aromas that waft onto the street and peer briefly through the front doors' etched-glass windows before entering. The well-heeled diners frown and whisper as the sisters make themselves comfortable at a prominent table. Mr. Delmonico hurries over.

"Mrs. Woodhull, Miss Claflin, how nice to see you."

"Hi, Mr. D," Tennie says. "We'll have two tomato soups, please."

"It's after six, Mrs. Woodhull," Mr. Delmonico says to Victoria.

"Yes, thanks to your delectable catering, our party ran later than expected."

"Sis was too busy jawin' to eat any of your fine spread, and I thought a little soup would be the perfect topper for all them rich delights," Tennie says.

Victoria cringes at her sister's grammar but doesn't correct her, knowing from experience it is futile.

"I, uh—" Mr. Delmonico looks uncomfortable and crooks his arm toward the women. "Here, let me escort you out. We can pretend you just stopped to have a word with me."

"We take our lunch here every day!" Victoria says, stunned. "We engage in business with these men regularly." She glances scornfully around, turns back to the restaurateur. "I have just paid you several hundred dollars for our event, and we would like some soup. Are you saying that because we are not accompanied by a puppet in pants you won't serve us?"

"I'm sorry, Mrs. Woodhull. It's not me, you understand. The law says no unescorted women after six."

Victoria's cheeks spot red; her eyes flash. Tennie, however, hops to her feet and sashays out. Victoria and Mr. Delmonico watch curiously as she hails their coachman. Everyone stares as the tiny African-American man in scarlet velvet suit and gleaming knee-high patent leather boots nervously follows Tennie to the table. She motions him into a vacant chair and smiles sweetly at Delmonico.

"Tomato soup for three, please."

"I'll have that brought out right away, Miss Claflin," the restaurateur says, biting back a laugh. "And it's on the house so no one can say I sold you food."

The coachman looks around at the sea of gaping and glaring white faces; his forehead glistens with sweat. Tennie pats his hand and winks at a snobbish couple at a nearby table, causing them to sputter with rage.

"Why must a woman have an escort to be reputable?" Victoria fumes. "What a comment upon the utter falsity and double standard of

19

the social conditions under which we live! We should have just left and never come back!"

"My god, Sis, lighten up. Like he said, it ain't his fault. When you're President it's the first law you can change."

Chapter 3

The morning of Victoria's announcement, the Reverend Henry Ward Beecher, a stocky man, mid-fifties, saunters down the exterior steps leading from the second floor of his ostentatious home in the wealthy Columbia Heights section of Brooklyn. Opening the front gate of the wrought-iron fence that surrounds his mansion, Beecher pulls a stack of newspapers from a covered box. He gazes across the East River for a moment, eyes intense under heavy lids. Although Manhattan is usually visible across the water, today clouds shroud it.

Beecher runs his fingers through his graying, shoulder-length hair and hurries back to his second-story parlor. The room is a clutter of conspicuous consumption. Oriental rugs are laid on top of one another (having taken up every space on the floor). There are dozens of knickknacks and plaster busts, a plethora of fresh flowers, and an assortment of new inventions: Singer sewing machine, carpet sweeper, and bicycle. Beecher whistles at the dozens of songbirds that sing from cages scattered around the room and settles into an overstuffed chair by a large picture window. An Australian Sheepdog snoozing on a blue Persian rug raises its head briefly, and then rolls onto its back and returns to its slumber, feet in the air and belly exposed.

Beecher opens the *Herald* and barely acknowledges his wife Eunice who brings a tray of tea and crumpets. A prune-faced woman with dull gray hair pulled into a tight bun, she looks old enough to be his mother although she is only a year his senior.

Beecher's sudden laugh startles her, and she sloshes the tea.

"Father!" she scolds.

"Sorry, Mrs. B. . . . What do you think about a woman running for President?"

"It'll never happen in our lifetime."

"Ah, but it has. Mrs. Victoria Woodhull, the Queen of Wall Street, has now declared."

"Oh, well, you know she can't be serious."

"She sounds serious enough. Sit. Listen."

21

Eunice hands him his tea and perches on a nearby footstool. Her look of love almost eases the stern line of her thin lips as her husband reads in a rich, baritone voice.

"'I anticipate criticism, but I trust that my sincerity will not be called into question. I have placed myself before the people as a candidate for the Presidency of the United States, and having the means, courage, energy, and strength necessary for the race, intend to contest it to the close.'" Beecher lays down the paper, actually impressed. "How's that for a new type of woman, Mrs. B?"

"I deplore the masculine aggressiveness of the new woman."

Henry Ward sighs and takes a large gulp of tea. Eunice picks up the paper and reads aloud.

"'If the women can be allowed to vote, Mrs. Woodhull may rely on rolling up the heaviest majority ever polled.'" She lays the paper down with a loud slap. "Well, I say praise God we can't vote. A woman's place is in the home. And you, Father, should stop helping those suffragists." Her lips curl in distaste and she practically spits the word into the air. "You're only involved because Theodore Tilton is heading Susan Anthony's group and you enjoy the challenge of being on the opposing side with Mrs. Blackwell."

"I advise you never to let Lucy Stone hear you call her Mrs. Blackwell. She will tear you to shreds."

"That's another thing I can't understand. Why would a woman not take her husband's name? It's disrespectful."

"I'm going down to the office." He stands and pecks her cheek. He takes a crumpet and tosses a second one to the dog—who jerks upright and catches it in midair. "This is a fine topic for tomorrow's sermon. I must think on it before I open my doors to the downtrodden. Come, Job." He walks briskly out, the dog at his heels.

~ ~ ~

As dusk deepens into night, Reverend Henry Ward Beecher is still in his office, which is downstairs at the rear of his home. This area is as ostentatiously decorated as his upstairs parlor: same clutter of artwork, flowers, and birds. One wall holds a bookshelf full of gilt-bound books, most of which have never been opened. A wide chair rail along the other three walls is littered with knickknacks, figurines, and dozens of highly polished gems.

Henry Ward perches on the bench of a gleaming concert piano, absentmindedly fondling sparkling pieces of amethyst and rose quartz as he watches Lib Tilton's tiny, olive-skinned hands dance lightly across the keys. Except for her very ample breasts, the woman beside him looks more like a schoolgirl than the mother of four she is. When the song ends, Henry Ward turns her toward him and runs his fingers through the long ebony ringlets that flow from a precise center part on Lib's head.

"As always, my dear, your melody ministers to my soul and refreshes me. It was a hectic afternoon. So many people with problems."

"I have no greater joy than to comfort you, Reverend. It amazes me that you make yourself available for two hours every day to whoever needs you. It must truly take a toll."

"It is a testament to your own caring spirit that you recognize that. Sweet angel Libby, you rescue me always." He stands and pulls her to her feet. Although he's only five-foot-nine, he towers over her by almost a foot.

"Do you say the same to our church soloist? I hear she visits—"

"Now, now, Libby, do not let the green-eyed monster cloud those beautiful eyes. Come, be my muse as I prepare my sermon."

"Have you chosen a text?"

She takes his offered hand, her eyes adoring him as he settles them on a loveseat.

"Yes. Proverbs thirty-one. 'Give not thy strength unto women, nor thy ways to that which destroyeth kings. For who can find a virtuous woman? Her price is far above rubies.'" His eyes hold hers; his voice seduces.

"I wish my husband would attend this sermon." She grimaces as she thinks of him.

"Yes, I miss his presence in my front pew. I was worried I wouldn't see you. That Dory had taken you to the President's party in the District. I am surprised he didn't."

"Are you really? How often has he said he would give five hundred dollars if I were not by his side?" Lib quells her bitterness. "But why have you not gone to Washington?"

"And miss the opportunity to spend time with you? I would give five hundred dollars if you were *always* by my side." He kisses her passionately.

~ ~ ~

The same Saturday evening, in Washington, D.C., hundreds of carriages deposit guests adorned in black-tie evening wear at the White House entrance. The cloudless sky glitters with stars, lending a wonderland quality to the affair.

In the White House master bedroom, President Ulysses S. Grant chomps on a cigar as he buttons his shirt and stares out the window at the arrivals. At forty-eight, he retains a military bearing that compensates for his short height, but the poor man has no élan whatsoever. Even in a tuxedo he looks rumpled. Luckily his wife's vibrant personality offsets his dullness. Julia Grant is primped and gowned and sits at her dressing table reading aloud from the *Herald*.

"Mrs. Woodhull says: 'Blacks were cattle in eighteen sixty, but a Negro now sits in Jeff Davis' seat in the United States Senate.' That's largely because of you, Ulys."

"I'm sure she doesn't say that."

"No, but she should have. What she does say is, 'Political preachers paw the air, with no live issue up for discussion.'"

"What issues does Mrs. Woodhull think need discussing?"

"She lists a whole plank of them: Equal rights, equitable wages— Oh, this is interesting. She calls for a global government with arbitration powers, a gathering of nations, if you will. And a universal language to facilitate that. I suppose that will be that Alwato stuff Mr. Andrews invented."

"Not bad. Idealistic, but not bad."

"Of course she throws in birth control and divorce reform to please the women."

"Can you help me with this?" Grant holds out his cummerbund. Julia lays down the paper and walks over to her husband. He sucks in his stomach. "Who's this dinner for again?" Ulysses asks.

"Prince Alfred Ernest Albert, Duke of Edinburgh, dear. Queen Victoria's third son."

"Maybe that's what set The Woodhull off. Maybe she's envisioning two ruling Victorias. God help us."

"We need to get you out walking more, Mr. President." Julia fastens the cummerbund and pats her husband's bulging midriff.

"Mrs. Woodhull had better not mess up my re-election."

"She won't. I surely would have had a dream." Julia gives her husband a final, adoring appraisal and pecks him on the cheek. "My goodness you are handsome."

"I can't breathe in this thing. Am I putting on weight?"

"Sometimes you really don't listen to me, do you?" Julia laughs and prods him toward the door.

The reception is in full swing when they enter the ballroom. The frescoed walls sparkle under large, crystal chandeliers hanging down the length of the room. A military band plays Stephen Foster's "Tioga Waltz," and several couples spin around the dance floor. Guests snake down a receiving line.

Grant groans as he sees Belva Ann Lockwood and Mary Walker approaching. He studies Belva Ann, a short woman, forty-years-old, with pointed features and dark, expressive eyes.

"Mrs. Lockwood's going to give me sarce about the Indians again, isn't she?" he whispers to his wife. "Who's the man with her?"

"That's not a man. It's Mary Walker. You remember her. She was a surgeon in the Ohio army and invented those little postcard receipts for registered mail."

"What's she doing in tails and top hat? Is that a Medal of Honor around her neck?"

"Ulys, I swear your memory is as short as a toothpick. She earned the medal sitting in a Confederate jail, and since she got used to dressing like a man in the war, she's preferred such attire."

"Where's their escort? They can't attend without an—"

"Oh, Ulys, don't be an old fuddy-duddy. They probably came with Mr. Stanton." She picks a piece of lint from his sleeve and pats his backside. "Now hush and smile."

Grant bites down on his cigar and grimaces as frumpy Mary Walker shakes his hand vigorously.

"I see you're still smoking that cigar, Mr. President, even though studies are now showing tobacco may bring paralysis and insanity."

"Studies be damned. My cigar *keeps* me sane."

"Any thoughts about Mrs. Woodhull's announcement?" Belva Ann asks, twisting one of the dark curls that frame the fusion of tresses piled high on her head.

"Well, I hear she's prettier'n me."

"She also addresses issues the two major parties ignore."

"Does this mean the women will support her?"

"Nothing personal, but I will," Belva says. "And as head of the D.C. suffragists, I'll encourage the group to do the same."

"Mrs. Woodhull's taken your mind off the Injuns, has she?"

"Not at all. I guarantee that Mrs. Woodhull will reform the politicized hogwash you call an Indian Commission."

Grant smiles grudgingly; Julia moves the line along.

Across the dance floor, Senator Benjamin Butler and Theodore Tilton watch the dancing. The contrast between the two friends is almost laughable. The Adonis-looking Tilton is six-foot-four and appears several years younger than his thirty-three years. He is clean-shaven with a long, flowing, sandy-colored mane and finely chiseled features. Butler, twenty years Tilton's senior, is two feet shorter. Black, oily straggles of hair hang from his bald dome to his shoulders. His bowed legs, long, sharp nose, drooping right eyelid, sagging jowls, and unkempt walrus mustache have earned him the nickname Beast. Fortunately for him, his

Civil War fame, acute intelligence, and magnetic personality override his grotesque appearance.

Henry Stanton, husband of suffragist Elizabeth Cady Stanton, walks up, puffing his ever-present pipe. Stanton is a slender, charming man with rust-colored hair trimmed above his collar. His unruly mustache and sideburns seem at odds with his otherwise impeccable grooming. With Stanton is former slave turned statesman Frederick Douglass. Douglass is almost as tall as Tilton, an imposing black man with a wild bush of graying hair and fierce dark eyes. His mustache curves around his stern mouth and connects with a short, neatly trimmed beard.

"How is Mrs. Butler doing?" Douglass asks Butler. "Have they been able to diagnose her?"

"They tell me it's the heart. She could go on for years or die tomorrow," Butler says sadly. "I pray she outlives us all."

"I wish I could say the same about Elizabeth," Stanton says. "I swear the only reason we're still married is that I spend most of my time in Washington, and she is either out stumping or in Jersey with the children. You gentlemen can thank your lucky stars your wives are content to be homemakers."

"Elizabeth removing the word *obey* from your wedding vows and refusing to respond when addressed as Mrs. Stanton should have been a clue, Henry," Tilton says with a wink.

"Well, you know what they say," Butler says, rolling his cigar across his lips. "No man is a hero to his wife since she sees too much of him in unheroic moods."

"Mr. Stanton and I were just talking with the President," Douglass says, glancing at Grant. "He is a bit disturbed about this Woodhull woman."

"He should be more concerned about Horace Greeley," Tilton says. "The Liberal Republicans are fed up with the shenanigans of this administration and are talking of splitting from the party. And the Democrats will nominate Horace as well. Can we say President Greeley?"

"I think I'd rather say President Woodhull," Douglass says with a chuckle.

"Grant may have reputation, but Greeley has him beat on character," Tilton insists.

"I wonder which The Woodhull has?" Butler asks.

"I'd say neither," Stanton comments.

"My question is: Will the Suffragists support her?" Douglass says. "Even without the vote, we all know how women influence their husbands."

"My wife has no influence on me," Theodore says.

"Just give her a little more time in the woman's movement." Stanton puffs his pipe and chuckles.

"I don't know how women can hope to govern when they can't even agree on how to fight for the vote," Butler says, chomping on his cigar.

"Which is why I've called this meeting for Wednesday," Theodore says. "Will you be there, Frederick?"

"I plan on it, if I can stomach being in the same room as Beecher. Does he still aspire to a Congressional seat?"

"He aspires, but also knows he reaches more people, makes more money, and has more power in the pulpit."

"All important to the Reverend," Stanton says.

"Where is he tonight anyway?" Douglass asks. "I didn't think a celebrity hound like him would miss the opportunity to mix it up with a Prince."

"Apparently the President didn't invite him," Tilton says. "He was quite put out about it, but I'm sure he's finding some sweet young thing to lick his wounds."

"Speaking of sweet young things, I understand Mrs. Woodhull is quite the looker," Stanton says. "Perhaps you should make her acquaintance, Theodore. See what she's about."

"Well, you know I'll always take one for the boys."

"Calm down, Dory," Butler says. "Even if Mrs. Woodhull's intentions are serious, even if the women join forces, even if the

Democrats and Liberals vote the same, the President will get the nomination, and it will take God himself to unseat him."

~ ~ ~

By Monday morning the skies have cleared, leaving New York City fresh and warm. The sun glints off the buildings of New York City's major dailies—the *Tribune, Sun, World, Herald, Times, Ledger, Evening Telegram,* and *Evening Post*—strung out along Park Row.

Horace Greeley hurries down the street to his office, several newspapers tucked under one arm and a gaudy orange umbrella hooked over the other. His wispy white hair sticks straight out from his wide-brimmed hat and his long white duster billows around his spindly legs. The coat is his trademark; he wears it on even the hottest summer days. Horace enters the *Tribune,* where he is editor, and hangs the umbrella on a doorknob.

"Dog bust it, where are my glasses?" He fumbles desperately through his pockets. "Aha!" He pulls out tiny, wire-rimmed spectacles and puts them on as his managing editor, Whitelaw Reid, comes into the office behind him.

"Did you read the news in Saturday's *Herald*?" Whitelaw asks.

"I have it right here. And, how many times do I have to tell you one item is new, several items are news."

Whitelaw Reid rolls his eyes as Greeley flops the newspapers onto his desk, which has been specially designed to reach chin-level when he sits.

"What's the world coming to, huh?" Whitelaw asks.

"For Ashley Cole to call Mrs. Woodhull's announcement a powerful document on behalf of women's rights is drivel. Ridiculous drivel. Is she dating him or something?"

"Her sister probably is. Tennie dates every man she meets."

"Including you?"

Whitelaw gives a derisive snort.

"There's one thing," Horace says. "Where is it?" He leans his chin on the desk and raises the paper close to his eyes. "Oh, here it is. 'The present position of political parties is anomalous. They are not inspired by any great principles of policy or economy; a great national question is wanted. That question exists in the issue of whether woman shall be elevated to all the political rights enjoyed by man.'" He lets the paper drop to the desk. "That's well stated, and Cole is correct that she has the novelty of being a beautiful woman. I haven't been nominated yet, Whitelaw, and I know there are many folks who don't like me. Mrs. Woodhull could ruin what little chance I have to be President."

"I can help with that, Horace. She's from my home state, you know, and I've still got friends in Ohio. No one knows anything about her life before she blew into New York like some flimflam carnie and got Vanderbilt to stake her on Wall Street right before last fall's market crash. I've often wondered how the three of them came out of Black Friday smelling like roses. There's got to be dirt somewhere in her past."

Horace considers. Whitelaw presses.

"You know she's hooked up with that Free-lover Stephen Pearl Andrews. His cooperative community—what was it called? Modern Times? Disgusting times is more like it. People cavorting around naked, dying of bean diets."

"Now be neighborly, Whitelaw. Pearl used to work for me, and he's brilliant. Speaks close to forty languages. Not to mention that his bringing Pittman's stenography to the States has made this newspaper considerable money by allowing us to transcribe and print political debates and the like. And cooperative communities aren't all bad, albeit rather Utopian. Nathanial Hawthorne and Bronson Alcott had the same thing at Brook Farm, and Nathan Meeker has founded one in Colorado he calls Greeley, after yours truly."

"But no one's dying in those."

"Modern Times attracted some crazies. Pearl was sick about it and got out. Just like I got away from Dr. Graham's strict cracker and grain diet, although sometimes I'd welcome it over the beans and rancid skilly Mrs. Greeley delights in serving me."

"Sorry, Sir. I didn't realize your feelings about Andrews. But I'd still like to check out The Woodhull."

30

"I don't want to sling mud. On the other hand, the *Tribune* must comment on the matter." He thinks for a moment. "For now, let's say that the woman seems sincere so the *Tribune* will investigate her qualifications. Get that into the afternoon edition. If she's got anything to hide, maybe she'll just disappear."

"So that's a go to dig?"

"Yes, Mr. Reid, that's a go. But no printing what you find without my approval."

Chapter 4

The six Claflin children, ranging in age from Tennessee at two to Polly at sixteen, sleep peacefully in the attic of a rustic log cabin. Suddenly the front door bangs open, and Buck Claflin stumbles in, drunk and yelling.

"Wake up and git on down here, you little heathens!" He rattles the ladder to the attic. "C'mon, be quick about it! Every second gets ya another lash."

The children scurry to line up before their father as Roxanna plops in the rocking chair and rants in German for Gott *to save her family's souls. The wails begin as Buck makes a big production of selecting a willow branch from the rain barrel by the door. The whip lashes, and eleven-year-old Victoria flinches and bites her lip as her skin welts and blood drips down her shins, but she refuses to cry out.*

It is dawn and the children are in tatters before Buck is spent.

"The Claflins are born to stick together when the going gets rackety," he growls. "And don't nobody forget that!" He sprawls across the bed, bloody whip still in his hand.

"Come, kinder, *kiss your father and thank him for correcting your sins and saving you from the fires of* Holle.*" Roxanna herds the battered, sobbing children toward him. Buck swats them away like flies. Victoria, holding Tennie, is last.*

"Just once, Papa," she whispers. "Just once couldn't you give us a fatherly kiss back?"

Buck's only response is a drunken snort. Victoria carries Tennie slowly up the ladder and crawls painfully onto the cornhusk mattress. A sudden downpour pelts through the leaky ceiling as they huddle under a dirty blanket and listen to their parents make loud, violent love below.

~ ~ ~

Victoria wakes suddenly from her nightmare. She slips out of bed and creeps through the dark to Tennie's room. Shakes her gently.

"Tennie, wake up."

"Huh? What's wrong?" Tennie jolts upright.

"I've been reading the papers, and I don't like what Mr. Reid says in the *Tribune*. What if he finds out about . . . well, everything?"

"My god, Sis, who cares? We've got nothing to hide. Mr. Greeley himself championed the Fox sisters' Spirit rappings, and we've never been the frauds they were. Sure we humbugged once or twice, but only to help people. Politicians do it every day to help themselves." She gives her sister a comforting hug. "You're a bona fide American success story, Sis. You should sleep like a baby. Like I was."

"You're right. I will never change my course because those who assume to be better than me desire it. The consciousness inside me is above such petty malice. Thank you for reminding me that I am driven by a power much stronger than Whitelaw Reid!"

"Sure. No problem. What are sisters for, right?" Tennie rubs her eyes and yawns. Victoria tucks the covers around her, kisses her forehead, and tiptoes out.

Unfortunately, a short time later, Colonel Blood snores softly beside her as Victoria tosses and turns in another dream.

~ ~ ~

The naked Claflin kids toss fitfully in the summer heat as ten-year-old Victoria looks out the uncovered attic window at her mother, who stands on a distant hill, arms raised and praying loudly. "Gott, I beg you for my ehemann's *soul. Buck flaunts homemade money and would be workin' on the chain gang if Victoria hadn't eaten it when the sheriff came. Now he's spent our meager funds on some fool thing called insurance for that rackety old mill and is a-fever to hunt gold in Californee. He's heading to* Holla, Gott, *unless you save him for us!"*

Suddenly, a loud explosion shakes the night. Flames burst from the mill and lap toward the starless sky. Victoria and her siblings rush to join their mother at the blaze, where they frantically scoop water from the creek and fling it uselessly on the fire. As the mill starts to crumble, Victoria spies the torches of approaching townsfolk, and the Claflins cheer in relief. Their joy turns to horror, however, when they hear yells of "arsonist" and "insurance fraud" and see buckets of tar and bags of feathers.

"Oh, Lordee!" Roxanna screams. "Run, children, run! Your father's done burned down his own mill!"

As the Claflins scatter, someone torches their house. The brittle abode is consumed in seconds. Flames crackle and pop behind them as Victoria grabs Tennie into her arms and flees. Buck charges up on a horse, hauls his wife up behind him, and gallops away. The children race after them, mob at their heels.

~ ~ ~

The next morning, Victoria, tired from her restless night, stares out the window of their carriage as their white steeds clip-clop through the partially developed Central Park. Her mood is as dreary as the drizzly April day. Tennie is beside her, deep in thought. Suddenly, she brightens and breaks the silence.

"I know! I'll get Ashley Cole to interview me about that manslaughter charge in Iowa. That's the worst of our past. I'll explain Hebern and Pa ran the Cancer Hospital, and the lady was dying no matter what they did. I'll give them statistics about how many people we cured compared to docs with degrees."

"No! I absolutely forbid it! Commenting on anything only makes things worse. Promise me, Tennie. No interviews."

"My god, I promise."

After another period of silence, Victoria speaks without turning.

"Papa never once kissed us, did he?

"My god, wasn't it bad enough him *shtuppin'* ya, without him slobberin' all over your face?"

Victoria gives her sister a shocked look.

"What?" Tennie says. "You think I don't know what you did for me? I woke up every time Pa climbed that ladder and reached for me.

'You need a woman not a baby,' you'd say. If I'd'a understood what he was doin' to ya out in that mill, I would'a grabbed his own gun and shot him. Sometimes I don't understand how you can even look at him."

"He's our father. We have to forgive him."

"Why? Because he beat it into us?"

"It's just the way it is, Tennie. Fathers can pretty much do what they want with their children."

"That doesn't make it right. Do you think Ma knew?"

"I don't know. But I do know that if we harbor hate or resentment, Buck and those like him win. I don't want to talk about this anymore."

"My god, Sis, I didn't mean to roil up bad memories."

Tennie glances out the window as they pass the lavish Fifth Avenue Hotel. She whistles as she sees Frederick Douglass help Lucretia Mott from a carriage. Almost eighty years old, the grandmother of the woman's movement is serene and kindly looking, despite deep-set eyes and bushy eyebrows. She is garbed in Quaker gray. Several other women enter the hotel. Another group converges from down the street.

"My god, Sis, look at that! It's a whole passel of suffragists. Wonder what's going on. Hey, maybe it's about your announcement. We should crash the party! Introduce ourselves." She reaches for the button to call the coachman, but Victoria pulls her back.

"Don't be ridiculous! They have to come to us. It's the only way they'll ever accept us."

~ ~ ~

The meeting at the hotel isn't specifically about Victoria, but she is definitely part of the conversation as the two warring factions of the woman's movement come together to discuss merging their groups. The American Woman's Suffrage Association, headquartered in Boston, is the more conservative of the two, focusing only on suffrage and working toward that goal on a state-by-state basis. Their leader Lucy Stone, who looks younger than her fifty years due to expressive eyes and high cheekbones, leads the way into the hotel, followed by co-editors of the AWSA's *Woman's Journal*, Mary Livermore and Julia Ward Howe.

"Is the next issue of our newspaper about ready for press?" Lucy asks as they ride the elevator, the first in an American hotel, up to the meeting suite.

"Very close," Mary Livermore, an unpleasantly plump and masculine-looking woman with bulbous nose and thick eyebrows, reassures her. "Louisa May Alcott's first letter from Europe has arrived. With her new book *Old Fashioned Girl* becoming as popular as *Little Women*, it should boost circulation considerably."

"I hope she remembers to feel out the interest in a world peace movement while she is abroad. We must do something about all these wars and terrorist activities." This comes from Julia Ward Howe, famous for penning "The Battle Hymn of the Republic." Julia is about the same age as Lucy and Mary, but has not aged well. Her hair is white and brittle, deep lines crease her high forehead, and her cheeks sag from bug eyes to hanging jowls.

"Ask Louisa to send an article about that," Lucy suggests. "Did Mr. Emerson send his essay on women?"

"His trip to San Francisco delayed that, so he sent a piece on the Over-Soul for now," Julia says.

"Good. But keep reminding him about the woman essay."

"About Mrs. Woodhull— Are we going to print a reaction?" Julia asks.

"My reaction is unprintable!" Lucy's fury reddens her face. "We will never mention that woman in our journal!"

They reach the suite, and Lucy quickly puts on a smile as they take seats beside their group's president, Henry Ward Beecher. Several of Susan B. Anthony's National Woman's Suffrage Association members are already positioned across the room. This contingency sees other issues, such as divorce reform and birth control, as interconnected with suffrage and in need of address. They think a Constitutional Amendment is the best way to achieve the vote.

The room is soon full of an 1870 Who's Who crowd of women—all shapes, sizes, ages, and wealth—with a few male supporters sprinkled among them.

Susan pats her dark hair that is parted in the middle and pulled into two rolled buns at her nape. Clutching her well-known red shawl tightly to her, she fumes as she opens the *Herald*.

"Did you ladies see this announcement?" She reads aloud. "'Mrs. Woodhull, the lady broker of Wall Street, independent of all suffrage tea-parties and Grundy associations, proclaims herself a candidate for the occupancy-in-chief of the White House.' Suffrage tea-parties, my foot! How dare she!"

"In honesty, Susan," Isabella Beecher Hooker, Henry Ward's 48-year-old sister, says, "Ashley Cole wrote that, not Mrs. Woodhull."

"Well, she said this." Susan glares at Isabella, who raises her finely chiseled chin defiantly. Susan reads on, growing angrier by the minute. "'While others of my sex devoted themselves to a crusade against the laws that shackle women, I asserted my independence. While others prayed for the good time coming, I worked for it. While others argued the equality of woman with man, I proved it by successfully engaging in business. While others sought to show that there was no valid reason why women should be treated, socially and politically, as being inferior to man, I boldly entered the arena of business and exercised the rights I already possessed.'" Susan slams the paper shut. "It's like she thinks we've been twiddling our thumbs."

"Elizabeth Cady wired that she is rather intrigued by the whole business," Belva Ann Lockwood contributes.

"La-de-dah and lullaby! Lizzie has been my best friend for many years, but lately she has teetotally flunked our cause."

"Susan, dear, sometimes people just need a break. Not everyone is as single-minded as you," Lucretia Mott chides gently.

"So you think this is okay? A woman running for President?"

"I have no objection to a woman being the neck to turn the head right. I'm just not sure I wish to see her assume the *place* of the head," Lucretia admits.

"You know, we may just be upset because we never thought of running a candidate," Isabella says with a mischievous grin.

"Belle! This is not a laughing matter!" Susan admonishes, one eye wandering into a crossed position. "I tried to interview her for *The Revolution* when they first opened their bank on Wall Street. She wasn't there, but I spoke with the sister Jennie."

She shudders, remembering.

"I think it's Tennie," Belva Ann says.

"Jennie, Tennie, or Henny Penny, who cares? She was terribly impolite. Why she immediately took off her hat as if we were old friends! Disgusting. But those prostitutes are teetotally serious about succeeding in their every endeavor, even if they have to step on our cause to do it. And they have the money and intelligence to do so."

"Then we shall simply have to wait and see," Lucretia Mott says. "The election is two years away and much can happen between now and then."

Others join the group and Susan's pique is assuaged, at least for the moment. Gossip buzzes through the room. Gorgeous Laura Cuppy Smith, an outspoken Spiritualist and noted lecturer in her early thirties, compliments Paulina Wright Davis' perfectly coiffed white hair and stylish dress. "Is it a French design?" she asks. "I've seen nothing to equal it in Demorest's catalog."

"Thank you. It *is* French. I bought it as an anniversary present since Mr. Davis once again forgot the date."

"Mr. Howe missed ours, too," Julia Ward commiserates, breaking the conversation barrier between the opposing groups. "Men have no idea how even a small remembrance kindles a wife's desire. Perhaps I'll buy myself a gift as well, although it certainly won't be an expensive Parisian frock."

"To each her own," Paulina says. "But I am determined to do my part to remove the impression that we suffragists are frumpy, old, masculine women."

"Amen, Paulina!" Laura Bullard says. "You're one of the reasons I joined this group." At 30 years of age, Laura is heiress to a syrup dynasty and the wealthiest member of Susan B. Anthony's group. She is beautiful and chic.

Conversations stop as Benjamin Butler hurries into the room, late as usual. Having been waiting for him, Theodore Tilton immediately claps for attention.

"Ladies and Gentlemen, we are here to discuss what I believe is a serious crisis in our fight for suffrage—the widening division between our two groups. Unless we stop arguing about small differences and unite in our efforts, I fear we will never see women vote."

"Why can't we just focus on suffrage? We can vote and still retain our status as women of the home," Lucy Stone says, advancing her group's philosophy.

"Because some women are not as fortunate as you," Belva Lockwood counters. "Your husband is sympathetic to our goals. He allowed you to keep your own name and encouraged you to earn a college degree even though no woman had done that before. But not every wife has such support. Too many are shackled to drunkards who rape, abuse, and suppress them. Would you really advocate staying married forever if your husband was one of those? If he insisted on calling you Mrs. Blackwell instead of Lucy Stone no matter how much you protested?"

"Perhaps if women knew they must lie in their beds, so to speak, they would consider the matter more thoughtfully before committing to wedlock," Julia Ward Howe says in derision.

"Not all women have a choice," Paulina Wright Davis argues. "With fathers of the same caliber as their husbands, many have been sold into marital bondage."

"Oh for goodness sakes," Mary Livermore says. "Since we freed the Negro, nobody's forced into bondage anymore."

"Did you really just say that?" Laura Cuppy Smith's mouth gapes in disbelief. "It certainly *is* still happening to women."

"We've made great strides," Belva Lockwood says. "But there are still laws forbidding women to own property, laws that require her to turn over her earnings to her husband, laws that give her no say over her children's treatment, laws that deny her the right to refuse sex to her husband even if she is about to bear him a thirteenth child or more!"

"Good lord, I can't imagine birthing that many children. A woman might never recover," Laura Bullard says.

"Some women don't," Paulina says.

"Women can't serve on juries or testify against their spouses," Belva continues, pressing the case. "And God help the wife who runs away. She can legally be dragged back like a slave and beaten to an inch of her life. Those laws will not change until women are allowed to vote against them."

"We agree that the vote is the way to change injustice," Lucy says. "That's exactly why we want to gain suffrage as quickly as possible. We just believe the most rapid route is state-by-state reform."

"Do you really think it would be faster to change thirty-seven state laws instead of one federal one?" Laura Bullard asks. "That makes no sense. And what about the territories that will one day join the Union? Will we have to fight for the vote in each of them, too?"

"Wyoming already allows women to vote."

The room dissolves into argument until Tilton finally claps for silence.

"Ladies, please, this is getting us nowhere."

"We started this whole thing, they should bow to us," Paulina says. "Tell them, Lucretia!"

"I think we should listen to Mr. Tilton's proposal," Lucretia says.

"Finally a sane voice," says Tilton. "Now what I propose is a *new* organization with a clearly defined agenda that incorporates all of our ideas. Each side may have to give a bit, but wouldn't the reward of a strong, united front be worth it? My wife suggested calling the merged group the Union Suffrage Association. Libby's tiny brain seldom has a good idea, but I like the suggestion and would be proud to serve as president."

Lib reddens. Several of the women purse their lips in anger. Susan Anthony quickly moves the discussion along.

"No offense to you and Mr. Beecher, Theodore, but Lizzie Cady thinks our officers should be women and I tend to agree."

"What about Mrs. Woodhull? Maybe it'll satisfy her need to be president of something," Henry Ward suggests. When loud protests fill the room, he holds up his hands. "It was a joke, ladies. A joke." Only Lib laughs.

"Most of thee know the story behind this shawl," Lucretia Mott says. She stands and holds her white shawl at arm's length to display cut-off fringe. "It had beautiful long fringe when a friend gave it to me. Of course, as a Quaker, such ornamentation caused a hullabaloo at Meeting. I liked the fringe, but the fight would have detracted from our fellowship and labors so off it came. I wear the shawl still to remind me to pick my battles. I think, with reflection, we can come to a compromise here today."

Unfortunately, it is not to be. As the sun sinks low outside the window, a frustrated Theodore ends the meeting.

"May I offer a final thought?" Butler says as the ladies begin to leave. "As we go away from here, consider this: If we don't pull ourselves together, Mrs. Woodhull may well walk away with the victory that we have all fought so long for."

Chapter 5

It's moving day for Victoria.

Flowers line the front of her new abode at 15 East Thirty-Eighth Street in Murray Hill, the prestigious neighborhood between New York City's Madison and Fifth Avenues. The house is the tallest, most elegant on the block, with ten-foot windows accented by black walnut sashes and glistening plate-glass panes.

The marbled entry is so spacious it dwarfs the statue of Demosthenes. Other rooms feature floor-to-ceiling mirrors, gold-and-crystal chandeliers, luxurious Oriental rugs, purple velvet drapes, and plush lavender carpets. There is a library with mirrored ceiling, mahogany paneled walls, built-in bookshelves, and a large billiard table. On another floor is a fully stocked playroom.

Buck wears a stylish suit and strolls around the ballroom, tapping his gold-tipped cane against the marble floor. He looks up at the gilt-and-glass dome that is hand-painted with pictures of Venus, Apollo, and Aphrodite. Incense burners hanging down the length of the room fill the air with sandalwood-scented smoke. Buck coughs harshly and spews phlegm into the white fountain in the middle of the room, from which rises a white marble statue of Daphne and Apollo entwined.

In the huge, modern-for-its-day kitchen, Roxanna bosses three maids and a cook, four of twelve new servants. In the first-floor parlor, Victoria directs the placement of a white grand piano. Songbirds sing from a large greenhouse opening off the parlor, and Tennie whistles gleefully along as she arranges urns of flowers on the jade mantel.

Colonel Blood throws open the French doors in the master bedroom and walks out onto the broad balcony with majestic Corinthian columns. Victoria soon joins him, and his arm encircles her as they take in the phenomenal city view. Overcome with joy, Victoria melts him with kisses.

Later that night, Victoria relaxes in a velvet chaise lounge on the mansion's flat rooftop and watches the sun disappear. Reflections from gaslights dance across the rippling East River in the distance. Victoria caresses the watch-chain at her neck and watches in peaceful musing as stars twinkle to life. Twisting her diamond thumb ring, she falls into a trance.

A short time later, Tennie's arrival snaps Victoria back to reality. She speaks without turning.

"This is the best part, Tennie. I feel so close to the Universe up here. Look! There's Orion. And Venus." She pats the chaise beside her. "Come. Sit a minute. The heavens are glorious tonight." Victoria watches Tennie perch, not relaxing. "Demosthenes was just here."

"I thought I felt him leaving. Did he give you the sign so you can finally spill the beans about your big surprise?"

"Yes. It's time." Tennie waits impatiently, but Victoria just stares into the heavens.

"My god, Sis, I'm exploding from curiosity!"

"I want you to go see the Commodore with another business proposition."

"My god, tell me what it is and I'll go tomorrow. I've been missin' the old goat anyway."

~ ~ ~

The next morning, Tennie C. waits in the foyer of the Vanderbilt mansion, tapping her foot impatiently. Organ music emanates from the parlor, accompanying a soprano-tenor duet of "Nearer My God to Thee." Tennie grimaces at several sour tenor notes. Gratefully the song ends, and Mrs. Frank Vanderbilt opens the front door.

"I'm terribly sorry, Miss Claflin, but my husband is indisposed." Mrs. Vanderbilt starts to close the door on Tennie, but a bell jangles from the second floor.

"What happened to that mad-dog hymnin' down there? Who's a-gabbin'?" Vanderbilt roars from his bedroom.

"Just one of your well-wishers, Cornele," his wife says. "But she's leaving now."

"What's her handle then?" Cornelius bellows.

43

"It's me, Old Boy. Tennie C."

"Well, shoot on up here, girl. You know the way."

Frank's eyes fire daggers as Tennie curtsies to the furious wife, bounds up the steps, and taps on the bedroom door.

"I got no time to waste on formalities, Little Sparrow. Git on in here." He grins as Tennie skips into the room, Frank fuming behind her.

"G'on, leave me in peace for a while," he says to the nurse who has propped up his pillows. He nods toward his wife. "And take her with you." Frank starts to protest, but his glare stops her in mid-sentence. "You wanna go to the asylum like the first Mrs. V.?"

"God have mercy on your soul," Frank mutters as she leaves.

"Lock that door, Little Sparrow, and c'mon over here."

"It's good to see you, Old Boy. I've been a-missin' ya," Tennie plops down on the bed and tugs playfully on the Commodore's whiskers.

"I'm the most powerful man in America, and they still try to run me. I get a little cold and they act like I'm dying. Wishful thinkin', I reckon."

"I had a message from the Spirits that my best old boy might be needin' some magnetic fingers, so I hurried on over."

"The spirits weren't lyin', Little Sparrow. I have the bed on saltcellars and still feel the energy sappin' away. I got whist to play and horses to race. Hain't got time to hang out in this hellhole. And all them whinin' prayers Frank and her bishop insist on sendin' up to heaven are prob'ly makin' me sicker."

"My god, the energy ain't all sapped off'n you yet, Old Boy. Lie on down and let me work on raisin' you up." She pulls off his quilt and nightshirt, exposing remarkably taut skin. He rolls onto his stomach, and her fingers dance over his neck and back.

"Can we contact mama Phebe when you're finished? I sure do miss her."

"Whatever you want, Old Boy. I was thinking of asking the spirits about a business venture I aim to propose to you anyway."

"If you'd only married me, you wouldn't have to propose nuthin'. You'd'a had it all."

"My god, Old Boy, I tried marriage once, and it weren't nothin' I cottoned to."

"I didn't know you had you a husband. Still got him?" He rises on one elbow and squints at her. Tennie gently pushes him back down, and her fingers resume their dance.

"Nah. It was long ago. I was young and pretty; he was young and pretty. He played the horses and cards like you do and had diamond rings on every finger. And those fingers were quite talented, if you get my meanin'. He turned me from a gal to a woman the first night, and we had fun for a while. He's the reason I'm so good at playing whist with you. In fact, that's what split us up."

"How's that, Little Sparrow?"

"Well, we was traveling with the Claflins' medicine show hawking the elixir with my picture on the bottle, and one night I won ten bucks off a man camped beside us. John B—that's what I called my husband—he said I had to give him the money since he was my husband. I told him, 'I earn it, I keep it' and sent him packin'."

She slaps Vanderbilt's back playfully.

"Now, roll on over. Let me see if you got any music left in that instrument of yours."

Later the same afternoon, Stephen Pearl Andrews hands Tennie, Blood, and Victoria each a copy of his thick new tome, *The Basic Outline of Universology.*

"My god, this thing is heavier than an elephant after breakfast," Tennie whispers to Blood. "And probably as full of crap."

Blood bites back a grin

"This is brilliant, Pearl. I cannot wait to study it," Victoria says, leafing through the book and taking in several pages at a glance.

"Yes, we'll delve into it anon. But first we must strategize about Victoria's campaign." Blood lays the book aside.

"Yes, yes. Quite right," Andrews says. "I saw Horace Greeley at the Liberal Club today. He is in an awful *tumulte* about the announcement."

"My god, wouldn't it be a rip-roar if Sis got the nomination he's hankering for?"

"The only way that can happen is if we make people aware of her," Blood says.

"I have the 'Petticoat Politician' column in the *Herald*. A lot of people read that," Victoria says.

"In New York, yes," Pearl says. "But we must reach more. *Beaucoup, beaucoup* more."

"First we must educate people to take me seriously," Victoria says.

"We also have to deal with the misunderstandings of your belief in free-love," says Pearl. "We can point out that Daniel Webster and William Pitt were *scandaleux bon vivants* but also great statesmen. Since some proclaim me the Father of Free-love, I will write an article to explain the philosophy. I'll point out that Henry David Thoreau first coined the phrase in a poem back in 'forty-two."

"Good. Government has no more right to interfere with morals than with religion." Victoria says. "We must show society that love can be nothing but free. Even Mr. Beecher preaches that love is God and God is love, and is not God's love the freest of all?"

"Of course the idea of Victoria as a novelty must be emphasized," Blood says. "People like novelty and will vote for such."

"My main appeal, though, is my daring," Victoria says. "And the fact that I combine a singular masculine grasp of reality with womanly intuition."

"Let's not forget it's your destiny," Tennie adds.

"All good, but none of that will win an election," Andrews says. "We must focus on issues people want to vote on: Woman's suffrage, of course, but also regulation of monopolies, laws to protect laborers and promote equality."

"It shouldn't be too difficult to score there," Blood says. "Democrats are as ineffective as a limp rag, and Republicans haven't anything to trumpet now that abolition is won."

"We must emphasize that we want fairness for all, nothing more and nothing less," Victoria says. "Who can argue against that? I also want to include abolition of the death penalty to our plank, since this is nothing but murder by a community."

"Absolutely," Blood says.

"And we want a one-term Presidency followed by a lifetime seat in the Senate," Victoria says. "This will not only temper corruption in administrations, but provide wise voices in Congress to guide future Presidents."

"And don't forget national public education," Andrews adds.

"My god, that's a great idea."

"But again, we must figure out how to make the general populace aware of these ideas. Which brings us back to square one," Blood says.

"And that's where my surprise comes in!" Victoria smiles mysteriously.

"Wait'll you guys hear this! Tell 'em, Sis! Tell 'em!" Tennie can't contain herself and blurts out the news. "We're starting a newspaper!"

Chapter 6

On April 23, Victoria is working at the desk in her parlor when Colonel Blood arrives with a tall, thin man about Andrews' age. The man's white linen suit is a sharp contrast to his coal black hair and goatee.

"Victoria, this is Dr. Joseph Treat, president of the American Association of Spiritualists," Blood says. "He has invited you to speak at their upcoming meeting."

Dr. Treat strides across the parlor to shake Victoria's hand. "If you consent to address us, I will pledge my group's support of your candidacy in whatever manner we can be helpful."

"My god, that's a few million votes!" says Tennie.

"I am not a public speaker, Dr. Treat, but I will trust the Spirits to help me."

"I understand you have been guided by Demosthenes, as well as Napoleon and Josephine, since you were barely able to walk."

"Everything I do is spirit-guided."

"Which is why Victoria is running for President," Blood says. "We are entering a new age, and we must be led by someone who believes in such a world and communicates with it."

"Quite true. Quite true," Treat says. He scratches his sharp, pointed nose.

"Of course, to make the idea more palpable to the public, we rely on Abe Lincoln's well-known spirit consultations, as well as Julia Grant using her precognitive dreams to advise our current President," Victoria says, glancing in surprise at the carved mahogany grandfather clock that chimes five P.M. "Oh, goodness, I am sorry to have to dash off, Dr. Treat, but it's my daughter's birthday. We have promised dinner at Delmonico's and then the theater. I must get ready." Victoria holds out a hand. "Thank you for joining our endeavor. My husband can work out the details of my appearance before your organization."

"*Namaste*," Treat says, kissing her hand.

"*Namaste*," Victoria responds, familiar with the standard Spiritualist greeting. She starts toward the door and almost collides with a maid who is wringing her hands and clearly her throat nervously. Concern fills Victoria's face. "What is it, Kate?"

"Th-th-there's a man who wishes to speak with you, Ma'am."

"If it's no one we know, please ask him to leave his card."

"Um, Ma'am, um, he says he's an old friend of the family. I-I think you should see him."

"I'll take care of it, Victoria," Blood says.

"That's okay. I'll just see who it is on my way upstairs."

Seconds later, Victoria is stunned to see the short, rotund man slumped on the foyer bench. Alcohol and morphine abuse make him look almost twice his forty-four years. He rises shakily when he sees her. His hat drops to the floor. His jaw twitches.

"Halloo, my little chick."

"Doc." Victoria is so shocked her voice comes out in a hoarse whisper. She quickly pulls him into the library and closes the door. Her mind travels back in time.

~ ~ ~

Lost in a daydream, fifteen-year-old Victoria collides with twenty-eight-year-old Dr. Canning Woodhull in front of the Mount Gilead, Ohio post office. Startled when he steadies her, Victoria almost swoons at the sight of his sooty eyelashes and lustrous black hair.

"Halloo, my little chick! I'm the new doctor in town, and I want you to go with me to the Independence Day picnic." He smiles a broad smile of perfect teeth as a rakish curl falls onto his forehead. Victoria is immediately madly in love. By November they are married.

A week later they have settled into a one-room log cabin. The place is a pigsty, with a clutter of papers and dirty clothes, a dying fire, and bare cupboards. Victoria is reading Hard Times *by Charles Dickens when Canning stumbles in. Seeing he's drunk, she ignores him. The next thing she knows her book is in the fire and another one hits her in the stomach. She ducks and dodges as Canning hurls everything he can grab. Running out of ammunition, he backhands her across the face and sends her flying. She crouches like a cornered animal as he smashes a chair against the stove and comes at her, measuring the rung against his thumb.*

"Perfect! Just the width of my thumb. Do you know what that means, Mrs. Woodhull?"

She shakes her head, shrinking back.

"It means that according to the law I can use this stick to discipline you. And that's just what I aim to do!"

She stands and faces him, stone-faced and defiant, as the splintered oak strikes her skin.

Later, Victoria sits on the floor by the barren fireplace shaking with cold. Her entire body is swollen and bruised. She rocks back and forth, digging at a sliver in her thigh.

"My god, Sis, I knew it!" Victoria looks up in a daze as Tennie bursts into the house. "I was helping Ma with the washin' and saw Doc beatin' you plain as day. So I hitched a ride to Cleveland. What has that scoundrel done? I'll get one of them new Colt pistols and shoot him dead. My god, it's cold in here. Why's the fire out?"

"Doc's left me, and I don't think he's coming back."

"My god, you ain't been wed a week. He'll be back."

"I don't even know if I want him back. All he does is drink. Doesn't do any doctoring that I can see. We've got no money. He's no different than papa, Tennie."

"Good riddance then. Come home, Vic."

"No. When you're going after your destiny, you can't go backwards."

"Then I'll stay. We'll set up shop, save our money, go to New York City. My god, let's get some heat in here."

~ ~ ~

Spring soon buds outside the window of the much cleaner house. Canning has returned and sits drinking his breakfast. A knock interrupts the trio's meal. Tennie jumps up. Opens the door to the sheriff.

"Landlord wants you out by the end of the week," the sheriff says, thrusting an eviction notice at her.

"Out? Why?"

"Landlord won't abide devil work in his house." The sheriff taps the sign beside the front door that reads: Mrs. Victoria C. Woodhull and Miss Tennessee Claflin, Clairvoyants and Spiritual Healers.

"Oh my god."

The next day, Canning waits on a wagon loaded with their few pitifully belongings while Victoria and Tennie hug each other desperately.

"You write from Chicago, Sis," Tennie says. "And try to go to some of them women's meetings they have there. You'll find your destiny yet."

"Don't tell Mama, but I think I'm in a family way," Victoria whispers in Tennie's ear.

"Oh my god."

~ ~ ~

As 1854 ends, a Chicago blizzard rages outside the unheated tenement apartment where sixteen-year-old Victoria writhes in pain. It takes several agonizing hours for her drunken husband to bring their baby into the world. As Doc sloppily ties off the umbilical cord, he doesn't notice that blood still seeps from his son's tiny naval

Sweat dripping down his face, Canning lays the infant on Victoria's stomach and stumbles out the door. The baby's wails echo shrilly through the room as Victoria looks at the cobweb-covered cupboards. The icicles on the bedposts. The cold hearth holding only a blood-soaked newspaper. Cuddling her son beneath their worn, grimy blanket, she promptly passes out.

New Year's Eve revelry finally rouses her. She tucks the blanket around her son and crawls painfully across the dirty wooden floor. Grabbing the poker from the hearth, she staggers to the window. The pane is already cracked so even her weak swing shatters it. Clinging to the windowsill, Victoria cries for help.

For the next month, Canning is nowhere to be found, and Victoria survives on the kindness of an aged neighbor lady. Then, as February wraps Chicago in bitter cold, pneumonia takes her rescuer. The day after the old woman's funeral, Victoria resolutely dons a calico dress and light shawl. Pulling a pair of rubber boots over her bare feet, she marches out into the ice-crusted city with her infant son. She stomps into the corner saloon and seconds later emerges and stalks away. Her cheeks are red with cold but hot with rage as she stops at Mrs. Petty's Boardinghouse, where boarders are dining on roast beef and fried potatoes. Canning sits by his mistress, nuzzling her neck between bites of food. Everything stops as Victoria appears in the doorway looking like an avenging angel. The food's aroma makes her swoon, but she squares her shoulders and walks boldly to the table.

"I am here for my husband, scoundrel though he be," she says, motioning toward Canning. "Let me tell you a story about this man you dine with." She holds out her baby. "This is his son, Byron, so named because since birth the boy has been as melancholy as young Lord Byron himself. Why? Because his own father left him and me to die while he came to live in luxury with you."

Victoria sways again, almost passing out. A boarder offers a chair. Another fills a plate with food and sets it in front of her. Mrs. Petty takes the baby and dribbles warm milk into his mouth. Everyone glares at Canning, whose jaw jerks crazily. He ducks his head and refuses to look up as Victoria relates the sordid story of her son's birth. When she has finished, Mrs. Petty stands.

"Mr. Woodhull, you are no longer welcome here. Go home and be a better husband and loving father." She packs up some food and wraps Byron in a clean fuzzy blanket.

With encouraging pats from all, Victoria walks triumphantly out the door, chastised husband shuffling behind.

~ ~ ~

Hearing there is a need for doctors in the boomtown of San Francisco, Victoria takes control and moves her family West. She hopes the warm climate will be good for her sickly son and that steady work will redeem her husband. Unfortunately, the weather is steamy when they arrive and Canning shows no ambition to look for work, so support of the family again falls to Victoria. After a horrible stint as a cigarette girl in a saloon and an uninteresting turn as a seamstress to an actress, she finds herself on stage starring in The Corsican Brothers with popular actor Frank Lawlor. She is an instant hit.

But a week later an apparition of Tennie calls her home.

Over the next several years, Victoria's dreams of an exulted destiny are buried under continuing Claflin drama. Finally she has had enough. She moves her family to New York City, planning to join the fight for woman's rights. Unfortunately, almost as soon as they arrive, Victoria becomes pregnant and her health falters. Canning finally earns a little money at a hospital, but they live in a tiny attic apartment above New York City's Union Square and almost starve to death.

On April 23, 1861, a quarter of a million people—the largest gathering in the country's history—assemble in Union Square for a rally in support of the Civil War that has just begun. The din of speeches and cheers rises to the tiny apartment above the Square, drowning out Victoria's screams as Canning delivers their second child, a daughter Zulu Maud.

Between caring for her two children and helping with the war efforts by rolling bandages and tending the wounded, Victoria's destiny seems a long way off. Then, in July of 1863, a military draft is instituted and riots explode on New York streets. Victoria flees with her family back to Ohio.

The Claflin chaos quickly drives Canning back to the bottle, and he now adds drugs to the mix, reviving his nervous tic and abusive ways. Victoria wakes one morning to find her husband passed out drunk yet again. She watches him for a long time, trying to cry. Unable to, she slips a note into his hand, smooths his tangled hair, and kisses his forehead.

"Forgive me," she whispers. Taking ten-year-old Byron and three-year-old Zulu Maud, she walks out the door without looking back.

~ ~ ~

"I'm dying and I got nowhere to go."

Canning's voice snaps Victoria out of her reverie. His lips tremble and he falls forward, out cold at her feet.

The next day Byron yelps for joy when Canning regains consciousness. Canning turns glazed eyes toward the boy. His voice is a hoarse whisper.

"Is this my son?"

"He missed you, Doc," Victoria says. Tears spring to her eyes as Byron hugs his father.

The nurse gives Canning a shot of morphine, and he sinks back into oblivion while Victoria gathers the Claflin clan and informs them that Canning will be staying.

"When he's well enough, he can take care of Byron," she explains. "He was a good father when he wasn't sick, and it is obvious that Byron remembers and loves him." Naturally, there's a huge uproar. Victoria has to shout to be heard. "Enough! This is my house, and if you have a problem with my decision you can leave! Now, I expect Doc to be treated like a member of this family. I've hired a nurse, so no one should be put out."

"It's not right havin' two husbands in the same house," Roxanna wails, wringing her hands. "They'll say you're a Free-lover for sure now! They'll put us on the street! Holy Mudder of Israel, we'll lose it all!"

"This is a simple act of charity," Victoria says. "No different than Tennie and I supporting all of you out of the goodness of our hearts."

"Victoria's got a point," Buck says, shocking Victoria. "The Claflins stick together. I reckon Mr. Woodhull's a Claflin now, too."

Chapter 7

The following Saturday evening, in a small auditorium in Troy, New Jersey, Dr. Treat introduces Victoria to the members of the American Association of Spiritualists. Blood, Andrews, and Tennie nod encouragement from the front row as she steps forward, takes a deep breath, and begins.

"I'm afraid you'll have to excuse my lack of expertise in the public forum," she tells the audience. "Dr. Treat apologized for the small size of the crowd this evening, but I must confess it is an answer to my prayers." The audience laughs, relaxing her a bit, and she begins her speech. "I had my first psychic experience on my third birthday." Victoria's mind travels backwards as she tells her story.

~ ~ ~

Three-year-old Victoria claps excitedly as her mother cuts a small johnnycake and pours on syrup. As her siblings fight over who gets the biggest piece, Victoria suddenly faints and cannot be roused. The family jabbers in confusion, and Roxanna shrieks for Maldron to fetch Nurse Rhodes. Victoria's eight-year-old brother dashes out the door, and Buck carries his daughter to the bed. His gruffness disappears as he gently lays her down. Roxanna whirls toward the other children.

"See what you've done with your arguing and misbehaving? Go away before your father gets the switch!"

The children scatter, but Buck doesn't notice. Aware only of Victoria's tiny hand resting in his calloused palm, he caresses it gently as Roxanna fills a basin with water and sponges her daughter's brow. The unconscious Victoria, meanwhile, is in a beautiful meadow with an older woman.

"Nurse Rhodes, is it you?" she asks.

"Yes, my child. Come walk with me." Victoria takes the woman's hand, and they walk through patches of bright yellow daffodils. A Monarch flits by, and Victoria giggles and gives chase. She doesn't

notice the angel that floats from the sky until they collide. Victoria stares in awe as the angel beckons to the old woman.

"Can I come too?" Victoria asks.

"No, my child," the angel tells her. "You must lead the fight for truth. Stay now and do not be afraid."

Victoria flings herself at Nurse Rhodes, but the woman tenderly loosens the toddler's fingers from her skirt and follows the angel into the sun.

At the same time, back in the Claflin home, Maldon runs in the front door, gasping for air.

"Nurse Rhodes can't help. She just died," Maldron says. Roxanna's wails grow louder; tears fill Buck's eyes.

Still in the meadow, Victoria squints into the bright light and sees a large man in chiton and laced sandals. He wears a crown of laurel, and his voice booms like thunder.

"You are destined for wealth and fame, Victoria. You will live in a city surrounded by ships and rule your people. Listen for me, and I will guide you."

"Who are you?" Victoria asks, but the figure just melts into the sun's blinding glare. Victoria blinks and opens her eyes, back in reality. She glances at her parents, who doze beside the bed. She strokes her father's cheek, startling him awake. "Why are you so sad, Papa? I was only visiting Nurse Rhodes in the garden. Then she went with an angel, and I saw a big man with a loud voice."

"Mary, Mudder of Jesus," Roxanna wails. "Our daughter is blessed by the spirits!"

~ ~ ~

Victoria returns to the present and becomes aware of the audience as she concludes her account.

"It is time for our nation to be led with Spirit guidance, and I am the candidate who will do that. I ask for your support in lifting our country up to the heights of goodness our forefathers envisioned."

She is overcome by the standing ovation.

Chapter 8

On Sunday evening, some weeks later, Victoria hosts her first salon, the in-vogue pastime for an informal exchange of ideas. She looks stunning, with a white rose pinned to the bosom of her long, deep purple gown. Chandeliers glisten off frescoed walls and censers fill the air with a lavender-scented haze. Fresh flowers surround the fountain housing the statues of Daphne and Apollo. A small band plays softly as the guest book quickly fills with well-known names of businessmen, politicians, entertainers, reformers, and Spiritualists.

"If I can convert you from the avaricious capitalistic philosophy, others will surely follow your lead," Andrews tells John D. Rockefeller, joining Blood and the oil tycoon who are discussing Rockefeller's new Standard Oil Company.

"And how will I do that exactly?" Rockefeller asks.

He is immediately sorry he asked as Andrews launches into a long-winded dissertation about the subject until Blood steps in to save him.

As soon as everyone has arrived and been greeted, Victoria seeks out Esther Andrews, Pearl's wife. She has just returned from an extended period of study of homeopathy in France, and Victoria is anxious to hear her ideas.

"Pearl says the regimen of fasting, herbs, and massage you learned on the Continent will add years to his life," Victoria says.

"I hope so. By the way, I stopped in your ladies room and was pleased to see you do not offer cigarettes as is the popular trend."

"Nor will I ever. Studies show that tobacco from cigarettes is the most harmful of all. Our bodies are temples of God, and I refuse to introduce poison to it or make it easy for my guests to do so."

"Bravo!" Esther kisses Victoria's cheek. "Pearl tells me your husband suffers from arthritis. If he eats only what flies or grows above the ground and walks daily, he will improve."

"I will remember that. We must set aside a date to chat more about your work with homeopathy." Victoria turns to embrace Mrs. Treat, a rather mousy little woman, who joins them. "Mrs. Treat is a strong advocate of meatless diets," she tells Esther Andrews. "She has recently converted me, and I can already see a difference in my stamina."

"I am now exploring the causes and treatments of hysteria," Mrs. Treat says.

"The new epidemic in middle-class women," Mrs. Andrews says. "Such a convenient disease! It's not fatal but requires endless attention."

"That was true at the beginning, but now men are using it as an excuse to suppress women. Every day I have some man drag his wife to me for a clitoridectomy to cure her hysteria."

"No!" Victoria and Mrs. Andrews say together, shocked and clearly disturbed.

"Yes. They are removing the essence of our womanhood simply because we want to join the suffragists or have a say in rearing our children. I won't do it."

"Men are so afraid of our woman power, which they relate, as they do everything it seems, to our sexual urges," Victoria says.

"Very true," Mrs. Andrews agrees. "It's amazing how otherwise intelligent women go to clinics and submit to the stimulation of their breasts and clitoris, and when they respond according to their God-given instinct, they permit these butchers to remove the very fountain of their femininity and spirituality."

"Maybe we should do the same to men," Mrs. Treat mumbles. "Stimulate their privates, and when they respond, amputate."

As short time later, Victoria assembles everyone for a program of poetry and exhortation, and then introduces the evening's entertainment.

"There is a Ouija board set up behind that curtain over there, and we'll have a séance in the main parlor," she announces. "There is also a billiards table in the library just across the hall if anyone would care to challenge me to a game."

"I'll take that challenge!" P.T. Barnum calls out. The famous showman is a stocky man with round face, receding black curls, and deep-set eyes. He is flamboyantly dressed in a bright blue suit, gold brocade vest, and gold top hat.

"Be careful, P.T.," Blood calls back. "Victoria will wipe the table with you!"

"Of course there will be dancing as well," Victoria says, smiling broadly. "But before we disperse to our activities, I want to thank you all for having the courage of your convictions and for supporting our ideals. With woman's increasing involvement in matters outside the home and my candidacy for President, a Golden Age is just around the corner. We mustn't mind what the world says or try to be popular. Instead we must come out from the ruck of grumblers who criticize only and do our duty to help our fellowman. And love one another. If we love freely and unconditionally we accomplish what God has put us on this earth to do. *Namaste*."

Dancing begins, and Johnnie Green watches Victoria and Blood glide around the dance floor. As a new song starts, he cuts in.

"May I conduct a short interview with you for the *Sun's* article about this evening?" Johnnie asks as they twirl away.

"Certainly. Come with me." Victoria leads him from the ballroom and up to the second-floor parlor. She motions him to the settee and pours him a whiskey. "I've watched you writing periodically this evening. Read me what you have so I may see the tone you are taking." She hands him the drink and sits beside him.

Johnnie blushes but reads.

"Mrs. Woodhull's salon last evening was a squeeze of diversity. Spiritualists, radicals, and respected bankers mingled in the Zodiac palace that smelled like Heaven itself. The salon resembled those of Mademoiselle Roland during the first French Revolution, a rendezvous for men and women of genius. But the highlight of the evening was the queenly and charming Mrs. Woodhull. Clothed in a flowing gown the color of overripe mulberries, a delicate white rose nestled tastefully on her bodice—"

"So this is to be a piece for the fashion page," Victoria says, interrupting him to tease.

"Well, uh, no."

"Mr. Green, since you are interested in my apparel, I will show you something." She stands. "Please help yourself to more beverage. I won't be a moment."

She hurries out, and Green meanders through the adjacent greenhouse, admiring the exotic plants and whistling at the songbirds.

"Sis asked me to keep you company. Would you like that, Johnnie?" Tennie's voice startles him, but in a pleasant way. She lights a cigar and offers him one. When she perches on a bench, he rests a foot beside her and balances his forearm on his leg to lean close.

"Miss Claflin, have I told you that you look stunning?"

"Thanks, Johnnie, but enough flattery and formality." She pulls his head down and plants a long, sensuous kiss on his lips. "How's it feel to kiss a competitor?" she asks coyly.

"How do we compete, my dear?"

"Sis and I are startin' a newspaper! *Woodhull & Claflin's Weekly* is gonna give the *Sun* a real run for its money."

"Really?" His journalistic instincts overcome his passions, even though Tennie nibbles his ear.

"My god, it's all Q.T., so don't do more'n hint of a surprise in your article, okay? Sis'll pull up my dress and spank me for spilling the beans." Tennie hops up, raises her dress, and pats her behind with childlike glee.

"Tennessee Celeste, quit teasing Mr. Green!"

Johnnie blushes, looks toward Victoria, and almost swallows his cigar! She wears navy pants, cuffed and buckled at the knee. Powder blue stockings show off her shapely legs. A white shirt, blue-patterned tie, and blousy, dark-blue, mid-thigh-length tunic complete the ensemble. Victoria pivots and turns.

"Mrs. Woodhull, that attire is far too scandalous for our times. If you appear in public, you'll be arrested on the spot!"

"Oh, no, Mr. Green. When I'm ready to appear in this, no policeman will touch me."

"It's her inauguration outfit, Johnnie! What do you think?"

"I think you are dangerous women, and I do not trust myself alone with you another minute." The sisters laugh as he tips his drink to them and makes no move to leave.

Chapter 9

Tuesday, May 10, is a gorgeous spring day. Birds tweet loudly from the square black canopy that juts over the front entrance of New York City's Apollo Theater. The red-lettered sign atop the three-story white building is the only color on this dingy street in Harlem as hundreds of women converge for the NWSA convention. Inside the auditorium, Theodore Tilton directs last-minute preparations. He looks relieved when Elizabeth Cady Stanton hustles in. Elizabeth is plump and jolly. Her bouncing, sausage-shaped white curls draw the eye away from her sagging jowls and heavily lidded eyes.

"Elizabeth! Thank god you're here! Maybe you can get Susan out of the state she's in."

"For heaven's sake, what now? Where is she?"

Tilton nods at a door off-stage; Elizabeth hurries into the room. Susan stares out the window, one hand clutching her red shawl and the other rubbing the bridge of her nose. Tears glisten as Elizabeth envelops her in a hug.

"Oh, my darling empress," Susan says. "Everything is dissolving before my eyes. Maybe it's turning fifty. Maybe I'm too old to fight the fight anymore."

"If you're too old, then I certainly am!" When Susan doesn't respond, Elizabeth gives her a probing look. "What's really going on, Susan?"

"I'm turning *The Revolution* over to Laura Bullard and Mr. Tilton. Maybe her family's money and Mr. Tilton's expertise can keep it running."

"So Theodore is to run our organization *and* our newspaper? How male of him."

"What's it going to take to win the day, Lizzie?"

"I don't know. But something will come along to rekindle us. It always does."

Chants rise in the auditorium.

"Susan dear, we can either sit here and feel sorry for ourselves, or we can walk out there, resign, and go upstate for a month-long water cure. Maybe sitting in a hot spa will help us figure out a new direction for our fight. Since I am obligated to preside today, I vote for the latter."

"At least there's something we can vote on," Susan mutters, following Elizabeth out.

Tennie is in the crowd, hidden under a shapeless Quaker dress and puffy bonnet. She assesses the suffragists as they take seats on the stage and grins in approval as Tilton walks to the podium.

"We shall never have a government thoroughly permeated with humanity until men and women unite to form public sentiment and administer that sentiment through government," Tilton says. He waits for the crowd to quiet and continues. "Ladies and Gentlemen, I present our organization's founder, Elizabeth Cady Stanton."

In minutes Elizabeth has the crowd in her hands.

"The idea that woman is inherently weak is a grand mistake. She is physically weak because she dresses in a way that would kill a soldier. With heavy bustles, yards of material to drag around, and steel bones that pinch and contort our bodices as we gasp for breath—why, many physicians say it is almost impossible to find a perfect female skeleton. Hoops, trains, high heels, chignons, and panniers—they're all man's handiwork. And what does woman get out of it? A limping gait, feeble muscles, and cultivated fears!

"And it's not only our clothes. Our systems are full of toxins from the cosmetics we use to improve our God-given beauty, which doesn't need improvement at all. You've seen the advertisement for Hagan's Magnolia Balm that boasts it will make a woman of thirty look like a girl of sixteen. I ask: What sensible woman of thirty, with all the marks of intelligence and cultivation that well-spent years give, would desire to look like an inexperienced girl of sixteen?"

Tennie leaps to her feet and whistles loudly. The rest of the women quickly join her, then quiet as Elizabeth continues.

"It is a shame what women must endure in life. In addition to confining fashion and poisoning potions, you have the hairstyles. It's bound, loosed, cultivated—all based on what is perceived to please man! We force it into curls, pile it high, and hold it with a thousand pins that exert constant pricklings on the skull. But let us cut it short to make it easy to attend to, and we are labeled fast women!"

Tennie pats her Quaker bonnet to be sure it still hides her short curls.

"In conclusion I say that beauty cannot be put on and off like a garment. It depends on intellect, sentiment, and affections of the soul. We cannot be one thing and look another. There are indelible marks in every face showing the real life lived. We must begin here and now to let our real selves show and teach our girls that true beauty begins within."

On Friday, the final day of the women's convention in New York, an American News delivery wagon drops two new publications at a Wall Street newsstand. The first is an unprofessional thing called *The Christian Union*. The front-page headline reads "The Gospel of Love." Henry Ward Beecher is listed as editor, and Beecher family members have penned every article. The wiry vendor sneers as he opens the stack.

"Just what the world needs," he mutters, "another Beecher horn."

The other new paper is *Woodhull & Claflin's Weekly*. The masthead reads "Onward & Upward" and lists Victoria C. Woodhull and Tennie C. Claflin as editors and proprietors, Stephen Pearl Andrews as editor-in-chief, and Colonel J. H. Blood as managing editor. The front page holds a prominent ad for the Woodhull, Claflin and Company banking house and the paper's mission as laid out by Stephen Pearl Andrews:

> **There is something radically wrong in modern society when wealth and luxury are on the increase but happiness and contentment are on the decrease. Therefore, this newspaper will give you a thousand times more than mere news. It will be a walking University, settling great questions of government, labor, and life in a way that a child can understand.**

People bustle by, grabbing papers and tossing him change as the vendor leafs through the *Weekly's* fifteen slick pages. There's something for everyone inside: A sports page with baseball scores and gambling odds on upcoming horse races; theater and book reviews; a financial column with stock reports; and a persuasive article on the new diet fad of Vegetarianism. There is an article on Spiritualism, and the first installment of George Sand's serialized novel *Malre Tout* (*In Spite of it All*), translated into English by Andrews. Headlines hit all the major stories: "Paris Sieged by Prussians; Rome Named New Capitol of Italy; James Gang Strikes Again." The *Weekly* also reprints Victoria's announcement of her candidacy for President. The vendor is so deeply engrossed in his reading the clip-clop of approaching horses startles him. He jumps up when he sees Victoria, Blood, and Tennie in the open carriage.

"Capital paper you got there," he says when the carriage stops. "I'm reading every word."

"But is it selling?" Victoria asks.

"See for yourself, Mrs. Woodhull." He gestures at a nearly depleted stack. "I'll sell as many as you can deliver."

"Then we'll all get rich, my man," Blood says.

"You've also made the cover of the *Daily Doings* again," the vendor tells the sisters. He gestures toward the men's sporting magazine that features a picture of Victoria and Tennie.

"My god, we must've been on that cover more than anyone else ever," Tennie says. "Can you hand me one?"

"Better on the cover than the racy pages within," Blood remarks.

The same evening, Lib Tilton huddles in a red shawl and lounges on a red velvet reclining sofa watching her husband and Elizabeth Cady Stanton play chess. The Tiltons' three-story brownstone, in a middle-class neighborhood not far from Beecher's more affluent one, is a study in Bohemian comfort. Cushioned sofas are interspersed with heavy walnut chairs carved with cherubs' faces and each with its own ottoman. Fresh flowers provide a vivid contrast to the bleak Gothic architecture, which includes winding passageways and mysterious staircases. A large crayon sketch of Horace Greeley hangs above a carved pipe organ, looking out of place among several original pieces of art.

"Good convention this year," Theodore remarks to Elizabeth as he moves a knight. "It was bold of you and Susan to offer to resign. It certainly revitalized everyone."

"Let's hope so. We were serious, you know."

The front door opens, and Susan B. Anthony marches in.

"Did you know about this, Mr. Tilton?"

She tosses a copy of the *Weekly* on the table beside the chessboard. Theodore picks up the paper and whistles.

"I did not."

"Those Wall Street harlots have some sense of timing," Susan bemoans. "Debuting their paper when everyone active in the suffrage movement is in the city is teetotally rude!"

"May I see?" Elizabeth asks. Theodore hands Elizabeth the paper, and she flips through it, pausing to read. "'This Journal will support Victoria C. Woodhull for President with its whole strength and will advocate suffrage without distinction of sex.' Hmmm. Interesting." She flips a page and reads again: "'I will be in fashion, if I die for it!' said the ambitious belle, whose locks were not of the ruling tint. And dye she did.' That's d-y-e dye. Clever. I must add it to my speech on the ridiculousness of today's fashions." She turns another page and reads: "'Mrs. Rolles has knocked one objection against woman's suffrage right out of sight by inventing a cradle that can securely and continuously rock the babies while women go to vote.'" She chuckles.

"I don't see any humor in this, Lizzie," says Susan, her eyes misting. "I think I shall retire."

As Susan walks to the stairs, and Lib follows to tuck in the children, Elizabeth lays down the paper and blocks Tilton's king.

"Checkmate!"

~ ~ ~

The following Tuesday, the women return to Apollo Hall, this time for a protest rally over a recent trial verdict that epitomizes woman's lot.

Victoria and Tennie are among those in the standing room only crowd as Susan B. Anthony speaks from the podium.

"This protest is about women rising en masse to say we will no longer tolerate statutes that keep women indissolubly bound to men they abhor. It's about women forcing complete codification of our laws! It's about women rejoicing over every female slave that escapes a discordant marriage! Ladies, I give you Abby Richardson to tell her story."

Abby walks to the podium, nervously fingering her hair that sorrow has turned gray overnight. Her brown eyes are swollen from tears, and she flutters her long, thick lashes as she struggles with her emotions and begins.

"Daniel McFarland and I met at a hospital benefit in Madison, Wisconsin. I was seventeen and he was forty, well spoken and boasting of landholdings and wealth he wanted to lavish on me. He told me he would train me to be a star. Lured by his promise of love, and also fame I suppose, I married him.

"My first beating came when he discovered I was pregnant, something he said would destroy my chance at stardom. After battering me for an hour, he abandoned me for dead. After our son Percy was born, the abuse continued, so I fled to my parents' farm in Vermont." Tears moisten Victoria's eyes, remembering her similar sorrow, as Abby takes a moment to regain her composure so she can continue. "But I believed in the sanctity in marriage, so when my husband came begging and promising reform, I succumbed. Of course, the minute I was back in his clutches, the nightmare began again.

"Daniel drank constantly and beat me for a look or a sigh. Oft times with no provocation whatsoever. When our second child died at birth, he threatened to make me drink prussic acid. Another time he threatened to cut open his chest with my sewing shears and spill his blood on our son. He kept loaded pistols around to shoot me at a moment's notice, or so he said."

"My god, makes Doc look almost like a saint," Tennie whispers to Victoria.

"I was too ashamed to tell anyone and too terrified to leave my son with him so I could work, so we ended up in horrid destitution. My parents turned their backs on me when I went back to Daniel, so that help was no longer available. Unable to stand by and watch Percy die of starvation, I finally told my tale to Anna Dickinson, who told Albert Richardson, one of the *Tribune's* chief journalists and a man I knew from my work as part-time theater critic for that paper.

"Albert found my husband two different prestigious positions, both of which he failed to hold due to his alcoholism. When I was offered the role of Nerissa in *The Merchant of Venice*, I found the courage to separate from my marriage, and because of his earlier kindness, Albert and I became friends. And fell in love. All we wanted was to be together. I moved to Indiana, which has more expedient and humane laws than New York, and filed for divorce.

"When I returned to New York eager to marry Albert, my former husband got wind of the plans. On November twenty-fifth, at 5:30 in the afternoon, he slunk into the *Tribune* and hid in the shadows until Albert came to collect his mail. Then he fired one bullet point-blank into Albert's left side." Women weep as Abby composes herself before continuing. "When it became clear that Albert's wound was a mortal one, the Reverends Beecher and Frothingham granted his dying wish for us to be married. Three days later, with his hand clasped in mine, my truest love died."

Overcome, Abby signals Elizabeth Cady Stanton to take over. She sobs into her handkerchief as Elizabeth takes the podium.

"Last week a judge rendered an utterly preposterous verdict against Albert Richardson's cold-blooded killer! That a man can be declared not guilty by reason of insanity after patiently waiting to fire his shot is lunacy itself. But to turn custody of an innocent child over to someone who, by law, is either a murderer or insane is a crime almost too heinous to grasp. And why? Solely because of the fundamental falsehood that wives and children are man's property! We had to rise up in protest!"

Victoria is entranced as Elizabeth's voice resounds through the auditorium. She is literally gaping in awe by the time Elizabeth builds to her conclusion.

"When that all-male jury found the murderer McFarland to be temporarily insane from legitimate anger, when that all-male jury not only set the killer free but gave him custody of twelve-year-old Percy in order to turn that innocent lad into a despotic male like themselves—that, dear women, was the Dred Scot decision of the woman's movement! And we . . . will . . . not . . . accept . . . it!"

Victoria is on her feet, leading the standing ovation.

Chapter 10

The Grand Opera House at Twenty-third and Eighth is seven-stories high and gaudily ornate. Fisk and Gould have just completed remodeling the building and are hosting an open house. New York's elite and powerful attend in formal dress. An orchestra plays Tchaikovsky's "Romeo & Juliet," as outlandishly dressed Napoleon Sarony, famed for his photographs of celebrities, takes pictures of the arriving guests. The men of Wall Street nod briefly at Victoria, Tennie, Blood, and Andrews as they arrive, then quickly steer their wives away. Victoria's cheeks spot red, but Blood takes her hand and whispers in her ear.

"Looks like they don't want their wives to meet your debonair husband."

"I wish I had Tennie's ability to not care so much. To have more fun," Victoria says, pecking Blood's cheek and glancing at Tennie, who flirts with banker Luther Challis, though he has a teenage girl on his arm.

"We'll work on that tonight." Blood slips an arm around her waist, and they follow the crowd into one of the building's six theatres, where showgirls present portions of the enormously successful play "The Twelve Temptations." A blonde chorus line juggles balls of fire, dodging the sparks and cinders that fall around their scantily clad bodies. One girl, seriously burned, flicks off the pain and dances on.

"I cannot watch this. That poor girl is hurt, and all in the name of entertainment," Victoria says. "It's ridiculous."

"Let's go to the other theater," Blood suggests gently. "Fun? Remember?"

"Fun. Right. But I'm going to address this insanity in the next *Weekly*."

They make their way to a second showroom where Fisk's mistress, in shimmering gold gown, belts out a song from atop a cascading waterfall. Brunette showgirls dance in the water below her. The rhythm of the water has a calming effect on Victoria. By the time they move on to the ballroom, she is smiling and ready to dance. Guests quickly fill the dance floor as Jim Fisk, the Regiment's ostentatiously dressed Colonel, conducts the Ninth Regiment brass band, the biggest and best in the country.

Victoria and Blood flow together in fluid motion, he dashing in tails and she a vision in deep purple gown accented by a white rose at her throat and a fashionable purple hat. Coming out of a dip, however, she sees her father, black eye patch askew, flirting outrageously with Luther Challis' teenage date. Buck is so drunk he falls against the tiny girl, almost knocking her over as he reaches for a glass of champagne from a passing tray. Victoria blanches, grips Blood's arm. He follows her gaze to Buck and smoothly and casually dances them toward him. Victoria breaks away and strides to her father.

"What do you think you're doing?" Her voice hisses from between her clenched teeth. Challis' date scoots away.

"Don't go getting' all high-falutin' on me, girlie. You think you're the only one fit to hobnob with the gentry? You're from my same cloth no matter how much you deny it. You wouldn't know any of these people if I hadn't introduced you to Mr. Vanderbilt!" He slugs back another glass of champagne and hiccups loudly. His words slur. "And that pretty young lady came up to me. There's some that find this patch alluring." Buck grabs another glass of champagne, downs it, and wipes his arm across his mouth.

"You're despicable!"

Buck raises a hand to slap her, but Blood is quick. He grabs Buck's wrist in mid-air and squeezes. His voice is low but firm.

"Let's go. Now! Before I break every bone in your wrist."

"Father, please," Victoria begs. "Don't make a scene."

"There won't be a scene. He's leaving," Blood assures her, his eyes steady on Buck.

Buck growls, but realizing he is outmatched, allows Blood to maneuver him out the door. He stumbles to his horse, Blood's hand still tight on his arm.

"Listen to me, Old Man. Victoria may be a forgiving spirit, but I am not. If you ever embarrass her like this again, I will beat you to a bigger pulp than you did your children and personally escort you out of our lives. Is that understood?"

They stare each other down for a moment before Buck hiccups and hoists himself onto his horse. He spits on the ground beside Blood before galloping away. Blood returns to the party, where Victoria waits by the door.

"I'm sorry for interfering, Victoria."

"No, you were right. This wasn't the time nor place for a showdown. I'll deal with Father when we get home. I can't find Tennie. Where is she? I want to leave."

"If we leave now, he wins. Let's dance. If Tennie doesn't show up shortly, we'll go find her."

Victoria glances around. Freak show curator P. T. Barnum yammers excitedly to Stephen Andrews about Heinrich Schliemann's excavation of Troy. The elite women of the Sorosis Woman's Club talk of French fashions and bemoan the turmoil in Paris that has postponed their trips abroad. J.P. Morgan and John D. Rockefeller discuss the Morgan family's fifty-million-dollar loan to France for their war with Prussia. The large, eclectic contingent from the art community chatter about Wagner marrying Franz Liszt's daughter, Cosima von Bulow, as well as the continuing popularity of artists Currier and Ives. Victoria is relieved to see that the altercation with her father has pretty much gone unnoticed. Only one woman catches her eye and smiles sympathetically. Victoria takes a deep breath and shrugs.

"You're right. If he knows he's ruined our evening, he'll do it again."

"That's my gal." Blood steers her back to the dance floor.

Tennie and Luther Challis, meanwhile, walk through the Erie offices in the left wing of the Opera House. Tennie gapes in awe at the freestanding safe that rises from its granite foundation in the basement, straight up through seven stories to the roof. Challis pulls her into Jim Fisk's office, with its gaudy, in-vogue wallpaper and dozens of original works of art and Egyptian hieroglyphics. A massive, carved desk sits on a raised dais by the window, and a blue velvet sofa stretches along one wall.

"We should get back," Tennie says. "Your date must be looking for you."

"Aw, she's not old enough or bright enough to find her way out of a paper bag. Don't you want to kiss me?" Before she can reply, Challis gives her a long, passionate kiss. She responds as passionately, and he maneuvers them onto the sofa. Lips locked, they slide into a prone position. When they come up for air, Challis grins. "See? I'm not the ogre you made me out to be when we had our little fuss at the French Masked Ball last fall. Do you realize this is the first time we've been alone together since then?"

"Oh, yeah, I had forgotten that."

"What madness it was. Wild, orgasmic madness! A magnificent orgy!" He lips move back to hers, but Tennie pushes him away.

"You were with teenagers that night, too. What's the deal with that, Luther? Does a grown woman scare you?"

"Mr. Maxwell invited them."

"Just like you to blame your friend. I could see you were the one getting them corned. And then you took them to the whorehouse across the street just so you could come back with the blood of a virgin on your finger."

"Hey, she asked for it and loved it."

"You're a liar. Sis and I found her cryin' in a corner after you and your friends were done with her. She wasn't more'n fifteen years old, for god's sake. We tried to help her when her father disowned her, but it wasn't many weeks later she slit her throat. My god, Luther, thanks for remindin' me what a blackguardin' masher you are. It's brought back my senses and spoiled my appetite." She starts toward the door, but Challis hooks the curve of his umbrella handle around her neck and jerks her backwards.

"Oh, no, Miss Claflin. You're honor-bound to take care of what you started here. Now, quit kickin' up a shine and do it."

She claws at the umbrella, trying to loosen it from her throat as he jerks her back down on the sofa. She gulps in long breaths as Challis discards the umbrella and dives on top of her. Her laugh startles him.

"Oh, Mr. Challis," she coos. "I was just testin' to see if you truly desired me. Shall I show you the magic I give to the Com?"

"Yes, yes! Show me your magic. Take me to Eden."

She rolls on top of him, running her hands lightly through his hair, over his face, and down his neck. He closes his eyes and groans with pleasure as she rips off his shirt and tie and flicks her tongue across his broad, fuzzy chest. Sliding down his body, she undoes his pants and feverishly pulls them off. He writhes in anticipation as she flings them across the room and bends toward his erection.

Suddenly, his moan of ecstasy turns to a cry of pain! Standing quickly, Tennie gives another twist to his genitals and sashays to the door.

"My god, what a scumbag," she says, giving him one final, derisive look.

He flies off the sofa and dives for his pants. But he isn't fast enough. Tennie is gone.

Chapter 11

A few days after the Fisk/Gould event, Tennie stands across the street from the Vanderbilt mansion. With her are an Italian organ grinder and his monkey, both clad in green velvet jackets, fancy red caps, and hoop earrings. She tosses a peanut to the monkey as Mrs. Vanderbilt climbs into a waiting carriage.

"Right on time, Mrs. Frank. Thank you," she murmurs, watching the horses clop off down the street that is covered with straw to muffle the noise. She pushes bills into the monkey's cup. "When I give the signal, go under the window and play as loud as you can," she tells the grinder. "Don't stop 'til I'm inside."

She dashes across the street and hides in the stairwell leading to the servants' quarters below the mansion. At her wave, the organ grinder positions himself beneath the tall front windows of the house. She nods, and he cranks up his hurdy-gurdy, churning out noise as fast as he can. Tennie covers her ears to shut out the tinny blares.

It takes only seconds for the butler to storm from the house, money in hand. The grinder cranks faster—and continues until Tennie has dashed up the steps and into the house. As soon as the door closes behind her, the monkey grabs the money and the music stops.

The Commodore is sick, and his illness has not softened his temper. He jerks his head away from a nurse who tries to brush his hair.

"Get away from my hair! I bet you sold a lock to that rascal Fisk and dastardly Gould. Is that how they got my power?"

Tennie stops in the bedroom doorway and watches the nurse load a syringe. Tears fill her eyes at seeing how frail the old man looks. Mustering a grin, she strolls into the room.

"I thought that was you I heard yellin' all the way down on Wall Street. What's got you so hepped up, Old Boy?"

"Little Sparrow!" He pinches the nurse's bottom. "G'on outta here! Miss Claflin can take care of me for awhile."

"Just let me give you this shot first, Sir," the nurse says. "You'll have a heart attack if we don't settle you down."

"I don't need no mad-dog sedative. I need to get my hands on them blasted blowers. They hornswoggled me for the last time! Git on over here, Little Sparrow." He turns to the nurse and gives her a swat. "And you skedaddle!"

"My god, Old Boy, you ain't gonna get your hands on anybody if you have a stroke." Tennie sashays to the bed and caresses the Commodore's hair, calming him.

"I'm gittin' too old for the game, Little Sparrow." Vanderbilt lies back and sighs loudly. "Them blowers Fisk and Gould got me good again. Hain't hardly got no pride left."

"Is this about the huge cut in cattle-hauling prices?"

"You know it. I took Central's cattle fares down from a hundred and twenty dollars a load to forty so people could afford meat for their summer barbecues, and them blasted robber barons slashed Erie rates to a buck. I had to match it."

"Is that what you're mad about?"

"What I'm mad about is that Fisk and Gould bought up all the cattle in Buffalo and shipped 'em on my train, leavin' no space for higher-paying cargo. Six thousand head! And they sold them at a pretty profit to boot."

"Them mashers!"

"Didn't cost me millions or nuthin', but it's the idea of them sittin' in their office laughin'. I hain't used to being laughed at, Little Sparrow, and I don't like it."

"My god, they'll soon sink in their own dunghill, Old Boy." She pulls his whiskers playfully. "In the meanwhile, it's good to hear you roar. Gets my blood a'pumpin'. Now, how's about a little somethin' to take your mind off your troubles?"

~ ~ ~

While Tennie cavorts with Vanderbilt, Victoria and Blood go over a mock-up of the *Weekly's* next front page, although the sexual tension between them makes it hard for them to concentrate.

76

"I am glad we lead with the story about Georgia finally rejoining the Union," Blood says, futilely attempting to stick to business. "The United States is whole again, and we can finally heal from the terrible war."

"And thank goodness Mrs. Lincoln finally has her pension, although it's outrageous that, after five years of practically begging, she is only allotted three thousand dollars a year. We spend almost that every month, and the woman gave her husband for this country for goodness sakes!"

"You are so beautiful when you're fired with righteous indignation. We must get you on the lecture circuit."

"No. No. I cannot. Had the Spirits not taken over and spoken through me at the Spiritualist convention, I surely would have fainted."

"But, Darling, in San Francisco you performed on stage with one of the greatest actors of our time. Surely you can't have stage fright."

"That was different. I was playing a role, speaking clever lines written for a character. If people didn't like what I was saying they would blame the playwright."

"As President, speeches will be required of you."

"Being President will give me the confidence. For now I am content to have my say with my pen."

"Well, today your pen has said enough." He takes the pen and lays it on the desk. "Have you forgotten it's our anniversary?"

"I don't think my body will let me forget. I know I'm not the only one who's had trouble concentrating the last few minutes. You are so sexy." She loops her arms around his neck.

"Shall we go dine and celebrate?"

"Or should we stay and consummate?"

Victoria's eyes tease, and their lips find each other hungrily, as they had the first time they had met.

~ ~ ~

On a warm, summer evening in 1865, Tennie accepts the fees at their shop in St. Louis, while Victoria tells fortunes. A handsome young man with lush chestnut hair and sideburns extending down to a handlebar mustache enters. He is dressed in a Union uniform and his right arm is in a sling. His erect bearing and deep chocolate eyes make Tennie flutter, but he is not smitten by her charms as most men are.

"I am Colonel James Harvey Blood," he says. "Commander of Missouri's Sixth Regiment, St. Louis City Auditor, and President of the St. Louis Society of Spiritualists. I am familiar with Mrs. Woodhull's reputation and wish to consult with her." He hands over his money, and Tennie waves him into the parlor where Victoria sits at a mahogany table. A kerosene lamp bathes her in an ethereal glow. As Blood walks toward her, Victoria can hardly breathe. Sparks almost sizzle off her skin as he kisses her hand. She immediately falls into a trance.

"I see our futures linked," she tells him. "Freedom from your constricting bonds of marriage awaits, and a destiny ordained by the powers of air."

Within days, they take to the road, James abandoning his wife and daughter and Victoria leaving Zulu Maud and Byron with Tennie. Traveling through the Ozarks in a brightly colored carriage with a gold, ball-fringed top, Blood is a charming and persuasive hawker. At every stop, long lines wait to have their fortunes told by the lovely seer Victoria.

In the evenings they relax by their campfire and Blood produces book upon book, which they read aloud, their legs entwined. He introduces her to classics by Jane Austin, the Bronte sisters, Shelley, Keats, Wordsworth and Lord Byron. One night Blood brings out a heavy tome by Adam Smith, known for his laissez-faire economic theory. Another night he reads the philosophy of Arthur Schopenhauer. Victoria is enthralled.

"Love is the beginning of knowledge as fire is of light, but literature is the thought of thinking souls." He tells her another night, quoting Thomas Carlyle.

"I have never known a man like you," she says. "You worship me like I am the Queen herself and at the same time inflame my mind with grand ideas. To love you is as natural as breathing. It makes me wonder how I remained true to Canning after my love for him had fled."

"You did it because women are taught blind obedience to man. It is hard to break the conditioning of a lifetime, but thank the Spirits you have!"

"Blind obedience. Yes, that's it. And so many suffer worse than I did. Even wives treated kindly are afraid to express their sexual feelings lest they be castrated, thrown into an asylum, or flung aside to the life of a prostitute. That must change."

Another evening, James introduces her to the writings of John Stuart Mill, including his famous On Liberty. Blood watches with fascination as she flips through the material, reading aloud ideas that excite her.

"'Ask yourself whether you are happy and you cease to be so. . . . A person may cause evil to others not only by his action but by his inaction. . . . One person with a belief is equal to a force of ninety-nine who have only interest. . . ." Laying down the book, Victoria finally tells Blood about Demosthenes' prophecy. He immediately insists they be off at once to follow her destiny.

"We will return to St. Louis, pay off my debts, give my wife and daughter money to find their own true loves and destinies. Then we'll retrieve Zulu Maud and Byron and make our way East."

"James Harvey Blood, you are my soul's true mate and my hero above all others."

~ ~ ~

Victoria's thoughts return to the present to find Blood has brushed the papers off her desk and set her on it. He stands facing her, shirt thrown open. Victoria draws back to catch her breath; sadness flits across her face.

"James, do you ever think about the family you left behind? Do you miss them?"

"Sometimes when I look at Zulu Maud, I think, *Carrie's the same age.* But Zulu seems much more my true daughter. Even at five, Carrie was like her mother. Money, society, and religion were all that mattered to them. Have I ever thanked you for saving me from all that?" He kisses her.

"Have I ever thanked you for surviving that awful war and finding me?" She pushes his shirt down his arms, flinging it aside. His chest is firm, with a light sprinkling of chestnut hair. She kisses four bullet scars: One on his right shoulder, another on his right arm, and two on the left side of his chest. She slides off the desk, unbuckles his trousers, and pushes them down his legs, kissing a final wound on his left thigh.

"What a glorious time we had traveling the Midwest and sealing our love," he says, his voice husky with emotion.

"You taught me everything. Everything! Sitting by the campfire reading Abigail Adams and Mary Wollstonecraft and all the other brave women who spoke out for justice. All I now am is because of you." Victoria's tongue explores his mouth, and he needs no persuasion to enter her.

Chapter 12

The late-August heat drives Victoria, Tennie, Blood, Andrews, and nephew Channing Miles to the water. A gentle breeze moves their small sloop across the Upper Bay that is alive with sailboats of all sizes and shapes. As Blood and Channing trim the sails, Victoria stares across the water toward Oyster Island and falls into a trance. Seconds later, she shakes herself back to reality.

"Well, that was interesting," she says.

"I knew you were in a trance. What'd you see, Sis?"

"I saw an island. It looked like Oyster Island, but it was called Ellis Island. And hundreds of ships were docking there, with thousands of people coming ashore. And then a giant woman whose skin shone like copper rose out of the water. She held a flaming torch of liberty high into the air and wore a crown with seven rays of enlightenment shooting off it. Everyone cheered."

"My god, she's you! It's a sign you'll win the election!"

"Perhaps so." Victoria smiles at the thought before becoming all business. "But only if we get to work. The Universe does its part and we must do ours. By the way, it was a wonderful idea to bring our planning meeting here, Channing. Even this small breeze feels delightful."

"Thanks, Aunt Victoria. And thanks, too, for sending me to Admiral Farragut's funeral. He was always my hero. Oh, and I met Mrs. Grant! She mentioned you running for President and said that if women could vote and Mr. Grant wasn't running she'd vote for you!"

"Well then, let's get to work to make both those things happen," Victoria says.

"I second that," Andrews agrees. "This boat rocks too much. I'm getting *beaucoup malade*."

"You do look a little green, Prof Pearlo," Tennie teases.

Victoria consults her notes and starts handing out assignments.

"Pearl, I want you to cover Sara Lippincott's lecture against the death penalty. Channing, pull the section on Margaret Knight, the female

Edison in Boston, from Matilda Gage's new pamphlet *Woman as Inventor*. We'll do a piece on Knight's latest patent, a machine that makes square bottoms on paper bags."

"My god, that's a great idea! I hate how they always fall over and spill everything."

"James, will your report on the insurance industry be ready for this issue?"

"It should be. I have proof of at least three companies that are devouring their shareholders' capital with exorbitant salaries for their officers. And the new trend seems to be to deny claims with no explanation and cancel policies on those who file for benefits."

"And we must warn about the falling real estate market," Victoria says.

"Yes, I have an article already prepared," Andrews says. "Investors buying on margin have created a giant bubble that is about to burst, sending all those properties into foreclosure."

"Good," Victoria says. "If we don't correct the situation now, it will sting the whole economy. It is amazing how to the external eye our country is at the height of prosperity, yet there is scheme upon scheme to rob the poor and make the wealthy richer. Pearl, put a notice in this issue that we have employed the ablest detectives to investigate bankers, brokers, and business leaders with the intent of publishing the names and frauds being perpetrated."

"My god, we can start with the bogus Mexican bonds," Tennie says. "And the carpetbagger operations in North Carolina that enrich the state's railroads at taxpayer expense."

"We must include politicians," Blood contributes. "If people realize the vast amounts of money that gratuitously and dishonestly go to our leaders, they will be more inclined to vote for an honest newcomer like Victoria. Someone who will ban the whole lobbying business."

"Good point," Victoria agrees. "Now for our book selection I've chosen Anne Stephens' *Married in Haste*."

"Is that one of her dime novels?" Andrews wrinkles his nose. "We don't want to cheapen the *Weekly* with that trash."

"Of course not. And it isn't. This novel makes some excellent satirical points about marriage." Victoria flips through her papers. "For our feature, Tennie will do the article on prostitution she's been harping about. It is time to awaken public investment in the subject."

"I beg to differ, Victoria," Andrews says. "That sanctimonious zealot Anthony Comstock is on a rampage. We mustn't jeopardize the paper by printing anything he can label obscene, and he casts a very wide net."

"No one is going to intimidate me into pulling back from the truth! Dr. Beecher discusses prostitution in vivid detail from his pulpit, so why shouldn't we address the issue? Who keeps the poor hookers in business for goodness sakes? If the pious men in the Plymouth pews did not patronize them—"

"All I'm saying is we need to be careful. Comstock is looking for a scapegoat."

"My god, I got statistics and everything," Tennie says. "Did you know there are more than six hundred whorehouses in New York City alone? Not to mention the zillions of hourly-rate hooker hotels and dubious dance halls. If a man's got money, he can get a woman anywhere, anytime, and the cops don't care. And it's the women who are ostracized and hauled off in the Black Maria, never the men. Why aren't the terms *libertine* and *rake* as opprobrious to men as are *strumpet* and *whore* to women? I was talking to Annie Wood—"

"She runs that brothel that specializes in girls bred of slaves by their masters, right?" Channing asks.

"Channing, how do you know about that?" Victoria scolds.

"I've been there," Channing teases. Then, seeing Victoria's horrified look, he laughs. "I'm kidding. I read about it in *A Gentleman's Guide*. They say it is the city's most interesting and expensive house because of its Southern charm and gentility. And Annie displays her gals' lovely caramel skin by draping it in white silk."

"Channing Miles, do not ever let your mother hear you talking about such things! Maggie will have my head."

"I'm not stupid, Aunt Victoria."

"Anyway, moving on," Andrews says impatiently.

"Thank you," Tennie says. "My point is that it's the rich who sponsor prostitution because they're the only ones with the money to pay hookers what they have to charge to cover their expenses. Annie's gals pay her fifteen bucks a week plus two bucks for every man they service, just for room and board. Then you have the bribes. Patrolmen get ten bucks plus wine and favors. Captains and sergeants get up to thirty!"

"Let's tread lightly. We don't need the police riled up against us," Blood warns.

"True, but like I said, we're not in this business to pussyfoot around," Victoria says.

"My god, everybody's affected by prostitution," Tennie continues. "Ten percent of American women have whored at least once, and nineteen out of twenty men visit brothels regularly."

"Don't forget that French study linking prostitution to economics," Victoria prods. "The disparity between what men and women earn for the same job must end. Even worse, when a woman sews all day to earn forty-five cents for a cloak sold for forty-five dollars, is it any wonder she turns to prostitution where she can at least obtain a fair return for her services? And we can't forget the District!" Victoria's face flushes with righteous fervor. "Whorehouses are well known as the third house of Congress. Lobbyists give hookers thousands of dollars to influence the Senators who visit them. No wonder Whitelaw Reid calls the women demi-reps. And the stooge politicians are so skillfully manipulated while in sexual paroxysms they don't even realize they're being bought."

Andrews is ready to move on, but Victoria has more to say.

"In a future issue we'll discuss how a wife in a loveless marriage is as much a prostitute as the woman who sells her body at a brothel. The only difference is the twenty-five-cent marriage license that allows the wife to be legally debauched. And sadly, many don't even have a choice in the matter, their families having given them to a man simply because he has a notable name or lucrative business. 'You'll learn to love him,' they are told. Ha! There never was a love that was *learned!*"

"Well, if you want to stir things up, darling, I think that'll do it." Blood's eyes gleam with pride.

"Again I say, let's be careful," Andrews says. "If that vice czar Comstock shuts us down, we're not going to be stirring up anybody about anything. Now, can we get off this subject and off this boat before I roil the waters with my *vomito*?"

A few days later, a huge crowd gathers along New York City's Fifth Avenue to watch P. T. Barnum's new traveling circus head out on its maiden tour. Emblazoned on the sides of the ornate lead wagon are the words: P. T. BARNUM'S GRAND TRAVELING MUSEUM, MENAGERIE, CARAVAN AND CIRCUS. There are a hundred wagons in all, twenty of which are covered with painted pictures of the freaks they carry, including the diminutive Admiral Dot and various giants, albinos, tattooed men, and bearded ladies. Ten glassed and barred wagons hold wild animals. Monkeys leap about, chatter shrilly; lions and tigers and bears pace and roar; elephants bellow. The spectacle is so exciting no one seems to notice the unbearable stench.

Vanderbilt sits in a place of honor with his wife Frank and son William. He sneaks a wink at Tennie, who has positioned herself across the street and sashays flirtingly whenever Frank isn't looking. Victoria and Vanderbilt exchange friendly waves.

"Is this not the most incredible thing, Cornele?" Barnum says, joining the Vanderbilts.

"I'm surprised you were taking such a cumbersome show on the road," Cornelius remarks.

"Well, since the ASPCA clamped down on most of the dog-fighting in the country—"

"Or drove it to secrecy."

"Whatever happened to it, they had to find another reason to exist. Medical students who use animals in their labs kept them busy for a time, but now they're after me worse than ever. It's disgusting. They investigated years ago and know I treat the beasts as well as I do the freaks."

"They all look well enough cared for," Vanderbilt agrees, glancing at a wagon where a lion shakes its fluffy mane.

"After three fires I may just forget about having a stationery museum altogether." A trumpet blares and Barnum tips his hat to the Commodore before hurrying to the open carriage that will lead the parade. With great fanfare, they are off. Tennie claps in delight with the crowd, but Victoria sees an earlier, more personal caravan in her mind.

~ ~ ~

Victoria is fourteen and Tennie seven when Buck brings home a rickety old cart with sagging tailgate.

"Hebern, get your ass out here!" Buck yells. Victoria's twenty-year-old brother hurries outside as Buck sets two cans of paint beside the cart. "Paint this wagon barn red and put the yellow on the wheels. That'll give a flow of health and attract the customers."

"Customers? What're we doin', Pa?"

"We're taking our show on the road."

Later the next day, Buck brings two large signs with ornate, scrolled lettering and gold-flourish borders. One reads: Magnetic Life Elixer Proprietor Dr. Reuben Buckman Claflin. The other says: Amazing Child Clairvoyants. Manager: Dr. Reuben Buckman Claflin. As soon as the paint on the wagon dries, Buck nails a sign to each side.

In the backyard, under Roxanna's direction, Victoria, Tennie, and Utica stir a black caldron over a small wood fire. Inside is a mixture of mostly alcohol and laudanum, with a handful of powdered lobelia, a good amount of sugar, and a few dashes of ground marijuana plant. Buck strides up with labels for the bottles that say: Miss Tennessee's Magnetic Life Elixir For Beautifying The Complexion and Cleansing the Blood. Warranted To Be Perfectly Harmless and Purely Vegetable. Directions: A Teaspoon Three Times a Day One Half Hour Before Each Meal. Persons Taking The Elixir Should Be Careful in Their Diet. Price $2,00 Per Bottle. The sisters giggle at the sketch of Tennie for the label.

"My god," Tennie says. "I look like an old lady. How's Pa going to bill me as the wonder child?"

"Maybe he'll tell them you're aging backwards or something."
They dissolve into giggles.

The bottles are soon filled, labeled, and packed. The show hits the road.

The first county fair is already underway by the time they lurch in. The air is saturated with noise as a brass band plays, a carousel blares hurdy-gurdy music, and children yell and scream and race about. Buck reins up to a choice spot. Hopping down, he drops the tailgate and begins his spiel. A crowd quickly gathers.

By autumn they are rich and roll back into Mount Gilead, Ohio to a large cheering crowd and great fanfare.

~ ~ ~

Loud cheering startles Victoria from her reverie. She shakes her head to banish the memories and glances around, afraid someone has read her thoughts. Tennie, on the other hand, glows with excitement.

"My god, Sis! Don't it remind you of the Claflin medicine show?"

"Tennie, hush! Someone will hear you!"

"My god, why are you so ashamed of our past? We made great money and for the most part honestly."

"People will use it against us nonetheless."

"My god, I guess you're right about that. If Mrs. Grundy was a real person instead of just a symbol of public opinion, I'd slap her silly."

Chapter 13

"Do you like the new masthead?" Victoria asks Tennie, proudly showing her the mock-up for the upcoming issue of the *Weekly*.

"'Progress! Free thought! Untrammeled lives! Breaking the way for future generations!' It's perfect, Sis."

"And look. I put the article every woman in town is going to want to read right beneath that."

"Mother of the Suffragists to speak at Apollo Hall,'" Tennie reads. "My god, the ladies are fools if they don't at least acknowledge the free publicity."

"I'd like to run this article in the next issue," Andrews says, interrupting to hand Victoria a sheaf of papers. "It's a personal thing, but I think it's newsworthy."

"Pearl, you don't have to clear your editorials with me."

"This involves a powerful man, and since it derives from personal animosity, I may not be the most *objectief* about it."

"'Henry Ward Beecher arraigned and charged by Stephen Pearl Andrews with a series of falsehoods, slander, moral cowardice, and other conduct unbecoming a Christian minister,'" Victoria reads. "What's this about, Pearl?"

"I have a long score to settle with Mr. Beecher on the grounds of moral vacillation and cowardice. The man's a pompous hypocrite who preys on the women in his congregation even while denigrating my name from his pulpit and, recently, yours and Tennessee's, too. He may take up the glove I throw down or not, but he will not escape being held to the strict logic of his public and private deportment unless he repents. You will see it is Mr. Beecher as a symbol of the hypocrisy of organized religion that I attack."

"Yes, I see that. A valid perspective. God knows I hate hypocrisy more than anything."

"Hopefully I can taunt him into responding. For all his faults, the man sells newspapers."

"Just don't get us into a libelous situation."

"Not to worry. Anything we could accuse him of he's probably done."

A few days later, Victoria and Tennie attend Elizabeth Cady Stanton's lecture at Apollo Hall. Whispers about the *Weekly's* attack on Rev. Beecher sizzle through the crowd as they take their seats. Fortunately, attentions quickly turn to the stage as Elizabeth takes the podium.

"We are in the midst of a social revolution. Conservatives say woman's political equality will destroy the family. Reformers say it will make the family stronger. I stand with the latter. The religious element has been played upon woman to subjugate her. But the question is not whether marriage is an indissoluble tie by holy sacrament, but that, as a civil contract, for how many and what reasons it can be dissolved. So long as by our laws no man can make a contract for a horse or piece of land until he is twenty-one, how do we permit the boy of fourteen and girl of twelve to make a contract more important than any other? And hold them to it, come what may!

"I say we are all Free-lovers at heart, despite how society uses that term to sully us. The truth is that the freer the relations between human beings, the happier we are. Many a man who is tyrannical today would become kind and considerate if he knew public sentiment would protect his wife in leaving him. Likewise many a wife who is now peevish and fretful, if she knew her husband could sunder the tie honorably and reputably, would soon change her manners."

"Oh, Tennie, of them all, I so want to meet Mrs. Stanton." Victoria leaps to her feet, clapping wildly, as Elizabeth concludes. The entire audience is with her.

"My god, just walk up to her and stick out your hand."

"No. We must meet as equals. I just pray it will be soon."

~ ~ ~

On October 27, clouds hide the moon and stars, casting an eerie pallor over New York City. Rain pelts Victoria's carriage as it moves slowly along the waterfront.

"Holy Toledo, Grant's really serious about this honest election stuff," Tennie says, staring out at the Federal troops in the streets.

"I feel like I'm back in the war," Blood says, watching the soldiers set up camp in the old forts along the water's edge.

"But why are our tax dollars paying for these men to sit here for two weeks?" Victoria asks. She shivers and pulls her cloak closer. "Why couldn't they just come in on Election Day? It feels very strange in the city tonight."

"Everything's felt screwy to me today," Tennie says. "Maybe it's because I'm twenty-five now. Maybe I'm finally maturing."

"Good Lord, I hope not." Blood grins. "The world needs more free spirits like you."

"My god, I hope I never lose that."

"What do you think Tweed's chances are of remaining the Boss with all the military around?" Victoria asks.

"Same as if the troops weren't here," Blood says. "It'll just cost him a few more of those millions he's embezzled from us citizens. His men won't be burning boxes or threatening people like the old days, they'll be buying votes."

"Why are we going to this thing again?" Tennie asks. "Sitting home with a hot toddy and a warm man is more my style for a birthday."

"I know. I'm sorry. But the Spirits said it would be fortuitous for us to go, so go we must."

The carriage moves slowly through the 50,000 men who surround Tammany Hall. They all wear red, and each holds a burning torch that sizzles and pops in the downpour. Soggy placards featuring snarling tiger heads droop on their sticks. The men step aside as Victoria and Tennie hop through the mud and puddles to enter. They are the only women attending and are escorted to front row seats. As they sit, the 300-pound Boss Tweed doffs his hat to them and walks to the podium. Though large of frame, he is somewhat handsome, with soft, deep-set, blue eyes, and short, neatly groomed mustache and beard. His hair has almost receded off the top of his head, but it, too, is precisely trimmed and groomed. He oozes charisma.

The crowd's roar is so loud Tennie covers her ears off and on during the entire two hours of the rally and sighs in relief as Tweed concludes. A short time later, the sisters and Blood greet the political boss in the receiving line.

"So you're the queens of Wall Street," Tweed says, shaking Tennie's hand and then taking Victoria's.

"That's one of the things they call us," Tennie replies.

"This is quite the event, Mr. Tweed," Victoria offers.

"Bill to my friends, Ma'am. I've been thinking of paying you ladies a visit for a while now. See with my own eyes our forthcoming President. Which of you is it?"

"Not me," Tennie says.

"I must say I find your newspaper fascinating," Tweed says, smiling at Victoria.

"Even though we haven't mentioned you?" Victoria asks.

"With all the lies that Bavarian Tommy Nast and the *Times* and *Tribune* have been printin', I'd say it's more *because* you haven't mentioned me." His laugh is loud and hearty.

"We'd be happy to put you on our gratis list, Mr. Tweed."

"Nah, I always insist on paying my way, and the other fella's, too, actually. Something for everyone, I say."

"Since every piker has his price, I guess that keeps you mighty busy," Tennie says.

"Well, there never was a time you couldn't buy a small fry or broke bloke."

"At least you're frank about it," Victoria says. "Of course, you realize we are neither small fry nor broke. Our paper and brokerage firm are both vastly successful."

"I've observed that." Tweed gives Victoria a penetrating look. "I've also been thinking about your campaign and how woman's suffrage relates to it. If you get to Washington, give Ben Butler a call. The Beast has the keenest legal mind in Congress and is sympathetic to the cause of women. You might find him helpful."

"Is he that homely little man with the weird eye?"

"Tennie! I apologize for my sister, Mr. Tweed."

"Don't," Tweed says, laughing heartily. "I like an honest, spunky woman. Ben Butler may not be much to look at, Miss Claflin, but he wields phenomenal power on the Hill."

"Then we shall be happy to make his acquaintance," Victoria says. "I appreciate the referral."

~ ~ ~

Tuesday, November 8, 1870, is New York State's Election Day. Victoria and Tennie go to the polls, but a marshal bars them from entering, reminding them that women can't vote.

"Oh, we are not here to vote," Victoria responds. "We are here in our capacity as newspaperwomen. We would like to write some inspiring paragraphs about democracy."

"Perhaps you've heard of our rag. *Woodhull & Claflin's Weekly*? She's Woodhull, I'm Claflin," Tennie contributes. The marshal still hesitates, exasperating Victoria.

"I am a candidate for the Presidency and as such am curious to see how the whole process works." Her voice is sharp, but Tennie steps forward and flutters her eyelashes at the man.

"Our friend Mr. Tweed suggested we stop by," she says.

"Why didn't you say so? Any friend of Mr. Tweed's is welcome."

Inside the voting station, an inebriated voter with tangled whiskers, unruly black hair, and rumpled clothes approaches the registrar. The voter's odor is so foul the sisters cover their noses with their monogrammed hankies.

"Name's Michael Murray," the voter growls.

"Don't' see no Michael Murray," the registrar says, studying his lists while he pinches snuff up his nostrils. "There's a Michael Murphy."

The sisters watch as the would-be voter pulls a crumpled scrap of paper from his pocket. He sways a little, squints at the page and adopts an Irish accent. "Sure and it's Michael Murphy, Sir."

"That's better." The registrar hands him a voting sheet.

The man makes his mark and drops the ticket into a loosely taped box. Victoria and Tennie follow him out. He enters a barbershop around the corner and the sisters peek in the window to see the man cleaned, shaved, and given a new jacket. One of Boss Tweed's men gives him a new scrap of paper and tucks a crisp five-dollar bill into his pocket. Muttering his new name, the man returns to vote again.

The next morning, Victoria is not surprised that the corrupt Tammany Hall has retained control of New York. She is furious.

"Women must get the vote or I don't have a chance of being President and changing this rotten system! Tennie, you are going to Washington."

Chapter 14

On Sunday, November 13, 1870, the parquet floors of Victoria's Murray Hill mansion bask in the glow of candles from cut-glass chandeliers as Victoria welcomes the usual notable guests to her salon. The dancing has already begun when General Benjamin Butler arrives. He surveys the room, rolling his cigar across his mouth and singing "Shoo, Fly" under his breath, a habit that relaxes him. Tennie spies him and hurries over to introduce him to Victoria.

"I am so pleased you could join us," Victoria says.

"Your sister can be mighty persuasive, but I must say, you are even more exquisite than she described."

Butler kisses Victoria's hand and winks at Tennie.

"I hope she didn't strong-arm you."

"If I can handle entire armies and the population of New Orleans, I think I can handle one little minx."

"Would you care to dance?"

"My corns are bothering me, so how about we just go somewhere quiet and talk?" He glances ruefully at the toes pushing out through his well-worn carpet slippers.

"Of course. I was hoping you'd say that." Victoria takes his arm, and they make their way to the sitting room off her bedroom. "Look what I've arranged for you!" She pours him a whiskey and presents him it with a plate of donuts.

"I see you've done your homework, Mrs. Woodhull. Donuts and whiskey, my consistent evening snack."

"I like my guests to feel at home."

She perches on the sofa beside him.

"I appreciate the gesture." He takes a bite of donut. "Hmmm. These are excellent."

"You have a reputation for getting things done, Mr. Butler. The number of votes in New York's recent election exceeded the number of registered citizens, so it is clear that women must be enfranchised in order to sway an honest election. Have you any suggestions to offer?"

"I do actually. You must present a memorial to Congress."

"A memorial?"

"A statement of your case. The House Judiciary Committee rules on all petitions to change the law. You have to make your case directly to them."

"But no woman has ever been admitted to those chambers. How will I—"

"Leave that to me. I warn that you may be jeered, but you *will* be remembered. Every new thing must begin somewhere, and since you've been bold enough to achieve a few firsts in your life already, I think you deserve to win another. I will help you with the woman's cause as I helped the Negro with his."

"I would be honored. What would be your fee, Sir?"

"I have counseled three Presidents, commencing with Mr. Lincoln during his battle to free the slaves. I advised Mr. Johnson until his policies demanded his impeachment, which I then conducted. Now President Grant frequently asks for my expertise to escape the scandals caused by his naivéty and blunders. This country has more vitality than any other on earth if it can stand two more years of him. What is such expertise worth to you?"

"To gain the vote, I will meet whatever price you ask."

"Since you seem to have the forbearance to follow your beliefs, my fee will be zero." Butler smiles as Victoria audibly exhales. He hands her his card. "Here is my card to use as your referral at the White House. Since Grant's administration is intolerable and I can't stand Mr. Greeley, I welcome you to the ballot."

~ ~ ~

Late in the evening of November 19, 1870, as weary members of Ohio's suffrage association leave the Cleveland Auditorium, Susan B. Anthony paces in the anteroom, ranting to Elizabeth Cady.

"I cannot believe our groups rejected merging again! This is the teetotal end of it! Our battle is against the men who prevent us from voting. I have neither time nor energy to continue fighting our sisters."

"Agreed."

They hide their despair as Paulina Davis steps into the room waving the latest issue of the *Weekly*.

"La-de-dah and lullaby, what's the prostitute done now?" Susan asks.

"'Startling Annunciation!'" Paulina reads the headline. "A new political platform proclaimed! Woman's right of suffrage fully recognized in the Constitution and completely established by positive law and recent events. Sixteenth Amendment a dead letter!'"

"Oh, good Lord!" Susan grabs the paper.

"I don't think the Lord had any part of it," Elizabeth says dryly. "Maybe Demosthenes did. I wrote Mrs. Woodhull a few months ago, and she has done exactly what I asked. I wonder what she means by dead letter? That indicates a law is in place but not enforced."

"Mrs. Woodhull has presented a written memorial to Congress and now Mr. Butler has arranged for her to address the Judiciary Committee," Paulina says.

"No! The General has teetotally betrayed us!" Susan turns to Elizabeth. "If a woman finally enters those halls, it should be you, my darling empress!"

"I guess none of us used the same persuasive tactics on Mr. Butler," Paulina comments dryly.

"Fiasco. Teetotal fiasco. She's going to brand us all Free-lovers." Susan sinks into a chair, skims the article.

"Now, Susan, it's not that bad," Elizabeth says. "Any woman who will speak on the legalities of woman's suffrage, obviously under the guidance of the knowledgeable General Butler, can only help our cause."

"I don't agree. And the irony of her timing—"

"Timing? Why's that?" Paulina asks.

"She's presenting her memorial opening day of our convention. It's like she delights in thumbing her nose at our efforts."

"So what are we going to do about it?" Elizabeth asks.

"Perhaps we should embrace her," Paulina says.

"Never! Never . . . never . . . never!" Susan stomps her foot, her glare a thunderbolt.

Chapter 15

After a picture-perfect Christmas at the mansion, Victoria, Tennie and Zulu Maud go to Washington D.C., still aglow with holiday joy. The wide avenues shooting off in all directions from the ornate Union Station amaze them. As do the luxurious accommodations at Wormley's Hotel, just blocks from the White House. Refreshing themselves quickly with the hotel's specialties of turtle soup and blue crabs fresh from Chesapeake Bay, they walk to Capitol Hill.

Although Pennsylvania Avenue is still icy from a recent storm, it bustles with activity. Trains chug past, cinders flying. Streetcars clang up and down the street. Carriages and horses make their way precariously through the throngs that gawk at our nation's premier residence. Outside the large iron gates surrounding the White House, vendors sell balloons, candy, and flags of all sizes while the downtrodden beg for handouts. Victoria, Tennie and Zulu Maud stand amid the swirl of humanity and stare in awe.

"Behold our next address," Victoria says. "I see it so clearly."

"Me too. It's right in front of us," Tennie jokes.

"Oh, Mama, I thought the hotel was grand, but this is even grander!" Zulu Maud exclaims.

"My god, let's not stand here all day gapin' like tourists. Have you got the Beast's card?"

Victoria holds up the card, and they walk up the flower-lined gravel path to the front door. They are ushered into a receiving room filled with many men and a couple of women. Some of the visitors tiptoe about as if in church, whispering and examining everything like it is a sacred souvenir. Others lounge comfortably on Victorian sofas, chatting about politics, including Joseph Rainey's swearing in as the first freed slave serving in the House of Representatives. Tennie grimaces at the gold frescoed walls, the drab orange-striped draperies, and the slightly worn furniture.

"My god, this place needs sprucing up."

"Oh, Tennie, it's the grandest house in the country. Think of all the history within these walls. Abigail Adams wrote her letter for the women. Mrs. Lincoln grieved her lost sons and husband. We could soon eat off their same dishes and sleep in their same beds. It is almost too incredible to consider."

A somber-looking black man in a black tuxedo steps into the room. Victoria stops rhapsodizing and looks at him expectantly.

"The President is receiving," he says. "Everyone with proper referral, please step forward and present it." He checks credentials and only a few follow him to see the President. They are all men except for the sisters and nine-year-old Zulu Maud.

Grant's study is sparsely and plainly furnished; the air reeks of cigar. Julia Grant pours her husband a cup of coffee as his guests file in.

"My afternoon refreshment," Grant says, holding up his cup. "Not whiskey as the press has led you to expect." His eyes twinkle. "A lesson to not believe everything you read, all news being filtered through the private notions of the reporter."

"What do you think about the Democrat's victory in New York, Sir?" a man asks.

"I'm downcast about it. But give them enough rope, and they'll do the usual hanging with it."

"Let's hope they start with Boss Tweed," another man says.

"It's easier to spoil a rotten egg than it is to damage that man's character," Grant says.

"What are your views on woman's suffrage, Mr. President?"

"Go get him, Mrs. Woodhull," a man calls out. The men hoot. Julia Grant arches a brow and grins at her husband.

"So this is the third contingent of women we've heard so much about," Grant says. "I'm told that if you align yourself with one of the established suffrage groups I might lose my house." He stands and grins, mocking her. "Would you like to sit in the chair you hope to one day occupy?"

"Flattery will not side-step the question, Mr. President."

"She's a sarcey one, isn't she?" He cocks an eyebrow at the men, and they laugh as he sits back down. He chews on his cigar, gives Victoria an assessing look. "I was telling Mrs. Grant the other day that we should give married women two votes. Then both husband and wife would be represented at the polls." The crowd laughs. Victoria presses.

"Will you support an amendment?"

"*That*, Mrs. Woodhull, rests with the Supreme Court."

"God help us if we've no other refuge."

~ ~ ~

On January 11, 1871, the marble hallway outside the House Judiciary Committee chambers buzzes with activity. Newsmen, including Henry Stanton for the *New York Sun* and Frederick Douglass for the *New National Era*, circulate, scribbling notes. Joining them is Emily Briggs, famous for her social and political commentary, "The Olivia Letters," a *Washington Chronicle* standard for years.

Congressmen stand in small groups and talk in low voices. A few gawk at Victoria, who waits with Tennie and Blood, nervously twisting the diamond ring on her thumb. She and Tennie are dressed alike in conservative, navy blue business suits: ankle-length skirts and jackets with masculine-looking coattails. Victoria has a white rose pinned to her navy velvet neckband. An Alpine hat with small lavender plume tops her short curls. A rustle down the hallway gets everyone's attention.

"My god, would you look at that," Tennie says.

Victoria turns ashen when she sees Susan B. Anthony lead a knot of women toward them.

"My god, they look like buzzards swooping in for a feast," Tennie mutters.

The suffragists converse with several waiting Congressmen, then huddle near the chamber door, ignoring Victoria, except for discreet, assessing looks. Victoria assesses them back, whispering softly for Spirit guidance.

"James, would you please find me a glass of water? See if you can hear what they're saying."

James ambles away, purposely passing closely and slowly by the suffragists in order to eavesdrop.

"I refuse to speak to her," says Isabella.

"A Beecher should be the last person to criticize," Paulina Davis says. "Your brother, after all, preaches to at least twenty of his mistresses every Sunday."

Susan glances at Blood, and he hurries off.

"I confronted him, you know," Isabella says.

"No! What did he say?" Paulina leans forward eagerly.

"'I tread the falsehoods into the dirt from whence they spring and go on my way rejoicing,'" Isabella mimics her brother's pomposity before continuing in her own voice. "Then he thanked me for my love and silence, saying it would be barbaric to drag the 'poor, dear child of a woman into this slough.'"

Blood passes the women again, carrying a glass of water and cocking an ear toward them.

"So far as I can see, if anyone's dragged a dear child into the slough, it is Henry Ward," Paulina says.

"Enough, ladies! This is not the time nor place for gossip," Susan scolds sharply.

"Oh, Susan, as if you didn't know every word we've said is true," Paulina says.

"What are they saying, James?" Victoria asks, as she takes the glass and drinks, her eyes on the suffragists.

"Something about Mrs. Hooker's brother preaching to his mistresses. And then they said something about dragging a dear child into the slough and leaving her there."

"Do you think they meant me?"

"My god, Sis, they wouldn't call you a dear child."

"No, more a brazen hussy, I'm sure."

John Bingham of Ohio, a tall man with graying hair and white mutton-chop sideburns, arrives. Bingham is the Judiciary Committee Chairman and famous for presiding at the Lincoln assassination trial, leading the prosecution in Andrew Johnson's impeachment trial, and framing the Fourteenth Amendment.

"I wonder what Mr. Bingham will say when I use his own Amendment to support my case?" Victoria muses as the Congressman throws open the chamber doors. The hallway begins to clear.

"The women are all going to be in love with you by the time you finish, Darling," Blood says, patting her hand that is white-knuckled on his arm. "Don't forget you have the Spirits on your side."

The suffragists follow the Congressmen into the room. With Blood and Tennie flanking her, Victoria moves woodenly forward, her face as white as her rose. Moments later, they are all seated around a long conference table. When she is called, Victoria stands, takes a deep breath, and removes her hat. The Congressmen smirk. Victoria glances at the suffragists, then quickly away. She looks at Tennie, who winks, and Blood, who hands her the Memorial. She exhales in relief as the ever-tardy General Butler rushes into the room, humming "Shoo Fly" and rolling his cigar in his mouth. He nods encouragingly. She smiles tremulously and begins to read, her voice a breathless whisper.

"To the honorable Senate and House of Representatives of the United States, in Congress assembled, respectfully showeth: That this memorialist was born in the State of Ohio and is above the age of twenty-one."

"Speak up! You can't be heard!" Bingham's deep-lidded gray eyes are filled with arrogance. The Congressmen chuckle and feign indulgence. Victoria takes a deep breath and closes her eyes. Her cheeks flush; her blue eyes flash. Her voice is loud and clear as she begins again, ignoring her notes.

"That she is a citizen of the United States, as declared by the Fourteenth Amendment to the Constitution of the United States, which states specifically, 'All *persons* born or naturalized in the United States and subject to the jurisdiction thereof are citizens of the United States and of the State wherein they reside.'"

The Congressmen stop snickering and glance with raised eyebrows at Bingham as Victoria continues, her voice firm but melodic.

102

"And whereas the Fifteenth Article of Amendment to the Constitution provides that 'the right of citizens to vote shall not be denied or abridged on account of race, color, or previous condition of servitude.' And whereas, nevertheless, the right to vote is denied to women citizens of the United States, your memorialist respectfully petitions your Honorable Bodies to make such laws as are necessary to execute the right vested by the Constitution in the citizens of the United States to vote without regard to sex."

With a steady, challenging glance around the room, Victoria takes her seat. The suffragists seem ready to burst with excitement.

"Thank you, Mrs. Woodhull," Bingham says. "The committee will take your petition under consideration, and a report will be issued. This meeting is adjourned."

In a whirlwind, the suffragists encircle Victoria, all talking at once.

"Brilliant! Brilliant!" says Paulina.

"The greatest step forward in the history of the woman's movement has been made this morning, and you have made it!"

Isabella kisses her cheek.

"You were magnificent, Mrs. Woodhull," Belva says. "I couldn't have presented a better argument myself."

"And she's studying law," Isabella offers.

Even Susan B. Anthony's stern face softens as her eyes sparkle with renewed hope.

"Congratulations, my little chick-a-dee-dee! You have changed the entire focus of our movement and won us the day! We are taking you to lunch, and you must repeat your speech for the ladies at our convention this very afternoon."

"You are called of God, Mrs. Woodhull," Isabella chimes in. "You have found the argument we've been praying for!"

~ ~ ~

While Victoria, with Zulu Maud at her side, woos the women over lunch, Blood visits the President and reminisces about the war, Tennie changes into comfortable, masculine attire and goes to Congress. She immediately charms D.C.'s good ol' boys.

103

"What's it like to be the only dames on Wall Street and surrounded by men day in and day out?" one asks her.

"I rather enjoy it," Tennie says, garnering a hearty laugh. "But seriously, when we went to Wall Street we did not intend to let our petticoats take up any more room in the street than the other brokers' trousers. My god, why shouldn't women just as well be stockbrokers as keep stores and measure men for shirts? We just couldn't see a difference, so we went where we could make the most money. Isn't that what you beaks do? Go where the lobbyists pave your pockets with gold?"

Meanwhile, in the Senate restaurant, curious Congressmen observe the animated chatter of the suffragists. Susan finally stands, holds the end of her red shawl in her fist and waves it triumphantly, announcing to the room.

"Since I determined to wear my red shawl until women got the vote, Washington has come to expect its robin red-breast of woman's rights each spring. But soon Congress will no longer have to see me trudging up their steps. Mrs. Woodhull has won us the day!"

Susan sits back down as the men clap politely, some with sneers, some with smiles. Lunch is served, and Victoria breaks the awkward moment of silence that ensues.

"I am so thrilled to finally meet you, Miss Anthony. I have read *The Revolution* faithfully, knowing I wanted to work for the cause in some capacity, although I never dreamed it would take so long."

"Well, you are with us now, little chick-a-dee-dee, and we are not letting you go."

"This is the first convention I've organized, and your speech will be a grand coup, though of course I can take no credit for that," Isabella says.

"When did that ever stop a Beecher from taking credit?" Paulina teases.

"You're a Beecher? As in the popular pastor of Brooklyn?" Victoria says.

"Alas, yes. I have quite a family name to live up to."

"Better than having one to live down." Victoria chuckles softly, then quickly changes the subject as the women exchange glances. "Will Mrs. Stanton be at the convention?" she asks. "I heard her speak recently, and her views on marriage are similar to my own."

"Unfortunately, she has stayed home to celebrate her daughter's birthday," Isabella pouts.

"You will meet her soon," Paulina says. "Let me caution you, however, to call her Elizabeth or Mrs. Cady. I believe if Lucy Stone had wed first and set the idea in place, Lizzie would have officially kept her maiden name after marriage. She hates being referred to as an 'appendage of man,' as she puts it."

Susan changes the subject before Paulina can gossip more.

"Your argument today was so logical I cannot believe we had not thought of it." Her gaze circles the restaurant. "I just hope these Congressmen don't sweep us under the rug again. It is hard to continue the fight, wondering if we shall ever succeed."

"Oh, we will succeed, despite the guerrilla opposition," Victoria proclaims. "The world is a looking-glass, giving back to everyone what she reflects. Look at the world as a place of equality long enough, and it must become fair."

"I love that," Isabella declares.

"Hello, ladies, I hear you stirred up the Hill today," Senator Charles Sumner says, stopping at their table. A big man with bushy hair and sideburns, he is more intelligent than his oafish appearance makes him seem.

"Hello, Senator," Susan replies. "Actually it was Mrs. Woodhull who did the stirring, but our kettle is now aboil so you gentlemen best watch out."

"So you're the woman who has the President all heated up. With all the grief he's giving me lately, you just might get my vote." Sumner holds out a large, fleshy hand to Victoria.

"I would be most pleased to have it, Sir."

"Put the ladies' bill on my tab," Sumner tells a passing steward.

"They think they can buy us off with a lunch here and there," Susan mutters as he walks away. "Just once it would be nice if one of them would step up and pressure their fellow Congressmen to give us the vote."

"I heard the President was removing Sumner from chairmanship of the Foreign Relations Committee," Paulina gossips.

"No!" Susan exclaims. "He's held that appointment for a decade."

"But he's blocking plans to annex Santo Domingo as a colony for the freed Negroes, and the President is not happy."

"Surely he won't be so vindictive as to humiliate the Senator like that," Isabella says.

"Belle, dear, sometimes you are so naïve," Paulina declares.

"Well, better naïve than unkind," Isabella pouts.

~ ~ ~

By early afternoon members of the national suffrage group fill Lincoln Hall, the largest, most prestigious auditorium in the Capitol city. As the speakers wait to make their entrance onto the platform, Frederick Douglass taps on the anteroom door. Isabella rushes over to hug him.

"Oh, thank you again, Mr. Douglass, for consenting to speak. It is such an honor to include you on our program." She leads him over to Victoria, who sits alone attempting to calm her nerves. "You must meet our new savior. Don't you agree Mrs. Woodhull made a most convincing argument for our cause this morning? She is repeating it this afternoon." She turns to Victoria. "Mrs. Woodhull, I present our great statesman, Frederick Douglass."

"I am honored. I've heard so much about you, Mr. Douglass." Victoria stands and shakes his hand.

"And I, you," Douglass says, his eyes twinkling.

"I'm sure it has not been with the same high praise." Victoria laughs softly.

"Always remember, Victoria, no man can put a chain around the ankle of his fellow man—or woman—without finding the other end fastened about his own neck. We are both a novelty, and any novelty takes time to catch on. But if there is no struggle, there is no progress. I have always preferred to be true to myself, even if I incur ridicule, since the alternative incurs my own abhorrence."

"I make that my maxim as well. Oh, Belva is motioning. It is time to begin. Perhaps we can talk more another time?"

"We'll make a point of it."

They follow Belva onto the stage. A buzz of speculation fills the auditorium when Victoria takes her seat with the other dignitaries. Isabella walks to the podium and greets the crowd.

"This morning, in Capitol chambers never before entered by woman, I, among others, witnessed an historic moment. Mrs. Victoria C. Woodhull offered an argument to Congress that so impressed us we have persuaded her to deliver it again this afternoon so that you might all share in the moment. Although she is inexperienced as a public speaker, she has consented for the sake of our glorious cause. I give her to you now: Mrs. Victoria C. Woodhull."

There is polite applause as Victoria steps timidly forward and begins to speak.

"I am often compelled to do things from which my sensitive soul shrinks, but I obey a power that knows better than I can know and that has never left me stranded and without hope. As I spoke at the Capitol this morning, these spirits surrounded me and protected me, as they do right now. And so I do their bidding."

When Victoria concludes her presentation, the entire assemblage is on its feet. Whistling. Stomping. Throwing hats and hankies into the air. Isabella rushes forward, shouting above the chaos.

"Ladies and gentlemen, Mrs. Victoria C. Woodhull, who this very morning single-handedly won the war for woman's suffrage! No longer will we fight for our rights. We will assert those rights we clearly already have! This little woman has bridged with her prostrate body an awful gulf over which womanhood will walk to freedom!"

The crowd's roar is deafening. Isabella motions Victoria back to the podium. The others on the stage gather around. A camera flashes.

Victoria stands sphinx-like and silent among the suffragist leaders as the applause goes on and on. Susan shouts to be heard.

"In this age of rapid thought and action, of telegraphs and railways, the old stage coach won't do. Victoria Woodhull has teetotally caught up the spirit of the age and advanced our cause by many years. Women everywhere are forever in her debt. Resolve, then, that it is the duty of women to apply for registration to vote, and where they fail to secure it, lawsuits will be instituted."

The crowd agrees as one.

"Opposed?"

"I don't oppose," yells a woman in the front row. "But good Lord, we are all going to jail!"

"Then they shall drag us proclaiming our rights!" Victoria shouts. "I hereby pledge ten thousand dollars toward any legal fees we might incur!"

A chant rises and fills the room.

"Long live Victoria! Long live Victoria!"

Chapter 16

The morning headlines tell the story:

New York Times: **The Cry of the Suffragans Was Anthems to Woodhull**

New York Star: **NWA Convention Has Had the Wind Completely Taken Out of Its Sails by That Lively Little Yacht, Mrs. Woodhull**

New York Tribune: **Mrs. Victoria C. Woodhull and Her Sister Chief Ornaments of the Woman's Convention and Congress**

The Commercial Appeal: **This the Bravest and Best Movement the Women Have Yet Made.**

President Grant scowls as he listens to Attorney General George Williams read the *Philadelphia Press* account. "'General Grant might learn a lesson from the pale, sad face of this unflinching woman. She reminds one of the forces of nature behind a storm.'"

"I want that Memorial put where the woodbine twineth!" Grant orders, chomping on his cigar.

"I'll try, Sir, but Butler's involved in the thing so he won't vote against it. And Loughridge can't be bought."

"Don't give me details. Just get it done. That woman is going to have the whole gaggle of them rising up worse than the South did. I ain't presiding over another goddamn war."

A couple days later, Elizabeth Cady Stanton is on a train, sleeping so soundly she does not stir as the train stops at the Philadelphia depot and Susan B. Anthony boards. Susan is pleasantly surprised to see her friend and sits across from Elizabeth. As the train begins to move, Elizabeth wakes with a start and looks around, orienting herself.

"Susan, is it really you, or am I dreaming still?"

"It is really me, my darling empress."

"Well, glory be! It's good to see you, my friend. Are you going as far as Chicago?"

"Eventually. I have a couple of dates in Michigan and Indiana first. I'm on a whirlwind tour for the next three months, and I'm tired already."

"I know what you mean," Elizabeth yawns. "Thank goodness for trains so we can sleep on the way. Lordy, remember the old days of wagons and sleighs and stagecoaches?"

"I try to forget. Especially the night our carriage got stuck, and those wild boars and rats kept attacking. That was the teetotal worst."

"I was beating off a boar and saw a rat crawl right over your arm!" Elizabeth shudders. "Between that and the blizzards, and sleeping in attics that were either freezing or stifling—I don't think I could do it today. We really believed in our cause, didn't we?"

"I still do, Lizzie."

"Well, Susan, so do I. I haven't let up on my lecturing one bit. Just because I don't have time for weak-willed women who march around with banners for two days and then go home and kowtow to husbands and forget about voting doesn't mean I've given up. How was Isabella's convention, by the way?"

"Surprisingly well organized. And I know you've heard about Mrs. Woodhull. Lizzie, she is nothing like we expected. She is humble and refined and has a power when she is speaking that you have to experience to understand."

"I read her Memorial in the paper, and the legality of her argument cannot be disputed. My father was a brilliant attorney, and even he could not have presented our case so well. But do you really think victory will come so easily?"

"Even if the Committee shoves us under the rug like they've done in the past, if we make a showing at the polls, we'll have to be heard by the Supreme Court. That is surely a faster way to our goal than by Amendment."

"So Mrs. Woodhull isn't an ogre after all, hmm?"

She gives Susan a teasing look.

"She is charming and utterly forgetful of differences of sex. Maybe it's true that when the old guard gets weary a new one appears to pick up the cross."

"I cannot wait to meet her. I'm very interested in her views on marriage."

"That's funny. She attended your lecture in New York and said almost the same words about you!" Susan glances around, and then leans forward to speak confidentially. "If I could find a man like Colonel Blood, I believe I might even consider marriage. I used to say Bob Ingersoll could do it, but Mr. Blood is even more handsome and charming. He is devoted to his wife, and they are truly equals. He's in full agreement with her first husband living with them. They explained about the man's illness and how he cares for the idiot son. It was a brave, compassionate act for her to take him in."

"What about the sister? Jennie is it?"

"Tennie, which is short for Tennessee. She's a wild one, but she has an innocence that makes even her bawdiest actions appear natural and inoffensive."

"Why, Susan, I declare those sisters have mesmerized you."

"If Victoria has won us the vote, I shall champion them both forever."

~ ~ ~

Sunrise colors the sky above her Murray Hill mansion, where Victoria sits on the roof peacefully sipping orange juice. She glances away from the celestial beauty when she hears Blood approaching. He can hardly contain his frustration as he hands her the February 6 *Tribune*. Disbelief turns to rage as she reads the headline: **Committee Tables Woodhull Memorial; Butler and Loughridge Issue Minority Opinion.**

"Tabled it? They can't just table it without a decision! Can they, James?"

"They're the power. They can do anything they want."

"Are they bulls who by sheer force can butt an object out of the way?" Victoria grumbles, skimming the article. "It is as cool a dodging of an issue as ever was made in the halls of Congress!" Victoria tosses the paper on the table and paces.

"In their minority report, Butler and Loughridge call it the strongest, most exhaustive argument for woman's suffrage ever," Blood says. "Butler says suffrage is an inalienable right of every citizen and that your Memorial clearly proves women are citizens."

111

"They cannot table me! I'm going to Washington."

Throughout February, the sisters seem to be everywhere in the Capitol city, except the hallowed chambers. The House refuses to hear Victoria's new petition, or take any action on her first.

"My god, I'm not surprised," Tennie says. "A Congressman told me the Committee got a petition from several connected women: wives of politicians, wealthy socialites."

"A petition? That said what?"

"Oh, the usual religious hogwash. The Holy Scriptures set woman in the higher sphere of wifedom and motherhood so that's how it should be. The additional burden of voting is unsuited to woman's—how'd they put it? Oh, yeah—'physical organization.'"

"Tennie, they force me to the platform to respond."

"My god, it's about time."

The blustery February air does not keep people from coming to Lincoln Hall to hear Victoria speak. Banners over the entrance proclaim: Only Criminals, Idiots and the Insane May Be Deprived of the Ballot. The capacity crowd goes wild as Isabella Hooker walks to the podium.

"The objective of this lecture is to present the legal and moral arguments in favor of enfranchising one half of U.S. citizens. If neither political party is ready to take on the issue, a new party will spring up that will grind the status quo to powder! Our one demand is not for reformed laws with crumbs and favors, but equal justice." Isabella motions for quiet as audience members roar their approval. "I now present the first woman to see clearly that woman's suffrage is already plainly guaranteed by Constitutional amendment: Mrs. Victoria C. Woodhull." Victoria steps forward to thundering applause.

"When I was before Congress," she begins, "I said to Mr. Bingham, 'I want to vote because I am a citizen.' He replied, 'You are not a citizen.' 'What am I then?' I asked. 'You are a woman.' I told him I knew that before I came to Washington." The crowd explodes in laughter, relaxing Victoria. She takes a drink of water and continues.

"I make no pretense of oratory, but I am fighting for freedom. I and others of my sex are controlled by a government in the inauguration of

112

which we had no voice and in the administration of which we are denied the right to participate, though we are a large part of its population." Victoria's face is flushed, her eyes flash, and she speaks without notes. The crowd hangs on her every word.

"I am subject to tyranny! Taxed in every conceivable way. For publishing a newspaper, I must pay. For engaging in my banking business, I must pay. Of what is my fortune to acquire each year, I must turn over a certain percentage to the government. I must pay taxes on tea, coffee, and sugar. To all these things I must submit so that man's government may be maintained—a government in which I am denied a voice and from the edicts of which I have no appeal." She takes another sip of water as the audience erupts. Finally quieting them, she continues.

"To be compelled to submit to these extortions is bad enough; but to be compelled to submit to them and also be denied the right to cast my vote against them is a tyranny more odious than that which, being rebelled against, gave this country its independence!" She takes another sip of water, letting the applause carry for a moment.

"In conclusion, I say that women must rebel against men as men rebelled against King George. Every woman who desires to vote should take the steps required to be qualified. If they do not wish to vote, I will stand alone and reiterate my claim. But I do not believe I stand alone."

Victoria leaves the stage to a deafening standing ovation. In the anteroom, Butler flusters around her, his cigar rolling excitedly across his lips.

"Impressive! Absolutely impressive! I have one word of advice, if you would like it."

"I would be honored for any advice you give me, General."

"Put down the water. You'll be amazed at the intensity of your speeches when you are thirsty." He laughs. "What am I saying? If you were any more intense, you'd start the building on fire!"

"Then I shall save the water to throw on the flame!"

"Oh, no, never put it out. It gives you irresistible attraction. Now, where are your printed speeches?"

"Sir?"

"Always print your speeches and make them available to the press. Sell them at the door. People believe the written word." Butler starts to leave but turns at the door. "And don't lose your passion! Incredible! Supremely, powerfully incredible."

Chapter 17

The Claflins are having their usual rowdy breakfast. Stephen Andrews is staying at the mansion while his wife is in Europe, so Victoria's sister Polly has moved her family to a hotel. Utica is also missing, sleeping off a binge. Their absence hasn't lessened the chaos, however, which Victoria, home from Washington, ignores as she flips through her mail and nibbles at her food. She is startled when Roxanna slaps at the letter in her hand.

"Don't be eating and working at the same time," her mother scolds.

"Oh, Mama, this isn't work. Look, a letter from Miss Anthony!" She beams as she reads it aloud. "'I have just read your speech of February sixteenth. It is ahead of anything said or written. Bless your dear soul for all you are doing to help strike the chains from woman's spirit.'"

"Did you tell Ma about the letter you got from Elizabeth Cady yesterday?" Tennie asks.

"Oh, Mama, it was glorious."

Victoria hops up and rushes out of the room.

"Victoria, get back here and sit down. You'll get *krank* jumping up and down like a *kaninchen*."

"I just wanted you to hear what Mrs. Cady wrote, Mama," Victoria says, rushing back in and pulling the letter from its envelope. "You like her. She says 'We have waited six thousand years for equality, and the time has come to seize the bull by the horns, as you are doing in Washington and Wall Street.' Isn't that great, Mama?"

"But printing all them pamphlets and speeches," Buck snorts. "How you gonna make money doing that?"

"The paper is doing well, Sir," Andrews says.

"And the brokerage house is adding clients daily," Blood adds. "Besides, sales at Victoria's lectures will cover most of the printing costs."

"Ach! Must I hear your voices at my breakfast?" Roxanna covers her ears with her hands. "It is you two who are destroying my daughters.

You drive Polly and Benjamin out. You got Maggie's innocent boy Channing down at the paper corrupting his mind. One day I will stab you both in your sleep."

"Mother!"

"Then I shall have to put you on my knee and spank you," Blood tells Roxanna, eyes teasing.

"Stop it, you two." Victoria's reprimand is automatic because her attention is on an official-looking letter that she slits open. Her gasp is followed by an exasperated sigh as she hands the letter to Blood.

"What is it? Something about Utie's arrest?" Roxanna asks, trying to get a look.

"Utica got arrested? For what?" Victoria asks, shocked.

"Being on a ran-tan and kickin' up a shine," Buck says.

"My god. Drunk and disorderly. That's just great."

"This isn't about that," Blood says. "It's a suit filed against us by that ungrateful Annie Swindell."

"*Gott behute! Gott behute!*" Roxanna rushes from the room shrieking.

"My god, Sis, isn't she the one you hired part-time to help her out when her investment lost money?"

"It is. This is what makes conducting business with most women so difficult. As much as we wish every female could be as savvy about man's world as we are, most aren't there yet." Victoria turns to Blood. "When's the court date? I have lecture engagements I can't cancel."

"March 28. Good lord, that's today! This must have come while you were in Washington."

"We'd better get to the courthouse. I don't want to lose by default."

"This is what I'm sayin'. You need to stop stirring things up and tend to your business." Buck waves his fork to punctuate his admonishment. "We'll be back in the poor house, you watch."

"If I lose every penny and awaken the women so we gain the vote, it will be worth it. This fight is not about money. It's about power. When mothers and daughters have equal power in corporate and political arenas men like you will no longer be able to take advantage of us."

116

She glares at Buck, who stands abruptly.

"I'm going to the track," he says. "At least things are sane there."

Late that afternoon, the spectators and reporters in the courtroom are all weary from a long day of arguments. Despite Victoria's testimony that a guilty verdict would set a dangerous precedent for bankers on Wall Street, the judge rules against her. Annie smirks as the court orders Woodhull, Claflin and Company to repay her original investment plus court costs.

The next day, Victoria stares morosely at the *Tribune* headline: **Swindell Swindled!**

"I cannot believe one of the most reputable papers in our city focuses on a frivolous civil trial over all other news! It is because we are women, and I have some power as candidate for President. Our opponents are going to use this to crucify us, Tennie." She firms her shoulders and sets her jaw. "So be it. If they want war, they've got war."

To gather support, Victoria visits Lucretia Mott at her home in Pennsylvania. Drinking tea at the long wooden kitchen table, they are soon chatting like old friends.

"Whitelaw Reid is claiming the *Weekly* is obscene and coercing newsstands into removing it from their shelves," Victoria laments.

"Don't feel alone, dear. Mr. Greeley closed the *Tribune* to Elizabeth Cady and Miss Anthony years ago. Men are so threatened by us, their fragile counterparts."

"I shan't change my course. There is something providential and prophetic in the fact that my parents conferred on me a queen's name that forbids failure. All I am I have become through sorrow; it has given me a consciousness that is above petty malice."

"Good for thee!"

"Is not freedom recognized and worshipped as a goddess in our country and her image stamped upon our coin? So why does my advocacy of freedom in matters of love strike such terror?"

"Unfortunately I believe the phrase free-love has become one that draws a picture of promiscuity," Lucretia says.

"But promiscuity is the very antithesis of free-love! Of course the highest sexual relations are monogamous, spiritual, and continuous. I actually pity the woman who is pure simply because the law makes her so. But we have gotten the meaning of love all warped now from what Christ preached. His love existed to *do* good not merely to *get* good. Love is something you should give even if you have no hope of getting anything in return. Such unconditional love is the only cure for the immorality and deep damnation by which men corrupt and disfigure God's most holy institution of sexual relations. If that makes me a Free-lover, then I am proud to be one. As Thomas Carlyle said, 'The Public is an old woman. Let her maunder and mumble as she will.' I will not falter in my beliefs!" Victoria blushes. "I am sorry to get on a soapbox, but it is the one subject that riles me more than suffrage. If I can do nothing more than teach people to love one another purely and selflessly then I will have done the work God put me on earth to do."

"Oh, my dear, I am glad to hear thy incontestable logic on the subject. It makes me wish to be called a Free-lover." Lucretia chuckles. "Although I don't suppose that will ever happen."

"You have won my heart, Mrs. Mott."

~ ~ ~

The following day Victoria travels in pouring rain to visit Lucy Stone's group in Boston. She finds Julia Ward Howe and Mary Livermore at the *Woman's Journal* office. They are not pleased to see her, but grudgingly invite her to sit.

"Mrs. Howe, first let me say that my sister Tennie and I think your proposed International Peace Organization is a noble idea." Julia doesn't soften, so Victoria plunges ahead. "It is why I believe you are the one to lead the way to unite our two groups. Before we can have world peace, we must have peace among ourselves, don't you think?"

"You dare talk to me of peace when your very presence causes more distance than ever between the women?"

"For heaven's sakes, what have I ever done to you?"

"Don't act all innocent, Mrs. Woodhull," Mary Livermore says. "I lived in Chicago at the same time you did and am therefore aware of several disgusting incidents involving your free-love activities. You may be accepted by that radical Elizabeth Cady and flighty Isabella Hooker, but we Stoners believe in marriage and family values."

"'If woman's suffrage is right, it makes no difference if its advocates are Free-lovers, Spiritualists, or Methodists,'" says Victoria, barely controlling her temper. "Those are your very words from a few years ago, Mary. And yet today it apparently makes a great deal of difference."

"It is a woman's prerogative to change her mind."

"So be it. I did not come to argue with you. I greatly admire all the service you have given to humankind, Mary. I understand you were the main reason we were able to almost eradicate scurvy in our troops during the war."

"Mrs. Woodhull, if you came to flatter us into accepting you, you have wasted your time," Julia says. "Now if you'll excuse us, we are busy."

"I cannot fight lies and innuendos nor will I try," says Victoria. "But, as the English proverb says, 'Those who live in glass houses shouldn't throw stones.' I can name several in your organization who live in brittle tenements, beginning with you, Mary. I understand you intend to leave your marriage." Mary opens her mouth to protest, but Victoria waves her off. "I apologize. The freedom I claim for myself I also accord to everyone else, so I will throw no stones except to protect my own house. But when you say that the hundred and fifty thousand readers of a paper that advocates suffrage earnestly and persistently are not representative of the movement simply because I publish that paper you speak a lie! I suggest you be careful, or you are liable to convict yourselves when the spirit of truth finally predominates over your assumed policy of falsehood." Victoria stands and swirls around, calling back over her shoulder. "Good day, Ladies."

~ ~ ~

Elizabeth Cady Stanton, Susan B. Anthony and Isabella Hooker are immersed in salt waters at the Water Cure Institute in Upstate New York, but Elizabeth is far from relaxed.

"I have received a letter from Anna Dickinson expressing her concern over Mrs. Woodhull's involvement with our organization," she says. "She fears it will do more harm than good."

"Yes, she expressed the same to me," Susan says.

"Anna has never thought enough of our movement to make one speech on our platform, so it ill behooves her to question your wisdom, or anyone else's, in welcoming anyone to our ranks who is ready to share in the labor," Isabella says. "Not to mention Anna's intimate relations with Whitelaw Reid, Ben Butler, and who knows who else. A third, secret lover, by her own admission. For her to call Victoria a Free-Lover is like the pot calling the kettle black, for goodness sakes."

"Point taken," Susan says.

"Lucretia Mott and her friends were completely charmed by Victoria." Isabella offers. "Lucretia said her explanation regarding free-love was logical, Biblical, and irrefutable."

"Unfortunately logic, even Biblical logic, is often trumped by illogical fanaticism. So we must proceed cautiously," Susan says. "Victoria seems refined today, but her history may harm us."

"It is impertinent for us to pry into any of the woman's affairs," Elizabeth says, slapping the water in anger. "We have had enough women sacrificed to sentimental, hypocritical prating about purity. It is one of man's most effective engines for our division and subjugation. If Victoria must be crucified, let men drive the spikes and plait the crown of thorns not us."

"Well, la-de-dah and lullaby, Lizzie hasn't even met the woman yet and she is riled to her defense," says Susan. "Wait until she gets a teetotal dose of the Woodhull's magnetism."

"On the other hand, Julia Howe and Mrs. Livermore were not impressed in the least," Isabella says. "They and Lucy had a good laugh at Victoria's attempt to reconcile our groups. I can't imagine what possessed her to even try."

120

"At least she's trying something," Elizabeth retorts.

"All right, ladies, we came to relax, remember? Let's table the subject to another time." Susan leans back and inhales deeply of the lavender-fragrant steam rising around them.

~ ~ ~

Toward the end of April, Victoria is catching up on correspondence when Isabella Beecher Hooker sweeps into her parlor. Seeing Victoria at her desk, Isabella marches over.

"My darling queen, I have come just in time!"

"In time for what, Belle?"

"To do this." Isabella tears up the plain brown paper Victoria has been writing on and holds out a box of elegant stationery. "Your notes have been a dreadful eyesore to me since I first laid eyes on them. Much too mannish. If you are to be our accepted standard bearer, you must be exquisite in neatness, elegance, and decorum. You are no longer just a banker and businesswoman but a prospective queen. You have the means, and these lovely furnishings show you know how to use them."

"If fancy paper will make what I have to say more palatable to people, I will use it until I die."

"Good. Thank you."

Byron wanders in, Zulu Maud at his heels. Victoria introduces them. Zulu Maud curtsies politely, but Byron grins his toothless grin and wanders out, Zulu Maud following. Victoria stares sadly after them.

"My son is—"

"Oh, Darling Queen," Isabella interrupts, "there is no need to explain. I think it's brave and wonderful that you have not locked him away in an asylum like most people do in such situations. There are ministers who don't have your Godly and compassionate nature."

"My great hope is that one day Byron will understand how much I truly love him."

"Perhaps he does already but just can't express it."

"Perhaps he does."

Victoria stands and leads the way to the sitting area.

"Can you teach me how to call Spirits at will like you do?" Isabella asks, delving into a plate of cookies as Victoria pours tea. "I have believed in the spirit world all my life and have seen many examples of its power, but they have been mostly spontaneous."

"Everyone has the ability. It takes only practice and belief to manifest it," Victoria says. "Let me show you an experiment I was trying earlier today." She walks to her desk and returns with a couple of two-inch pieces of broom whisk, one straight and one bent into a V. Holding the straight piece between the thumbs and forefingers of each hand, she has Isabella hang the V-shaped piece over it so the tips hover in the air. Isabella's eyes widen as the bent piece moves slowly along the straw between Victoria's hands, inching to the left.

"Oh, I love these kinds of games! Let me try."

Victoria hands her the straw, and Isabella is astonished as the V-shaped piece moves of its own volition for her, too. She moves the bent straw back to the middle and tries again.

"It's caused by the magnetism flowing through us," Victoria says. "When Tennie and I heal, we use this magnetism to align the imbalanced organs and tissues that are causing the illness." Her eyes sparkle with mischief. "Of course healing magnetism is not to be confused with animal magnetism."

"Animal magnetism?"

"The magnetic current that constantly flows between the sexes and creates mutual warmth when in the presence of each other. Sexual vitality if you will. The essence of the Free-love philosophy is that our affection should be at liberty to flow with this natural attraction. Studies are finding that the healthiest humans are those with the greatest sexual vitality. One renowned physician at Cincinnati Medical College proved that if both body and mind are satisfied in the sexual act, no disease arises."

"That's an interesting theory," Isabella says.

"Show me a person suffering from a chronic complaint, and I will show you someone who either has improper sexual relations or none at all. It's why we cannot know equality until women have the right to govern our own bodies. Nature continues on its course no matter how much the law attempts to restrain or suppress it; hence so many of us are weak and sickly."

"So if I have more intercourse with Mr. Hooker my arthritis will go away?"

"It might. As long as you allow yourself to reach the highest state of ecstasy each time. It helps the Colonel with his inflamed joints. Of course, even if you don't cure your ailment, you will still have experienced the most divine pleasure available to humanity."

"We must get off this subject before my face remains permanently red!"

"Okay, to change the subject, let me ask you: What is your biggest pet peeve?"

"Boredom. I tell my children that boring is the only thing I will not accept them becoming. What's yours?"

"Hypocrisy. People point fingers and call me a Free-lover because I had the compassion to take in my ailing first husband, yet they are everywhere having secret affairs. And then you have Christians who sit piously in pews on Sunday and lie, cheat, steal, and kill the rest of the week. One of these days I will expose all these sanctimonious hypocrites!"

"Bravo, my dear! Just do it on fancy stationery."

A couple of nights later, Colonel Blood escorts Victoria, Paulina Wright Davis, and Elizabeth Cady Stanton to Daly's Theater on Fifth Avenue to see "Delmonico's," a new play about their favorite restaurant that stars the popular Clara Morris. Sitting in prime box seats, they chat as they wait for the play to begin.

"Colonel, thank you for escorting us," Paulina tells Blood. "It is so frustrating to want some entertainment and have our menfolk busy."

"When I am President, attending without a male escort won't be forbidden," Victoria says.

"You'll still let us tag along, won't you?" Blood asks, winking. "There are few things more pleasant than being in the company of three lovely ladies."

"Victoria, you are blessed," Paulina says, practically swooning.

"Even Susan said she might consider marriage if she could find a man like you, Colonel," Elizabeth says.

The Colonel smiles and bows gallantly.

"I am even more blessed this evening," Victoria says.

"Why is that, Dear?" Elizabeth asks.

"Why to be meeting you at last, Mrs. Cady. When you wrote asking me if Demosthenes had some new argument for suffrage, I knew we'd be fast friends should we ever meet."

"I must admit Demosthenes responded in the most magnificent way. Anyone who does not now see that suffrage is already ours should be institutionalized!"

"Apparently that includes the entire male population of our government," Blood says.

"Then we will keep hammering away." Victoria turns to Paulina. "You, too, have my deepest admiration, Mrs. Davis. Is it true that your lectures include an anatomically correct female mannequin so as to teach women to know their bodies?"

"Yes. I believe we must talk about these topics so clearly and so often that the stigma of doing so is finally removed."

"Exactly!"

"Which is why I am glad to see you'll speak at Apollo next week," Paulina says. "That hall draws a good crowd."

"I hope I do well. Lately I have been distracted by the assault of Harriet Beecher Stowe's pen. It was bad enough when she mocked me with her story in their newspaper, which is little read, but now she plans to release *My Wife and I* as a book. Everyone knows she means the character Audacia Dangyereyes to be me, though I've never smoked a cigar in my life."

"Mrs. Stowe should be the last to ridicule you," Paulina huffs. "Her own brother is a Free-lover!"

"What?" Victoria is shocked.

"Oh, yes. The great Henry Ward is rumored to have had many affairs, but we have firsthand information of one. Tell her, Lizzie."

"I have it from Mr. Tilton's own lips that for two years the Reverend preyed on his wife's vulnerability over the death of their infant son, until she finally succumbed."

"Libby confessed last July and her husband beat her something fierce," Paulina adds. "That's how Susan and Elizabeth found out. And apparently on Christmas Eve, the men even forced Libby to abort her baby, since they didn't know who the father was."

"No! That poor woman!" Victoria's eyes narrow in anger.

"And it's not as if Mr. Tilton hasn't had his own affairs. He's sleeping with Laura Bullard, for one," Paulina adds.

"Even worse, Beecher has now convinced the Tiltons to sweep the entire matter under the rug," Elizabeth says. "It's rumored he put up money for Tilton to start his *Golden Age* paper after Henry Bowen fired Theodore. I swear I would like to strip the mask right off that hypocritical scoundrel. As Susan says, 'For a man so blest and overflowing with soul food to dally with a revering devotee is teetotally inexcusable.'"

"That man manipulates spiritually thirsty women so cunningly they would do his bidding if, like a heathen priest in Hindu-land, he told them to fling their children into the Ganges!" Paulina tsks. "Poor Libby can be blamed for weakness, but it's that sanctimonious cur who seduced her."

"Now I have another Beecher to abhor," Victoria says. "If Rev. Beecher is *preaching* virtue and damning others to hell for what he does himself, he is the biggest hypocrite of all. Is only Belle a dear?"

"Oh, Belle definitely has her Beecher moments," Elizabeth says. "Oh, the play begins."

"You must tell me the whole story later," Victoria whispers to Paulina as the curtain rises to reveal a remarkable likeness to the Wall Street restaurant.

Chapter 18

In May, when the NWSA holds its annual spring convention at the Apollo in New York, Horace Greeley and Whitelaw Reid decide to attend.

"Good Lord, they have filled the place," Horace comments as they take their seats. "Last year they rattled around in one corner." He opens his long duster and leans on the handle of his bright orange umbrella.

"They're still mostly all talk. That won't get them a federal amendment."

"Shh, Elizabeth is starting the program."

"Victoria C. Woodhull stands before us today a grand, brave woman, radical in social, political, and religious principles," Elizabeth says. "The processes of her education mean little, the grand results everything. Let's show our pride in Victoria C. Woodhull!"

The applause is thunderous. It takes only moments for Victoria to mesmerize the crowd.

"The Democrats are not as antagonistic to the true interests of the country as are the Republicans simply because they haven't the power. But where they have the power, their leaders do not hesitate to make use of it to their own aggrandizement. It will be suicidal to attach ourselves to either of these parties. So we have only one course left. Women may have no government, but we will have our rights! We have besought and argued, but we have failed. And we . . . will . . . not . . . fail!"

"This woman is not to be swept under the rug, Whitelaw." Horace says, leaning over and practically shouting to be heard above the din.

"We will try just once more," Victoria continues. "If the very next Congress refuses women all legitimate results of citizenship, we give deliberate notification that we shall call another convention and frame a new constitution and erect a new government complete in all its parts!"

Hankies and hats fly in the air. Women stand on chairs, waving hands and cheering. Victoria shouts to be heard.

"We mean treason! We mean secession! And on a thousand times grander scale than was that of the South! We are plotting revolution! We will throw off this bogus republic and plant a government of righteousness in its stead! A government that will not only profess to derive its power from the consent of the governed, but shall do so in reality!"

Greeley and Reid realize they have leapt to their feet and are applauding with the others. They sit quickly, embarrassed.

"This is dangerous talk, Horace!"

"It is indeed. And there isn't a thing we can do about it. If she is silenced now, the women will rise up like we can't even imagine. Not only will they vote, they will run the country and everything in it."

"Frightening. Very frightening." The men turn their attention back to the stage as Victoria continues in a more moderate voice.

"Because I have advocated radical political action, because I have called for a new party and announced myself as a candidate for the Presidency, I am charged with being influenced by an unwarrantable ambition. First I will ask: Why is ambition in women bad but in men enviable? Then I will state, once and for all: I have no personal ambition whatsoever. All that I do I do because I believe humanity will be advanced thereby."

"I don't think I've ever seen Miss Anthony look so alive. She's almost beautiful." Reid nods toward Susan B., who sits on the stage her face aglow with inspiration.

"Mr. Reid, this is a spirit to respect, perhaps to fear, certainly not to be laughed at. Mrs. Woodhull is to be praised for having the courage of her convictions, and I would not be true to myself if my editorial tomorrow did not say so and, God help me, recommend that others emulate her."

"Now, Horace, remember what you always say: 'Fame is vapor, popularity an accident, riches take wings. Only one thing endures, and that is character.' And that is one thing The Woodhull does not have."

A woman shushes them as Victoria finishes her speech.

"In conclusion, I declare that if women will do one-half their duty until Congress meets, our government will be compelled to pass such laws as are necessary to enforce the provisions of the Fourteenth and Fifteenth Articles of Amendment to the Constitution. But should they fail, then for secession!" Victoria bows and sits as the crowd chants her name.

Paulina Davis rushes to the podium, yells above the noise: "Ladies and gentlemen, the Joan of Arc of the Woman's Movement!"

~ ~ ~

The next day, the mid-afternoon sky is overcast as Harriet Beecher Stowe climbs the flower-lined steps to Victoria's Murray Hill mansion. At 60, Harriet is pleasingly plump, with curly, graying hair. Her normal jovial tomboy personality is at the moment hidden behind a scornful frown. Victoria has been expecting her and opens immediately at her knock.

"Mrs. Stowe, how glad I am to finally meet you!"

"My sister Belle seems to think you are God's instrument for righting social injustice so I promised to meet you with an open mind," Harriet says tersely, ignoring Victoria's outstretched hand.

"That's all I ask. I am flattered by Belle's words but assure you I am just an ordinary woman who believes in equality for all." Victoria steps outside. "Let's ride in the park while we get to know each other. Perhaps the sun will peek through on us after all today."

Almost as soon as the women sink into the plush velvet seats of the carriage, Harriet begins to lecture.

"Do you not realize, Mrs. Woodhull, what a dangerous proposition it is for a woman to challenge man's power? Women of good breeding and proper antecedents can gently persuade men, but this moral influence is the only one that women should wield. Those who attack marriage and advocate free-love destroy civilization. People will soon behave like animals. The sacredness of marriage has already been mangled and torn asunder in the name of progress. Woman's independence begets marital degeneration. If you do not understand this, you either misunderstand woman's role entirely, or you are possessed by powerful and malignant spirits."

With Harriet giving her no opportunity to defend herself, Victoria looks out the window to control her temper. She watches the afternoon promenade through Central Park as Harriet drones on.

"Feminine power is to be exercised in the home. Our first obligation is to maintain domestic harmony. My soul is downcast at the ignorance and mistaken zeal of you crusaders. Mrs. Stanton and you free-love roost of harpies who follow her imagine that the remedy for the evils that oppress our sex is to introduce woman to political power and make her a party in the scramble for governmental office. Never mind that men will never accept a woman President. Or that it's unnatural for us to govern. Who can look at this danger without dismay?"

"I certainly feel no dismay about it! Mrs. Stowe, it appears that I am not party to a conversation but merely attending a lecture. You speak like a missionary trying to convert a heathen."

"If you act like a heathen, decent folks will treat you like one! Only a lady willing to be slopped into every dirty pail of muck like an old mop would run for office. And for you to do it while you flaunt a Free-love lifestyle— Someone ought to do to you what my father did to me: Hold your head under water until you lose your will to be foolish."

"I'm surprised to hear you condemn me when several distinguished editors, clergymen, and lady authors of this country, many of whom you know and all of them supposed models of domestic purity and virtue, not only hold my opinions on free-love but practice it! Your own brother included!"

"Hank has never been false to his marriage vows!" Harriet hisses through lips tightened in anger.

"Oh? Then why of all your brothers did he spring to your mind just now? Do you have irrefutable proof of his virtue?"

"Well, of course no one can—"

"I have proof in the form of confessions, and I will tell you the explicit details of that proof."

"Stop!" Harriet punches the bell that calls the driver. "Return us to Mrs. Woodhull's at once!"

The driver glances at Victoria, who shrugs and nods. Harriet stares straight ahead, her lips clamped in a thin line. She puts her hands to her ears as Victoria lays out all she knows about the Beecher-Tilton affair. White with anger, Harriet punches the coachman's bell again and orders the carriage be stopped right where it is. She practically falls onto the street in her haste to depart.

"I will strike you for this, Victoria Woodhull! I will strike you dead!"

"Strike as much and as hard as you please, Mrs. Stowe. Just don't be like a snake in the night! I like to see who my enemies are!"

Chapter 19

Victoria's carriage reins up in front of her Wall Street firm just as a sheriff's deputy is leaving. She hurries inside, entering the inner office as Blood opens an envelope and curses.

"Oh, God, what is it now?" she asks.

"Pearl would call it *Commedia D'elle Arte*," he says, handing her the subpoena. Her mouth drops open as she reads.

"This is insane! Does mother really think she can sue you for alienating Tennie and my affections? Why, the judge will laugh the case right out of court! I am going home this instant to tell her to withdraw this ridiculous claim!"

Having failed to get her mother to drop the suit, on the afternoon of May 15, Victoria and Blood join the entire Claflin clan in the Essex Market Police Court. Roxanna takes her place at the defendant's table with her attorney, Mr. Townsend. Blood is at the plaintiff's table. Victoria and Tennie sit directly behind him. Victoria wears a deep purple suit; a red rose offsets her dark blue necktie. Tennie looks almost conservative in her navy suit. Victoria fingers the watch-chain at her neck nervously as she glances at the handful of curious spectators and the few reporters in the press galley. The judge climbs to the bench, but before he can sit Roxanna rushes forward, wringing her hands.

"Judge, my daughters were good and affectionate girls until they got in with this man Blood. He has corrupted my babies and weaned them from their affectionate and never-to-be-consoled mother. He has threatened my life several times. Once he said he would not go to bed until he had washed his hands in my blood."

The judge bangs for order, gives Roxanna's attorney, Mr. Townsend, a stern look.

"Keep quiet, old lady," Townsend tells Roxanna. "Come back here and sit down!"

"But I want to tell the judge what these people are!" She drops to her knees before the bench. "I was afraid for my life when I lived in that house. It was nothing but talk about lunatic asylums and murder. That man Blood ain't got no bottoms in his pockets. I hear him telling my sweet Tennessee to secure the attentions of this married man or that so he can blackmail them to pay for his fancy suits and expensive games of whist. If my daughters had sent him flying as I told them, they'd be rich now."

"We are rich, Mama," Tennie calls out.

"Order! Mr. Townsend, control your client!"

The judge bangs his gavel furiously. Townsend rushes forward, shushing Roxanna as he drags her back to her chair.

"Now, let us proceed according to law," the judge says. "Mr. Townsend, call your first witness."

"I need no Bible to tell the truth," Roxanna declares as she scuttles to the stand and ignores the outstretched Bible.

"If you do not swear on the Bible, Madam, you cannot speak."

Roxanna pouts as she places her hand on the Bible.

"As *Gott* is my witness I can no more tell a lie than President Washington could." She plops into the witness chair and begins to rant. "So help me *Gott*, there is the worst gang of Free-lovers living in our house. Mr. Andrews is a blasphemer who taunts me daily that our blessed savior Jesus Christ was no more than a common man like himself. And now he and Mr. Blood are bringing in the communists. There's a litter of 'em in every room."

Victoria's sister Polly testifies next, saying that she often heard her mother wailing as Blood assaulted her in private. She also says that Victoria invoked spirits to threaten her mother with the asylum and put a 'strange and unnatural' spell on Tennie.

Utica is so drunk when she takes the stand that the judge has to strain to understand her slurring words as she accuses her sisters and Blood of withholding her medications, which of course she doesn't say are alcohol and illicit drugs. Victoria is frustrated by the time Blood is called. Several women in the audience whisper and flutter as he steps forward with military precision and in his melodious baritone swears to tell the truth. Attorney Townsend sneers as he begins his questions.

"Tell us, Mr. Blood, when did you marry Mrs. Woodhull?"

"In eighteen sixty-six, Sir."

"Was Mrs. Woodhull divorced when you married her?"

"I believed so."

"Were you not afterwards divorced from Mrs. Woodhull?"

"Yes, Sir."

"Victoria, this man is not your husband under *Gott*!" Roxanna cries out, leaping to her feet. "Drive him from your house today before the holy *Mudder* of Israel calls her wrath down upon you!"

The judge glares. Townsend restrains Roxanna. She sniffles into her hankie as he returns to questioning Blood.

"Following your divorce, how long were you separated from Mrs. Woodhull?"

"We were never separated. We continued to live together and were afterwards remarried." He gives Roxanna a pointed look.

"Have you seen Dr. Woodhull, Mr. Blood?"

"Of course. I see him daily. We live in the same house."

"Do you and the Woodhulls occupy the same bedroom?"

Blood snorts derisively in response.

"Colonel, tell the court why Dr. Woodhull lives with you and who supports him," Blood's attorney advises.

"Dr. Woodhull came to us destitute and dying. Out of compassion, my wife took him in. Under our care and kindness, he experiences many good days now and has become invaluable to us. Mrs. Woodhull's son suffered a fall when he was young, and his father's medical treatments are crucial to the boy's enjoyment of life. The firm of Woodhull, Claflin and Company supports the entire household, as well as my mother-in-law, even since she moved out."

"Are Mrs. Claflin's charges against you true?"

"They are in toto false. I have never been violent with Mrs. Claflin. Well, one day she was particularly vexing and I teased that if she were not my mother-in-law I would turn her over my knee and spank her. But that is as harsh as I have ever been to the woman. I saw enough violence when I fought at Shiloh that I go out of my way to preserve peace."

Blood's attorney has no questions so the judge tells Blood he may step down.

"I have heard enough today," he says. "We will resume testimony at 10:00 A.M. Court is dismissed."

With a whack of his gavel he is gone.

The next day, not only are all the Claflins back in the courtroom, but the press galley overflows with newsmen. The morning's headlines have brought a horde of spectators as well. Physicians, lawyers, reformers, servants, brokers, and men of leisure in velvet coats and top hats fill every available seat and spill into the hallways. Victoria is called first, and the curious onlookers strain to get a clear view. In response to Townsend's first question, she testifies that she was married to Woodhull at a young age and later divorced him.

"And yet he continues to live with you in addition to the man you claim is now your spouse?"

"Mr. Townsend, my relationships with Dr. Woodhull and Colonel Blood are not matters for this court's consumption as neither has any bearing on this ridiculous charge my mother has made. Let us get back to the issue at hand. Colonel Blood always treated my mother kindly. Sometimes she would say he was the best son-in-law she had. Other times she would abuse him like a dog. At those times, he would ignore her. She has threatened him with poison, prison, and death in his sleep, but I never knew him to put a hand on her."

"Is it true that on the first of April of this year you evicted your mother from your home on Murray Hill?"

"No, Sir. My mother went to board with my sister of her own accord. Woodhull, Claflin and Company has continued to pay all bills for her maintenance. I can produce receipts."

"If what you say is true, Mrs. Woodhull, why would your mother distress herself to file a complaint against Mr. Blood?"

"You will have to ask her, Sir."

When Tennie takes the stand, she waves to the reporters and kisses the Bible with a loud smack, causing the room to erupt with laughter. Attorney Townsend approaches with a stern look, but Tennie greets him with a friendly nod and stares directly into his eyes for a long moment. She smiles when it flusters him.

"Please state your name for the record," the judge says.

"My name is Tennessee Celeste Claflin, the martyred one."

Before Townsend can get a question out, Tennie is off and running, speaking directly to the judge.

"Your honor, since I was eleven years old I have told fortunes with my mother. Victoria and the Colonel got me away from that life. They're the best friends I ever had. For almost as long as I can remember we have supported almost forty Claflin deadheads, working as Spiritualists, fortune-tellers, and trance-physicians." She gives Roxanna a pained look and glances quickly away. Victoria signals her to be quiet, but Tennie continues jabbering. "I have power, and I know my power. Commodore Vanderbilt knows my power. I have humbugged some, sure, but only to keep my family together. And I am through with that life!" Tennie finally realizes she's rambling and looks at Townsend. "Hadn't you better ask some questions, Sir?"

"Well, thank you for finally allowing me to, Miss Claflin," Townsend says, earning laughter from the spectators. "Can you please tell the court why your mother quarreled with Mr. Blood?"

"My god, who knows? The Colonel was never anything but kind to her. I don't see how he stood all the abuse she heaped on him. I blame this whole thing on my sister Polly's husband. That blackguard Sparr has been blackmailing people and using my name to do it."

"That is not relevant," the judge says.

"My god, I have been accused of being a blackmailer. I want it ventilated to clear my name." Tennie pulls a bunch of papers from her purse. "These are letters signed with my name for the purpose of blackmailing eminent persons in this city." She looks at the judge. "It was my sister Polly and her lamebrain husband who did the blackmailing, so think about that when you think about their testimony!"

"Miss Claflin, those letters are ruled out."

"No! I insist on clearing my name! They have made me out a bad woman and that can't stand."

135

"Counsel, please approach the bench," the judge says, banging his gavel. The two attorneys come forward. As they consult with the judge, Tennie springs from the chair and rushes to Roxanna. Grabbing her mother into her arms, she begins to sob.

"My god, Ma, I didn't mean to call you a deadhead!" When Polly tries to pull her mother away, Tennie brings her into the hug as well. "You're not a deadhead either, Polly. Vic and I are happy to give you everything we have."

The crowd is abuzz. The judge bangs for order.

"Miss Claflin, you have not been dismissed!"

"My god, Judge, I am afraid Ma will die under this excitement."

"If no one has any more questions for her—" At the judge's questioning look, both attorneys shake their heads. "Then Miss Claflin, you are released. Mr. Townsend, do you have any more witnesses?"

"No, Your Honor, prosecution rests."

"Does the defense have any questioning to be done?"

"No, Your Honor."

"Then it is my ruling that this case be dismissed. Court is adjourned."

The following day, Victoria stews while Tennie plays minor chord rifts on the piano. The morose melody matches their moods. They hardly react when Andrews arrives with an armful of newspapers.

"Well, they have done it," Andrews says. "French workers have revolted. The communards have engaged government armies in a bloody battle in Paris. The Palais-Royal, Ministry Building, and Rues de Rivoli and Royale are all in flames, and the fire is spreading to Porte Saint-Martin, the Hotel de Ville, the Bastille, and Bercy!"

"Has the news mitigated coverage of our trial?"

"I'm afraid not, *mon tenez le premier role*." Andrews hands her the papers. "Under the front-page headline 'Free-love is Free Lust' Mr. Greeley claims you share the couch with one husband but bear the name of another to show your impartiality towards them."

"The front page? Really? Shouldn't New Yorkers be worrying about the fate of their poor working brothers and sisters in France instead of stimulating themselves with our private pain? Don't they know if things continue the way they are going in America our own citizens may soon rise up in the same way?"

"This revolt has to have sent shivers up and down Wall Street and Madison Avenue," Pearl comments. "These same conditions exist in the restless, working class Americans who grow more destitute as the rich amass more and more wealth."

"And yet they focus on destroying me." Victoria glances through several more papers, speed-reading. "My own mother has given the hounds their bones," she moans. "They are dredging up our entire past. This one calls me a brazen, unsexed snake of a woman, and this one laughs at the open, shameless effrontery with which I have paraded my name as a Presidential candidate."

"My god, Sis, why don't you just stop reading that trash?"

"No, it's important to know what is said so I can respond." She turns white as she picks up the *St. Louis Times*. "Oh, no, this article talks about Ohio. They've discovered Papa's pilfering at the post office and burning down the mill for the insurance."

Victoria sighs and lays the paper aside.

"My god, they can't blame you for what Pa did. You were a child!"

"Maybe, but the sins of the father—"

"What's the Bowen of contention have to say?" Andrews asks, nodding toward the *Independent* on top of the dwindling pile. Victoria picks up the paper.

"I'm almost afraid to look. You know the Beechers are behind whatever Henry Bowen prints." She finds the article and reads, "The suffrage question was not a little fanned by the sudden revelation about the private life of Mrs. Woodhull. Mrs. Stanton, Miss Anthony and Mrs. Hooker have been foolish to give a prominent place on their platform to such a woman.'" Victoria swipes at a tear. "Oh, dear."

"I will respond forcefully in the *Weekly*," Pearl consoles.

"Mary Livermore says in the *Woman's Journal* that we ran a grand and peculiar house in Chicago. She knows that we only told fortunes, but she sure implies something more."

"My god, don't assume people will think that, Sis," Tennie says. "They can look all they want, but they'll never find proof that any of us were prostitutes, because we weren't."

"Listen to this one," Victoria says, opening the *Cleveland Leader*. "'She has made herself a prominent figure in the Woman's Suffrage Movement and now that her shameful life has been exposed, the enemies of female suffrage will point to her as representative of the movement.' Oh, how will I ever face the ladies again? My dreams and destiny are crushed in the dirt by my very own family."

"My god, Sis, dozens of great statesmen have had and still have colorful backgrounds and crazy relatives."

Tennie plays a minor riff.

"Benjamin Franklin had an illegitimate child," Pearl agrees.

"That's gotta be a graver sin than anything they can accuse you of," Tennie says.

"The difference is that he was a man and I am a woman."

"Well, you can either bury your head in the sand and waste away hidden in your house, or you can go out and fight it head on. I'll be with you either way." Tennie bangs her hands down on the piano.

"Of course I won't hide away. No matter what they say and do to me. I just needed a tiny pity party."

"Thank god."

The maid rushes in and hands a note to Tennie.

"What is it, Tennie?" Victoria asks.

"The Commodore. He's summoned me."

A short time later, Tennie pokes her head into Vanderbilt's bedroom, lugging a painting.

"I brought you a gift, Com. It's the painting you always liked at our office."

"That Frederic Church thing with the spectral sky?"

"Yup. *Aurora Borealis*. It's an original, ya know."

She props the painting on the dressing table.

"That sure brightens the room, Little Sparrow."

Tennie hops into bed and cuddles against the Commodore, running her fingers through his wispy hair. He takes her hand and kisses it, then lays it on his chest and pats it gently.

"I'm sorry I dragged you into that court mess, Old Boy."

"Me, too, Little Sparrow. You are dearer to me than anything, and I will never forget your kindness to an old man. But I will be seventy-nine years old before the month is out, and I am mostly infirmed. Can't hardly hear a thing anymore; my heart is skippin' every other beat; I got a hernia, kidney stones, constipation, and an enlarged prostate."

"My god, why ain't you called me for a healing?"

"My family says our friendship proves my senility and threatens me with the asylum if I do not denounce you. I still hold the power of the purse strings, but I am tired."

"Don't fret it, Com. I understand. But let me fix some of your problems before I go, okay? Roll over on your stomach. I'll get to work." As Tennie massages the old man, she jabbers about their early days.

"My God, I remember when I first met you. For once Pa's horse-tradin' and drinkin' paid off. We hadn't been in the city more'n a month when he found out at the saloon that you welcomed visits from healers. He went to watch ya race in the Park, set up a meeting, and *voila*."

"Your Pa is a scoundrel," Vanderbilt says, "but I looked over my balcony at you two gals—Victoria so refined and delicate and you all plumped up and pretty as a peach—and I knew I'd tolerate anyone to get to know ya. I was a grievin' widower at the time, Sophie only recently dead, and seein' you was like seein' an angel from God." He pauses, smiles. "When Victoria contacted mama Phebe, I could literally smell the soap-and-lavender scent of her dear departed soul."

"My god, everyone was scared of you but me. I knew there was a gentle lamb 'neath all that cussin' and bellerin'. I think our daily healings helped you. And gettin' rid of that rich diet you was eatin'."

"You know I wanted to marry you, Sparrow. Got my blockhead boy Billy so upset he went out and found what he called 'a more dignified replacement.' Frank's a pretty enough thing, but if you'd'a said the word, I'd'a married you instead, the hell with what society had to say about it."

"I reckon I loved you more than any man ever, Old Boy. I'm sorry I couldn't be what you needed, but even sorrier public opinion had a say in all of it. That old Mrs. Grundy oughta keep her nose out of personal business."

"Well, that's hindsight, I expect."

"Yup. We had us a good run, though."

"That we did. I am gonna sorely miss ya, Tennessee. Snip off a piece of what hair I got left, Little Sparrow. That'll give you some of my power to see you through."

Chapter 20

The media assaults on Victoria continue. Both Victoria and Andrews take on the muckrakers in the *Weekly*, but when Harriet Stowe harpoons her in the *Hartford Courant*, Victoria has had enough. She dashes off an angry open letter to the *New York Times*. When it appears in the Sunday edition, she sends a note to Theodore Tilton. He comes to her office the following morning. Victoria runs her gaze up his tall frame to the handsome face and flowing hair, motions him to sit.

"I appreciate your prompt response to my note, Mr. Tilton," she says.

"We have traveled in the same circles for quite some time, and I have been anxious to meet you. I must say you are even more beautiful than people have described."

"I have also heard much about you."

"All good I trust." His eyes flirt. She ignores his charm.

"Mr. Tilton, organized hypocrisy has become a main feature of modern society, and poltroonery, cowardice and deception rule supreme. The continuation of such falsity will eradicate honesty from the human soul before a generation has passed. Someone must lead the vanguard against it." She hands him the Sunday *Times,* which is folded open to the Letters page. "Would you please read the marked portions of this letter?"

Her gaze is steady. He purses his lips, amused, and reads.

"'I put myself before the public voluntarily, knowing full well that my opinions and principles would be subject to criticism. I accept that. But I do not intend to be made the scapegoat of society. Many of my self-appointed judges preach against free-love openly but practice it secretly. For example, I know of one man, a public teacher of eminence, who lives in concubinage with the wife of another public teacher of almost equal eminence. I shall make it my business to analyze some of these lives and take my chances in the matter of libel.'" Tilton lays down the paper and gives her a wary look.

"Do you know to whom this letter refers, Mr. Tilton?"

"How can I tell in a blind card as this?" Tilton tosses his long curls behind him with forced indifference.

"I refer to the Reverend Henry Ward Beecher and your wife." Tilton's bravado vanishes. "I can read by your expression that my charge is true." Tilton is too stricken to speak, so Victoria continues. "Understand that I do not condemn Mr. Beecher for loving your wife, or vice versa. But I deplore his hypocrisy in condemning his flock for what he does in private."

"So what is it you want?" Tilton's voice is hoarse with trepidation.

"An introduction to Mr. Beecher will suffice for the moment."

"We are short of Harlem, I tell you! Up a creek! You must meet with her, Hank. She means to ruin us both!" Tilton tells Beecher a short time later. He paces, agitated.

"She is bluffing. Our best defense is silence."

"I tell you she does not bluff."

"Well, who will believe her?"

"Do you really want to take the chance of finding out?"

"Then do whatever it takes to pacify her," Henry Ward says, the fear in Tilton's eyes finally convincing him of the earnestness of the situation. "I will support you from the sidelines, but I cannot be seen with her. It would open the can of worms from another direction. Turn on that famous charm, good man. I have faith that you can have her writing our praises in a week."

Henry Ward is more pessimistic as he reads another letter Victoria has published in the *Times:*

> I ask by what equity and justice is a woman accused on the mere imputation of offenses that her accusers may commit without condemnation? To go behind a man's hall door is mean and cowardly. This is the polemical code of honor between men. Why is a woman treated differently? I claim as a matter of justice that the same rule be observable toward woman as toward man. This is natural equity, and I will use my every resource to see that it is achieved.

Tilton is even more concerned than Beecher, and despite his wife's furious objections, invites Victoria to dinner. When she arrives, Theodore greets her with a kiss and ushers her into the parlor. He introduces her to Lib, calling Victoria one of the most intelligent and honest souls he has had the privilege to meet.

"It is a pleasure," Lib says, kissing Victoria's cheek. "I sense already there is no subterfuge in you at all."

"Quite unlike my wife," Theodore says, chuckling wryly. Lib blanches, and Victoria swings an accusing look toward him.

"Mr. Tilton, your wife is wasting away in guilt for something about which she should feel no shame. You do not need to deliver maudlin sentiment, mock heroics, and dreadful suzz over actions as natural as the seasons."

"I believe I am quite noble. I have forgiven and forgotten the lies and betrayal that went on for two years while I was working my fingers to the bone for my family."

"There is nothing to forgive. The false social institutions under which we live have humbugged you into thinking you ought to feel and act in this harlequin way. And you do not seem to have forgotten anything."

"Then help me be the better man."

Lib blushes at her husband's obvious flirtation and looks relieved when a bell signals dinner is served.

"Saved by the bell, Mr. Tilton," Victoria says. "Shall we preserve the niceties and enjoy non-combative conversation while we dine?"

The Tiltons readily agree, and over dinner they become comfortable enough to slip into first-name basis.

"So you haven't told me, Theodore, what do you think of a woman running for President?" Victoria asks.

"I have always demanded the ballot for women, but should we have a woman for President? I would thank God if today we had a *man* for President!"

"So you are not a fan of Mr. Grant's?"

"Not in any way, shape, or form. Horace will drive him out of office next year, you watch."

"I prefer to think I'll be doing the driving."

"I have no doubt you could do it." Tilton's eyes fill with lust. Victoria holds his gaze.

"I sense that you mean that," she says.

"I do. In truth, women have governed us poor men from the world's creation. Hasn't the chief bone of contention between us from earliest ages been Adam's rib out of which God made Eve?"

"Did we really just hear a man admit it is women who hold the power?" Victoria asks Lib with a grin.

"I imagine you could get a man to admit to most anything, Victoria," Lib says. "Perhaps you can share your secret."

"I believe you have enough secrets already, my dear." Lib blushes. Victoria glares. Theodore speaks quickly to prevent their attack. "Seriously, though, I believe women should have the right to do whatever they can do well, whether it be in business or politics or in the family."

"If men were permitted to do only that which they do well, what a host of poor fellows would be thrown out of employment," Victoria teases.

"Touché." Tilton stands and lifts his glass. "With that I am off to my study so you ladies can have a nice chat."

Lib and Victoria adjourn to the parlor, where Lib leans forward and grabs Victoria's hands, earnestly pressing her case.

"I must tell you how this whole sad situation happened so you will understand. Rev. Beecher has been my pastor since I was a teenager. My father was dead, so the reverend was my paternal figure. He performed our marriage and became not only our spiritual mentor, but dearest friend. He and my husband and Mr. Bowen were like the Brooklyn Trinity. So close. When I saw Dr. Beecher was in danger of squandering his spiritual promise by lounging with fawning admirers, I consecrated myself to keeping him on task. I thought to show that I could inspire his purity and fidelity by showing my own."

"A noble, Christian goal."

"When he asked my help with writing his novel *Norwood*, I was flattered. He opened his heart to me like Theodore never had. His visits were refreshing and comforting."

"That's understandable. I have seen tonight that rumors of your husband's abuse of you are true. That can be demoralizing."

"Perhaps. But no excuse. And it was more. I saw my friendship with our pastor as a means of furthering the cause of religion. I loved Theodore with steadfast commitment, but I also began to love Henry Ward for the higher power he represented. The power of God's forgiveness. He told me he saw a similar strength in me. That he found in me a haven from the demands of his position. He said he needed my, as he called it, divine mercy in order to speak as forcefully from the pulpit as he did. I knew both men loved me, and I somehow thought this was God's way of drawing all of us closer to him. I longed to bring us into that trinity of pure souls again.

"Unfortunately, over the hours of our work and with my husband's extended absences, I found it increasingly hard to distinguish reality from art. The struggles of the *Norwood* characters revealed the strange forces and desires of my own world." Lib stops, staring into the distance for a moment. Victoria waits for her to continue. "I began to feel a spiritual . . . passion with Henry Ward. I offered him maternal sympathy, and he gave me . . . mystical inspiration. It was so different from what Theodore and I shared. So I convinced myself that my love with Mr. Beecher, though laced with guilt, wasn't truly wrong.

"Last July, while reading the novel *Griffith Gaunt*, a dam was opened to my self-understanding. I decided to face the truth, sever ties with Beecher, and ask forgiveness of my husband. But was it not a greater sin to burden Theodore's heart? Since he knows, he has subjected me to blow after blow." She pauses, thinking a moment. "But I have faith we can grow strong again and love more ardently, if only you do not reveal our secret." When Victoria does not immediately promise discretion, Lib tries another strategy. "My daughter Flory is aware of the suffering of her mother. She is the same age as your Zulu

145

Maud and endures pain a girl her age should never know. My other children are even younger. I beg you not to bring public condemnation down on their innocent heads."

"Lib, I have endured and continue to endure unbearable suffering for my own parents' actions. And my children, dearer to me than life, suffer from the current attacks on me. I would cut off my right arm before I intentionally hurt any child."

"I invited you to my home because my husband insisted," Lib says, dabbing at a tear. "Having missed the convention at which you spoke, I confess to judging you by the unsavory stories in the newspapers. But I see you are a purer, more honest woman than I am, and I am ashamed."

"Lib, dear, your only shame is allowing men to take your right to happiness. If you wish, I will help you reclaim that."

"But my happiness comes from being the pure, devoted wife my husband demands. It is all I live for. I would give my life to regain Theodore's love and trust."

"Then you shall have it again. Just do not throw pearls before swine. Seize your power and stand up to him."

Theodore comes in, interrupting.

"I have your carriage waiting, Victoria. I will see you home."

"That won't be necessary. I have found my own way many times."

"I insist. It is my responsibility as your host."

~ ~ ~

Victoria's carriage stops at the Murray Hill mansion, and Tilton offers a hand as she alights. As soon as her feet are on the ground, he grabs her in a passionate kiss. She pulls away.

"Mr. Tilton! How can you kiss me so and then scorn your wife for doing the same with your pastor?"

"Mrs. Woodhull, you cannot deny that you desire me as I do you. I saw it in your eyes all through dinner."

"Mr. Tilton you are the perfect Adonis with whom any woman of sentiment and refinement would fall in love. The most popular man in America, they say. But I do not desire you."

146

"I can change that." His kiss brushes lightly on her neck. "I will make fantasies you haven't even dreamed of come true."

"Mr. Tilton, you are totally depraved." She steps away.

"Thank you. Depravity is a very good doctrine. If only people would live up to it." Her soft laugh encourages him and he leans in to kiss her. She places two fingers on his lips.

"Mr. Tilton, I have one fantasy you have in your power to make come true."

"And what is that, my beauty?"

"To introduce me to Rev. Beecher as I have asked." She pats his cheek. "And I shan't wait forever."

Chapter 21

By the end of May, Paris is in ruin as the last fortress of government falls. The human devastation is high: over 20,000 dead and 40,000 in jail. But the Claflin family drama again bumps the news from the front page: Benjamin Sparr is found naked and dead at a brothel hotel in a seedy neighborhood, and their sister Polly accuses Victoria and Tennie of killing her husband and robbing him.

"How can they print this? We've been charged with nothing. It is another crucifixion!" Victoria fumes when she sees the headline:

Bewitching Brokers Charged with Murder and Theft

She tosses the newspaper aside, ranting to Tennie. She looks expectantly at Blood as he rushes in.

"The autopsy shows Sparr died of apoplexy due to booze," he says. "You will not be arrested."

"Unfortunately the damage is done." After a moment she stands, her eyes determined. "We must forget all this nonsense. If the public continues to see me as a spectacle, I will use it as a tool for social protest. I will no longer deny accusations. I will insist they shouldn't matter. We must refocus our efforts on what is important. With Mr. Tilton groveling to placate me, we can use his influence to forward my campaign."

"I also bring good news," Blood says. "The members of Section 12 of the International Workingmen's Association have voted you their president."

"That will give us clout to address desperately needed labor reforms!" Victoria says, brightening. "Hopefully the Communists will prove more courageous than the suffragists and come out strongly for my campaign."

~ ~ ~

Throughout June the assaults continue from all sides. She still hasn't gotten her meeting with Beecher, but with Lib visiting friends in Schoharie for the summer, Theodore Tilton showers Victoria with attention. They ride horses through Central Park and sail on the bay.

They take a rowboat down the Harlem River. Over a romantic picnic on the sunset-drenched beach, he woos her with a poem he has just written, called *French with a Master*:

Teach you French? I will, my dear!
Sit down and con your lesson here.
What did Adam say to Eve?
Aimer, aimer, c'est a vivre.

French is always spoken best
Breathing deeply from the chest
Darling, does your bosom heave?
Aimer, aimer, c'est a vivre.

He takes Victoria's contented smile as an invitation and steals a kiss. When she does not immediately pull away, he continues his seduction in a deliberate, poetic sort of way. With unhurried movements, he cradles her face on his fingertips.

"*Aimer, aimer, c'est a vivre,*" he whispers huskily, letting his hot breath linger at her ear. "To love to love is life. Sate me with your love, and I will give you the introduction you say you must have."

Her legs turn to butter as his hand brushes as light as a butterfly's wing up her thigh. She moans, succumbing to the slow-dance of his fingers on her skin. As darkness swallows the shore, they make love under the glittering diamond sky.

The following day, Theodore rhapsodizes to his old college friend Frank Moulton, who has been serving as a go-between in the cover-up of Beecher's affair with Lib. Moulton is as tall and handsome as Theodore, and although he refuses to attend church or accept organized religion, is known for his honesty and integrity.

"Victoria is a most remarkable woman. She rides horses like an Indian, climbs trees like a chimpanzee, and can walk all day without tiring. She swims, rows, plays chess better than Elizabeth Cady, excels at billiards, and literally floats about a dance floor. I don't think there's anything she can't do. I find myself unable to resist her. Maybe I should have let my wife cleave to her lover, leaving me free to pursue this wondrous soul."

"Mrs. Woodhull already has two husbands in her house." Moulton scoops a long wave of red hair from his forehead and fingers his bushy handlebar mustache as he cautions Tilton. "She probably does not want or need another. Besides, Dory, why buy the farm when you can have all the milk you want out of the cow without it?"

"Meet her and you will understand."

Indeed, both Frank and his wife Emma are smitten when Theodore brings Victoria to dinner. Thrilled to be introduced to his friends, Victoria afterwards takes Theodore to her favorite spot, the Murray Hill rooftop.

"Your husband doesn't mind my being here?" he asks as they fondle each other on a chaise lounge.

"Not at all. James and I practice the doctrine we preach. In fact, he said that a woman who could not love you must be dead to all the sweeter impulses of nature."

"You are an amazing woman. Is there anything you can't do?"

"Well, it appears I am unable to meet Mr. Beecher."

"Soon, my beauty. Meanwhile, I have another idea."

"And that is?"

"*The Golden Age* will publish your biography, my honkidory darling. You can tell me your story and have full approval on the final pamphlet. I believe if people know the truth about you, they will love you as I do."

I love it! Let's begin right now!"

"Why not?"

They adjourn to the library, Theodore transcribing as Victoria dictates.

"I was born on September twenty-third, eighteen thirty-eight, just as the sun was dawning pink-gold over the horizon," she begins. An hour later, Victoria is deep in a trance, reliving memories Theodore commits to the page.

~ ~ ~

Victoria watches in disgust as her siblings beg at a neighbor's door for food. Scoring a few scraps of bread, they scamper away, devouring the treats like wolf pups on a rabbit. As soon as they are out of sight, Victoria knocks on the door.

Twenty-one-year-old Rachel Scribner answers.

"Please, Ma'am," Victoria says, "I apologize for my brothers and sisters. Are there any chores I can do in payment for the food your mother gave them?" She looks up through tangles of blonde hair, her face red with shame.

"There are no chores, but come in and keep me company. I get so lonely with no one my age around, and I sense that you are wiser than your years. What is your name?"

"I am Victoria, Ma'am. I was born the same year as Queen Victoria's coronation, so I am named after her."

"So let's see, that makes you five, correct?"

"Yes, Ma'am."

"Well, Victoria, I am Rachel, and we shall be friends."

"Are you sure it's alright? Most parents don't want the Claflins around."

"You let me worry about that. Come, let's have milk and johnnycakes. And then may I wash your hair? I am thinking of becoming a hairstylist, and it will be good practice for me."

The days pass quickly as Victoria's new friend teaches her to read and write, praising her quick intelligence.

"My goodness, child," Rachel tells her, "you can look at a page one time and know all the words. That is amazing. Are you sure you've had no formal schooling?"

"No Ma'am, I've attended only a few days. There is always so much work to do: making soap and candles, baking bread, hauling wood and stoking fires, ironing, harvesting the garden, taking care of Tennie and my squalling nieces."

"You do all that? You poor thing." Rachel wraps her in a big hug.

A few months later, cholera spreads through the town and takes Rachel in an instant. When she hears the news, Victoria runs to the apple orchard, spinning wildly until the Rachel's spirit appears and takes her through a white light to a world of beautiful homes, well-dressed people, and singing children. That night Victoria tells her family about her vision.

"Rachel and I had the best time."

"Rachel is dead, you ninny," her brother says.

"I don't care. I saw her. Susan and Greta gave us tea—"

"Our sisters are dead, too," Polly says. "They couldn't give you anything!"

"They could and they did. They took me to the angels, and we played with flowers. They showed me where the devil lives. He had a red scarf over his face and horse's feet."

"Oh, my blessed Victoria," her mother says. "You have seen your sisters in the world beyond. You are truly blessed."

"Oh good grief!" Twelve-year-old Polly stalks away.

~ ~ ~

Victoria comes out of her reverie and smiles sadly at Theodore.

"My siblings ridiculed me mercilessly. I couldn't have endured it had not my spirit-guides assured me I would one day have a sister who wouldn't laugh. When Tennessee arrived, she fulfilled that promise. I don't know what I'd do without her."

A few nights later, Theodore and Victoria are again working on the biography.

"Shall I read what I've written about the Claflins?" he asks.

"Oh, yes!"

"'Such a family of cats and kits, with soft fur and sharp claws, purring one moment, fighting the next, never before filled one house with their clamors since Babel began. They love and hate, do good and evil, bless and smite each other. The whole brood is of the same feather, except Victoria and Tennessee. Victoria is a green leaf, and her relatives are the caterpillars who devour her.'"

152

"I like it," Victoria says, rewarding him with a kiss. "We must add Papa's motto, which was ingrained into us with a whip from the time we were born: The Claflins stick together, no matter what. Despite the beatings and the misery he and Mama still bring to our lives, that motto was brainwashed into us, and unfathomable as it may be, we will never cast them away."

Chapter 22

In mid-July, Isabella pays another visit to Murray Hill, wrapping Victoria in her arms and planting kisses on her cheeks.

"Oh, my darling queen, how are you enduring the gossip? Is it true you're trysting with Golden Boy Tilton? Ah, I can see by your face that you are."

"Am I terrible? I initially meant only to use Theodore to meet your brother, after he refused your own requests on my behalf. I threatened Theodore with exposure of their little secret if he did not introduce me. But now he has so captivated me I am powerless to resist him. He is no more intelligent than my husband, but has an outgoingness James will never have. It's an incredible aphrodisiac.

"And the sex. Oh, my. James is a tender, caring lover, while Theodore has this . . . animalistic aggression. Sometimes to the point of savagery. It brings a release like I have never known." She is almost panting at the thought and laughs as she sees Isabella turn as red as the roses on the mantle. "My goodness, I believe I have raised the temperature in here at the very thought."

"I will tell you a secret few know." Isabella leans close, whispers, "I have my own paramour. I think for the same reason."

"Well, good for you, Belle!"

"And it isn't a woman like people have speculated." Isabella giggles. "It is Senator Pomeroy. I still love my husband with all my heart, but he is always so busy with his work. Like you said, I must protect my health. Mustn't I?"

"Of course you must! Just don't let your brother's hypocrisy make you ashamed to admit it."

"I am not ashamed, but I also cannot be open about it. My husband is not like yours. He does not understand the capacity of a human heart to love more than one person. It would destroy him. You are fortunate to have a spouse who accepts your need for others."

"Yes I am." Victoria chuckles. "Although sometimes I question whether it's acceptance or weakness. Of course then I remind myself he's a war hero, so I don't suppose there is any weakness about him."

~ ~ ~

"My god, are you really without Pretty Boy tonight?" Tennie startles Victoria as she plops down beside her on the mansion's rooftop. "I thought he had become attached to your hip."

"Lib is returning this evening so I told Dory he needed to be home to greet her."

"Well, good. I'm bored. You got Pretty Boy and your lectures and your campaign, the Colonel has the brokerage firm, and Professor Perlo has the *Weekly*. What have I got?"

"Aren't you still seeing Johnnie Green?"

"My god, we have an occasional pork—"

"Tennie, don't be crass."

"I want to do something to help you become President."

"I was thinking about that. Do you want to run for Congress? That will give me a friendly face in Washington when I'm elected."

"My god, do you think I could?"

"Why not? How hard can it be?"

"But how? Where?"

"The German district. You'll be perfect! With the *Weekly* set to be the first in the U.S. to publish Mr. Marx's recent interview, and Pearl translating Marx's *Manifesto* into English for publication, the Germans will love you."

"Maybe if I tell Ma she's forgiven for the blackmail scheme, she'll help me bone up on my German. I ain't used it much lately."

"Good. That'll keep her out of the Colonel's hair."

"Speakin' of the Colonel, I've comforted him a time or two, but he sure misses ya. How long is Pretty Boy gonna be around?"

"I don't know. I may be in love. When I am in his arms, the world is full of joy. I don't think I've ever smiled so broadly or laughed so hard."

"Oh my god." Tennie studies her sister's flushed face and the luster in her eyes. "You've got it bad, don't you?" She sighs wistfully. "Maybe someday I'll understand all the rhapsody."

"You will, honey." Victoria gives her a hug. "In any event, Theodore says my biography will take at least until September to complete, and then he's offered to help write the speeches for my next tour."

"Demosthenes writes your speeches."

"Someone must transcribe them while I trance."

"The Colonel always did a fine job at that."

"Yes, but I am still waiting for Theodore to introduce me to Mr. Beecher. With all the Reverend's hypocrisies, he has the reputation and power to legitimize me to the public. No one will dare criticize me as immoral when I have the endorsement of the most renowned and powerful preacher in the country."

"My god, that's true."

"And I enjoy spending time with Theodore and the Moultons. They are intelligent and interesting, which makes for an evening of stimulating conversation. If all Christians were like Emma, this would be a grand world. And Frank has proven he needs no church to be a good man. Now that Lib has returned, I look forward to spending time with her as well. Her letters to me have taken on a much more positive and independent tone, so I think mine to her have done some good. Besides, it's summer and it's fun to be romantic in the summer."

"My god, if Pretty Boy is loosening you up, I guess I'll let ya keep him a bit longer."

"Oh, you will, will you?" Victoria laughs and ruffles Tennie's hair.

A couple of nights later, Victoria and Theodore walk along the almost deserted beach at Coney Island Point. They stroll past Tilyou's Surf Bath House where a sign reads: "Bathers Without Full Suits Positively Prohibited." They stop at Charles Feltman's hotdog wagon, disappointed to find it closed for the night.

"Oh, shoot, I wanted to try one of those new hotdogs," Victoria pouts. "Have you had one yet?"

"You're the only hot thing I want," Tilton says, nuzzling her neck.

"There's only one thing to do in such heat!" She grabs his hand and runs toward the lapping waves.

"There is no way on God's earth you're—! We have no suits. We'll get arrested."

"Pooh on all that. I'm going in!" She throws off her clothes and dives in, beckoning seductively. Tilton, unable to resist, joins her. They float on the waves, arms entwined until Victoria breaks the mood. "Theodore, I can wait no longer. You must schedule an interview with Mr. Beecher immediately. His support is critical to our success."

"Darling, please don't spoil this perfect passion with thoughts of causes or weak-livered preachers." He kisses her hotly, but she pulls him under the water. When they come up for air, she wraps her arms around him.

"Promise to do it within the week, or I will hold you under until you drown."

Tilton's lips chase hers, but her legs wrap around his, submerging him. She pushes on the top of his head until he finally shakes loose and comes up gasping.

"Okay, I promise!"

"That's better. And I shall hold you to it."

Their lips lock, and it takes only seconds for their loud cries of release to echo across the waves.

Chapter 23

The sisters spend the first part of August lecturing. At a meeting at Cooper Hall, Victoria speaks to the International Workingmen's Association.

"Dear friends, last month, on the streets of this city, the Irish poor saw their peaceful march for a decent life turn into a slaughter, with forty-seven citizens killed. If we do not address the concerns of the less fortunate among us now, we may soon have a revolt bloodier than that of the French. So tonight we will return to square one. We will examine the nation's railroad monopolies, which were the first to enslave the workingman. We will examine our factories where women and children work unbearable hours for subsistent wages. We will even look at the life of Christ and see that he and his disciples 'had all things in common.' They were communists of the strictest sort. And so are we!"

~ ~ ~

Tennie takes to the stage at Irving Hall, addressing the German-American Progress Association of the Eighth Manhattan District. The American and German flags hang side-by-side at the back of the platform, and the crowd is mostly men. Tennie presents her lecture in German, using her body to animate her words. By the time her speech ends, the entire room is infatuated with her.

"In closing I say that just as religious American has the privilege of going to church on Sunday so must the right be equally secure for you to drink your glass of lager beer in peace and quiet on the Sabbath, so long as you do not disturb the public order!"

Applause and cheers ring through the hall as the Association president presents Tennie with a huge basket of brightly colored flowers.

"Gentlemen, our soon to be Congresswoman, Tennessee Celeste Claflin!"

"*Es ist alles wahr wodurch die besser wirst*! Through truth you know better!" Tennie shouts, and sashays off the stage.

~ ~ ~

As September begins, Tilton stops into the *Weekly* office and proudly proffers the newly printed pamphlet, *Victoria C. Woodhull, A Biographical Sketch by Theodore Tilton*. Victoria opens it excitedly, running her eyes quickly over the thirty-three pages before returning to read portions aloud.

"'Known as a rash iconoclast, she beats her daily gong of reform. To see her is to respect her—to know her is to vindicate her. She may have some impetuous headlong faults, but she possesses the mad and magnificent energies that (if she lives) will make her a heroine of history.'" Victoria smothers Tilton with kisses. "Thank you thank you thank you. You are poet extraordinaire!"

The following evening, Henry Ward Beecher stands by an open birdcage, cooing at a songbird that sits on his finger. The door bursts open, causing the bird to flutter frantically and fly away. Its song turns to a discordant squawk as Tilton storms in, waving a letter and roaring.

"Are you behind this? Have you betrayed me yet again?"

"I don't know what *this* is, Dory." Beecher catches the bird and calmly returns it to the cage before he responds.

"The Board has scheduled a dismissal hearing for me."

"You rarely attend service, so what does it matter?"

"You know as well as I do that membership in the church is an important credential for society. You must stop this—"

"How can I without endangering us both? You flaunt your relationship with that—that . . . woman. That pamphlet you wrote about her literally gushes with adoration."

"My association with Victoria was to protect both our hides, remember?"

"I never asked you to parade your ridiculous cupidity about town and pen a harlot's praises!"

"I promised to do whatever it took to protect us, and that is what it took."

They glare at each other for a long moment. Beecher finally sighs.

"Calm down, Dory. Continue to keep the Woodhull reined in, and I'll see what I can do with the Board."

"Don't see to anything! Do it! If I am ousted, I will not go down alone."

"I said I would take care of it."

"I have held her off as long as I can, but Victoria insists on meeting you without further delay."

"Then you must convince her it would be unwise. Come, my friend, surely your gift of charm—."

"If *your* gift of charm had not seduced my wife, we wouldn't be in this mess." He stalks to the door and turns. "I suggest you prepare yourself. I have told Victoria you will see her Friday night after your prayer meeting."

Friday evening arrives and Henry Ward fusses nervously at the mirror, then pats his dog Job and paces. When he hears the knock at his office door, he quickly sits at his desk. Pulling a few smooth, round stones from his pocket, he rolls them around in his hand (a nervous habit), takes a deep breath, and awaits his visitors. Victoria and Tilton enter, and Victoria shocks Beecher by walking boldly to his desk.

"Mr. Beecher, it is a pleasure to meet you at last." He returns the gems to his pocket and takes her offered hand—but drops it immediately, as if it were a hot coal. She notices, and smiles as she sits. Tilton begins to sit as well, but Victoria touches his arm. "I'm sure Lib would be pleased if you returned home early this evening, Dory. Mr. Beecher and I are both mature, reasonable adults. I hardly think we need a chaperone." Her look brooks no argument and at a nod from Beecher, Tilton leaves in a pout. Victoria turns to the reverend with a challenging smile. "Now we can say what is on our minds, Mr. Beecher."

"Henry, please."

"I feel to finally meet you has been an achievement as great as the recent ascent of Stevens and van Trump to the peak of Mount Rainier. Although I understand I am not the first to have scaled *your* peak." He blushes at the accusation, but quickly recovers and returns her banter.

"You never know how accessible most men are. The secret is to approach by the right door."

"I understand now why your congregation is full of women," she says, surprised that she is responding to his charisma. "Your charm is quite potent. Have I reached the right door?"

"And I now understand Dory being taken with you. You, too, have extraordinary magnetism." Nervous, Henry Ward walks to the window and perches on the sill, clears his throat. "What may I help you with, Mrs. Woodhull?" Beecher's full, sensuous lips curve into a patronizing smile. He is back in control.

"Nothing at the moment. I simply wanted to meet you so your opinions of me are based on firsthand knowledge instead of the unfounded character assaults which have been put forth against me, including those from your sister."

"I apologize for that. I have asked Harriet to desist."

"I appreciate that."

He fidgets as she walks toward him and is relieved when she veers toward the overflowing bookshelf and peruses the book titles.

"I have recently been honored with the distinction of writing the introduction to the English translation of Goethe's *Elective Affinities* which will be published in the U.S. next year. Are you familiar with the German classic?" she asks.

"Yes, although, since I don't know the language, I have not read it."

"You would enjoy it. I will see that you get a copy in English. You have an impressive library."

"Where is human nature so weak as in a bookstore?" He chuckles and walks over to her.

"I can think of one place."

"I'm sure you can." He holds her gaze for a long moment, shakes loose. "Books. Yes. Nothing else so beautifully decorates a house. I confess, however, that though I love books as objects, I find my mind refuses to concentrate sufficiently to enjoy reading them. I read for three reasons: To know what is going on in the world; for knowledge to use in my work; and to bring my mind into a proper mood."

"Have you read the *Kama Sutra*?" Her eyes tease. "That book brings *me* into a proper mood. And with the pictures, it doesn't take much actual reading to achieve its purpose."

"I decline to answer on the grounds that I might incriminate myself." She laughs outright at that. Her eyes sparkle seductively and the preacher quickly changes the subject. "I am fascinated with the theories of government espoused by your partner Mr. Andrews," he says. "Unfortunately, they are unrealistic."

"And why is that, Henry?"

"They assume all men are perfect. In truth, most still need external law to keep them from utter ruin."

"Do you?" She chuckles and pulls a book from the shelf to give him a reprieve. "Phrenology. My father wanted my sister and me to read heads." She flips through the book, pressing different spots on her head. "I understand you used to practice the science with Dr. Fowler. Would you read me?"

"Unfortunately I remember only the one bump that is abnormally enlarged on me." Beecher returns the book to the shelf, but remains close. His eyes are sultry gray.

"And what trait does your head say is so dominant, Henry?"

He places her hand on the back of his neck. She strokes the large bump at the base of his skull ever so lightly.

"Can you feel it?" he asks. "That is the bump of amativeness. I have been told that this excess of need is what lends zest to my sermons. Have you heard me speak?"

His hand has now found her nape, and he is not surprised to find an equally large bump there. Suddenly nervous, he pulls away and slips his hand into his pocket to jingle the gems. Her hand stays on his neck, her fingers feathering through his hair, at odds with their conversation.

"I visited your church once, but since I could only attain a seat high in the balcony, I was unable to feel the full force of your charisma. Meeting you— Hmm, perhaps your amativeness *is* the reason your church has flourished these many years."

"Perhaps."

"I sometimes think it would be just reward for their stupidity if husbands were shown why their wives are so earnest in religious matters. Everyone knows that the churches would totter and tumble if it were not for the ladies. Many churches besides Plymouth are made up mostly of women, half of whom are in love with their pastors. And it is safe to say the feeling is often reciprocated, as it appears to be at Plymouth. I have heard your private beliefs are akin to my own." Sparks are almost visible as she continues to caress his neck. "Ah, yes, I see we *are* two of a kind." Her breath vibrates against his ear, and he almost kisses her. She pulls back slightly to look into his eyes. "Yet you refuse to preach truth. I cannot understand how you can call damnation down on those who practice what you do yourself! I swear the Church and State both do no more with their laws and sermons than make hypocrites of the masses!"

"Mrs. Woodhull, the secret to preaching is to break no images, touch no sore spots, and open no new trails. I tell my congregation what they want to hear and entertain them at the same time. Marriage is the grave of love, and I know it. Every time I join a young couple to the yoke of it I feel that I condemn them to a life of unhappiness. But if I confessed that, I would preach to empty pews. I must let my people have the truth a little at a time, as they are ready for it. Milk for babies and meat for strong men, as they say."

"And the gospel of love for women?"

"Even the Bible says God is love."

"And yet you denounce free-love. Doesn't the Bible say we should love freely and unconditionally?"

"Yes, but the connotation of that phrase in today's society is a little different than the biblical meaning."

"You know, the Jews hurled the name *Christian* with withering contempt upon the early followers of Christ. It was the most opprobrious epithet they could invent. But the name *Christian* is now synonymous of all that is good, true and beautiful. So shall it be with free-love."

"Are you a religious person, Victoria?"

"I believe in the Golden Rule and Abe Lincoln's rule."

"Abe Lincoln's rule?"

163

"When I do good I feel good; when I do bad I feel bad. Whether you call that being religious or not is immaterial to me. Organized religion is too complicated and corrupt. I doubt if Christ's disciples could even gain fellowship in today's church palaces, since they were nothing more than the humblest of fishermen with no social standing. They certainly could not afford a pew at Plymouth Church."

"You do speak your truth, don't you?"

"Of course. What is your truth, Henry? Did you—do you—really love Lib?"

"To the depths of my soul. That's why I do not believe God will condemn me for my acts with her."

"Why, Reverend, you have just enunciated the doctrine of Free-love." Victoria sits on the settee and pats the space beside her. "Come sit by me so we can explore this further."

"Mrs. Woodhull, are you trying to seduce me?"

"I have never felt that two kindred spirits attempting to connect was seduction. I believe that sexual intimacy—not marriage, not the Church—is God's most holy institution. If people enter into sexual relations as if they are communing with God, the act is never wrong."

"I couldn't agree more." He crushes her to him in a paroxysmal kiss and murmurs hoarsely, "Shall we visit Eden?"

Chapter 24

On September 23, Victoria and Blood lie together on a chaise on the mansion rooftop. The night is warm for September, and Blood opens his shirt for Victoria's caresses. Victoria's fingers dance across his skin.

"I wish I didn't have to leave you, James, but we desperately need the lecture fees. Being involved in the media campaign against Tweed has hurt us terribly. I never realized how many of our advertisers were under his thumb. Of course we had to do it once proof was presented that Tweed's government has swindled our city treasury out of almost two hundred million of our hard-earned dollars over the past six years alone. The cost for the still uncompleted county courthouse stands at twelve million, a third of which is fraudulently spent. It's unconscionable that they spent over seven thousand dollars for a single thermometer and one order of stationery cost almost two hundred thousand!"

"Shh, My Love, no causes or worries tonight," Blood says, kissing her forehead that has furrowed in outrage. "Tonight we celebrate the birth of your wonderful being. Three is the luckiest of numbers, and I predict your thirty-third year will be a banner one."

"I hope so. Sometimes I feel so old. If only there was someone competent to run our banking firm and keep Pearl in check at the newspaper, you could come with us. I have neglected you these past months, first because of Theodore and now because of Mr. Beecher. Are you sure it doesn't pain you?"

"Of course not. I've enjoyed the schoolgirl radiance they have brought to you. It has made me love you more than ever. Variety is good for stoking passion."

"And yet, probably because of the freedom you give me to experience what I must, it is you I love most steadfastly." Her fingers trace his face, neck, circle lower. He moans and closes his eyes in pleasure.

"Every man has a lover he will wander the spirit world to find, and when this soul's mate is met, a new life dawns. You are that to me."

"And you to me, James. I wish everybody could find such love."

"We would have no more wars."

"There cannot be a single person who does not desire such a union. Who wouldn't sell all he has if it could be purchased?"

"Not a soul, My Love." He kisses her tenderly.

"While I am otherwise occupied, you are free as well, you know."

"Now where would I find another woman like you? Tennie is the most endearing little creature on this planet, and I content myself occasionally and lovingly with her, as you know, but I see her as a facet of you. Were it not for that I would be impotent to find release at all."

"I'm sorry to have ruined you," Victoria teases.

"Fortunately I do not believe, like the churches teach, that I will go blind and to hell if I see to my own needs." He grins and then kisses her passionately. "Still, it is good to taste you again."

With a low moan, they meld together under the moon.

~ ~ ~

Victoria's fall lecture tour is a flurry of cities. Tennie is in charge of publicity and venue after venue boasts record and diverse crowds.

In Cleveland, a crowd of 4,000 huddles under gaslights surrounding the city skating rink as Victoria tells them, "Marriage is an assumption by the community that it can regulate the sexual instincts of individuals better than they can. We have been so well regulated that there is scarcely a natural sexual instinct left in our species. A sister of a friend died recently. She had been married four years to a clergyman. At the time of her marriage she was in vigorous health. Beautiful. With a deep, love nature. Under any reasonable condition she would have gladly reciprocated the requirements of any man. But this beast to whom she was bound by law was scarcely human in his demands. His brutal approaches stultified this poor woman's sexual nature and undermined her health. By the birth of her third child she was doomed.

"On her deathbed she said she had sacrificed her life to what she believed to be her religious duty. She said that as many as six to ten times a day she had been compelled to submit to this brute who took no care for her comfort or pleasure. Even up to the moment of the birth of

166

her children and within hours thereafter, she was forced to submit to this sexual slavery. She told me, 'I was murdered by the legal rights marriage gave to this man whom I believed it my duty to obey or else be doomed to hell. I have prayed every night since my wedding night that death would set me free. I would not live longer if I could.'" An anguished murmur ripples through the crowd as Victoria concludes. "And this tale is repeated over and over again. Do you wonder why I cannot hold my peace? Perhaps you should wonder how I restrain myself as well as I have!"

~ ~ ~

In Des Moines, the auditorium is filled almost completely with men, since, on the Sunday before her lecture, one minister pronounced her a "hag of hell" and condemned women who attended her lecture as "lost to all decency and purity." As a result, after beginning with her standard opening—"Agitation of thought is the beginning of wisdom"—Victoria changes her message.

"Since you gentlemen have come to stimulate yourselves with my frank words about the sexual debauchery brought about by marriage, I'm instead going to speak about your children." An angry rumble reverberates through the lecherous crowd, which Victoria ignores. "The great statesman Frederick Douglass has said, 'It is easier to build strong children than to repair broken men' and I agree. Our offspring are the points to which our most earnest efforts should be directed. They have something more than minds to be developed. They have souls as well. And just as your wives are slaves to your passions, your children are slaves to your abuse, the penalty for which you escape unscathed.

"Recently, a man in Vermont whipped his son, lacerating the flesh from the small of the child's back to his knees. When a neighbor complained, the Justice of the Peace fined the father two dollars. The man paid the money, saying it was cheap. Cheap for him, maybe. Certainly not for his poor boy.

"When will parents learn to train and govern their children with kindness and love rather than harsh treatment and fear? When will they learn to spare the rod and save the child? No matter how diseased of soul they are, a man may become a father and entail upon his child unmentionable evils. It is a sad irony to think of the minister who whipped his son to death because the lad would not pray for forgiveness from sins he had not committed! And such murder is okay in our supposed Christian society! It is an outrage I can scarcely endure."

Victoria looks out across the sea of male faces, some of whom have the grace to look ashamed. She softens her tone as she concludes.

"Two kinds of men will go out from here tonight: Those provoked to contemplate their actions and those furious about the indictment against them. Which one will you be?"

In South Bend, Victoria talks about how her endeavors in the business world have prepared her to run the country.

"All this talk about woman's rights is moonshine! Women *have* every right. All they need to do is exercise them. My sister and I have done more for woman's freedom by being on Wall Street and publishing our newspaper than speeches will do in ten years. I intend to use the same effort and have the same success when I vote in the upcoming election—and when I am inaugurated President of the United States of America!"

By Sunday, October 8, Victoria has reached Chicago, where she speaks to a full house.

"Are you feeling helpless?" she asks the women in her audience. "Then let me assure you: The power is in the vote! Horace Greeley advises women to learn how to cook a steak and not to mind suffrage. But women don't want to just cook the steak. They want to be able to obtain it without being beholden to man, who thus has power over her very survival. This is where suffrage will come in."

"Are you going to vote November seventh?" She challenges a wealthy young woman in the front row, who nods fervently. Victoria focuses her gaze on woman after woman in the audience, asking the same question and smiling as they assent.

The lecture ends a little after nine P.M. and the sisters are astounded to discover the free room they have been offered is at The Palmer, an exclusive hotel owned by Bertha Palmer, an avid suffragist.

Unbeknownst to them, as they settle into their suite, a cow prancing restlessly in Patrick O'Leary's barn at 137 DeKoven Street in the South Division of Chicago tips a glowing lantern into the straw, which begins to burn. Flames quickly fill the barn. The alarm sounds. With brittle dryness, high winds, and a fire department exhausted from days of fighting wild fires outside the city, a row of wooden tenements is quickly engulfed. And the fire marches on, consuming everything in its path.

By midnight it has jumped the south branch of the Chicago River and rages toward the main business district. Fire crumbles the brick walls of banks, melting vaults and licking up money. It destroys the Courthouse, Customs House, and Post Office. Only five buildings are left standing in all of downtown as the blaze marches toward State and Monroe, the location of the hotel. Alarms are shouted through The Palmer corridors, waking Victoria, Tennie, and Zulu Maud. They evacuate with the others and watch from safety as the elegant establishment burns to the ground.

The rampage continues into Monday. The ground quakes as buildings implode and terrified families rush toward the lake to escape the flames. Michigan Avenue becomes so compacted it is impossible to navigate. Finally, everyone moves together and plunges into the water in a long, undulating stream of humanity.

On Tuesday, rain helps douse the searing inferno, but the task of rebuilding the city seems almost insurmountable. Victoria, Tennie and Zulu Maud stay to help. They unload supplies from trains until their backs ache. They sift through burned buildings until their hands are bleeding and raw and their hair grimed with ashes. They help a crying child find her parents. When they finally leave the city, they learn that Chicago has almost 300 dead. A third of its population is homeless. And Chicago is lucky. A forest fire in Peshtigo, Wisconsin has wiped out the entire city, killing fifteen hundred, destroying eighteen thousand buildings and scorching over a million acres.

"We must pray for them all," Victoria says, wrapping an arm around Zulu Maud and staring out their carriage window at a Gothic water tower standing alone amidst smoldering ruins. "Men and women are equal in tragedy. Seeing these poor folks left with nothing has made me realize again how very fortunate we are. We must always be grateful."

"Mama, since the courthouse burned all the documents about you and the Colonel being married and stuff, does that mean you're not married anymore?" Zulu Maud asks.

"Honey, marriage is like charity. It's in the heart that it's real."

Chapter 25

On Tuesday, November 7, 1871, twelve women, including Paulina Wright Davis, Mrs. Treat, Mrs. Andrews, and Laura Cuppy Smith congregate in Victoria's parlor.

"Who's ready to exercise her right to vote?" Victoria asks them, face aglow with excitement.

"We are!" the women respond in unison.

"Has everyone registered so we cannot be shut out on technicalities?"

"Yes!"

"As we march, let us think of our sisters that Belva Lockwood leads to the District of Columbia polls. Let us think of other sisters around the country who go to exercise their rights under the Constitution. Let us rejoice for our sisters in Wyoming and Utah, whose territories no longer deny them enfranchisement! Repeat with me: We are right! We are united! We are strong! We are woman! We are voters!"

Open parasols in one hand, voting tickets clutched in the other, the women march behind Victoria and Tennie—down the street and around the corner. By the time they arrive at the Sixth Avenue Furniture Store that serves as a voting station over a hundred people have gathered behind them. A path clears, and the women march through aisles of furniture to the rear of the shop. Victoria, leading the line, holds out her ticket. The Republican inspector reaches for it, but the Democrat inspector bats his hand away.

"We cannot take your vote, Ma'am."

"By what right do you refuse the vote of a citizen of the United States?"

"By the Constitution, Ma'am. Only men may vote."

"You are mistaken, Sir. Tennie, would you kindly read the relevant portions of the Fourteenth and Fifteenth Amendments to the Constitution?"

"Article Fourteen, Section One: All *persons* born or naturalized in the United States, and subject to the jurisdiction thereof, are citizens of the United States." She turns a page. "Article Fifteen, Section One: The right of citizens of the United States to vote shall not be denied."

"That is the Constitution verbatim, Gentlemen. Do you still refuse our vote?" Victoria asks.

"Yes. You cannot vote."

"On what legal grounds?"

"Because we were told to refuse you."

"Will you swear to that?"

"I'll swear to nothing to you."

"Are you aware that you are liable to a penalty of five hundred dollars for barring a citizen from voting?"

The crowd rumbles, distracting the inspectors. Laura Cuppy Smith quickly sneaks her vote into the box. Victoria whirls to face the onlookers.

"Under the election laws of the State, either these inspectors are guilty of a felony, or I am. Either they prevented a legal voter from voting, or I attempted to vote illegally! Under the laws of our land, one of us should be convicted of the crime. But is it a crime to be a woman? No! So why are women subjected to such blatant tyranny? If our rights as citizens are not recognized, we will revolt! By heavens, we will secede! I argue not a woman's right to vote. I argue for woman's duty to discharge her citizenship!

"Men say women are not educated to the proper standard to vote intelligently. This is bosh! The same may be said of our young men, who vote in every election. The way our elections are managed, no one but a few politicians and wire-pullers know anything about the personal merits of candidates, so our male citizens instead vote for whom they want to go hunting with, or who can best grease their palms in business. Women by nature are much more discriminating." Victoria motions to the women. "Ladies, let us adjourn to the courthouse to file suit against the inspectors and the government for refusing us our rights as citizens."

Victoria stalks down the aisle, the ladies at her heels.

Chapter 26

On November 19, Henry Ward rushes into Victoria's sitting room. She is not surprised to see that he is frantic, having sent him a ultimatum earlier in the day.

"Have you come with good news or bad?" she asks. "Will you introduce my lecture at Steinway tomorrow night or do I expose your sins?"

"I thought our bond was above such threats."

"It is time to stand up to your ideals, Mr. Beecher. If a person does not advocate what he knows is truth because it is unpopular, that person is a moral coward and a traitor to the conscience God gave him."

"You're right! I admit it! But spare me your judgment! You cannot grasp the wearing and grinding on my nervous system over this." Henry Ward kneels in front of her and holds her hands to his lips. Tears stream down his face. She is not moved.

"Slavery to your secret vice causes your suffering! Don't you realize that if you stand and banish these shadows, you will release untold hundreds from similar bondage?"

"Victoria, you understand me better than anyone. You have looked into my soul and found a twin to your own, except you are strong and I am weak. Where is your sympathy for an erring fellow man? I am not fit to stand by you who go there to speak truth. I should be a living lie and sink through the floor. Please, have mercy on a sinner as Christ himself has mercy." He is groveling, but Victoria is not swayed.

"Oh, for heaven sakes!" She holds out a copy of her speech. "Just read what I am to say. I assure you you'll find no coarseness in it!"

"No! I cannot bring myself to be a rung on the ladder you wish to climb."

"Perhaps it is not courage you are short of but honesty."

"Please, I beg you. Torture me no more."

"If I am compelled to go on that platform alone tomorrow, you shall have what you deserve."

"What are you going to tell them?"

"Everything. Including explicit details of our previous meetings."

"Then tell me twenty-four hours in advance that I might kill myself!"

"Mr. Beecher, you don't have twenty-four hours!"

The following evening an angry blizzard strikes New York. Even so, some 3,000 citizens brave sleet and whipping winds to hear Victoria speak. The storm fuels the rowdiness, and when the doors of New York's Steinway Hall are finally thrown open, the wet, restless crowd stampedes inside.

Victoria waits in the anteroom, clothed in a modest black dress with a pink tea rose on her throat band and gold watch-chain around her neck. She forces a smile as various friends stop in with good wishes, then steps away from the hubbub and motions to Tennie.

"Where is Mr. Beecher?"

"My god, maybe he croaked himself. No, wait, he doesn't have the guts."

By 8:15 P.M., the capacity crowd is chanting for Victoria.

"My god, Sis, you gotta go on," Tennie says. "Professor Perlo can introduce you."

"No! It is important for the audience's receptiveness to what I am to say that one of their own—" Anger flares her cheeks. "The devil be damned! I am going out there without an introduction and tell the truth!" She strides angrily toward the door, almost colliding with Theodore Tilton and Frank Moulton, who burst into the room. She breathes a sigh of relief. "Is Mr. Beecher with you?" she asks.

"He said if he had the courage he would meet us here," Frank says.

"Which means we can count him out," Tilton says.

"There isn't a brave man in the city to preside at my meeting. So be it. The chips will fall where they will!" She brushes past them and marches out. Tilton catches up to her.

"Will you introduce her, Dory?" Frank asks.

"Yes, by heaven. No one else has the pluck to do it." He steps ahead of Victoria and onto the stage. The reaction is deafening. Tennie gives

174

Victoria a hug, and leaving her standing off-stage with Moulton, hurries through a side door to sit in the front row with their parents, Blood, and Zulu Maud. Tilton quiets the crowd.

"Since I had a rare free evening, I decided to come hear what my friend had to say about the question that has occupied her for many years. Upon my arrival I discovered others had declined to introduce her because of objections to the lady's character. I know her character and vouch for it." Tilton ignores the few hisses and catcalls. "The great Frederick Douglass has said, 'To suppress free speech is a double wrong because it not only violates the rights of the speaker, but the rights of the hearer as well.' Now it may be that Mrs. Woodhull is a fanatic; it may be that I am a fool; but I would rather be both a fanatic and fool in one than a coward who would deny anyone free speech!"

"Are you going to tell them?" Frank asks Victoria.

"I don't know. But if I don't, let Mr. Beecher know it was Theodore who spared him."

"With as much pride as ever prompted me to the performance of any act, I introduce Victoria Claflin Woodhull." Tilton turns toward the wings and holds out an arm to Victoria. She runs her sweating palms down the front of her dress and strides onto the stage. He leads the applause, which swells as Victoria reaches the podium. She is amazed to see a standing-room-only crowd. She smiles tremulously at Blood, who nods in encouragement. She glances at Andrews, who is in the orchestra pit with a copy of her speech to cue her. Tilton and Moulton watch nervously from the wings as she takes a deep breath and begins.

"Society has always suppressed individual freedom, but each of us has an inherent right to self that cannot be delegated to any political or social entity. The Declaration of Independence calls it inalienable. It is not given to us and cannot be taken away. And this includes women!" Hisses and claps are evenly split. Most settle down as Victoria continues, although a loud hissing from an upper box seat persists.

"The court holds that if the law solemnly pronounces two married, they are married. But the law cannot compel two persons to love. They are sexually united by nature and married by God. Suppose a separation

175

is desired because one loves and is loved elsewhere. If the union is maintained by force, at least two of them, and probably three, are unhappy."

Tilton and Moulton exchange a panicked look.

"Now, by no means do I say there are no good conditions in marriage. On the contrary, a large proportion of these relations are commendable. I believe those good things will continue to exist if all marriage laws are repealed tomorrow. But as it now stands, there are two classes of people who benefit most from matrimony: The hypocritical priest who gets his fee for forging the chains and the blackguard lawyer who gets a bigger fee for breaking those fetters."

This earns whistles, stomps and applause. Above the din, the hissing continues from an upper loge. Exasperated, Victoria steps away from the podium and searches the crowd for the heckler.

"If the lady or gentleman in the audience who is hissing will—"

"It is not a gentleman or a lady!" yells a man from the main floor.

This elicits laughter.

"I'll tell you what I think from up here!" Utica shouts, standing from the box seat where she sits with friends.

Victoria looks up in horror as her sister sways with drunkenness. The crowd comes alive, boisterously taking sides.

"How would you like to come into this world without knowing who your father was?" Utica asks, slurring her words.

Hats fly in the air and hankies wave. There are cries of "Hurrah!" and "Answer that!"

"There are thousands of noble men and women in the world today who don't know who their fathers are!" Victoria retorts. "Does this make them less noble? And if the children argument is to be advanced to prove the right to control marriage, why should not laws also be enacted to compel people to eat and drink such things as doctors say are conducive to health? Is there any difference between the two at the core?"

"Always got a pat answer, don't you, Vic?" Utica hiccups loudly, and a male companion pulls her back into her chair. Relieved, Victoria continues her lecture.

"The first great error most married people commit is in endeavoring to hide from each other the little irregularities into which we are all liable to fall. Never discussing sex is false modesty. One day soon the Free-love doctrine will be accepted as normal."

"Normal like your idiot son?" Utica is on her feet again.

Victoria grabs the podium to control her anger, then walks to the edge of the stage and whispers for Tennie to help. Tennie rushes out as Victoria takes a deep breath and continues.

"Free-love is blamed for the troubles caused by the slavery of marriage."

"It's *you* who causes the—" Utica shrieks as a policeman grabs her. The crowd whoops as Utica flails against the officer.

"Let her speak!"

"She's got the right!"

"Brutality! Police brutality."

"Aw, she's drunk anyway. I came to hear The Woodhull!"

Tennie slips into Utica's box and waves the policeman away. Talking calmly, she coaxes her sister out. The crowd is in an uproar, and Victoria shoots Tilton a helpless glance. He walks quickly to the podium and bangs for attention.

"Order! Order! I am the chair of this meeting, and I say order! This meeting has been called for Mrs. Woodhull to express her views. Mrs. Brooker can present hers in her own time in her own hall. I introduce again: Mrs. Victoria C. Woodhull." The crowd settles somewhat under Tilton's authoritative presence. Victoria gives him a grateful look and resumes her speech.

"People may make marriage vows in perfectly good faith and repent of them in sackcloth and ashes within a twelve-month period. Would it not be the Christian way, in such cases, to say to the disaffected party, 'Since you no longer love me, go your way and be happy, and make those to whom you go happy also'?"

"Are you a Free-lover?" Whitelaw Reid yells from the crowd.

Victoria stops in mid-step. A gasp ripples through the room as she flings back her head and red spots of anger flame her cheeks. Her eyes blaze. Her voice rings clearly.

"Yes, I am a Free-lover! I have an inalienable, Constitutional, and natural right to love whom I may, to love as long or as short a period as I want, to change that love every day if I please! And with that right neither you nor any law you can frame have any right to interfere!"

Andrews glances desperately at Blood, but he is staring at Victoria with pride and love. Andrews shrugs and throws away his notes, since Victoria is obviously no longer speaking from the prepared text. In the back of the auditorium, Henry Ward Beecher stands in the shadows, hat pulled low and collar high to avoid recognition. He listens transfixed as Victoria takes a deep breath, and her voice becomes less combative.

"The highest kind of love is that which is utterly devoid of selfishness. Whose highest gratification comes from rendering the object of that love the greatest amount of happiness, let that happiness depend upon what it may."

Victoria walks to the edge of the stage. Her voice softens, and the room becomes still to hear her. "I dearly prize the good opinion of my fellow beings. I would so gladly have you think well of me. It is because I love you all that I tell you my vision for the future. The order of nature will soon determine whether society is right, or I am right. Let that be as it may. The love I cannot command is not mine. Let me not disturb myself about it nor attempt to filch it from its rightful owners.

"A heart that I supposed mine has drifted and gone. Shall I go in pursuit? Shall I forcibly capture the truant, transfix him with the barb of my selfish affection, and pin him to the wall of my chamber? No! Rather let me leave my doors and windows open, intent only on living so nobly that the best cannot fail to be drawn to me by irresistible attraction."

There is dead silence. Henry Ward's eyes fill with tears as Victoria gives the audience a long, pleading look.

"Contemplate this and then denounce me for advocating freedom if you can, and I will bear your curse with a better resignation."

With a final, tremulous smile, Victoria leaves the stage. There is scattered applause, but mostly stunned silence. Henry Ward quickly slips out a side door.

Police have to hold back the crowd as Andrews, Tilton, Moulton, and Blood escort Victoria and Tennie out the backstage entrance to their carriage. Victoria kisses Tilton on the cheek, ignoring the crowd's reaction.

"I will never forget the brave words you uttered tonight, Theodore. They created a magical influence on the audience and drew the sting of those who would harm me. Thank you from the bottom of my heart."

She climbs into the carriage.

"She said violent things, James," Tilton says, shaking Blood's hand. "Violent."

As Blood and Andrews join the women in the carriage, Tennie grins at her sister.

"My god," she says.

"Shall I break out the hemlock?" Victoria asks.

~ ~ ~

"Do the papers crucify me?" Victoria asks the next day as Blood skims the newspapers and she opens mail.

"The *Herald* doesn't." He reads from that paper: "'Woman's right to vote and to work had been talked about and the equal capacity of woman had been advanced, but nothing practical had been done. Victoria C. Woodhull stepped to the front, and grasping the hostile weapons, concentrated them on herself and undertook to receive the full charge of ridicule, obloquy, and detestation in the hope that the cause of women might triumph.'"

"I shall send a note of gratitude to Mr. Cole for his kind words."

"The worst, of course, is Henry Bowen's *Independent*. He writes that Demosthenes corrected his speech impediment by walking along the roaring coast and speaking with pebbles in his mouth, but that last night the great orator spoke with a mouthful of dirt."

He continues quickly to soften Victoria's anger.

"Most of the remaining papers say you handled the subject rather scholarly. Of course those were probably only reviewing your prepared speech." He chuckles. "It is the extemporaneous thoughts that may cause the trouble. Pearl said he almost had a *cardíaco de ataque* when you went off script."

"If it causes this kind of trouble, I'll do it again. I've got thirteen lecture invitations right here. With the wire service spreading the word all the way to the West Coast, the recognition can only help my campaign." She runs over and sits on Blood's lap, smothering him with kisses. "Oh, James, we can do this! We can really do this!"

An angry voice from the entry interrupts their celebration. Before they can react, their landlord blusters in and shoves a court order at Victoria.

"I'll not have Free-lovers living in my house! You have one month to clear out!"

Chapter 27

By year's end, Victoria has settled in a small but clean apartment, and on January 10, 1872, she goes to Washington for NWSA's annual winter convention. The huge Lincoln Hall is standing room only as Spiritualists and labor and other special-interest groups attend the meeting for the first time. Resounding applause greets the women who take seats on the platform. Victoria sits between Elizabeth Cady and Isabella Hooker. A weary-looking Susan, her red shawl hanging lopsided on her shoulders, walks to the podium.

"Since last year's convention in Washington, I have traveled fifteen thousand miles and spoken one hundred and eight nights. My message has been simple: The true woman will not be the exponent of another. She will be her own individual self, do her own individual work, stand or fall by her own individual wisdom or strength. Woman must take to her soul a purpose and then make circumstances conform to this purpose, instead of forever singing the refrain if and if and if."

Speaking seems to revive Susan, and she introduces Elizabeth Cady Stanton with some of her usual vigor. Elizabeth begins with an attack on the current Administration.

"President Grant, in his message to the people, has remembered all classes and conditions of men but has not said the word *woman* once. So he is not our candidate. And, personally, I'd rather see Beelzebub elected than Horace Greeley! Our next speaker may be our only hope for justice. Ladies and Gentlemen, I present Mrs. Victoria C. Woodhull."

"I am here to ask all evangelical bodies to organize for political purposes," Victoria says, wasting no time launching into her objective. "Let Spiritualists and reformers tear from their political banners the names Democrat and Republican, which have become a stench in the nostrils of thoughtful people, and throw to the breeze the more comprehensive name of Equal Rights."

"She is pushing too far too fast," Susa mutters to no one in particular. Her lips tighten into a thin line as Victoria thrills at the standing ovation.

When the convention breaks before the evening session, Victoria adjourns to the anteroom. Seeing Frederick Douglass, she asks if she can interview him for her newspaper. He agrees and they settle onto a settee in a corner.

"I understand you call yourself a 'woman's rights man,' Mr. Douglass. Is that true?"

"Absolutely. I believe that women should be given the vote for the same reason the colored man got it."

"Which is?"

"So she will have the same motives men have for making herself a useful citizen."

"You were born into slavery, am I correct?"

"Yes, in Maryland. I was the offshoot of the rape of my slave mother by her white master."

"But your father forced you to live and work with the slaves and suffer the same abuses?"

"Yes."

"The loss of freedom must be as bad—or worse—than any physical pain inflicted on a person."

"It changes who you are. Even though I always had the sense that no man could degrade my soul, the way slaves were treated went against my whole notion of goodness."

"How could you even understand what goodness was in such a situation?"

"When you're surrounded by evil, it's not hard to recognize goodness when you find it. Would you like to hear a story?"

"I would be most honored."

"Shortly after I was born, my mother was sold to another plantation some distance away. I was given to Aunt Katy, a slave who had dominion over all the black children and wielded her power with great cruelty."

"Against her own kind?"

"I prefer to believe it was because she feared losing her own status with the master. In any event, one day I offended her somehow. I can't remember what I did. Something minor. In punishment, Aunt Katy made me go all day without food. By sundown my stomach was growling and I was as weak as a runt dog. I begged for a crust of bread, but all she gave me was the promise that she would starve the bad out of me. Finally, I could stand it no longer. Sitting in a corner of the kitchen too hungry to even escape into sleep, I broke down and cried. As I sat there, a pitiful little creature, a woman I did not know entered our shack."

"Who was it?"

"My very own mother! Picture it, a wretched boy suddenly in the arms of the mother he's never known. She placed me on her knee and fed me a large ginger cake. That night, I knew for the first time that I was not only a child, but I was *somebody's* child. She was gone the next morning and I never saw her again, but I knew the truth of love and never felt so wretched again."

"But how did she know to come to you?"

"I thought for a long time it was a mother's instinct that had brought her, but now I believe it was only her Spirit sent to bring me a message that would lead to my destiny."

"Yes! That must be it! It's like Demosthenes appearing to me and pressing me to go on, even against hopeless obstacles."

"I have never told anyone that story, but I instinctively knew you would understand."

"I am deeply honored. I believe of all the men who serve our cause, Mr. Douglass, because of your own great oppression, you best understand why I fight so hard."

~ ~ ~

"I have been asked by men, 'Why did you drag Victoria Woodhull to the front?'" Susan B. Anthony says, leading off the evening session of the continuing NWSA convention. "Now, bless your souls, she was not dragged to the front. She came to Washington from Wall Street with a powerful argument and lots of cash. And cash is a big thing with

Congress." She chuckles with the audience before continuing. "If we need youth, beauty, and money to capture Congress, this is the woman we are after. Welcome, please, Victoria C. Woodhull for her keynote address."

Victoria, as always, enthralls the crowd and ends with a powerful rallying cry.

"Women citizens are entitled to a Constitution to represent them, and they have the power to inaugurate it. I do not propose that we wait sixty years for justice. I want it here and I want it now! Are you with me?"

The building shakes from the thunderous response.

The next morning, fearing the various reform groups clamoring to form a political party to nominate Victoria are sidetracking the convention, Susan B. chides the assembly.

"We don't endorse any sect, breed, or political power. We don't endorse temperance, labor reform, or Spiritualism. We *do* endorse woman's suffrage. And I tell you that I will endorse whichever Democrat or Republican puts woman's suffrage on his plank."

"But, Miss Anthony, why should we wait?" Laura Cuppy Smith calls out from the audience. "Why not form our own party and nominate Victoria? I am not a hero worshiper, but my whole soul does homage to this inspired representative of our cause."

"Thank you, Mrs. Smith," says Susan, trying to quell her annoyance. "Victoria indeed inspires us all. In fact, tomorrow she will be with us when we present our suffrage petitions to the Senate, which Belva Lockwood informs me contain twenty thousand signatures! But to rush too quickly ahead might endanger our gains. I—*We* have worked too hard to take the risk."

Later, Elizabeth Cady Stanton ignores Susan's warning to deflect the group from nominating Victoria and opens her part of the program with a rallying cry.

"The signs of the time indicate the formation of a third party in the presence of which the old parties will tremble," she says. "It behooves women to take up studies pertaining to the science of government since we may one day soon take over the rule."

"Perhaps the nucleus of that party is in this hall right now!" Stephen Pearl Andrews calls out.

The crowd begins to chant, "Woodhull! Woodhull!"

Elizabeth laughs and motions toward Victoria as Ada Ballou of Wisconsin jumps to her feet.

"I nominate Victoria C. Woodhull for President of the United States."

The crowd goes wild. Susan rushes to the podium.

"Such a nomination is premature. And the final moments of our meeting is not the time to begin discussion on the matter." She is furious when the crowd answers with loud boos. "For God's sake," she hisses to Elizabeth, "adjourn this convention now. Before The Woodhull takes us all down a path that will destroy us."

Chapter 28

"Look at this, Tennie! Just look!" Victoria fumes as she waves the February 24 issue of *Harper's Weekly* at Tennie. Tennie peers at the Tommy Nast cartoon that depicts Victoria as the devil, complete with wings and horns and holding a sign that reads "Be Saved By Free-Love." Nast has captioned the cartoon: "Get Thee Behind Me [Mrs.] Satan." It's not enough that *The Daily Doings* constantly uses our images on the cover of their salacious gentleman's magazine, but for this pious Methodistic Nast to burlesque me—!"

"My god, the picture harpoons the current state of marriage about right, though, with a haggard woman climbing a steep, rocky hill, a sotted husband and squalling child on her back. Seems like that's making your case for you."

"You may be right, Tennie. I will take that interpretation and use it to point out Mr. Nast's own ignorance!"

"My god, Sis, go get 'im!"

A few nights later, the length and breadth of Irving Place and the entire block surrounding New York City's Academy of Music is packed with a huddled, shivering mass of 12,000 people waiting to hear Victoria speak. Temperatures are frigid, but the crowd is so large it spills over onto Third and Fourth Avenues. Unfortunately there is only room for 6,000 inside, so tickets are scalped at ten dollars for reserved seats and thirty for private boxes. By seven o'clock, the elite are packed like sardines with the poor. When a woman faints and is carried out, dozens fight for her spot. She is the first of many to fall in the crush. A roar goes up as Victoria steps onto the stage. Her simple black dress is adorned with a red rosebud at her throat. Her cheeks flush, and her voice rings out from her opening words.

"Agitation of thought is the beginning of wisdom. The impending revolution has begun! A few days ago I became the first woman to address Painter's Lodge Number Five. Prior to the event, I mentioned to a Congressman my intention to speak on the relation between labor and capital, and he said, 'Speak to the laborers on finance? Why, you might as well talk Latin to cattle.'" Victoria smiles at the loud boos. "Exactly my reaction. I told this gentleman politician, 'Be careful lest you wake up to find it is these people, and not you, who actually *do* understand the question of finance.'

"In our paper, we have told you of companies floated to work mines that do not exist. We have told of railways that go nowhere. We have shown how banks and insurance societies flourish by devouring shareholders' capital in large salaries for their officers. And we will continue to broadcast such scandals until the people have had enough and rise up against them.

"A Vanderbilt may sit in his office and manipulate stocks to amass tens of millions of dollars from the industries of the country and he is regarded as one of the remarkable men of the age. Yet, if a poor child were to take a loaf of bread from a Vanderbilt larder in order to prevent starvation, she would be sent first to the Tombs and thence to Blackwell's Island. This inequality must end!" The crowd is surprised to hear her come down on her benefactor, which makes what she is saying all the more powerful. Their response is so loud the building shakes. It is several minutes before they are quiet enough for her to continue.

"An Astor may sit in his sumptuous apartment and watch the property bequeathed to him by his father rise in value from one to fifty million, and everybody bows before his immense power and worships his business capacity. But if one of his tenants does not vote Republican and so loses his job and cannot pay his monthly rent, the law sets the poor man's family into the street in midwinter. And whether they die of cold or starvation, neither Mr. Astor nor anybody else cares.

"And so the privileged class monopolizes the wealth of the country and has an enduring hatred for me because I am the friend of freedom and equality and justice. No one who has bartered principle for political or corporate purposes shall escape retribution. That law of compensation called karma shall enforce even-handed justice."

The stomps, whistles, and applause rise to the rafters.

An hour and a half later, Victoria has the audience wound to a fever pitch as she concludes.

"Not only has our government let us down, but Christianity is also a failure. It shuts itself away from humanity and stands idly by while people suffer. It is therefore the bounden duty of every Christian to support the political party that bases itself upon Human Rights. Since no such party exists, we must construct one and we must begin the construction now!"

Later in March, the reign of robber barons Jim Fisk and Jay Gould has come to a dramatic end. In January, Fisk is murdered as a result of a love triangle. Now his partner Jay Gould is ousted as President of Erie Railroad after an almost comedic foot chase and two-day standoff at the Grand Opera House. The news sends Erie stock into a spin, which Victoria uses to her advantage to bolster their coffers.

Then, in April, Canning Woodhull is taken off morphine and after a two-day vigil, with a final twitch of his jaw, he shudders and dies. Byron is so devastated by the loss of his father, he allows Victoria to hug and kiss him, almost undoing her.

The same day, the long-standing friendship between Elizabeth Cady Stanton and Susan B. Anthony almost dies as well, when they argue about the women supporting Victoria's candidacy.

"We will not use our spring convention to form a third party to nominate Mrs. Woodhull," Susan insists. "I cannot tell you how teetotally hurt I was to see your announcement in the newspaper that we would. That woman seeks to run our craft into her port and none other. Can't you see that?"

"But think, Susan. What if we really got behind her? What if we went all out for a woman President? Even if she didn't get in, it could lead to suffrage, not to mention pave a path for future generations of ladies to rule."

"If that is what you want to do, god speed. But I won't be a part of it, and you will not nominate her at my convention!"

"That's funny, I thought it was the *woman's* convention. The trouble with you, Susan, is that you get one idea and can't abide anyone who has two!"

The following week, the headline in Bowen's *Independent* reads: "Beecher for President! Will the great Reverend run?"

"Oh my god," Tennie says when she sees it. "They've actually just printed a letter from an E. F. B. of Brooklyn, New York. Now I wonder who that could be? His wife Eunice maybe?"

"What does it say?" Victoria asks. "Is he really going to run? Or is it just another Beecher stunt to thwart me?"

"'A new religio-political party to be formed in New York. Henry Ward Beecher proposed as its candidate for the Presidency,'" Tennie reads. "My god, Sis, he's trying to steal your nomination! The gall!" She reads on. "'Mr. Beecher's character, history and antecedents are known to everybody.'"

"Not yet, but they will be," Victoria mutters.

"'His influence is already felt over the civilized world. His sermons are more widely read than the utterances of any contemporaneous public teacher. Mr. Beecher is a liberalist in his views and teachings. Some would consider him radical.'" That brings a bitter laugh from Victoria as Tennie continues. "'He favors woman suffrage and equality of the sexes; he is the patron of temperance, peace, tolerance, and progress. Of his devotional nature it is quite unnecessary to speak.'"

Tennie closes the paper. "Apparently whoever wrote the letter doesn't know the reverend like you do."

"I swear, Tennessee, I am going to bring that man down, even if he takes me down with him."

~ ~ ~

The "Woodhullism" controversy continues to swirl through the women's ranks, but Victoria and Tennie are too busy lecturing to notice or care. Having sent a scathing note to Beecher and received his assurance that he is not interested in stealing her nomination, Victoria's optimism about receiving the NWSA's endorsement has returned. She arranges lectures to every group that will have her. Everywhere she goes, auditoriums are standing room only and flowers are showered onto the stage.

To American Labor Reform League:

"Eight-hour workdays must be instituted to preserve quality in family life. Child labor laws must protect our precious offspring. Adolescent factory girls live in disgusting tenement dormitories and slave all day to sew a wealthy lady's cloak for the paltry wage of two dollars. Children as young as six toil for long, backbreaking hours in squalid conditions for mere pennies. And meanwhile, the elite, with their fashionable attire and gilded coaches, enact civil statutes and regulate civil law to benefit themselves and oppress the poor. This must change, and it must change now!"

To the American Anti-Usury Society:

"The current parties, bought and paid for by the privileged classes, will not change the status quo. Greedy merchants and robber barons must be controlled by government regulations. My platform alone calls for this advance. A vote for Victoria Woodhull is a vote for you!"

At the Sorosis Woman's Club:

"You ladies must lead the way to end the practice of mercenary mothers who trot out their daughters at summer watering places as though they were so many equines to be hawked to the man who can pay the most money or who has the most prestige. It doesn't matter how he obtained his fortune. It doesn't matter if he has just come from the doctor with a diagnosis of a sexual disease. If he has the name and the means, daughters are 'sold' to these partners who they will be forced to remain with until death do they part, love or no love be damned!"

Another night, the auditorium resounds with shouts of approval as Victoria speaks on segregation, something most of the audience endures daily because of the color of their skin.

"Frederick Douglass has warned that designing white men are exploiting racial differences by segregating education. I am proud to join his campaign that calls for us to educate all children together. As President of the United States, I will pass laws to ensure that such integration is accomplished. If blacks and whites are educated equally and together, they will grow up to know that color makes no difference to the rights of man. They will see that this country is as much the country of one as the other and that both must work together to make it a strong and valuable nation.

"Mr. Douglass' detractors say that mingling races is not good for either race. I ask where is their proof of these assertions? Whites and blacks have mingled for generations and have produced some fine results. Mr. Douglass himself is a prime example. You'd be hard-pressed to show me a wiser more outstanding statesman than he is."

The entire audience is on its feet as Victoria concludes with her standard finish. "In closing I want to remind you that in a few days I will be an officially nominated candidate for the Presidency of the United States. I invite you to take an active part in my campaign."

The crowd is with her!

~ ~ ~

Victoria's campaigning pays off when a multitude of different reform groups attend the National Woman's Suffrage Association in May. Lib Tilton and Laura Bullard chat as they collect tickets at the door.

"Despite our differences with Lucy Stone's group, I hope we don't boycott Julia Ward Howe's proposed Mother's Day next Sunday," Lib says. "Honoring mothers for pledging not to send their sons to war will make a dramatic statement."

"Unfortunately, one day a year honoring mothers will not bring world peace."

"Not at once. But the idea has made me aware of how I can influence my sons' future stances on the subject."

"Oh, Lib, you live in a fictionalized world. There will never be a war-free globe, even if we honor mothers three hundred and sixty-five days a year. Not while men rule."

"Do you think we'll nominate Victoria today?"

"Not if Susan Anthony has anything to say about it."

The pair turns their attention to the front as the dignitaries file onto the stage and stragglers scurry to seats. The famous Hutchinson Family Singers lead the choir in singing "The Star Spangled Banner," following which Isabella offers a short prayer. She then introduces Elizabeth Cady.

"Good morning and welcome," Elizabeth says. "I have been asked to state at the onset of this meeting that it has not been called to make a nomination for the Presidency but rather to take the initiative steps thereof. We have distributed a platform of resolutions. In a moment, Mrs. Hooker will recap them for you. This afternoon we will hold discussions regarding them. And then tonight we will vote.

"There is one other matter that needs to be addressed before we begin. We regard this as a woman's meeting and request that the brethren hold their peace. Men have such loud voices they are apt to overslaugh the women who have waited so long for their hour to come. That being said, I now introduce Mrs. Isabella Beecher Hooker to present our resolutions." There is a smattering of applause as Isabella walks to the podium.

"We, women citizens of the United States, in national convention assembled in New York, proclaim the following principles essential to just government: Number one, we recognize the equality of all and hold that it is the duty of government to mete out equal and exact justice. We pledge to maintain the union of the States and to oppose reopening questions settled by the Thirteenth, Fourteenth and Fifteenth Amendments to our Constitution.

"We demand the immediate and absolute removal of all disabilities now imposed on rebels and women and demand for each individual the largest liberty consistent with public order. We demand civil service reform so that honesty and capacity become valid tests for public employment.

"We affirm that no form of taxation is just or wise that puts a burden on the people. Taxes should not be laid upon necessaries but upon the luxuries of life so that the rich and not the poor bear the burden. The highest consideration of commercial morality and honest government requires a thorough reform of our financial system so that it

192

provides a cheap, sound, uniform, abundant, and elastic currency. We oppose all land grants to railroads and corporations. Public domain should be held sacred to settlers and should guarantee an inviolable homestead.

"To address the corruption that has been an increasing characteristic of our government, we propose a one-term Presidency, with lifetime service in the Senate following. We believe in referendum and minority representation.

"We call for a national welfare system to help those less fortunate and those unemployed, and advocate humane treatment and methods of reform for criminals, along with the abolishment of the death penalty.

"It is the duty of government to secure the best advantages of education for all children by establishing a national public education system. And it is also the duty of government, in its intercourse with foreign countries, to cultivate friendships of peace. Toward this end, we advocate a congress of nations endowed with the authority to settle disputes between countries. For the promotion of all these vital principles and a party based on them, we invite the cooperation of all citizens, without distinction of race, color, sex, nationality, or previous political affiliations."

There is a standing ovation as Isabella takes her seat.

As suffragists file into the Hall for the afternoon session, Victoria hears Susan Anthony and Elizabeth Cady arguing in the anteroom. She steps into the shadows and listens.

"You are petty to refuse Victoria the stage," Elizabeth says. "Petty, petty, petty. And I refuse to preside at any narrow-minded meeting! I resign as newly elected president."

"Fine. I will preside. Will you also leave me in the lurch for a keynote speaker?"

"No, I won't make your task more difficult."

"Thank you. But there is to be no mention of supporting Mrs. Woodhull's teetotally fool scheme to get nominated!"

"Fine!"

Victoria is livid. She hurries away. When the afternoon session is called to order, she is noticeably absent. A murmur rumbles through the auditorium as Susan steps to the podium and calls for discussion and voting on the group's resolutions as presented by Isabella. Several of the points are watered down or discarded. Tempers flare, and confusion becomes evident. Finally Stephen Pearl Andrews stands.

"I would like to know by whose authority some of the presented subjects have been discarded," he questions.

"By the authority of those member delegates who are entitled to speak and vote," Susan retorts. There is uproar from reformers, but Susan shouts above it. "For the peace of this meeting only NWSA members will be acknowledged and heard."

"I have attended these meetings for two years," says an elderly delegate. "We have considered the suffrage question to death and begged of the present parties in vain. It is time to form a new party and nominate candidates. If this Convention refuses to meet its responsibilities, I retire from it." She walks toward the door amid loud and protracted applause. Several follow her out.

When the evening meeting is convened, attendance is considerably smaller. You can almost see the frost in the air as Susan introduces Elizabeth for her keynote address. The crowd is restless as Elizabeth speaks.

"The Republican party, in destroying slavery, accomplished its entire mission. Now, in fostering monopolies, it is building a commercial feudalism dangerous to the liberty of the people," she says. "The Democratic party died in the attempt to sustain slavery and is buried beyond hope. Thousands support these parties because there is no other and better place for them to go. They cast their votes for the lesser of evils. Thousands more remain aloof from politics altogether. I believe all these citizens will come out from their retreats and join a Human Rights Party.

"It is strange that men ask what possible benefit women can bring to government. They forget that, like the Negro, this cribbed domestic slave will be transformed in freedom. She will develop powers he never dreamt she possessed. We shall never know what grand womanhood is until women have full liberty. I therefore urge all ladies to exercise their rights under the Constitution and vote in the November election as members of a new political power!"

Susan Anthony rushes to the podium.

"What Elizabeth means is that we should wait to see what the party conventions do. If suffrage is not on their plank, then we will hold a convention to discuss our own presidential ticket."

"Excuse me! Excuse me! I've been here all day, and I'm tired of everyone talking in circles." Dr. Treat calls out. He jumps to his feet, white suit jacket flapping and hand angrily rubbing his goatee.

"Me too!" Wisconsin delegate Ada Ballou yells from another group, "I came hundreds of miles for a human rights meeting, and all I've heard is that women must vote. Who and what are we voting for?"

"Where's the Woodhull?" asks a man from the Labor group. "I want to hear what she has to say! We're never in doubt when she speaks."

A roar of "Woodhull! Woodhull!" rises from the floor. Susan practically spits her response.

"If you want to know what this meeting is for, I will tell you. This is a meeting for woman and her enfranchisement and that is all! Anyone not a member of the National Woman's Suffrage Association can leave now!" As several stand to go, there is a stir at the side of the stage. Susan pales as Victoria glides onto the platform. The crowd goes wild!

"Excuse the interruption," Victoria says. "But I have—"

"You are out of order! You cannot speak!" Susan protests.

The crowd disagrees, roaring "Let her speak!" and "We want the Woodhull!"

Elizabeth glances nervously at the growing agitation and whispers to Susan, "For God sakes, do you want a riot? Let her say a few words." Victoria ignores them both as she addresses the assemblage.

"I hereby move that this meeting reconvene tomorrow at Apollo Hall to nominate candidates!"

"I second that!" Ada Ballou says.

Susan stalks off the stage as Victoria continues.

"The eyes of the world are upon us. Our enemies have sneered at the idea of combining reform groups for organized action. They say that women don't know how to organize and therefore are not to be feared as political opponents. I say they are wrong. I have even heard some reformers say they don't want anything to do with those who don't belong to their particular society. I trust this policy may not succeed. All friends of humanitarian reform must clasp hands—"

The lights suddenly go out, plunging the auditorium into darkness. Victoria yells above the panic.

"Everyone who believes in human rights meet at Apollo Hall tomorrow at noon!" She leaves the platform, passing Susan, who stands by the power switches, oozing venom. Victoria gives her a bitter smile.

"Perhaps you should raise the lights so the exodus from this hall does not result in injuries and ruin your good cause."

Chapter 29

The following day, Friday, May 10, 1872, the sun warms the late morning air as a festive and motley mass of reformers, already sweltering in their summer cottons, await the opening of the great white doors of Apollo Hall. Red, white, and blue signs bob and wave with such slogans as: Government Can't Govern My Heart; Corruption in Government Must End; Wives Are Prostitutes, too; -and on one, Let Women Vote, the word *vote* has been crossed through and changed to *rule*. There is a carnival atmosphere and growing excitement as vendors weave through the crowd, yelling and selling. Newsboys wave newspapers, hawking the headlines.

"Read Mrs. Woodhull's First Pronunciamento!"

"Greeley chosen by the Democrats. Governor Brown of Missouri to be his running mate."

"James Gang kills cashier in Kentucky."

"More scandal brewing for Grant."

The hall is as festive inside as it is outside. Workers hustle about with last-minute details, draping American flags on walls, hanging posters and banners. At the sales table, Belva Lockwood sets out pamphlets and books, as well as reprints of Victoria's announcement of her candidacy and her memorial to Congress. There are also copies of various issues of the *Weekly*.

The anteroom is filled with rustic baskets of tulips and lilacs. Zulu Maud plucks a small bunch of lilacs from one vase and holds it under her mother's nose.

"Take a whiff, Mother. It'll calm your nerves." Victoria smiles and takes a deep breath of the bouquet, although she continues to twist the diamond ring on her thumb. "Must be a hullabaloo crowd out there," Zulu Maud says, glancing toward the half-open door. "The Colonel is grinnin' ta high heaven and pig's feet."

"Zulu Maud! What have I told you?"

"Sorry, Mother, but the Claflins talk like that, and if I get my point across, why can't I?"

"I can't control my family, but I can train you to do better. Proper grammar is a sign of intelligence and good breeding, and we must always use it."

"Mr. Vanderbilt talks like the Claflins."

"Fine. When you get as old and as rich as he is, you can talk any way you want. In the meantime, let me fix your dress, and then you can practice your poem." She straightens Zulu Maud's ruffled pink dress and plants a loving kiss on the top of her daughter's head. "Do you remember it?"

"Yes, Ma'am." Zulu Maud straightens her shoulders, takes a deep breath, and starts to recite in a singsong voice.

"Feel it, Zulu Maud. Say the words from here."

Victoria presses her fist to her heart and repeats the poem in a low, lyrical tone. Zulu Maud is spellbound as her mother squats to look into her eyes.

"You see?"

"Yes, Ma'am."

"That's my girl. You're eleven now and old enough to sway an audience."

"Yes, Ma'am. Where's Aunt Tennie?"

"She's helping mother and the servants make food for the victory celebration to save on catering cost."

"Aunt Tennie? She hates—Oh, I get it, she's keeping Granny away so she doesn't disrupt the convention, right?"

"Zulu Maud, don't be precocious."

"What's that mean?"

"I'll write it down, and you can look it up in the dictionary when we get home." Victoria glances around. "Where's the Colonel? It's almost time to start."

Minutes later the doors are flung open and the famous and infamous surge into the hall. A nearby church bell tolls twelve times. As soon as the gongs fade, the organ launches into "Hail Columbia." Stragglers quickly find seats as Zulu Maud, Blood, Paulina Wright Davis, and Laura Cuppy Smith enter from the wings and sit in the front row beside the Wisconsin delegate Ada Ballou. Stephen Pearl Andrews walks to the podium and leads the singing, then greets the crowd.

"Welcome everyone! I understand there are at least twenty-two states and four territories represented here today." He has to shout over the cheers. "So that means Victoria C. Woodhull has nationwide support!" It is several moments before he can continue. "To begin our program this afternoon, Mrs. Woodhull's daughter, Zulu Maud, will share a poem."

Zulu Maud scampers onto the stage, voice clear and full of passion, hands emphasizing the points.

> *O, woman, you've not known your place*
> *our power has ne'er been felt!*
> *O, come at once! Come fill that space*
> *That vacant has been left.*
> *Let us, Sisters, stand up free*
> *Equal with brother man;*
> *Then will our minds unfold to see*
> *What's needed at our hands.*

Victoria beams as Zulu Maud curtsies to loud applause and walks confidently back to her seat.

"Excellent job, Zulu Maud," Andrews says. "And now, ladies and gentlemen, down to business. Our first task is to determine what to call our party."

"How about the Human Rights party?" someone calls out.

"I like Cosmopolitical," Laura Cuppy Smith offers.

"Mrs. Woodhull has suggested Equal Rights Party, and I make the motion we accept that," Paulina Wright Davis offers.

"I second," Ada Ballou says.

"All in favor?"

The crowd yells "Aye."

"Opposed?" There is no dissent.

"All right. The Equal Rights Party it is.   We will now select committees. These will meet immediately following this session and give their reports tonight. Tomorrow we will have the ratification process. Let us begin with the Nominating Committee. Do I have volunteers?"

~ ~ ~

The committees soon reconvene in designated meeting rooms. Colonel Blood and the thirty members of the Resolutions and Platform Committee, including Belva Lockwood and a few members of the Section 12 labor group, sit around a large table. Blood passes out papers.

"I took the liberty of printing up the resolutions Victoria has suggested and which were read at the NWSA convention," he says. "We've reinstated those points that misguided group disallowed. These will give us a good starting point."

"Did you remember—oh, yes, I see it here: ownership of land, mineral, and water resources by the people. Good. Good."

"We want eight-hour workdays and protection for strikers. There are 60,000 of them in New York right now and Mother Jones is on her way from Chicago."

"That's Resolution Four."

"It is the duty of the government to guarantee employment to all unemployed persons upon equitable principles of time and compensation," Belva Lockwood reads. She glances around the group. "These resolutions seem comprehensive and complete. I say we go down the list and discuss and vote on each in turn."

At 6:30 P.M., Victoria and Zulu Maud are outside Delmonico's restaurant, scanning the sidewalk in both directions.

"I don't know why we can't just wait inside," Zulu Maud complains, fidgeting.

"Women aren't allowed in restaurants alone after six. You know that."

"It's a stupid rule."

"And that's why I'm running for President, Dear, to change such stupid laws. Stand still. A lady doesn't fidget. The Colonel will be—See, here he comes now."

"You're lucky you're not allowed on a committee," Blood says as he rushes up and ushers them inside. "It took some rather heated discussions to get all twenty-three resolutions accepted!" As the maître d' seats them at a prime table, Blood tells him, "We are in a hurry so Mr. Delmonico already has our order. His famous Chicken á la King for me and Eggs Benedict for the ladies."

"What about the nomination? Am I even being considered?"

"That's what delayed me. Laura Cuppy Smith was on that committee, and I waited to speak with her. Darling, you are at the very top of the slate!"

"Who else is on the list?"

"Let's see, Robert Owens, Jr., Elizabeth Cady Stanton. Some thought her moderation an asset."

"She won't be chosen since she's not even here. Oh, I wish she had defected, too. I know she believes as I do, and I truly thought she possessed the courage of those convictions. But I understand it is hard to desert an organization that you founded and ran for so many years."

"Judge David Davis is your strongest opponent since, as candidate of the Labor Party as well, he would have dual support. But the Internationals want Wendell Phillips because of his stand on unions, so that could split that vote. A temperance delegate suggested George Francis Train, but my committee couldn't even decide on a temperance resolution—"

"George wouldn't accept. He's running his own campaign and knows this is my opportunity. Oh, James, I think I've got this!"

Attendance at the evening meeting is double that of the earlier session. Blood begins the Committee reports, introducing the Equal Rights Party plank, which is quickly voted on and accepted. Andrews ushers through the remainder of the committee reports and calls for a short break.

"But don't stray far," he cautions. "The Woodhull will speak next!"

As expected, the audience reacts with wild anticipation. They stand as one and stomp, cheer, whistle and wave signs and fans for a full five minutes before scattering like flies. Victoria retires to the anteroom and is surprised when Isabella Beecher Hooker bustles in. She grabs Victoria into a hug and kisses her cheeks.

"Our convention is dry as an old bone without you," Isabella says. "They're harping over the same old stuff. Be strong in our society. Blah, blah. I am truly sorry I am as gutless as my brother. If I didn't feel it my duty to deliver my scheduled speech tonight, I would be here with you. But I promise to support your nomination."

"I understand, Belle. It's okay."

"You wouldn't believe the quarrel Elizabeth and Susan are having. This whole thing may end a long friendship."

"Oh, I hope not."

"Two minutes, Victoria," Blood says, coming into the room.

"I must get back," Isabella says, giving Victoria a hug. "Good luck, good luck, good luck, my darling queen!" She rushes out.

"That was just what I needed," Victoria says. "A blast of Beecher balderdash! Let's go do this! Come along, Zulu Maud." Zulu Maud scampers to her front row seat with Blood while Victoria strides onto the platform and sits. Andrews steps to the podium.

"In Nathanial Hawthorne's *The Blithedale Romance*, the outspoken character Zenobia says to Miles Coverdale, "'Thus far no woman in the world has spoken out her whole heart and her whole mind. The vast bulk of society throttles us, as with two gigantic hands at our throats! You let us write a little, on a limited range of subjects, but the pen is not for woman. Her power is too natural and immediate. It is with the living voice alone that she can compel the world to recognize the light of her intellect and the depth of her heart.' Ladies and gentlemen, twenty years after this truth went out in the guise of fiction, we have a Living Voice to speak not only for women, but for all of us. I give you the Representative Woman, Mrs. Victoria Claflin Woodhull."

The applause drowns out her name, but everyone knows to whom he refers. In seconds no one remains seated. They stomp and cheer and whistle until the rafters rattle. Victoria humbly and briefly soaks up the adoration, then leans forward with arms outstretched as if to invite them into a hug. It is her well-known cue for silence, and people hush and sit.

"Agitation of thought is the beginning of wisdom. Who will dare to attempt to unlock the luminous portals of the future with the rusty key of the past? Those of you who know me know I work only for the common good. To those of you who don't know me, I thank you for the faith you've shown in our common cause." Victoria's voice grows stronger, more compelling. The audience hangs on every word. "We seek, no, we *demand* fairness. One standard for all! From this convention will go forth a tide of revolution! A resistless force, if not fury, to purge this land of political trickery, despotic assumption, and industrial injustice!" Her voice softens. "But how can there be equality when one-eighth of the population is functionally illiterate? When the rich hoard wealth and corrupt politicians? Shall we be slaves to escape revolution?"

"Never!"

"I say away with such weak stupidity!"

"Away! Away!"

"Let us have justice, though the heavens may fall!"

The crowd is on its feet in a frenzy as Victoria sits.

"Mr. Andrews! Mr. Andrews! May I be recognized?" Judge Carter of Ohio calls out, leaping to his feet in the second row.

"Judge Carter, you are recognized."

"The time for talk has passed. I nominate Victoria Woodhull as the Equal Rights Party choice for President." There is a thunderous and extended roar of "Aye." Andrews bangs a gavel for silence.

"There are others on the slate. Shall I read them?"

"No!"

"Are there any opposed to Mrs. Woodhull's nomination?"

There isn't a single "nay."

"Victoria C. Woodhull is hereby nominated as the Equal Rights Party candidate for President of the United States."

Bedlam ensues. Hats sail in the air. Men leap onto chairs, yelling themselves hoarse. Women weep and wave hankies and hats. Andrews motions Victoria back to the forefront. Her face glows with happiness. When she speaks, her voice is choked with emotion.

"I sincerely thank you for the unanimity with which you accord me this distinguished honor. I feel this moment more deeply because I have worked heart and hand for our good cause for so long, sometimes meriting your applause and sometimes encountering your rebuffs. But I have always been faithful to my principles. *Our* principles! My gratitude knows no bounds for the great faith you have shown in making me your standard bearer. *Namaste.* I see God in all of you."

More pandemonium as Victoria leaves the stage. Andrews steps forward and holds up his hands for silence.

"Mrs. Woodhull will be receiving in the anteroom," he tells the gathering.

"Dr. Andrews, what about a Vice-President?" Laura Cuppy Smith asks.

"Oh, yes, thank you. That would have been a terrible oversight. The floor is now open for nominations for the Equal Rights Party Vice-Presidential candidate."

"I nominate Chief Spotted Tail," Belva Lockwood says. "From the Trail of Tears back in thirty-eight, through treaty after treaty that our government has failed to honor so as to steal their land, to the current wars being waged against Captain Jack and the Modoc, the Indian is still as denigrated as woman."

"What about Ben Butler?" Judge Carter proposes. "He's got experience in Congress and military service. If we are to win, we must consider these things."

"We need Laura Cuppy Smith for an all-woman ticket!" a woman in the back cries out.

"What about Henry Ward Beecher?" someone yells. "There was a letter proposing him in the paper recently!"

"Why would Mrs. Woodhull share her ticket with a hypocrite? He is everything she rails against!" Laura Cuppy Smith counters.

"I nominate Colonel James Blood," Paulina Wright Davis says. "We don't want him left a grass widower!" Even Blood laughs at that.

"We have the oppressed sex represented, why not the oppressed race? I nominate Frederick Douglass." This comes from prominent lecturer and author Frances Harper, a member of both oppressed groups.

"Isn't he stumping for Grant?" someone asks.

"All the more reason to nominate him and save him from the dung Grant's corruption will cast on him."

"But won't a Negro hurt our chances of gaining the throne? There is a terrible fear of miscegenation. Such a ticket would be a bold rejection of the prevailing racial view."

"Well, I am all for rejecting the status quo," Ada Ballou says. "I second the nomination of Frederick Douglass!"

"I agree," says Andrews. "We must have a ticket that shocks and instructs on universal rights and stimulates the national debate. A black-and-white ticket of Victoria Woodhull and Frederick Douglass will do it. Frederick Douglass has been nominated and seconded. All in favor?"

With only a few weak cries of "nay," Douglass is named Victoria's running mate. Andrews' voice cracks from hoarseness as he yells above the din.

"The Equal Rights Party hereby accepts Victoria C. Woodhull and Frederick Douglass as our nominated candidates. And I say that Horace Greeley and President Grant better step aside! The Equal Rights Party *will* be reckoned with! This meeting is adjourned."

Suddenly the huge white doors of the hall are flung open and Tennie enters in a black, high-crowned, Neapolitan hat and full military uniform. Behind her are the 400 soldiers of the 85th Regiment marching band. She waves her baton, and the band begins to play "Comin' Through the Rye." The music brings Victoria back to the stage as the soldiers march down the center aisle and Tennie hands out lyric sheets. The crowd claps and hums along with the band until Tennie hops onto the platform and shouts for attention.

"When the courageous Spencer Grays and the noble Veteran Guard combined their forces to become the all-Negro 85th Regiment, no white man would lead them. Hearing the Ninth Regiment had rejected me to replace their murdered leader Colonel Jim Fisk, these heroic soldiers asked me to be their colonel. Never have I accepted a task so happily and proudly. When my sister is President, this gallant unit will be our country's honored guard!" The band bows and keeps on playing softly as Tennie continues. "I've handed out lyric sheets for a campaign song I wrote for my sister. Let's all sing along!"

People stand on chairs, waving banners and flags. Hats hurl to the ceiling. Curious passers-by poke their heads into the auditorium. Most disappear in panic, but some join in the celebration as shouts of "Victoria for President!" fill the air. Audience members fall in behind the band, marching up and down the aisles and singing:

If you nominate a woman
In the month of May,
Dare you face what Mrs. Grundy
And her set will say?
How they'll jeer and frown and slander
Chattering night and day;
Oh, did you dream of Mrs. Grundy
In the month of May?

Yes! Victoria we've selected
For our chosen head.
With Fred Douglass on the ticket
We will raise the dead.
Then around them let us rally
Without fear or dread
And next March, we'll put the Grundys
In their little bed.

The after celebration is as vociferous as the rest of the convention, with excited well-wishers hugging and kissing and congratulating Victoria. Mrs. Joseph Treat is first.

"Congratulations, Mrs. Woodhull," she says. "I feel so encouraged just thinking about you in the White House. Maybe soon our medical professionals won't be charged with obscenity for educating women on birth control."

"I hope so. It's the best solution to the horror of abortion. I don't know why so few understand that."

"Ohio is fired up for you, Ma'am!" says Judge Carter from Ohio. "Even Governor Rutherford B. Hayes is impressed." As the judge moves on, Tennie bursts into the anteroom, motioning behind her for the band to keep marching and playing in the auditorium.

"What do you think of my song, Sis?"

"Oh, Tennie, it was wonderful. And nice addition of Mr. Douglass' name."

Johnnie Green, scribbling on his notepad, has followed Tennie into the room. He grins at Zulu Maud.

"You read the *Sun* tomorrow, sweetie. I'll have some fine things to say about that recitation of yours!" Zulu Maud blushes.

"That's nice of you, Mr. Green," Victoria says. "It means a lot."

"It's my pleasure. Be careful, Mrs. Woodhull. She's almost as good as you on the platform already." He winks at Zulu Maud and then turns back to Victoria. "Can I ask a few questions?"

"Now, Johnnie, you know the rules," Blood says, stepping in. "No interviews tonight. Only celebration."

"Just one statement for my article. Please, Mrs. Woodhull."

"I'll give you a mini-interview, Johnnie." She flirts as she leads him toward a corner.

"I noticed your mentor isn't here tonight, Tennie," Johnnie says. "I thought he might be."

"My mentor? Oh, you mean the Com? No, I 'spect Mrs. Vanderbilt is keeping him on a short harness. But listen, Johnnie, let's not talk history. Did you hear my campaign song?"

The celebrators eat, drink, and engage in merry conversations until Victoria yawns, suddenly exhausted. Blood eases them discreetly toward the door, but someone notices and calls out.

"Good night, President Woodhull. Long live Victoria!"

The entire room stands at attention and applauds as Victoria waves like a bride leaving for her honeymoon and slips out the door.

Chapter 30

Although Frederick Douglass declines the Vice-Presidential nomination of the Equal Rights Party, citing his support for Grant, Victoria leaves him on the ticket believing he will accept the post if she should win. She is pleased that he at least sends her a thoughtful note and wishes her well. It is the one pleasant spot in her days as word of her official nomination reaches the nation and the backlash begins.

It breaks Victoria's heart when Zulu Maud is expelled from her school, but she assures her that Professor Andrews will tutor her to be the smartest of any student. Then Victoria and Blood arrive home at dusk to more bad news.

"Pack up and get out now! I'll have no anarchists here!" Their landlady says, shoving an eviction order into Victoria's hand.

Late into the night, Victoria, Blood, Tennie, and the children walk the streets, stopping at every boarding house and hotel they see. No one will rent to them. The moon is high when they finally trudge back to their Wall Street office. The outer door is locked, so Blood lifts Zulu Maud up to the transom to climb in and unlock it from the inside. The weary family collapses on the sofas, chairs, and floor.

"This will be our home for the time being," Victoria declares. "It's comfortable enough and will free up money and energy to use in our campaign."

~ ~ ~

In June, the GOP nominates Grant, as expected. Senator Henry Wilson of Massachusetts is selected as his running mate, ousting Schuyler Colfax, the current Vice President rumored to be tainted by a new scandal brewing in Grant's camp, the underhanded dealings between politicians and the Credit Mobiliér firm.

The more liberal Republicans, splintering off from their party, back the Democrat's ticket of Horace Greeley and Governor Brown, even though Brown is known to be a raging alcoholic.

With James Black and John Russell representing the Temperance party, David Davis and Joel Parker Labor party candidates, Charles Adams, descendant of John Junior and John Quincy nominated by the little known Anti-Secrecy Society, and George Francis Train running as an Independent, the fall slate is set.

Despite herculean lobbying efforts by Susan B. Anthony, only Victoria's Equal Rights Party has woman's suffrage on their platform. But things are not going well. Returning from the lecture circuit, Victoria shuffles through legal papers while Blood attends to the bookkeeping. Because they are still living in the office, Victoria lowers her voice so the children don't hear.

"Look at this," she tells Blood, waving a handful of papers. "Suing, suing, suing. I don't know what anyone expects to get. I hardly own the clothes on my back."

"It's not just us. The whole country is in recession."

"Are the Equal Rights Party bonds selling at all?"

"Not enough. We've got to come up with money for filing fees soon if you are to get on all the state ballots."

"We must think of something. I haven't a chance as a write-in. As long as we merely talked and wrote, no one minded. But the moment a practical move was made, they began using any and every means to shut us down." She peruses another letter. "Oh, dear, Karl Marx and the Executive Committee have expelled our Section 12 from the International Workingmen's. That may cost us labor votes."

"Mrs. Woodhull?" Victoria groans as the bird-like building owner hustles into the room. "Mrs. Woodhull, I've been told you folks are camping out in these offices. If this is to be home as well as office, I must raise your rent. I want an additional thousand dollars a month and the entire year paid in advance."

"You know we can't possibly give you that."

"Then I suggest you start packing."

~ ~ ~

A short item in the *Weekly* is the only notice of the demise of Wall Street's Woodhull and Claflin Company. As Victoria and Tennie leave the building for the last time, Victoria looks sadly around the offices.

"Maybe we should have been content with getting rich investing other people's money," she bemoans.

"My god, Sis, Mrs. Grundy probably still would have been at us. Look at it this way, now we can devote more time to your campaign. And we'll find a perfect place to live. You'll see."

If Tennie meant her statement as a psychic prediction, her powers seem to have evaporated. With the children tagging along, Victoria, Tennie, and Blood walk the streets searching desperately for a new dwelling. Everywhere they go, doors slam and heads shake—at boarding houses, hotels, and offices. It is after midnight when they finally drag themselves into the Gilsey Hotel, a seedy establishment where ladies of the night ply their trade openly in the lobby. Victoria almost cries when the perky young male desk clerk actually smiles at them.

"We have a suite that I believe will house you all," he says cheerfully. "Just sign here." He hands Blood a key. "Go up to the third floor. It's the last door on the right."

The next morning, the hotel manager arrives as one of the soldiers of her regiment helps Tennie, looking sharp in her military uniform, into a carriage. The manager scowls and hurries to the desk clerk.

"What is that woman doing at my hotel?"

"Tennie C.? I rented them a room last night. Her and her sister and an honest-to-God Colonel! Well, Tennie's a Colonel, too, but—"

"You did what?"

"Shh, Sir, there's the other one. She'll hear you." The clerk nods toward Victoria, who is coming down the steps across the lobby. The hotel manager swings around and calls to her.

"Mrs. Woodhull! A word please."

The few slovenly guests lounging in the lobby stare as Victoria crosses to the desk and greets the man cheerily.

"Good morning, Sir."

"I'm afraid it's not a good morning for you. Apparently my young clerk was overzealous in renting to you last evening. You must leave immediately."

"But why, Sir? We have paid for a week in advance."

"I will return your money, Madam, but I will not tolerate your kind in my establishment."

"Men and their mistresses live here openly and you're worried about my kind? Unless you prove that I have committed a misdemeanor, I will not leave. Now I have a newspaper to put out. Good day."

Anger colors her cheeks as she intercepts Blood at the foot of the staircase. She takes his arm, and head high, walks out.

It is one of the hottest days of a hot summer and the setting sun has not lessened the record-breaking heat as a wilted Victoria and Blood return to the hotel late the same afternoon. Suddenly Victoria's eyes widen.

"Oh, my god! Zulu Maud! Byron!" Her children are perched atop the family's meager belongings, red with sunburn and numb with embarrassment. Victoria covers the distance in seconds. As she reaches them, two passers-by spit at Byron. Victoria turns on them, murder in her eyes, but Blood grabs her.

"Let them go. We need to tend to the children."

"I'll shoot that horrible man! They could have died! This heat has already taken hundreds and today was the worst ever! I'll rip his heart out!"

"Victoria, the children have endured enough today. Let's just get them away from here."

"Oh, baby, I am so sorry. How long were you out here, honey?" Victoria kisses eleven-year-old Zulu Maud's lobster-red arms as Blood and Tennie help Byron down off the luggage.

"Right after you left, Mother, but it's okay. I thought about when we went to the theater for my birthday so I stayed happy. And I told By stories because he wanted to find you. When people walked by and laughed at us, I pretended like I was slow-witted like By and couldn't

211

understand what they were saying. This'll make us strong, right, Mother?"

"You are already the strongest young lady ever. Honey, honey, honey, I am so sorry." Victoria gives her son a loving look. "Byron wanted me?"

They make their way to their sister Maggie's Magnetic Institute. Maggie almost faints in fright at the sight of them.

"*Scheis!* What are you doing here? Do you want to put me out of business?" She quickly lets them in, then locks the door and shutters the windows.

"You have to help us, Maggie. They put my children out on the street." Victoria points to her children's blistered skin.

"Good Lord! Come, Children, let me take care of your burns."

They are as gentle as possible, but the children, now shivering from sun poisoning, wince in pain as Maggie and Victoria apply ice packs and soothing aloe and wrap them in cotton sheets. Once the children are attended to, Maggie sits her sister down.

"Victoria, I have no room for you. You know I've got Mama, Buck, and Utie all living with me. There's just no space."

"I'm begging you, Maggie. We always made room for you."

"Papa taught us to stick together," Tennie pipes in. "My god, you gotta help us."

"Okay, okay. Let me think. Oh, wait, there's a house a block over on Twenty-fourth. The owner has gone to Europe for a year. I think his agent will rent to me. But for goodness sakes, you stay here. I'll put the lease in my name and hopefully he won't find out it's for you. Lock the door. And don't let anyone see you!"

The following day, safely ensconced in their new quarters, Victoria tries to rebuild. Unfortunately, between legal costs to fight the bogus lawsuits being lodged against them, the loss of advertising dollars, and the expenditures necessary to continue her campaign, there are no funds left to publish the *Weekly*. Heartbroken, Victoria clears her desk. The presses grind to a halt.

"They have taken both our businesses now," she mourns.

"My god, they can't say we didn't give it a run, though, Sis." Tennie tries to be strong, though tears trickle down her cheeks.

"Where are all my friends? They are a bunch of fair-weather cowards who desert me when I'm down."

"My god, why are you surprised? All they ever gave us was flowery talk. Never any bucks to back up their words. Even Belle, who says you are her queen and who can well afford to contribute, never gave us a dime."

The front door opens and closes and they look toward the sound. Victoria tenses at the sight of a short, frail, blond man, about thirty-five, walking toward them. His untrimmed beard spills over his vest, reaching almost to his waist. She relaxes, however, when the Colonel rushes to greet the man.

"George! Everyone, this is my brother George."

"Babysitter at your service, Ma'am."

George tips his hat gallantly, bringing tears to Victoria's eyes.

"You're a lifesaver," says Victoria, hugging him. "Our only recourse for survival is the lyceum circuit. At least people still pay to hear what I have to say. We will take Zulu Maud with us, but there is no one I trust to watch Byron. James explained about him?"

"Yes, Ma'am. And don't you worry. By and I will get along fine. And I will use my talent with numbers to stretch your coffers as far as necessary to keep the wolves at bay."

"You have my undying love and gratitude. When I am President you shall make a better Secretary of the Treasury than Alexander Hamilton himself!"

The last stop on their tour is the Spiritualists' convention, which convenes in Boston on September 11. Victoria, still their President, waits in the anteroom for the meeting to begin. Voices carry into the room as a man and woman walk by the half-open door.

"She only came to sell party bonds for her futile Presidential campaign," the woman sniffs.

"I ain't buyin' nothin'. I came to talk about spiritual concepts not politics."

"That's it! I am too tired to fight another battle," Victoria rants to Tennie. "I am going out there and resign! Don't they know I realize I won't be elected this year? Don't they see that, even if I lose, I am breaking new ground for women and justice? That it's for this reason I push myself night after day?"

Striding onto the platform, Victoria's manner is so electric the intuitive audience immediately feels it and is shocked to silence. She speaks without preamble.

"Why am I persecuted for demanding equality for women? Why am I shunned for declaring my freedom to love whom I please? There are dozens in this city who do the same but hide behind masks of respectability. Lucy Stone and her AWSA group delight in defaming me, but their ranks are filled with Free-lovers. Rev. Hanaford and Mary Livermore have both left their marriages. And everyone knows about Abby Hutchinson Patton's long-standing affair with Lucy Stone's husband.

"But the rot goes even higher up the tree of religion, just as the symbolic snake slithered up Eden's hypothetical apple tree. The Reverend Henry Ward Beecher preaches every Sunday to his mistresses, female parishioners robed in satin and respectability. If I withhold these facts, am I not abetting the hypocrisy?" Mouths gape. Eyes widen. Several women faint. Victoria is in a trance, unaware of the audience she continues. "If it be my mission to expose the hypocrisy of the American Pope and his exercise of free-love with Mrs. Theodore Tilton, to name just one of his paramours, so be it! I will tell you the details told to me by the Tiltons and Mr. Beecher himself, as the Reverend lay in my arms!"

The stunned audience listens with scattered coughs and frequent gasps as Victoria reveals everything she knows about the Beecher-Tilton affair. When she finishes, Victoria stalks off the stage.

~ ~ ~

Blood and Zulu Maud sleep as their train bounces and jolts through the Midwest. Victoria and Tennie are awake, however, and surrounded by newspapers. They flip through each, looking for any reports about Victoria's explosive revelations at the Spiritualist meeting.

"Oh, here's one," Tennie says, reading. "'Then Mrs. Woodhull said some slanderous things about an esteemed member of the clergy, which didn't stop the motley crowd from re-electing her as their president.'"

"That's it?"

"That's it." Tennie cuts it out for their scrapbook as Victoria checks the *Boston Journal*.

"Oh for goodness sakes, this one says I made accusations against people with 'impeccable reputations.' And that I swore profanely. I did not! If I swore at all it was divinely! Did I swear?"

"I don't think so," Tennie says, turning the pages of *The Memphis Appeal*, a small specialty publication. She stops at a deep inner page. "Oh, here's something about the convention by Mrs. Meriwether. We met her, right? Big, white-haired woman?"

"Yes. What does she say?" Victoria waits impatiently for Tennie to scan the article.

"Finally!" Tennie says. She grins and begins to read. "'Then Mrs. Woodhull fell into a trance. A sort of electric shock swept over the assembly, striking it to dead stillness, as if awaiting a thunderclap. Mrs. Woodhull tossed back her hair in high tragic style and poured out a torrent of flame. It made the flesh creep and blood run cold.'"

"Oh for heaven sakes."

"'Her features are delicate and clear-cut, her nose slightly aquiline, her skin smooth and pale, except when under the excitement of speaking. Then two crimson spots burn her cheeks and a lurid light springs to her eyes. When speaking, she has the fervor of a tragic actress. Her face, the saddest I ever saw, tells of wrecked hopes and a cruel battle with life. Her speech was not obscene but fiercely denunciatory. Fiery and scandalous.'"

"What about Beecher? Does she mention Beecher?"

"She does," Tennie says, continuing to read. "'Editors, teachers, preachers, she spared not one. She lifted some of Boston's own editors high and scorched them with accusations. Henry Ward Beecher suffered

215

the most. After setting the whole Beecher-Tilton scandal out in vivid detail, Mrs. Woodhull concluded by saying that she does not blame the Reverend for his infidelity but objects to his sanctimony in not owning up to his private practice of free-love.' My god, she doesn't give any of the specific details, but she says enough to get the curiosity worked up. Maybe we should buy up some copies, mark the article, and send them around."

"It won't do any good. No man will print it. If this thing is to be aired, we must find a way to revive the *Weekly*."

~ ~ ~

On Sunday, October 13, 1872, the Tiltons are among church members who organize outside Beecher's home for a parade to Plymouth Church in celebration of its 25th Anniversary. Flowers fly and drums roll as Henry Ward leads the procession. His pretty church soloist, dressed as a bride, clings to his arm. As the massive parade surges down the street, Victoria's broken-down carriage, pulled by scrawny nags, is forced to wait at an intersection for them to pass.

"My god! What a racket!" Tennie shouts, covering her ears.

Victoria doesn't respond. Her face is a raging storm as her thoughts snap back to the past.

Robust gospel singing stops in mid-note as Roxanna Claflin storms into a small Methodist church and parades down the aisle, her children in tow. Two-year-old Victoria is mortified as her mother grabs the pastor's wrist and screams at him, her German accent heavy with rage.

"You do not act like Christians here!"

"Please sit down, Mrs. Claflin. You're disrupting the service."

The pastor jerks his arm away.

"Nein, nein! You warn the children to stop pushing and laughing at my precious babies or the Holy Mudder of Israel will have her Son strike you dead!"

Roxanna slaps away ushers who hurry over. She marches her brood back down the aisle, turns at the door. Making the sign of the "evil eye," she bellows back into the room.

"*Gott curse you, black-hearted spawn of Satan, and your* mittel *wife too!*"

Victoria snaps out of her reverie and fumes to Tennie.

"I ought to go out there and tell those poor souls the truth about their saintly leader!"

"I don't think they would hear you for the noise."

"Then I'll stand on top of this carriage and make them! If I am doomed to perish, I'll take that hypocrite with me!"

"My god, Sis, you'll cause a riot! Those Christians will tear us to shreds!"

"Then when, Tennie? When will there be justice? Oh, if only we could get the money to raise the *Weekly* from the dead."

"My god, Sis, I'll get the money, okay? I'll think of somethin' and get the money."

A short time later, Cornelius Vanderbilt is in bed ill, although not too sick to grab lustfully at the nurse who tucks a quilt around him. She bats away his hand and looks gratefully at the relief nurse who rushes in, her hood still covering her head.

"Good luck with the old coot." The nurse grabs her shawl and can't leave quickly enough. Her replacement locks the door. The Commodore's voice is hoarse as she turns toward him.

"Go away," he grumbles. "Doggum it, I'm tired of nursing. Just give an old man peace to lie here and croak."

"Hey, Old Boy, it's me!" Tennie throws off her cloak and plants a big kiss on his sunken, veined cheek.

"Little Sparrow?" Life seems to seep back into his veins. "Well, I'll be hornswoggled." Vanderbilt pulls her close and gives her a loud kiss on the lips. She runs her hands gently through his snarled hair and beard.

"They ain't takin' too good of care of you, Com. You look a sight. Are you happy to see me, Old Boy?"

"Happy as a blushing boy. But I know you're comin' with some business, so give me one of them magnetic healings and whatever you're wantin' you can have."

217

"It's a quick moneymaker, Com. We need a pittance. Just enough for one more issue of the *Weekly*. I guarantee we'll sell so many copies we'll pay you back double in a week. Maybe I'll send it through Billy Boy. Wouldn't that chortle him. *Me* giving *you* money!"

"Double, huh? What's it gonna say that's worth more'n gold? On second thought, don't tell me. And don't tell nobody where you got the money. Agreed?"

"You got it, Old Boy."

The next day Victoria is at the new location of *Woodhull & Claflin's Weekly,* a small building at 111 Nassau Street. She writes furiously as Zulu Maud and Tennie clean half-heartedly and Blood and Channing ready the presses.

Victoria looks up, startled, as Buck storms in.

"Are you a fool? Did I raise a fool? I oughta take my hand to you!" Buck raises his hand as if to strike her, and Zulu Maud hides behind Tennie.

"Have a seat, Father," Victoria says, giving her father a cool look. "You're scaring Zulu Maud. Tennie, will you take her out, please?"

"I'm warning you, Victoria. Mr. Beecher has more power than you can imagine, and he'll unleash it all against you."

"If an omelet is to be made, some eggs have to be broken. Mr. Beecher will weather the storm and become a better leader for the honesty thrust upon him. After the first waves of public indignation, he will find that he still lives and that there are brave souls who stand by him. Then he will rise in his power and utter truth."

"You hain't seen nuthin' compared to what that man and that Church will rise up and do, and it won't have nuthin' to do with truth!" Buck bellows. "I'm warnin' ya. Don't say I didn't warn ya." He storms out.

"Is he right, Pearl?" Victoria asks Andrews, who is working at his desk and has heard the exchange.

"For once I think he is."

"But don't we have an obligation to compel Mr. Beecher to do the duty for humanity from which he shrinks?"

"We have avoided personal attacks for a reason, Victoria. And this is the most *dangereux* personal attack of all. Anthony Comstock, that self-appointed Commissioner of Vice, will not let it pass. With the Church and the Government behind him, he will lock us up and throw away the key."

"They won't. They can't! This is America, the land of free speech. And we will print only truth. Truth is more important than any man's fair fame! *Something* must be done to break down the walls of prejudice that prevent public discussion of the sexual problem!"

"All I'm sayin' is that I'm too old to sleep in a damp jail cell on a ratty old cot."

"But this isn't just about Beecher. It's about hypocrisy. It's about taking aim at the way the elite abuse their power. It's about revealing the tarnish beneath the gilding of position and reputation. That's why Tennie is also exposing that rapist Luther Challis' debauchery of innocent young girls."

"Must I give you a dissertation about the savagery of Christians? History is littered with those tortured and killed in the name of God. You have been called the Joan of Arc of the woman's movement. Do you want to die as she did?"

"Oh, good heavens. No one's going to burn me at the stake."

"Victoria, you've already experienced the wrath of society because of your candidacy and opinions about love. But I assure you it pales to what you will face if you go through with this."

"What if you set the story up with one of your erudite dissertations about the cesspool of modern society? And we'll present the exposé as an interview—you asking me questions for the facts and why I'm doing this. I can't let this go, Pearl."

"Whatever you say, Victoria. I say you will regret it, but it's your paper to do with what you will."

"Yes, it is. And we are going ahead, consequences be damned!"

Chapter 31

On the Friday evening before the paper goes to press, the sisters pass Plymouth Church and see Henry Ward leaving after his prayer meeting. They wait until he is gone and go inside. Their footsteps echo through the empty auditorium, which seems even more massive than it is. The place is dark, except for moonlight that streams through the windows and casts eerie shadows on the pews. Tennie's eyes are wide with fear as she follows her sister down an aisle.

"My god, Sis, this place is creepin' me out. Let's go."

"Look around, Tennie. Thousands sit in these pews every Sunday, searching for truth. And what do they get? Condemnation. Condemnation that makes them deny what the Spirit inside is prompting them to do—how God wants them to be—because this— this so-called *voice* of God stands up on his stage and tells them they cannot behave as he himself behaves! He chains them with fear and keeps them from the Gate of Heaven."

"My god, I don't know how the man lives with himself. What gets me is that he believes that love should be free just like you do. The only difference is that you think it should be free for everyone, and he believes it should be free only for those that he thinks are, I don't know, advanced enough spiritually, I guess. Who made him judge anyway?"

Victoria walks onto the platform and sits in Beecher's chair. Tennie yawns and slumps into a front pew. Victoria surveys the room for a long minute, deep in thought. Finally she speaks.

"He is wrong. He sins the sin of hypocrisy. And God help me, if I do not speak out, I am damned with him."

"My god, I'm glad that's settled. Let's go home."

"Let's talk this through one more time. We are including your article about Luther Challis to prove it is not a personal attack on the preacher, but one of the whole male zeitgeist. So with that article as well as the Beecher exposé, what will happen?"

"We'll be seen as heroines ushering in an age of truth?"

"I doubt that, but we've already lost our home and money, so there's not much they can do to us in those areas. We could be laughed or shamed out of town. I don't think I could stand that."

"We survived it before; we could again. There's a big world to run to. Canada, France."

"I don't think anyone will assassinate us. We're not worth the powder. . . . We could be arrested."

"For what? My god, by the time Professor Perlo got done tweaking things, the articles sounded almost scholarly."

"Libel? But truth can't be libelous, can it?"

"No. My god, there ain't nothing they can do to us except bluster and blow. Maybe a few will kneel down and pray for our souls. I say we go ahead."

"I agree. We are ready to face whatever consequences ensue."

"Good. Let's go." Tennie stands.

"But what will be gained for the betterment of the world? It kills me to do this to Lib. Exposing the affair will be seen as an act of cruelty toward her, the victim, and especially her children. To sacrifice them we must be sure this bombshell fulfills the higher purpose of social advance. Does it?"

"Well, it'll open some eyes and maybe help some escape their self-imposed prisons." Tennie yawns and plunks back down.

"Oh, I pray so." Victoria is silent, her thoughts racing. "I really think that once his sin is revealed and he is forgiven, Beecher will enter the higher regions of Christian life and be better able to interpret God's word. And I think Lib will find her marriage survives and is better for the removal of the shadows of secrecy her husband now lords over her."

"Right." Tennie yawns again. "Look, Sis, we've already written the articles, the presses are ready to roll, I say we go home to bed and let the chips fall where they will."

Victoria doesn't respond. She walks to the altar and drops to her knees. Tennie rolls her eyes and lies down in the pew. She is asleep in seconds. A half hour later, Victoria shakes her excitedly.

"Tennie, wake up!"

"Huh? What? Where are we?" Tennie sits up. She rubs her eyes and looks around. "Oh."

"Tennie, Christ came to me as I prayed! His eyes—the love—It took my breath away. Then, in a flood of inspiration, he illuminated my soul! He reminded me that Paradise was lost in Genesis through woman and regained in Revelation through woman. The message was clear: Through the revelation of truth by woman, the world will be saved! Christendom must be shocked. We will cast a thunderbolt into the center of the socio-religio-moralistic camp and strike their chieftain! The world may tremble at the blow, but it will be saved. And in twenty years no one will say that I was wrong."

"Thank god. Can we go home now? I've had enough church to last me a lifetime."

"You know, Tennie, I really do feel the presence of God here," Victoria says as she drapes an arm around her sister and they walk to the door. "That is greater than any human failings or sins, even those done in his name."

~ ~ ~

Ironically, on Sunday morning, Henry Ward expounds on morality to his congregation at the same time as the *Weekly* presses roll. When the first paper churns out, Victoria grabs it and quickly turns to page nine. A nervous smile spreads across her face.

"It is universal washing day," she says.

Chapter 32

October 28, 1872 is a typical Monday morning at the American News loading dock. While workers transfer newspapers to delivery carriages, one man sneaks a look at the *Weekly*. His eyes widen as he reads page nine:

> **We propose aggressive moral warfare on the social question, to begin in this article with the ventilating of the conduct of the Reverend Henry Ward Beecher in his relations with the Theodore Tilton family. Like the abolitionists used the exposure of sexual abuse of slaves to discredit that abominable institution, this exposure reveals one reverend, representative of far too many wayward Christian preachers, who are exemplars of religious corruption.**

The worker rushes to show his manager, who quickly charges down to the loading dock, yelling orders. A short time later, ignoring the protests of the *Weekly* staff, American News workers dump the hundreds of newspapers onto their office steps. Victoria and Blood quickly load their carriage and head for the Wall Street newsstand. The faithful vendor is happy to see them.

"Mrs. Woodhull, you're back!"

"Yes we are. And with a vengeance. Can you help us unload?"

"Why aren't you letting American News make your—" He suddenly realizes just how many papers they are unloading. "Holy cow, Mrs. Woodhull, you've got five hundred copies here. I can't possibly sell that many."

"I promise you'll be crying for more, my friend," Blood tells him.

Throughout the morning, they deliver the Weekly to vendors in three teams: Tennie and Andrews, Victoria and Blood, and nephew Channing and Blood's brother George. Trains already carry the message across the nation.

When newsstands open, shock and horror sweep the country like wildfire. Citizens devour the *Weekly's* "interview" between Stephen Pearl Andrews and Victoria:

> **SPA: I confess I cannot understand why you of all persons should find fault with Mr. Beecher.**
>
> **VCW: It is the paradox of my position that, believing in the right of Mr. Beecher socially, morally, and divinely to have sought the embraces of Mrs. Tilton, I still denounce him as a poltroon, a coward, and a sneak for failing in his position as representative man. I claim no condemnation for the actions of Mr. Beecher and Mrs. Tilton but only for the hypocrisy of the deed. If I do not reveal it, I am guilty of collusion.**

By mid-morning, as Lib Tilton lies in bed sobbing, vendors and newsboys mob the streets outside the *Weekly* office, fighting to replenish their depleted supplies.

"A blowout of entertainment for only a dime, huh?" one comments.

"A dime? Man, I'm selling them at ten bucks a pop and still can't keep 'em in stock!"

Inside, the press grinds away, and Victoria and Tennie can hardly count their stacks of money.

~ ~ ~

"Do not worry, Father," Eunice tells her husband when they see the news. "Everyone knows the woman lies. You're too great a man to be brought down by her ridiculous accusations. Mr. Bowen won't allow it."

"You're right, Mrs. B. When a man is unlucky enough, as he walks along, to be drenched by a torrent of dirty water thrown on him from an upper window, the best thing he can do is wipe himself off and continue on his way."

Beecher tosses the *Weekly* into the wastebasket.

Meanwhile, broker Luther Challis enters the New York Stock Exchange to whispers and stares. One agent pulls out a *Weekly* and reads aloud, "This scoundrel Challis, to prove he had seduced a maiden, exhibited triumphantly on his finger the red token of her virginity."

"Challis the Conqueror," another man shouts. The others pick up the refrain, roaring with laughter until Challis stalks out in a fury.

By early afternoon, the Wall Street newsstand cannot even be seen for the crowd stretching far down the block. An outcry arises when the vendor again runs out of the *Weekly*. Several wealthy patrons rush the man who got the last copy. The bidding war begins.

"I stood in line for hours and paid forty dollars," the man says. "I won't sell, but I'll rent it to you for ten bucks a read." A wealthy woman flashes a bill and snatches the paper.

"Five minutes," the man says. "Five minutes is all you get."

"They're printing more!" The vendor shouts, trying to ward off a riot. "I'll have new deliveries any moment."

~ ~ ~

"You must read this for yourself," Harriet Beecher Stowe tells her husband, livid with rage. "The words are too unspeakable." When he just stares at her, she sighs in exasperation and reads aloud.

> **SPA: Do you not fear this exposé may cause you trouble?**
> **VCW: What I do is for a greater purpose. The social world is in the very agony of its new birth, and somebody must be hurled forward into the gap. I have the power, I think, to compel Mr. Beecher to come forward and do the duty for humanity from which he shrinks.**
> **And let it be known that we have five hundred biographies of other oracles of society who live lives similar to those presented in this article.**

In Rochester, New York, Susan B. Anthony and thirteen other suffragists, after much wrangling, are finally allowed to register to vote. As they leave the registration station, reporters bombard them.

225

"Do you have a comment about Mrs. Woodhull's bombshell, Miss Anthony?" one asks.

"La-de-dah and lullaby, what has the prostitute done now?"

As Susan skims the page, her eyes widen in horror.

> **SPA:** There are rumors that you have attempted to blackmail the parties with this information.
>
> **VCW:** There is not money enough to purchase my silence. I believe it my duty to light up and destroy the heap of rottenness that, in the name of religion, marital sanctity, and social purity now passes as our social system!
>
> I know there are other churches just as false, other pastors just as recreant to their professed morality. But Plymouth Church is a great congregation, and Mr. Beecher a most eminent man. When a beacon is fired on the mountain, the little hills light up. This exposition will send inquisition through churches and conservative society. And that is its point.

"I have no comment to anything that harlot says," Susan says, handing back the paper. "Not now. Not ever."

In Washington, President Grant summons Ben Butler and Frederick Douglass to the White House to discuss the exposé.

"Henry Ward will be fine," Douglass assures him. "There's an entire community that won't let his reputation be sacrificed."

"That is true," Butler agrees. "I'm sure Beecher's Boys have already gathered."

"The good news, Gentlemen," the President says, firing up a cigar, "is that this will cook The Woodhull's goose, so I shouldn't have to worry about any competition from her on Tuesday."

Later the same evening, reporters bombard Theodore Tilton as he leaves the Pennsylvania auditorium where he has lectured. One hands him a *Weekly*. Tilton turns white as he reads.

> **SPA: Mr. Tilton confided this story to you?**
>
> **VCW: Yes. And I am persuaded that in his inmost mind he will be glad the skeleton is out of his closet. That he believes his feelings are wounded by this affair is the result of bogus sentimentality pumped into his imagination because our sickly phariseeism has humbugged him into a belief that he ought feel so.**

"The tongue's a wild beast no man can tame, and like a wolf, it now seeks to devour the chief shepherd of the flock, together with my own pretty lamb," Tilton comments. "A great wrong has been done to my wife . . . in whose sorrow I have greater sorrow. That is all I have to say." He stalks away.

Chapter 33

William Vanderbilt is surprised when Tennie pops into his office at New York Central Railroad, which he runs for his father. He is even more surprised when she hands him a bag of money.

"What's this?" William asks, taking the bag.

"My god, it's money, Billy Boy. Lots of money."

"I don't understand."

"Tell the Old Goat Tennessee Celeste Claflin paid double her debt as promised." She sashays to the door and turns, grinning at William's gaping mouth. "You might want to use some of that dough to hire decent nurses. And get the old boy out in the fresh air once in awhile, for god's sake."

Meanwhile, Blood is handing out bonuses to the *Weekly* staff when policemen burst in with warrants. The sergeant clamps cuffs on Blood while his men handcuff the others.

"What's the meaning of this?" Blood asks.

"You are under arrest for sending obscenity through the U.S. Postal Service. Where are Mrs. Woodhull and Miss Claflin?"

"I wouldn't tell you if I knew," Blood says.

"No matter. We'll find them."

The deputies spread through the facilities, smashing presses and ransacking desks and cabinets. They remove every document and every copy of the *Weekly* they can find. When the office has been stripped, the sergeant shoves Blood roughly out the door.

A short time later, church bells on Broad Street chime noon as Victoria's carriage travels down Wall Street. Suddenly U.S. marshals block the way. The carriage stops abruptly, and Victoria leans out the window.

"Why have we stopped?" She calls up to the coachman.

"Because you are under arrest," says one marshal, flinging open the carriage door.

Seeing every available space stacked high with newspapers, the marshal sprawls across the sisters' laps while his cohort grabs the reins. Victoria turns ashen and barely pulls the carriage door shut before the horses jolt away. Tennie laughs and bounces her knee to annoy the marshal, but even her face is riddled with concern.

At the Federal courthouse, police torch the newspapers in the street as Victoria and Tennie are led to an examination room. Victoria refuses to be intimidated.

"We may be women, but we know our rights! We demand a public hearing and will not say a word without our attorney."

As if on cue, a large man with a large head walks in. He has a crop of wavy gray hair and a full, walrus mustache. Diamonds drip off his pudgy hands and everywhere else on his person he can find to put them. His blue plaid pantaloons and bright red vest define flamboyance. His complexion is ruddy from alcohol, and he has a brusque British accent.

"I am Attorney William Howe," he tells the sisters. "Your father has asked me to represent you, if that's all right."

"My god, the man they call the voice of organized crime," says Tennie. "Considering some of the scumbuckets you've gotten off, no offense, you must be good. So it's fine by me."

Victoria shrugs her consent, too stunned to think clearly.

"They have destroyed your presses and taken the men to Jefferson Market Prison," Howe reports.

"My god, the Black Hole of Calcutta," Tennie says.

"Pearl too?" asks Victoria. "I fear for his health."

"No. Because of his advanced years, the judge let him go."

"Thank goodness. What about the others?"

"Your pressman Hume has made bail, and your nephew Channing will be released shortly."

"Mother and Maggie will never forgive me."

"Mrs. Woodhull, we must talk about your defense."

"Yes. The marshals said the warrant was issued to Mr. Comstock based on a complaint by three men. Who are they?"

"One is a postal employee; the others are obviously agents of Beecher. One attends his church and the other works for Mr. Bowen. I believe Comstock had the paper mailed to entrap you."

"That pious pit bull!" Tennie slaps the table in anger. Victoria shushes her with a look.

"Apparently the cowardly Christian community seeks to destroy you to cover up the rotten state of society," Howe continues. "But don't worry. I'll prove that what you printed is no more obscene than the Bible itself."

The next morning, Stephen Andrews visits the sisters in their cell.

"I'm glad you've been spared," Victoria tells him, kissing his cheeks. "You're not endangering yourself by visiting us, are you?"

"*Nyet*, my dear. Once the judge let me go, he cannot re-arrest me, unless I do something else. Which is why I have come. I wanted you to hear it from my own lips that I am deserting you—in presence only, never in my heart. I have been offered a position on *The Crucible* and have accepted. I am truly sorry, but I have my own destiny to fulfill."

"I understand, Pearl. I shall miss you greatly. You have advanced my education in social issues beyond what I could have imagined, and I will be eternally grateful. Perhaps I should have listened to you and Papa. . . . But Mr. Howe has every anticipation that we will be freed today."

Victoria gives Andrews one last hug as the warden arrives to take the sisters to their bail hearing. "*Namaste.*"

"And I say to you, as said in the Bible, *Mizpah*—may you go with God," Pearl says. "My little *minsk,* I shall miss your spirit," he tells Tennie, patting her shoulder.

"You've got your charms yourself, Prof Perlo." Tennie has a tear in her eye as Stephen Pearl Andrews walks out of their lives and they turn to follow the warden.

~ ~ ~

"The DA is a member of Plymouth Church and Beecher's relative," Howe whispers to Victoria as the District Attorney steps forward to address the judge. "It's a connection we can use against them."

"Your Honor, the state requests bail of ten thousand dollars each," the DA says. "The defendants are guilty of unjust and malicious libel against one of the purest and most revered citizens of our country. A man whose character it is well worth the while of the government of the United States to vindicate."

"Objection! My clients are not on trial for libel, and government vindication is outside this case!"

"Overruled. An example is needed, and we propose to make one of these women. Bail is set at eight thousand each. Hearing will be next Tuesday."

"Your Honor, Tuesday is Election Day. The courts are closed."

"I stand corrected. Hearing will be Monday, November fourth. Court is adjourned."

As the sisters are being led out, George Francis Train rushes in, his knee-high red patent boots clacking frantically against the floor. The charming, six-foot, curly-haired and bearded man is forty-one and dressed foppishly in a tight, black pants, purple brocade jacket and lime green satin vest. The yellow carnation in the buttonhole of his full-length, sealskin coat shakes as he raises his fist and yells.

"Don't worry, Ladies, I have just returned from my sail around the world, which everyone said could not be accomplished in eighty days, but I have done it. And you are my new cause! Your journal has voices from the seventh heaven and gabblings from a frog pond. It's an amazing paper with thought and information that can be found nowhere else! But it is not obscene! This is persecution! A violation of citizen rights under the First Amendment! George Francis Train will stand your bail and free you from the dungeon!"

Unfortunately, before bail can be arranged, Attorney Howe receives word that Luther Challis has obtained a libel warrant against the sisters.

"Libel is a more serious offense," he tells them. "If you are released now, you will be re-arrested and taken to Jefferson Market."

"Isn't that where James is?"

"Yes, but you wouldn't see him, and trust me, you don't want to go there. Spend the weekend at Ludlow Street Jail. The food is better and

231

accommodations more comfortable. This case will be thrown out on Monday, and we can then use Train's money for bail on the libel suit."

The warden of the L-shaped, redbrick county jail at Ludlow Street and Essex Market Place treats them kindly as he leads them through a maze of corridors to one of the 87 ten-foot-square cells.

"You'll find our quarters are not so bad," he tells them. "The jail is only ten years old and well maintained. A bit of trivia, if you like: It was named in honor of Lt. Augustus Ludlow, who in the War of 1812 prompted the badly wounded Captain Lawrence to utter his famous, 'Don't give up the ship.'"

"Good advice," Tennie says. "Sis and I will never give up our ship until they take away our last breath, right, Vic?"

Victoria forces a weak smile but remains silent as they turn down another corridor. The warden continues his tour-guide monologue.

"The long, wide windows, although barred, provide more light and ventilation than any prison in the country, and of course inmates enjoy time in the yard daily."

"So who are our roommates?" Tennie asks.

"Most are incarcerated for civil offenses, so they aren't dangerous. This is where they'll probably put Boss Tweed if and when he is finally convicted." They turn down another corridor. "We call this area Fifth Avenue." They stop at Cell 11, which holds two iron cots, a chair, and a washbasin. The clang of keys echoes down the corridor as the warden opens the door.

"You'll find the cots tolerable enough and sheets clean. I'm sorry our better accommodations aren't available. The head warden's family is occupying our guest quarters while his house is being remodeled. And a prominent merchant is sleeping off a binge in the citizen bedroom. But I promise to make you as comfortable as possible."

"This will be fine. Thank you," Victoria says. "We have never asked for favored treatment, only fairness."

"Perhaps these poems will be helpful for your defense," the warden tells Victoria, handing her a book by Alexander Pope. "He's written stanzas more indecent than anything in your article."

"Thank you, Sir," Victoria says.

"My wife is cooking you a hot meal, and we also have bathing facilities."

"My god, that's what I could use!" Tennie says. "The sanctimonious hypocrites have sullied my hygiene."

A short time later, she sits on one of the cots, half-dressed and smiling. She dries her hair with a ragged towel.

"My god, Sis, that bath was great. You should have one." She glances at Victoria, who sits on the other cot looking grave and distant. "My god, look at it this way. We'll have firsthand information for an article on prison conditions. You can bet the other prison reformers aren't advocating from such personal experience."

"I wonder how the children are. And James, in that awful place. Why didn't we realize this would happen?"

"My god, Sis, who could know the religious machine and male zeitgeist wouldn't let a small thing like the Constitution bother them? But we'll beat the charges. Howe may be corrupt and a blowhard, but he's good. Better'n good."

"Of all the scenarios I imagined, I never thought— To subject my daughter to the scorn— Thank goodness Byron—" Her voice catches. Silent tears flow down her cheeks.

Church bells toll six o'clock and the warden returns with a bountiful meal of boiled chicken and potatoes.

"My god, this looks delicious. Better than the skilly we was expectin'," Tennie says. "Thanks, Warden."

"My wife wanted to give you something special. We are both quite upset about your treatment."

A half-hour later, Johnnie Green and about 20 other reporters visit. Tennie grins as Johnnie hands her a cigar and lights it. She takes a deep puff.

"Sorry I can't offer you gentlemen some whiskey," she says.

"Are they treating you okay, Tennie?" Ashley Cole asks.

"The warden of this fine hotel is an upright guy. Make sure you praise him in your reports."

"Will you get out on Monday?" Johnnie asks.

"Our attorney thinks so. He says we got a good case if the Christians stay out of it. But remember this, gentlemen, Sis and I are martyrs to a cause that affects each of you. If newspapers aren't allowed to have their say, the status quo will turn us all into sheep to follow erring leaders."

"Tennie, be silent," Victoria commands. "Whatever you say can be used against us in court!"

"But enough of our tribulations," Tennie tells the reporters. "Go home and read Shakespeare, read Byron and Whitman, read the Bible. Read this book the warden gave us—you guys ever read Pope's *Rape of the Lock*?" Tennie shrugs as Victoria motions her to shush. "Anyway, go do some readin' and then come to court on Monday and don't let them tell us we are vile!"

Chapter 34

On Sunday morning, Plymouth Church is abuzz as the overflow of people spill out the doors and make the edifice an island in a sea of people. Deacons try to control the curious throng and stop reporters from entering. As the choir sings "Rescue the Perishing," all eyes fix on Beecher, who walks serenely to the platform, throws off his floppy hat, flings his cloak from his shoulders, and sits.

When the song ends, Henry Ward, eyes sparkling and face flushed, opens his Bible.

"Our text today is from the book of Luke, Chapter twelve: 'Beware ye of the leaven of the Pharisees, which is hypocrisy. For there is nothing covered that shall not be revealed; neither hid that shall not be known.'"

The congregation can hardly believe what they are hearing. They wait breathlessly for Beecher to comment on the scandal, but the Reverend adroitly avoids the subject the entire sermon.

When the doors swing open and the congregation files out, reporters rush "Tearful" Tommy Shearman. Nicknamed for his courtroom histrionics, Shearman is superintendent of Plymouth Church's Sunday school and Beecher's attorney. He pats his impeccably groomed hair and peers over the top of his gold spectacles when one reporter asks if Beecher refuted Victoria's charges.

"No, Sir," Shearman says. "That harlot's name was not allowed to stain the pulpit."

"Does he intend to refute them?"

"I do not think he will take the trouble."

"Will the Church Board investigate?"

"Not at all. We know our pastor and don't propose to take anything a woman like that says against him."

Johnnie Green, realizing Beecher is not greeting his parishioners as usual, slips to the rear of the church. He springs forward as Henry Ward sneaks out the door on Cranberry Street.

"Dr. Beecher! Will you comment on the allegations in the *Weekly*?" Johnnie asks.

"If a man meets with injustice, it is not required that he be roused to respond. It is by trials that God shapes us for higher things."

"So you're saying the whole matter is a fraud?"

"Entirely." Beecher brushes past Green, who calls after him.

"Is Mr. Comstock working as your agent against The Woodhull?"

"Absolutely not," Beecher says, stopping and turning to Green. "I do not even know the man." He strides away.

The same afternoon, Victoria and Tennie sit in their jail cell reading the Sunday newspapers. Tennie looks up from the *Brooklyn Eagle*.

"This article calls you the Archpriestess of Priapus. What does that mean?"

"Priapus is the Greek god of fertility," Victoria responds.

"My god, the one with the big phallus? I'd be his archpriestess any day!"

"It wasn't meant as a joke, Tennie."

"I know, Sis, but if you don't find the humor, they're gonna win the war." She cuts out the article and then picks up the *Dispatch*. "I like this one. It mentions me. Says I'm quite the looker with 'ruby lips, splendid teeth, well-cut features, and a bright, animated expression.' That's better than the *Mercury* sayin' I curse like a mule skinner and smell of cigars."

"'The female name has never been more disgraced and degraded than by these two women,' Victoria reads from the *Times*. "I should have known the *Times* would be against us." Tears fill her eyes. "Is there no one who supports us?"

"My god, the *Weekly* has been banned in Germany." Tennie says. "Ma's not going to like that."

"Speaking of—" Victoria nods toward where the warden ushers Roxanna, Buck, and Zulu Maud to the cell.

"Didn't I warn you this would happen?" Buck bellows.

Victoria ignores him and rushes to Zulu Maud. Wraps her in a big hug.

"Oh, darling, I am so sorry. I am a terrible mother. When I am out of here I vow to do better if you will only forgive me."

"You both get down on your knees right now and ask *Gott* to forgive you for not heedin' your father's advice," Roxanna orders.

"Please don't give us none of your gum, Ma," Tennie says, grimacing at the hard floor. "How 'bout if we just stand here and pray for a miracle to turn the locks and leave the doors ajar like what happened in the Bible?"

"I'm afraid Mr. Beecher is praying more richly to keep them secure," Victoria bemoans.

"I oughta take a whip to ya right now for bringin' this shame to our family," Buck says.

"My god, Pa, it's going to be fine. Thanks for hiring that pitbull Howe. He says we ain't said nothin' that ain't in the Bible itself."

"Please, all of you, no fights and no lectures," Victoria pleads. "Just let me hug my daughter and then take her away from this dismal place."

On Monday morning, Victoria and Tennie enter pleas of not guilty, and the Commissioner immediately sends them back to Ludlow Street Jail under additional bail. Attorney Howe steps forward, diamonds sparkling, to issue a protest.

"Your Honor, I request that a court date be set now and bail be reduced," Howe says. "Mr. Comstock has not presented one shred of evidence against my clients. This is flagrant and malicious persecution instigated for the revenge of certain persons in high stations. In fact, I demand these women be released. They have done nothing more than exercise their rights under the First Amendment to the Constitution of the United States and have published nothing more obscene than the Word of God itself!"

Spectators gasp. The commissioner bangs his gavel.

"Enough, Mr. Howe! Request denied. This court is adjourned."

That night Johnnie Green visits the sisters, bringing more newspapers.

"Me and the boys'll be around tomorrow to keep you company," he tells them. "But I brought Beecher's paper and Tilton's, too, so you can see what they have to say. It's a joke."

"Beecher comments?" Tennie takes the *Christian Union* and skims the paper. "The man's got a sense of humor, I'll say that."

"What does he say?" Victoria asks.

"There's an article headed Scandal, but it's not about us. It says 'no sin is more prevalent among professors of religion and less recognized as sinful than speaking evil of others.' He's one smooth chump, that preacher."

"This just says the editor will have something interesting to say in the next issue," Victoria says, tossing *The Golden Age* aside. "More non-saying, I imagine." She sits on the cot and stares at the cracks in the concrete floor, deep in thought.

"Well, at least they're not calling you harlots like Miss Anthony did," Johnnie says. "The good news is that Lucy Stone's *Woman's Journal* has been silenced, at least temporarily. There's been a huge fire in Boston. Took out most of the commercial district. It's just now been contained."

"My god, it's a good thing we're in jail. Them Stoners might've blamed us for startin' the blaze."

"They're not sure what the final damages will be, but it's bad. Most of the horses have some kind of flu so men had to pull the carts and reel the hoses. Between that and lousy water pressure. . . . Fire Chief John Damrell's been warning about the latter for a long time. Maybe someone will finally listen."

"As usual, nobody pays attention to common sense until it's too late," Victoria says.

"Oh, and speaking of fires," Johnnie continues, "Frederick Douglass has lost his home in Rochester. They suspect arson."

"Why would anyone want to harm Mr. Douglass?" Victoria asks. "He is a true man of honor. I shall send him a note." Victoria glances over as the warden appears with a telegram. Her brow furrows as she opens it.

"My god, who's it from, Sis?"

"Elizabeth Cady. Oh, I cannot—" She smiles as her eyes skim the page. "She has not deserted me! Listen: 'Dear Victoria, The grief I feel in the vile raking of you is threefold: sympathy for you, shame on the men who persecute you, and the danger in abusing one of our greatest blessings, a free press.'"

"My god, that's great!"

"Are you going to vote for me tomorrow, Mr. Green?" Victoria asks.

"Yes, Ma'am. I figure Mr. Grant's going to win anyway so I might as well make a statement with my vote. Several of us are."

"You will never know the depth of our gratitude."

Chapter 35

On November 5, Election Day 1872, Victoria languishes in jail, refusing visitors. She barely speaks, even to Tennie, but spends the day in a troubled trance while Tennie reads the headlines: "Grant wins in landslide!" "Women vote illegally!" "Equal Rights candidate in jail!" "Voter turnout exceeds ninety percent! Two party system emerges stronger than ever!"

"My god, Grant got like eighty percent of the electoral votes," Tennie says, quoting the *Herald*. "Took every state but five."

"He would have defeated Jesus Christ," Victoria says bitterly.

"Don't take it too hard, Sis. The good news is that by the time we beat these stupid charges, everyone in America will know your name and how you were persecuted for your honesty. You'll have their vote in four years!"

"We'll see what they do now, ladies!" George Francis Train's voice brings a weak smile to Victoria's lips. He waves his newspaper *The Train Ligue* as he strides to their cell. "I have challenged Master Comstock and his ass of a law by reprinting your entire exposé and comparing it for obscenity against Shakespeare, Alexander Pope, and the Holy Bible! I shall flood the newspapers with letters on your behalf and do whatever else I can, no expense spared. We must get you released. Speed is of the essence! I spent some time behind bars, you know. In Dublin in the mid-sixties, for serving the cause of freedom with the Feinian Brotherhood and the Irish Republic."

"You were the first to come to our aid, and we shall be the last to forget it." Victoria pecks his cheek, drifts into melancholy thought.

"Don't mind my sister, Mr. Train," Tennie says. "But the election . . . ya know."

"If it makes you feel any better, Mrs. Woodhull, my friend who helped tally votes said they counted almost three thousand write-in votes for you in New York before the Commission ordered them destroyed.

And who knows about all the states where you were actually on the ballot. I heard they were throwing those away, too, though."

"My god, we'll sue!"

"We're not suing anyone, Tennie. I've seen enough courtrooms to last a lifetime."

On Friday following the election, Federal marshals usher Victoria and Tennie from the jail wagon and through the noisy crowd gathered at Jefferson Market Court. Attorney Howe and Zulu Maud meet them at the door. As they walk to the courtroom, Howe briefs Victoria.

"This hearing is a preliminary on the libel charges, but the judge will also address the writ of habeas corpus we've filed to get James released. I want Zulu Maud up front and looking extremely sad. Can you do that, Zulu Maud?"

"How can she look otherwise with her family in jail?" Victoria asks, caressing her daughter's hair.

The din of conversation increases as they enter the courtroom. Blood is ushered in under guard. His presence calms Victoria, but also distresses her since his usual impeccable appearance is marred by the rumpling and stench of prison. With a tremulous smile, she sits with Tennie. Lined up on the other side of the room are the dark forces of the faux-puritans. Luther Challis wears a black suit, white necktie, and carries his black silk umbrella.

Victoria, however, is more interested in the other antagonist. She studies Anthony Comstock, who makes notes in a small, purple, leather-bound journal. At twenty-eight years of age, he is short, heavy-set, and bald on top. His thick, ginger-colored, mutton-chop whiskers do nothing to soften the sternness of his face. A scar on his right cheek dates back to the early days of his crusade against vice. He wears his standard outfit: a wrinkled black suit and crisply starched white shirt. A bow tie squeezes his thick neck, hanging askew at his muscular throat.

All rise as the judge bangs for order.

Buck testifies first, followed by George Francis Train. Then it's Tennie's turn.

"Yes, I have been intimate with the scoundrel Challis," she testifies. "But we ain't been on squeezing' terms since I figured out what a scoundrel he was."

"Maybe you got too old for him," someone yells out.

"Order in the court! I will not have outbursts, or I will clear the room!" The judge raps his gavel on the desk and nods at Tennie to continue.

"Mr. Challis had actually proposed to take my sister and me to the Masked Ball on the evening we wrote about, but at the last minute reneged. Since we had the costumes, we went anyway and saw who had replaced us as his date: Fourteen-year-old girls he and his friend might more easily take advantage of!

"I sent him a routine letter asking him to back Victoria's lecture at the Steinway," Tennie explains when questioned about a letter supposedly sent to blackmail Challis. "Two prominent banks and a certain popular preacher had already agreed to help sponsor the event."

Luther Challis, of course, refutes Tennie's testimony, denies even knowing her.

"Ordinarily I would not have attended such an orgy," he says of the French Ball. "But Mr. Maxwell and I were bored and decided to go slumming. We soon tired of the spectacle and went home."

"And you never kissed Miss Claflin or had other relations with her?"

"No, Sir."

"Tell me about this blackmail letter."

"Miss Claflin sent me a copy of an article derogatory to my reputation. She threatened to print it if I did not advance her two hundred dollars immediately."

"Did you pay?"

"No. I told her to print what she liked and I would see her in court. I tell you now that I will spend a hundred thousand dollars to secure her conviction and teach her that blackmail and libel are not the way to do business."

"Will you present this article Miss Claflin supposedly gave you and the accompanying letter?" Howe asks, jumping to his feet.

"No. I threw them in the trash where they belonged."

"So you have no proof of your accusation." Howe gives the judge a pointed look before sitting back down. Challis is dismissed.

"The French Masked Ball was an affair attended by the city's best men and worst women," Mr. Maxwell says, corroborating Tennie's testimony when called to the stand. "Miss Claflin's article clearly and accurately spells out the events of the evening. I heard Luther use the words in question myself."

Finally Comstock is called. He speaks before he is questioned.

"Your Honor, I cannot tell you the horror I felt as I read the filth these two harlots spewed in their paper."

"Objection!" Howe says.

"Overruled!"

"Isn't it true that you receive half the fines collected under your warrants?" Howe questions.

"Yes, but—"

"So Anthony Comstock looks out for himself as well as the Almighty, eh?"

"It is my Christian duty to bring confusion to the partisans of free lust! Debasing publications are sold on the streets as freely as roasted chestnuts, and they are nothing but feeders for the brothels! We are mired in a swamp of sin at the mouth of the foulest sewer, but I attempt each day to do something for Jesus!"

"Well I believe he would be sorely disappointed in you today, Mr. Comstock."

"Objection!" Comstock screams. "Do not allow this man to slander our Savior as these harlots have slandered his messenger in Brooklyn!"

"Mr. Comstock, you cannot object," the judge says, heaving a weary sigh. "Let's move on." He nods for Howe to continue his questioning.

"Mr. Comstock, you say Mr. Blood personally sold you the offending issue of *Woodhull & Claflin's Weekly*. Would you please point the Colonel out to the court?"

Comstock looks around, confused. He points to a stranger who sits in the front row and blushes as Attorney Howe laughs.

"Your Honor, please note for the record that Mr. Comstock has pointed out the wrong man."

Victoria is called last. Howe asks her when she last spoke with Luther Challis.

"Just the other day. Mr. Challis visited us in jail to bribe us into denying what we printed about him. The warden can confirm this."

"But neither you nor your sister asked for, or took, money in exchange for your silence?" Howe asks.

"That is correct."

She is next asked about Blood's involvement in the newspaper.

"The Colonel has nothing to do with the *Weekly*," she says. "He handled our banking firm and counsels us on financial matters. He was the city auditor of St. Louis, you know."

By late afternoon, the examinations are complete and the weary judge rubs his temples as he bangs his gavel.

"I've heard enough. I reserve my decision on this case until one week from today. In the meantime, I order Mrs. Woodhull and Miss Claflin to Ludlow Street and Mr. Blood to Jefferson Market Prison."

"Your Honor, bail must be set!"

The judge ignores Howe's protest.

"One week! Court is dismissed."

Back in jail, Victoria flips through newspapers. An item in the *Brooklyn Eagle* brings a smile.

"Finally someone besides our allies understands what is at stake in this case," she says. "Listen to this, Tennie. 'That penal consequences are set against mailing any materials Federal authorities may think are of a bad character, whether they are in fact or not, shows that, without knowing it, our citizens are living under a law more narrow and oppressive than any people with a written Constitution ever lived under before.'"

"My god, that's the truth. And they call this the land of the free," Tennie says.

Another week creeps by and the sisters are still in jail. Johnnie Green and other friends keep them apprised of the news. They are only slightly surprised to hear that Horace Greeley, after losing his wife and the election, and then being ousted from the *Tribune* by Reid, has gone insane and been committed to a mental institution. But even with visitors, the women become listless from the confinement. Victoria rouses slightly when Attorney Howe brings a report of Blood's bail hearing.

"Did they release him?" she asks.

"No. The judge ruled he was probably guilty of a misdemeanor— that's exactly how he put it—*probably* guilty. He did set bail, however. It's five thousand dollars."

"We must get the money!"

"I am more concerned about the two of you. It is a travesty of justice to hold you so long without a trial."

"We are comfortable enough."

"My god, we're even gettin' used to it," Tennie says. "'Cept for itchin' for a man, it almost feels like home."

~ ~ ~

As November draws to its close, the sisters are still locked up, the judge having again postponed their trial and denied bail. They sag wearily on their cots as Johnnie Green visits.

"I've got all kinds of news," he tells them.

"Tell away, Johnnie," Tennie says. "We're not going anywhere."

"Mr. Greeley died yesterday."

"My god, we expected it. Sis had a vision of a coffin following him around way back last summer," Tennie says.

"The Commodore has given each of the Greeley girls ten thousand dollars. Apparently Horace paid off Cornelius Junior's gambling debts when Vanderbilt refused to."

"My god, that's my Com."

"You'll get a kick out of Mr. Greeley's last words. He said, 'Be kind to Boy Tilton. He is foolish but young.'"

Tennie laughs. Victoria chuckles bitterly.

"Oh! And guess what! Miss Anthony has been arrested!"

"Get outta here!"

"Sure enough. For voting."

"I guarantee she isn't languishing in jail," Victoria says.

"Johnnie, can't you write something that will help us?" Tennie asks.

"I did, but my boss refused to publish it. Don't give up, though. Reporters are starting to agree that your right to a speedy trial is being denied. An inspired word from you, Victoria, might bring them out on your side."

"If only I had one to give."

~ ~ ~

The tolling church bells count off 32 days as the sisters wait for justice. Even conservative newspapers begin to ask when they will be tried. They finally get a bail hearing, but the amount set is thousands more than they can pay. That evening, Victoria is tossing in restless sleep when suddenly her eyes fly open. She bolts upright, shakes Tennie.

"Tennie! Wake up!"

"My god, Sis, what's wrong? Are we free?"

"Nothing's wrong. I've just had a dream."

"My god, who's gonna die? Please tell me Luther Challis."

"Remember when Demosthenes came in a vision and sent us to New York?" Victoria paces, her face flushed with excitement. "That was when, after visiting me for so many years, he finally told me his name. Remember? He showed me the house on Great Jones Street, and we found it exactly as I had envisioned it, down to the For Rent sign on the door! And the open book on the table in the study was there just like in the vision! When I saw the title—*The Orations of Demosthenes*—I knew there was a higher purpose for us here. We'd still be in Pittsburgh, or Indiana, or Ohio or something if I hadn't had that vision."

"My god, I prefer this cell, even if it does stink a bit. It's a great memory, Sis, but what's your point?"

"I had that vision in October of sixty-eight. The same month Mrs. Tilton and Mr. Beecher began their affair."

"My god, how about that for irony."

"Don't you understand? Part of my mission was to expose the affair! To tear the masks off the self-righteous hypocrites so Christian love could reign."

"Gotcha. But what about ruling in a city of ships and all that?" Tennie yawns.

"If everything else has happened as it was supposed to, I'll have my mansion back and rule my country one day, too. We must get out of jail and start planning our next campaign. Wouldn't our country's Centennial year be a perfect time for a woman to finally be President?"

"My god, it would! And I'm with you on getting out of here. These manless beds are makin' me old."

Chapter 36

"Gentlemen, did you read The Woodhull's letter in the *Herald* this past weekend?" Bowen asks two Plymouth Church deacons he has summoned to his office. When they shake their heads, Bowen picks up the paper, and reads, "'Suppose, Mr. Editor, that enemies of yours should throw you into a cell, suppress your newspaper, and prosecute your publisher. Would not every land ring with the outrage?'"

"Good Lord, that's martyr talk."

"Yes. And that's just a snippet of what she says. She concludes with: 'To the public I say that they may succeed in crushing me, even to the loss of my life, but from the ashes of my body a thousand Victorias will spring up to avenge my death by carrying my work forward to victory."

"Let's hope she don't die. She'll be the John Brown of the woman's movement."

"Exactly. And if they sit in jail any longer waiting to go to trial, they'll be martyrs without dying." Bowen hands the deacons a thick bag of money. "Here's sixteen thousand dollars. Bail them out. But for god's sake, keep my name away from it."

As soon as the deacons leave, Bowen pens a note.

~ ~ ~

"Ladies, you are free women at last," the Warden says as he unlocked the jail cell.

Tennie hoots in glee, but Victoria stops her from dashing out.

"Tennie, wait. It's a trick. We've authorized no bail."

"Nonetheless, it has been paid. Someone must have seen your letter in the *Herald* and been moved to help," the Warden says.

"Who posted bail?"

"It was anonymous."

"Maybe it was the Com," Tennie says.

"Would you contact Mr. Howe for us?" Victoria asks.

"My god, Sis, even if it's for just an hour, I'm taking the reprieve!"

"Mrs. Woodhull, your bail's been made. You have to go."

Ashley Cole is waiting for them at the prison gates. Tennie throws herself in his arms.

"Was it you, Ashley? Did you bail us out? I'll show you lots of gratitude if it was."

"Tennie, behave," Victoria says.

"I'd like to say yes, my little minx," Ashley says, "but I'm not sure who it was. I got an anonymous note suggesting it might be Mr. Beecher."

"I cannot believe it was," Victoria muses. "Unless. . . . Perhaps the man has a conscience after all."

Unfortunately, they are no sooner home then a new warrant filed by Comstock sends them back to jail. Comstock cackles gleefully as this time the judge sends them to the horrible Jefferson Market Prison at Tenth Street and Sixth Avenue. Their bail is another eight thousand dollars each.

Inside the tall iron gates, the sisters are led to one of the tiny, clapboard sheds where farmers once sold their produce but which now serve as jail cells. The sheds are in horrible disrepair and covered with grime, since they will soon be torn down to be replaced by a huge, Victorian Gothic penitentiary already under construction. Victoria stumbles as she and Tennie are shoved inside and the door slams shut. She screams as a rat, frightened from its quarters, runs across the floor. Victoria looks at the filth and inhales the rancid smell. She grabs the bars to keep from fainting. The one tiny window has no pane, and the frigid air coming through it has a putrid odor. Even Tennie seems dismal and concerned.

Luckily, Henry Bowen again secretly pays the bail.

~ ~ ~

"My god, you have gone completely gray overnight from all this insanity!" Harriet Beecher Stowe stops short as she bursts into Henry Ward's office.

249

"Now, Hattie, I was almost there already. But I'm sure that's not why you stormed in here."

"You're right. Did you bail those jailbirds out?"

"Of course not, although I'm glad they're free. Maybe this whole mess can now be forgotten."

"We are not wrestling with flesh and blood here, Hank. That wretched Woodhull is under satanic spirits. She is a snake who deserves a good swat with a shovel for precipitating this despicable foulness being dribbled over you." Henry holds a rose quartz to the light and doesn't respond. Harriet plops into a chair. "Do you not care that she means to ruin you? She applied for a license to speak in Boston, but I spoke to Governor Claflin and she is banned. He was only too happy to help so people don't think he's related to them."

"Hattie, why don't you leave the poor woman alone?"

"I have met the first Mrs. Blood." At Henry Ward's questioning look, she explains. "The Colonel's deserted wife. She moved to Farmington with their daughter, who Mrs. Woodhull has not allowed Mr. Blood to see."

"Now, Hattie, you don't know that. It could have been his choice. Or Mrs. Blood's."

"Mrs. Blood is a lovely, dignified, and accomplished woman. She says the Colonel was from one of the best families in St. Louis and had every prospect of turning his great honors from the war into a prosperous future. Hope and love is not yet dead in her heart, and I am praying for justice to put Mrs. Woodhull in the penitentiary and leave the Colonel free to be redeemed."

"Hattie dear, I'm sure Eunice will fix you a hot cup of tea and listen raptly to all your gossip. I must work on my sermon. It's about the rewards of loving. Perhaps you should attend services tomorrow."

"Fine. Just don't be too nonchalant. Mr. Stowe has had a vision, and this mess is not resolved!" She flounces out.

Chapter 37

On December 23, 1872, Victoria speaks in Springfield, Massachusetts. Her subject: "Moral Cowardice and Modern Hypocrisy." A large crowd waits to enter the hall. Everyone stares as a huge, red-faced old man stalks up and grabs a tiny, young woman. He knocks her bonnet off as he jerks her away by the hair.

"I forbade you to come, didn't I? Didn't I?" he screams. "You wanna be a prostitute like these sirens I can arrange that!"

The woman struggles against him, but he punches her in the face and slings her over his shoulder like a sack of potatoes. Her friends cluck in helpless anger as the man stalks away. When the meeting begins, the red-faced man is in the front row, smirking as Victoria addresses the assemblage.

"Governor Claflin, banning us in Boston, said they had enough bad women in Boston without permitting me to come and further demoralize them. They *do* have bad women, and I recently named some of them. Calling me a common streetwalker, the Governor refused to let me, as he put it, 'open my vile mouth in the city so recently honored by Mr. Beecher's presence.' Apparently Mr. Beecher's celebrity makes him sacred to his pseudo-Christian supporters. I say Governor Claflin is a disgrace to the Claflin name as well as a disgrace to those who seek and speak truth! I applaud Springfield's courageous mayor for going against the Governor's order and allowing us this hall in your lovely city. Not only is freedom of press threatened by our present prosecution, but now, too, freedom of speech is under attack. Let us have no gag law! The right to elucidate even unpopular opinions is the birthright of all in our American polity!

"We have been charged with a crime and confined in jail for daring to attack hypocrisy in high places! Have you studied the list of books this pious puppy Comstock has sought to burn? Great works by Byron, Cervantes, Swedenborg, Goethe, Dante, Plutarch, Hugo, and Spencer! What will be spared from his moralistic fanaticism? Mr. Comstock has shown how easy it is to ruin the usefulness of a person by innuendo and insinuation. We have been brought to public dishonor and disrepute while not a single piece of evidence to justify the charges has been advanced. We are persecuted, forced to wallow in the American Bastille, while the persons who condemn us almost unanimously re-elect a President who is embroiled in new scandal before he is even inaugurated!

"We are assaulted for printing truth and exposing injustice, while these same assaulters venerate men who have defrauded them of their hard-earned dollars! I must confess that I do not understand it." She has to wait for the boisterous agreement to die down before she can continue. "So I promise you here and now: They may ban us in Boston, they may shut down our presses, but never will they silence our tongues! I am accountable to a Higher Power and as long as I live, I will speak truth. I will be heard. And you may kill me afterward if you must."

Victoria leaves the stage to a standing ovation, and the sisters rush to catch a train. Taking a private compartment, Victoria counts the nights' receipts.

"It's enough, Tennie!" she says, a smile brightening her face. "We can free James!" She shivers and reaches for her wrap. "Oh, my cloak! I must have dropped it. I will not take one penny of James' bail money to replace it." She rushes to look for her cape, not noticing 18-year-old Bennie Tucker coming down the aisle until they collide.

"Thee forgot this at the hall, Ma'am. I ran all the way." He blushes and holds out her cloak.

"Oh, thank you. I had just missed it." Victoria impulsively grabs the darkly handsome baby face in her hands and kisses him on the mouth. "Is that sufficient reward for such a handsome young gallant?"

"Oh, yes, Ma'am!" Tucker's eyes are held spellbound by hers. "It-It is thrilling just to meet thee!"

Victoria feels herself sink into the deep chocolate glow of his adoration. But the train jerks forward, breaking their gaze. Tucker bows and dashes off. Victoria rushes to her compartment and blows kisses out the window as the train pulls away.

"My god, Sis, what's going on?"

"Just enjoying my freedom! Isn't he the cutest thing?"

"A might young, wouldn't you say?" Tennie says, her jaw dropping as she looks out at Bennie and his three young friends.

"Most men we know are married to women half their age, so why can't women seek younger companions? You of all people should know that neither love nor lust knows the barrier of age. I am going to see that young man again."

~ ~ ~

On Christmas Eve, Victoria huddles against the bitter cold as her carriage jolts toward Jefferson Market Prison. She clutches Blood's bail money and looks out on the Christmas-adorned streets sliding past the carriage. Suddenly, an apparition appears on the carriage window: Jefferson Market Prison is in flames. Victoria covers her ears as prisoners' screams become deafening to her. Real sirens jerk her back to reality. Fire wagons wail past, and Victoria calls to the coachman, her voice shrill with panic.

"What's burning? Can you see? Is it the prison?"

"It looks like Barnum's museum again, Ma'am. Lordee, what a sight! I'll try to get around it."

"We must get to the prison! The fire will go there next! Go through the flames if you must! Just hurry! Hurry!"

Smoke and the bellows of panicked animals fill the air. Victoria holds her hankie to her nose to shut out the smell of burnt hide. The coachman whips the horses, and the carriage flies down the road, careens to a stop at the prison gates. Victoria hails a guard. Paces as she waits for Blood to be released.

Finally the gate opens, and Blood is pushed out. He looks terrible. His hair is shaggy and unkempt; his untrimmed beard and mustache do nothing to hide his gaunt cheeks. He blinks under the bright lights as Victoria flies into his arms and presses her lips to his.

"I smell," he protests.

"I don't care." Victoria breaks away and pulls him toward the carriage. "We must hurry! Barnum's new emporium is burning and it's headed this way! I was afraid I would be too late. That you would die in this horrible hell!"

They can't stop touching each other as the carriage bounces away from the prison. They near Barnum's museum and the horses whinny in fear as the carriage jerks and jostles over smoldering debris. The stench is almost unbearable. P. T. Barnum stands on the corner, staring numbly at the ruins.

Luckily the fire has been contained and the nearby Academy of Music and Tammany Hall, as well as the prison, have escaped unharmed. A few flames still lick up the side of the crumbling, charred walls of the museum, reaching toward monstrous icicles that drip slowly to their demise. Elephants, rhinos, and giraffes sizzle in the streets. Victoria gags and begins to weep.

Blood holds her against him as the carriage races away.

~ ~ ~

An ailing Comstock glowers at an announcement for Victoria's upcoming "Naked Truth" lecture at Cooper Institute in New York City. Coughing violently, he wraps a sock tightly around his neck and shuffles out into the cold January air. He is weak from his constant hacking by the time he reaches the courthouse. Only fanatic zeal keeps him on his feet long enough to swear out new warrants.

Johnnie Green, on his way to work, sees police descend on the *Weekly* office. Spurring his black steed, he gallops away. Reining quickly at Victoria's house, he leaps from the stallion and sprints inside.

"What'd ya come back for, Johnnie? Need another kiss?" Tennie asks.

"Where's Victoria? They're coming for her!"

"My god!"

"What's happening?" Victoria asks, rushing down the hallway.

"You gotta go!" Johnnie grabs her hand and runs for the door. "Hide, Tennie! They want Victoria most of all, but they'll take you, too."

"Someone warn James!" Victoria cries as Johnnie pulls her out the door and up behind him on the horse. They gallop away seconds before marshals surge toward the front door.

Zulu Maud dashes out the back door to warn Blood. Roxanna shoves Tennie into a laundry tub, sets another tub on top of it and pours in a pail of water. She opens the door just as the police push it in. They search room-to-room, Roxanna on their heels yelling obscenities in German. They find nothing and don't stay long.

"Don't worry," the captain assures his men. "She's bold enough to show up at Cooper to speak. We'll grab her there."

"Hey! There's the Colonel!" a rookie yells. He points at Zulu Maud and Blood rounding the corner. Uniforms immediately swarm them and haul Blood away.

Victoria, meanwhile, makes it safely to the Taylor Hotel in New Jersey. She telegrams Laura Cuppy Smith, and the reformer dashes to her aid, having experienced ostracization herself when her single daughter had given birth and elected to keep her baby.

"Few remain to console us in our difficult times, and only you, leading champion of radicalism, have the courage to help me!" Victoria says, wrapping Laura in a grateful hug. "You'll read my speech if I am unable to appear tonight?"

"Absolutely. You are woman's one brave voice, Mrs. Woodhull, and we will never be free if you are silenced. I am your willing servant forever."

~ ~ ~

City police and U.S. marshals encircle Cooper Institute as citizens, huddling against the wicked cold, arrive in droves. Stephen Pearl Andrews is among a group that arrives as a marshal tries to turn the crowd away by announcing that Victoria is under warrant and will not appear. A few people groan and leave.

"Is she in custody?" Andrews asks the marshal.

"No, but she will be if she shows her face here."

"Victoria will turn heaven and earth not to disappoint her supporters," Andrews shouts to the crowd. "There's going to be a speech tonight, folks. You can bet on that. Let's go on in." He goes inside and others follow. The hall buzzes with gossip as people find seats.

"Even if she doesn't show, I'm going to sit a spell and warm up. It's as cold as I can remember out there tonight."

"Enough to freeze a cow's teat right off."

"They do say The Woodhull is lightning when she gets warmed up. We sure need somma that fire tonight."

"Comstock may be the one hounding them sisters, but it's that sanctimonious Beecher behind it. You know it is."

"The Woodhull will be here, and it will be fireworks. No way am I gonna miss the show!"

Among those entering is a frail, old Quaker lady. Her bonnet, plaid shawl, and gray cloak are pulled so tightly around her it almost looks like there's no one inside. She stumbles, and one of the marshals catches her.

"Let me help you, Ma'am. Where would you like to sit?"

"Eh, Sonny?" The old woman says, cupping a hand to her ear.

"Where would you—Never mind, let me take you down front." The marshal crooks his arm, and the Quaker woman clings to it, stumbling frequently as he leads her down the aisle. Noticing his captain glaring from the unguarded doorway, the marshal motions the old lady toward a seat and hurries back to his post.

A nearby church bell tolls eight o'clock. Feet begin to stomp. Louder. Faster. A chant rise: "Woodhull! Woodhull!" Laura Cuppy Smith walks nervously onto the stage. The crowd cheers, then snickers as the old Quaker woman wanders across the front of the room.

"Ladies and Gentlemen," Laura says, "as you may know, the enemies of free speech have another order for Mrs. Woodhull's arrest. She cannot appear tonight lest she be thrust again into an American Bastille." The crowd roars in protest. Laura glances at the Quaker lady who now wanders onto the stage, but continues. "I had hoped until this minute that Victoria would appear. Since it doesn't look like she will, I will read her prepared speech in her stead."

"No! I am here!" The old Quaker woman rushes forward, throwing off her cloak and bonnet. It is Victoria!

"Comstock is defeated!" Laura cries jubilantly.

A tumultuous roar rises from the floor, so loud it threatens to bring down the building. Victoria steps to the podium, arms raised, head thrown back, hair wild, breasts heaving, and eyes on fire! Police rush forward, but the crowd threatens riot. At the captain's nod, officers surround the stage and stand down.

"I thank you, Sir, for allowing my fans not to be disappointed," Victoria says to the captain. "When I am finished, you may take me to jail."

He dips his head in acknowledgement, and Victoria stretches out her arms to quiet the protesting crowd. Her voice is fired with righteous indignation as she begins.

"I denounce Anthony Comstock as a self-appointed agent of Christ, a tool of Mr. Beecher, and a Pickwick prosecuting official! Our articles about Mr. Beecher and Mr. Challis have been reprinted in several male-run newspapers, and no one else has been arrested. But officers of the law have ruined my business, stolen my private papers, and held me in prison for weeks on end. Even with these efforts, however, the truth cannot forever be suppressed! Let tyrants prepare to meet their doom! The day of judgment is at hand!"

The crowd goes wild. It is several minutes before Victoria can go on.

"I am conducting warfare on the frightful confusion known as our social system. The government and all the wealth of the country, backed by the church, is a formidable power against the people. But there is a new gospel rising. Join me as we prepare for the coming millennium and the absolute liberty of the human heart!"

The crowd leaps to its feet in a thunderous ovation. Victoria bows her head in humble acknowledgement, then throws open her arms in a gesture of crucifixion and steps to the front of the stage. Holding out her wrists to the marshals, she silences the crowd's protests with a shake of her head. As the handcuffs click shut and the marshals lead her out, the crowd stands as one, fists in the air, tears streaming down their faces. "Woodhull! Woodhull! Woodhull!"

As news of Victoria's re-arrest hits the streets, concerned newsmen pack into the Liberal Club to discuss the threat to freedom of speech and press. Johnnie Green leads the meeting.

"Gentlemen, Christian bigots are attempting to install themselves as God's vice-regents on earth. America's professed liberty of the press is no longer ours when a single person can consider the content of a newspaper immoral and force suspension of its printing and imprisonment of its publisher. Today it is Mrs. Woodhull. Tomorrow it may be us. We must immediately demand Mrs. Woodhull's freedom to speak in order to ensure our own!"

"Just because publishers put out a paper doesn't mean they can print anything they choose," Whitelaw Reid says, standing to face the group. "We must censor ourselves, something The Woodhull seems incapable of." Whitelaw is quickly shouted down, but Green mediates.

"Now, Fellas, Reid has a point. We must self-censure. You also know as well as I do that the articles Victoria published were very much self-censured. Christ, they were almost scholarly." Several men nod. Reid has no rebuttal, so Green continues. "But what we are seeing is the machinery of Government at the beck and call of a man who has made it his private obsession to deprive Victoria and her sister of their liberty. It is a mockery of our courts. Mrs. Woodhull's exposé has been printed in toto in at least thirty-five other publications, and Comstock has not attacked a single one of them."

"He's afraid to tackle the big boys," Ashley Cole says with a chuckle.

"Today, yes," Johnnie says. "But what about tomorrow? When Comstock has beaten Mrs. Woodhull to the ground, whom will he turn on then? Standing up now may be our only hope of preserving First Amendment rights for all of us!"

"I wouldn't have printed that filth," Whitelaw grumbles.

"Shut up, Reid," Jim McDermott growls. At the chorus of agreement, Whitelaw Reid shakes his head in disgust.

"Go ahead, boys, do what you must. But leave me out of it." He walks to the door, giving one parting shot. "Am I the only one not dangerously befuddled by those two sirens?"

Chapter 38

On January 14, 1873, the judge presides over a courtroom jammed with reporters and spectators as the obscenity trial against Victoria, Tennie, and Blood finally begins. Howe first calls Anthony Comstock to the stand. Diamonds flash as Howe buttons his bright orange vest over his rotund belly and addresses Comstock with contempt.

"When my clients were first hauled into court, there was much ado about an obscene attack on a venerated member of our Christian community. When asked for specifics of the obscenity, the prosecution cited the article about Mr. Challis. In order for us to fairly refute your charges, we must clarify which article offended you."

"The one about Mr. Challis, Sir. It contained language too filthy for even the coarsest of men to use."

"Your honor, I ask that this case be dismissed," Howe says to the judge. "The warrant under which my clients are held for obscenity cites the article about Mr. Beecher. Now the chief witness against them says another article, not named in the warrant, is the basis."

"I understand your concerns, Sir, but because of the importance of this matter, we will proceed."

"Very well." Howe walks to the table and picks up a *Weekly,* which he hands to Comstock. "Would you please read aloud any portion of the article about Mr. Challis you find offensive?"

"I cannot bring myself to use such words in mixed company, Sir." He throws the paper to the floor.

"Which words?" Howe picks up the paper and reads. "'. . . exhibiting in triumph the red token of her virginity'?"

"You will burn in hell." Comstock's voice is an ugly hiss.

Howe shrugs and lays down the paper. Picks up a Bible.

"I'm sure you will have no problem reading the Word of God." He opens the Bible to a marked spot and hands it to Comstock. "Will you read, please, what I have underlined?" He addresses the room. "For the record, I have asked Mr. Comstock to read from the book of

Deuteronomy, Chapter twenty-two." He turns to Comstock. "And if you could just specify the verse numbers."

"Verse fifteen: 'Bring forth the tokens of the damsel's virginity—'" Comstock's face reddens as the crowd snickers. The gavel bangs. Comstock tries to hand the Bible back, but Howe motions to keep reading, which Comstock does, haltingly. "Verse seventeen: 'These are the tokens of my daughter's virginity.'" Comstock slams the Bible shut. "This is ridiculous. I refuse to read."

"Very well, those two examples will suffice for our purposes. Mr. Comstock, will you tell us how the very same words are obscene in the *Weekly* but not in the Holy Bible?"

"It is the context, Sir!" Comstock stands, his face burning with rage. "Mrs. Woodhull's entire publication constitutes an obscenity! She and her sister live and breathe obscenity. When we arrest these people we habitually find the most disgusting set of Free-lovers cohabitating with them!"

"Objection," Howe says. "Character assassinations have nothing to do with the matter of law." The crowd erupts.

"Quiet or I will clear the court! Mr. Comstock, sit down!" The judge bangs for order.

"Your Honor, it is impossible to refute non-specific charges that change on the whim of the persecutors," Howe says to the judge. "I ask again that this case be dismissed."

"Although I do not agree with the publication of such explicit matters, I agree that the warrants under which Mrs. Woodhull and Miss Claflin have come to trial today are inconsistent with the testimony presented against them. I therefore rule this case satisfied by forfeiture of the bail amounts already paid. Court is adjourned."

~ ~ ~

At Blood's suggestion Victoria hires Spiritualist Dr. Joseph Treat to help at the newspaper so she can return to the lecture circuit. Tennie eyes the hawk-faced man as he shakes Victoria's hand and promises to serve to his utmost. She can't put her finger on why, but the man bothers her. Victoria seems to have no such reservations as she brings him up to speed.

"Somehow Channing has managed to keep the *Weekly* limping along throughout our legal ordeals," she tells Treat. "But it is too much to do alone, so we sincerely appreciate your assistance. We have regular articles from Mr. Train in the Tombs, that worst of all penal institutions to which he has been condemned for defending us."

"I understand he demanded the arrest of the Bible Publishing Company for printing disgusting slanders on Lot, David, Abraham, and Solomon."

"Yes. But, as is typical in this campaign against us, they arrested Train instead. His cell is on Murderer's Row, and twenty-two of the murderers have formed a club and elected him president. His correspondence about this, and even his discourse on the rancid stew they are served daily, provides excellent insight into our deplorable prison system."

"George says they continue to give him opportunities to escape, even leaving him unattended in the prison corridors," Blood adds. "But he is determined to remain a prisoner and go to trial in order to trumpet the travesty of justice being perpetrated against Victoria and Tennessee."

"Train's a loon," Treat says.

"My god, you may be right that Georgie's crazy, but not for the reason you think," Tennie says. "Having spent time in better jails than the Tombs, I cannot imagine suffering the bad air and general insalubries of that place just to make a point."

"Oh, no. Not again." Victoria walks to meet the marshals coming in the door. "What is it this time, gentlemen? I should think we had been arrested enough by now to satisfy everyone."

"It is obscenity again, Mrs. Woodhull. I don't know who has sworn it out, but it's for all three of you."

The sisters are stunned when this time they are taken to join George Francis Train at The Halls of Justice. The imposing citadel in lower Manhattan covers an entire square block bordered by Centre, Elm, Franklin and Leonard Streets. A massive structure of granite, its resemblance to an Egyptian mausoleum has earned it the nickname The Tombs. Built to house 200 inmates in three structures, many more are now crammed inside.

The sisters are white and silent as the guard locks Blood in a cell on the lower of four tiers of cells. The cell has only two cots but already three prisoners. Blood's face turns to stone, but he forces a smile and mouths "I love you" as the solid cell door, with only one small food slot, clanks shut. Guards yawn and spit. Inmates' eyes leer through the small opening in the cell doors as they jeer at the women being prodded down the corridor and up rusted, unsteady stairs to an overhead bridge that connects the men and women's facilities.

"This is called the Bridge of Sighs because the condemned must pass over it on their way to their hanging in the courtyard," the guard says. The smell of death assaults them as he points at gallows in the courtyard two-stories below and chatters on. "You're lucky we have separate housing for women. The Sisters of Charity provide spiritual services for you ladies and see that you are a little better treated. Where your men friends are, the prisoners receive no outside air and are only released for an hour a day to walk the iron gallery around the cells for exercise. At night the rats come out in force, gnawing on toes and nipping at ears."

"If ya don't mind, we'll pass on the guided tour." Tennie glares at the guard and grabs her sister as she swoons.

The women are turned over to the chief matron, who ushers them to one of the fifty five-by-eight cells facing Leonard Street. The solid door of their cell closes with a bang. They look around. Filth blocks most of the sun from penetrating the barred skylight, leaving everything a dull gray. Because the prison sets on marshland, it has sunk over the thirty-odd years since it was built, warping walls and ceilings and leaving cracks through which water trickles into pools on the stone floor. The sisters gag as vapors of mold and mildew fill their nostrils.

Darkness comes, and they huddle together, shivering from cold and fear under the one dirty blanket on the one iron bed with its musty, straw-tick mattress. They look at the walls that glow green with mold in the gray moonlight. They look at the one rickety chair, one splintered table, and one encrusted slop bucket. Sleet pelts against the skylight and drops around them.

"They are either trying to break us or kill us," Tennie says. "But we're not going to let them do either, right, Sis?"

"The *Weekly* is our only hope for justice."

"Do you think we can trust Dr. Treat?"

"Of course. Why not?"

"I don't know. Forget it. All this confinement cuttin' into my sex life's got me addled."

"You're addled; Mama's hysterical; Zulu Maud cries all day. Thank god Byron doesn't know what's going on. Everyone is being hurt because the status quo is out to silence me. Oh, Tennie, I had no idea the battle I was waging when we attacked the men. If I had, I surely would have fainted by the wayside. Sometimes I wish for Demosthenes' pen so that I might suck the poison out of it as he did when soldiers took him. But if God gives me the strength, I must see this through."

"You mean we, don't you? I'm the one who got us into the worst of it with my Challis article."

"No, this is my sacred duty, not yours. You're a baby yet. Not even thirty. You deserve better. I am taking you off the paper. At least then, if they keep up this insanity, they can't touch you."

"My god, Sis, haven't we always stood together? Isn't that what Pa taught us?"

"This isn't kids taunting us in church, Honey. This isn't even being run out of town for the sins of our father. They mean to destroy me, Tennie, and if they succeed, I need you free to take care of Zulu Maud and Byron and the Colonel. I need you free to let the world know what society has done!"

~ ~ ~

When Victoria and Tennie return to court, Attorney Howe immediately presents a letter Benjamin Butler has written to the *Sun* at the request of Isabella Beecher Hooker and Laura Cuppy Smith. In the letter, Butler, as author of the law under which the sisters are being held, states that it was written to cover lithographs, prints, engravings, and licentious books published for the corruption of youth It was never meant to apply to newspapers. Butler instructs that the women should be released as a mere matter of law. Howe immediately requests that all charges be dismissed, but the Commissioner is not swayed.

"Mr. Howe, I tend to agree with Senator Butler's premise and would be inclined to dismiss the charges, but this is a matter for the Grand Jury to decide. I therefore remand the prisoners under an additional eight-thousand-dollar bail each until—"

"Your Honor, this is an outrage! There is no legal ground—"

"Nevertheless, because of the importance and subtlety of the questions involved, and the anxiety of the community for a definitive ruling on the case, your clients will have to wait for the Grand Jury."

"Then at least reduce bail. These women, for a misdemeanor, have been subjected to bonds totaling sixty thousand dollars. That's nine thousand more than Tweed paid for feloniously looting our city out of hundreds of millions of dollars! This is not justice. It is persecution in its most odious form."

"Mrs. Woodhull and Miss Claflin came into our courts with unclean hands. Bail must be fixed to teach them it is no light matter to violate the law. However, I will agree to reduce it to monies already paid plus one thousand dollars for each woman and two thousand for Mr. Blood. Court is adjourned."

Victoria scrapes together the bail, and they are freed.

~ ~ ~

Anthony Comstock is furious at Butler's involvement in Victoria's case and rushes to Washington. He has already had his Senator friend introduce a bill in Congress that calls for 20 years in prison for selling contraceptives or for performing or having an abortion, but Comstock wants more authority. Authority that will allow him to lock Victoria up for life.

When his friend warns him that Butler has already found several parts of the bill unconstitutional, Comstock decides to personally present his case to the House Judiciary Committee. On the morning of his appearance, Comstock strides into Committee chambers, sets a battered brown suitcase on the table, and removes his private collection of vice.

"Esteemed members of Congress and of this Committee," he says. "The items I have laid out before you are corrupting our impressionable young men by turning their minds from the Lord and toward lust." He holds up pornographic pictures. "They view these types of images, and it incites them to debauch our sisters and daughters." He picks up various contraceptive devices and shows them around. "Tools like these allow those who breed bastards to mitigate the recompenses of their sin. They also provide an easy way out for women too lazy and self-absorbed to take on the role of motherhood for which she was created.

"And these items, gentlemen . . ." Comstock holds up various tools created for self-stimulation. ". . . these encourage the most repugnant of sins. The guilt and shame of turning God's holiest act into one of self-pleasure will soon bring our young people to ruin, perhaps even to death. Therefore, I humbly beg you, in the name of all that is holy, to approve the bill before you that bestows on me, as special agent of the United States Post Office, greater authority to eradicate such harmful and soul-sucking commodities from our society so that we might again be pure."

The bill passes. All it needs is Grant's signature.

The following evening, March fourth, Comstock attends the inauguration party to pressure the President. The event is a disaster. A storm hits with a vengeance and guests fight blizzard winds, bitter cold, and waist-high snowdrifts as they converge on the party that is unfortunately being held in a new, unheated pavilion on the Capitol grounds. Grant's speech is muffled by the wailing wind. Horn valves seize. Hundreds of songbirds freeze in their cages. Since the West Point and Annapolis marching bands have not been allowed to wear coats, several topple over from the cold. The roasted turkeys become so frozen that waiters must hack them with axes in order to feed the guests. Not many are eating, since they are shivering too much to hold plates. Whiskey flows freely to warm the crowd, causing much staggering and a few falls.

"Mr. President, the latest bill to restore this country to purity and glory awaits your signature. Are you going to sign it?" The President turns toward the voice and gives Comstock a blank look. Comstock holds out his hand. "Anthony Comstock, Sir. I am the author of the bill to protect our citizens, especially our youth, from terrible vice. It awaits your signature and I am asking you to sign it for the good of the country."

"I am considering it, but there may be Constitutional issues involved."

"Sir, look around you. I could attack vice at this very gathering. I've never seen so many enameled faces, powdered hairs, and obscene dresses as the women are flaunting. It is a blessing that the Lord sent this storm so they are forced to cover themselves. Except for Mrs. Grant and a smattering of others who still have some modesty, the women are caricatures of everything but decency. It's outrageous."

"Will this new law, if I sign it, allow you to end Mrs. Woodhull's reign of vulgarity?"

"Yes, Sir. Not only will we shut her down, but it will deter others from following in her footsteps."

"I'll give it further thought, Mr. Comstock." Grant walks over to Attorney General Amos Akerman and asks, "Is Mrs. Woodhull in or out of jail?"

"She is out on bail but returns to court tomorrow."

"Has she learned her lesson?"

"I don't think so," he says. He rubs his nose, lobster red from the cold.

"Then I'll sign Comstock's bill. How about the Susan Anthony situation?"

"We're stretching out the legal battle like you asked in order to harass her. Do you want her in jail, too?"

"No. She won't be cast off like The Woodhull, and we don't need a g.d. martyr on our hands."

"Mr. President, can I ask why you are so concerned about two insignificant women? Congress will never give them the vote, so why not let them talk all they want? Mrs. Woodhull's married to a flake—"

"Now, don't be putting down a good soldier. Colonel Blood and his brother George both took bullets for me at Shiloh."

"I stand corrected, Sir."

A scream and commotion on the dance floor draws their attention. They rush over. Dancers, shaking in their furs, stare in horror at a woman dead of heart failure at their feet. Although it's still early, the party is over.

Chapter 39

While Comstock plots to silence Victoria forever, she and Blood travel to Boston for the Labor Reform League convention. She is surprised when young Bennie Tucker, who had rescued her cape on her previous trip to the state, takes the podium to present the group's resolutions. He is nervous and her admiring gaze from the front row makes him even more so. Afterwards, she seeks him out. His face reddens, although his dark eyes shimmer with desire when she pecks his cheek.

"You have a true gift, Bennie. You made even dull and dry resolutions seem exciting."

"Thank thee, Mrs. Woodhull. It was my first attempt at public speaking."

"Really? I couldn't tell. It is heartening to see someone so young engaged in the business of reform. It leaves me hopeful for our future." Her eyes lock on his.

"I intend to be an anarchist for the rest of my life."

"Ah, yes, I see the fire of your soul in your eyes and feel your energy. Do you feel mine, Bennie?"

Tucker glances nervously at Blood, whispers a quick "yes," and flees.

That evening, for Victoria's keynote address, Bennie Tucker sits with Blood, Tennie, and Zulu Maud in the front row. His puppy-dog eyes never move from Victoria's face as he hangs on her every word.

"The last time I tried to speak in Boston, the governor banned me. I am grateful to the Labor Reform League for granting me this opportunity to present my views to your city, even though it closed the best halls to this convention. I also want to thank everyone for paying your hard-earned dollars to attend this lecture and for being faithful with your subscriptions to the *Weekly* so we can continue to publish it. With your support we shall preach the message of truth and justice wherever we will be heard.

"I know it's not been easy. Our country suffers a severe recession. Last year over four thousand businesses failed. Former stalwarts of our economy are on their backs. Greed and plunder have fattened the bellies of the rich and bled dry the poor. Farms are in foreclosure because it costs more to produce crops than can be made from them. Textile mills and coalmines are shut down, and those factories still running have suspended most of their workers and cut the wages of the rest. And in the midst of all this, our government is misusing your and my tax dollars to serve the whims of a self-righteous moralist and to protect a practicing hypocrite!

"According to the *Tribune,* last year Mr. Comstock seized one hundred and thirty-four thousand pounds of books, over two hundred pictures, sixty thousand rubber articles, and fifty-five hundred playing cards, all of which he deemed obscene and lewd. Yet none of these peddlers are haunted and jailed as I am. You know this little vice czar reads every book from cover to cover twice before giving it to police." Loud boos. "And he watches peep shows for an hour before proclaiming them obscene." More boos. "It's hypocrisy at its height.

"Further, Mr. Comstock allows something I consider grossly more obscene than any of this so-called pornography to go unchallenged. I refer to the advertisements featured in respectable newspapers: 'A beautiful boy, three months old, available for adoption to a wealthy couple.' 'Wanted for adoption, a little girl, two to three years of age, light hair and blue eyes preferred.' Tackling such blatant buying and selling of illegitimate babies to protect the reputation of the so-called Christian families to which they have been born is a game worthy of Mr. Comstock's zeal. Yet he turns a blind eye to such outrage and says *I* am the one out to destroy the family.

"And let us look at the charges of libel leveled against my sister, my husband, and me. It is interesting to note that Mr. Beecher, about whom eleven columns of the most intimate details were printed in our paper, has not said one peep about libel. Yet the whole machinery of justice is invoked to silence me and keep certain men from being irritated. This is the injustice I suffer. The government's involvement in my persecution demonstrates that woman's subordination by class and gender has the force of government behind it.

"But it is not only women who face a double standard. It is also the poor. Many of you face threats against your very existence because of rich man's laws and his failure to acknowledge your suffering. Too many of you, as Edgar Allan Poe so famously said, 'robotically follow the tintinnabulation of the bells that tell you when to work, when to lunch, and when to drag your weary bodies home to bed with hollow bellies.' This is unacceptable! We must stand together and demand justice and not stop demanding it until we breathe our last breath!"

Bennie jumps to his feet, leading the standing ovation.

Following the lecture, there is a reception at the luxurious Parker House, famous for introducing the European plan of serving continuous meals from their kitchens and for coining the term *scrod* to identify the white fish catch-of-the-day. The scrumptious buffet is complete with Parker House rolls and Boston cream pie, both inventions of the hotel chefs. Maneuvering next to Bennie Tucker, Victoria takes a deep whiff of a freshly baked roll, declaring that the aroma is almost orgasmic. She laughs softly as the young man's face turns as red as the pickled beets.

"My husband tells me you were very energetic in setting up for this event," she tells him.

"It was my pleasure to be of service, Mrs. Woodhull."

"I would ask you to dinner to make my appreciation more concrete, but we must catch a train— I understand you're planning a trip to our city soon?"

"Yes, Ma'am."

"If I am not in jail, please call on me so I may properly reward your efforts on my behalf."

"Hearing thee speak is reward enough."

"Is it?" She laughs softly and pats his cheek. "Then stop by simply so we can get better acquainted. If you are so inclined, we might offer you a position on our staff."

A week later, Bennie takes Victoria up on her offer and visits her in New York. Blood is writing at the table and Victoria is lying on the sofa when the maid ushers the young man into the parlor.

"I have a terrible headache, and my husband is preoccupied. Will you place your hand on my forehead to heal me, Bennie?" Victoria says without rising.

"I-I know nothing about healing, Ma'am."

"I will show you." She places his palm on her forehead, letting her hand linger on his. "You have great magnetism. My pain is easing already." She caresses his hand; her eyes seduce.

Blood gathers his papers and walks toward them. Bennie blanches, jerks back his hand, but Blood continues to the door.

"I am going to the library to finish my work. There is entirely too much magnetism in here," he teases. Bennie stares uncomfortably at the door as it closes behind Blood.

"What will thy husband think of this?"

"Oh, he knows, but do you?"

"Do I know what?"

"That I should dearly like to sleep with you!"

"Oh."

"Would you like that, Bennie?"

"It would, um, it would be my first—"

"How can that be?! You are much too handsome to be withheld from the female race. Those chocolate eyes are made for gazing into, and those lips look . . . delicious." Her finger traces the outline of his lips. She inhales his scent; her breath quickens.

"But thou art married."

"Yes, but we do not own each other." She pulls the fidgeting Bennie toward her, unbuttoning his shirt. "Let me show you other healing techniques I know. Have you heard of the Kama Sutra?" Her kiss prevents his answering. He groans in pleasure.

"Oh, Ma'am."

"If our Spirits are to meld, Bennie, you must call me Victoria." She giggles, rolls him onto his back on the sofa and straddles him. Her hands

272

slide down the firm flesh of his chest, followed by her exploring tongue. She undoes his pants.

"Hail, Victoria," he gasps.

Much later, Victoria walks the flushed and glowing Tucker to the door and gives him a tender kiss.

"Be sure to come back this evening for another lesson," she whispers.

"Thou art like something I never imagined." Bennie can barely choke out the words, he is so overcome.

"Would you mind stepping into the library on your way out so my husband knows you are no longer with me?" She pats his behind gently and sends him down the hall.

Blood looks up cordially as Bennie timidly pokes his head into the library.

"I-I'm just saying good-bye, Sir."

"You will visit again this evening?"

"I have been invited."

"Splendid. We shall see you then. Thank you, Mr. Tucker. You have brought a glow to my wife's cheeks. She has been through so much, it's nice to see her joyful. In fact, to prolong such good health and happiness, I would like to offer you a position as our assistant. We leave on the lecture circuit in a few days and need another hand to help ready the halls."

"It would give me great pleasure, Sir."

~ ~ ~

As Victoria and Tennie make plans for the West Coast lecture tour, Dr. Joseph Treat publishes two pamphlets for them to sell at events: *Martyr'd Woman of the Nineteenth Century* and *Victoria the Brave*. He delivers the first copies to Victoria the night before they depart. She scans them quickly, pecks his cheek in thanks.

"I, uh, I thought perhaps I might read them to you," Treat whines.

"Unfortunately, we must finish our packing. But I will read them before I retire."

273

Treat looks disappointed as she walks him to the door.

"My god, that old goat's got it bad for you, Sis," Tennie says as soon as he is gone. "I'm betting he'd let you cure his celibacy."

"Tennie! He's a sweet man, but no way am I interested in him romantically. My mind is all wrapped around a younger man at the moment."

"Thank god. Treat gives me the willie-jillies. Can't we find someone else to run the paper while we're gone? What about Bennie? He wants to be a journalist."

"Didn't I tell you? Bennie's going with us!"

"My god, you're kidding. I hope you warned him they don't call it the Wild West for nothin'."

"Tennie, Tennie, what am I going to do with you?"

"Share the youngster for a start."

~ ~ ~

Although it's a drizzly day in San Francisco, Victoria takes the group on a tour of where she lived and worked those many years ago. The saloon where she worked as a cigarette girl is boarded up and about to fall down, but the theater where she performed is as vibrant as ever. Maggie Mitchell is appearing there in the title role of *Fanchon the Cricket*, an adaptation of George Sand's *La Petite Fadette*. Zulu Maud is thrilled when they attend the matinee performance.

In the evening, Victoria opens her "Scarecrows of Sexual Freedom" speech to a full house.

"My brothers and sisters, I am going to tell you plain truths tonight about educating for perfected sexuality. The more I see the little sexual fibs prevalent in society, the more I despise them. Let us teach our children to speak truth by speaking it ourselves and telling them the secrets of sex instead of stories about birds and cabbage patches. We must provide demonstrated sexual training as a preparation for marriage, establish a family planning program, and control births before conception so that the horror of abortion becomes a thing of the past."

Two hours later, Victoria concludes her speech with a fiery call to action.

"We must have sexual emancipation of women! Women must not only be allowed to refuse sex if there is no love but to find pleasure in it if there is!"

The crowd loves her. And Bennie most of all.

Chapter 40

On May 6, 1873, National Woman's Suffrage Association members turn out en mass to celebrate the organization's 25th anniversary at Apollo Hall. Elizabeth Cady Stanton is the first of several featured speakers who recount the movement's history.

"My anger at woman's plight began as a child when, hidden in my father's law office, I heard Widow Campbell crying. Her husband had died and her stepson was throwing her out of the only home she had ever known, the family farm she had inherited that now was, by patriarchal law, her stepson's property.

"When I turned seven, our black servant took me to court to watch my father argue cases. I remember a woman whose daughter had been sold into prostitution and her son hired out for hard labor so that her husband could have his whiskey. And the law prohibited the poor woman from having any say in the matter!

"I could go on and on. But when, in eighteen forty, the World Antislavery Society refused to allow women to speak at their convention, it was the final straw. I ranted to Mrs. Mott that we should organize to change the laws, and the seed for our movement was planted. Our first convention was at the Seneca Falls Methodist Church on July nineteenth, eighteen hundred and forty eight. Our Declaration of Sentiments was approved as written, including the right of suffrage Mr. Douglass and I had fought so hard for. The reaction was fierce. My husband left town in a fury. My father disowned me. Other women were beaten to an inch of their lives. But we persisted. Though ridiculed, spat on, and ostracized in the twenty-five years since that fateful day, we have made gains! Unfortunately, these gains are not universal and we still don't have the vote. So we will continue our fight until women are equal to men in every area of life, from the bedroom to the boardroom, to the big White House in Washington D.C.!"

Later in the afternoon, as the speeches wind down, Laura Cuppy Smith steps to the podium.

"Mrs. Hooker was too ill to attend our meeting, so I thank Miss Anthony and Elizabeth Cady for allowing me to read her letter to this assembly." She opens the letter. "Even though Mrs. Woodhull has been barred from our meeting today, Mrs. Hooker, in her letter, says—" Laura ignores the strangled hiss from Susan and reads, "'In applauding the accomplishments of the past twenty-five years, I pay tribute to the work of Victoria Woodhull, a tender mother, young and inexperienced, but with a heart bolder than a lion and a will firmer for right than granite rock. From the reluctant Congressional committee she wrung the first recognition that women citizens of the United States have a right to the ballot and laid the foundation for absolute equality.'"

There is thunderous applause as Laura returns Susan's venomous glare with an innocent look and walks off the stage. Elizabeth Cady bites back a smile.

Following the meeting, Ashley Cole interviews Elizabeth Cady Stanton and Amelia Bloomer, President of the Iowa Woman's Suffrage Association. Amelia is 55, with short, tightly curled hair and dark, bushy brows.

"Mrs. Cady, I'm sure you've seen that Mrs. Woodhull has reprinted her exposé of the Beecher-Tilton affair," Ashley begins. "Do you still deny her story?"

"I deny nothing, Mr. Cole. I am simply disposed to be more cautious in talking about the matter."

"Then there was an affair."

"Oh, goodness, everyone knows it," Amelia breaks in. "And this committee the Reverend has asked Henry Bowen to form to investigate the matter is a total sham. Of course they will find their pastor pure. How can they do otherwise?"

"Mr. Cole, I thought this was to be an interview about the suffrage movement," Elizabeth says, cutting Amelia off.

"I apologize. Let's talk about the pantaloons that are named for you, Mrs. Bloomer: How did you design such an outfit?"

"Actually Mrs. Cady's cousin, Libby Smith Miller—Gerrit Smith's daughter—designed them. Bloomers were only named for me because I promoted them in my newspaper."

"And millers, of course, would not have been a good name, having been long associated with grain." Elizabeth says dryly. Cole looks puzzled, but then "gets it" and chuckles.

"Those pants were so practical," Amelia muses, remembering the comfort of being out of corsets and stays.

"So why did you stop wearing them?"

"Ridicule, Mr. Cole," Elizabeth says. "When husbands and children refuse to be seen with you, and school boys follow you chanting bunkum, eventually it becomes not worth the effort."

"Goodness, sometimes that stupid ditty still rings in my ears," Amelia says. "'Gibbery, gibbery, gab, the women had a conflab, and demanded their rights to wear the tights, gibbery, gibbery, gab!'" She covers her ears with her hands and shudders.

"Do you think your group and Lucy Stone's will ever work together?" Ashley asks.

"Lucy Stone has rejected every overture and refused all compromise," Elizabeth retorts. "If you want to know anything else about her and her group, I suggest you go down the street to their convention." She stands, ending the interview.

Chapter 41

As spring moves toward summer, justice seems to take a holiday. First, in May, George Francis Train is acquitted of obscenity on the grounds of insanity, but then sentenced to an asylum. Luckily for George, the deputies escorting him allow him to escape, and he flees to England.

In June, Susan B. Anthony's trial for voting is another travesty when the judge refuses to let her speak and instructs the all-male jury they must find her guilty. She is fined one hundred dollars, which she refuses to pay.

Victoria receives a blow to her legal battles when Attorney Howe abruptly drops her as a client. Her only hope is Charley Brooks, a dashing Irishman in his forties, who offers to represent her pro bono. As they discuss her situation, he speaks with a heavy Irish brogue and sweeps his heavy red hair from his forehead often. She finds it endearing.

"Take heart," he tells her. "Leave everything to me."

"You don't know how nice it is to finally hear a man say that to me. You have restored my faith in both man and God."

Toward the end of June, a hot summer rain pelts the streetcar in which Tennie and Victoria ride. Victoria looks peaked and holds her fist against her chest.

"My chest hurts, Tennie. I can't seem to breathe."

"My god, no wonder. It's stifling in here." Tennie fans her with a newspaper. "Hang on. We'll be home soon."

"All this . . . in . . . and out of . . . court, I fear the stress . . . might kill . . . me." Victoria fights for breath.

"My god, stop that kind of talk right now! If you were going to die I'd have had a vision. Charley will get everything resolved. I have a feeling about *that*."

The streetcar stops. The sisters disembark. The rain revives Victoria somewhat as they walk the few blocks home. Zulu Maud meets them at the door.

"I'm going to rest a bit," Victoria tells her daughter. "Can you bring me some tea in a bit?"

"Yes, Ma'am." Zulu Maud heads for the kitchen, Tennie following. Suddenly they hear a thud.

"My god! It's Sis!" Tennie rushes to the staircase, calling for Blood.

Victoria is passed out on the landing halfway up the stairs. Blood oozes from her mouth; her face is gray and clammy. The entire Claflin clan appears and huddles around her. Roxanna sticks a mirror under her nose. There's no breath. James is too horrified to speak, but his look sends his brother George dashing for the doctor. Byron tries to go after George, but Zulu Maud grabs his hand; they follow Blood as he carries Victoria up the stairs.

Roxanna, wailing and praying in broken German, applies a hot mustard plaster to Victoria's chest. Tennie wraps steaming towels around her sister's feet. Blood holds Victoria's hand in a bowl of almost scalding water. Nothing brings a response. Zulu Maud stands by Buck, who sits in an armchair and puffs furiously on a pipe. They both stare numbly at Victoria, tears in their eyes. Byron stands nearby, confused by all the commotion. He runs to George, who arrives with the doctor. The family waits breathlessly as the doctor checks Victoria's vital signs. When Roxanna doesn't move aside for him, Buck finds his voice and orders her out of the way.

"Oh, it don't matter, Mr. Claflin," the doctor says, stepping away. "Your daughter's got a ruptured blood vessel in her lung. She won't last the night. If it makes your wife feel better to doctor her, it won't hurt anything."

"My god! My god! My god! You're wrong! You're wrong!" Tennie flails at the doctor until Blood puts his arms around her to calm her.

"Tennie, Sweetie, that won't help." He kisses the top of her head. "Go wire Johnnie Green. You know how Victoria loves to see her name in the paper. We should have a stack to read to her when she wakes up."

"That's a good idea, Colonel." She swipes at her tears and takes Zulu Maud's hand. "C'mon, Zulu Maud, you can help me."

~ ~ ~

Early Saturday morning, newsboys run through the streets waving papers and yelling the headlines:

"Woodhull dying!"

"Mrs. Woodhull on death bed!"

"Bewitching Broker fights for life!"

Blood purchases a copy of each newspaper and brings them to the bedroom where Tennie and Zulu Maud keep vigil with Victoria.

"My god, I've tried everything, and she won't wake up." She looks at Blood with haunted eyes.

"I'm sure her body just needs to shut down for a bit so it can use all its energy to heal itself," Blood says. "Our systems are amazingly self-sufficient that way. Why don't you read to her, Tennie? When I was wounded and unconscious, I still heard the conversations around me."

"Good idea, Colonel." Tennie swipes at her tears and picks up the *New York Graphic,* which carries the story on its front page, as do all the newspapers. She reads through sniffles. "Her influence over people of intelligence and refinement, women as well as men, is a phenomenon which has yet to be satisfactorily explained.' I'll explain it. It's because she always acts with unconditional love."

Tennie passes the day reading aloud from the papers, while Zulu Maud cuts out each article and pastes it into a scrapbook.

From the *Democrat:* "'At death's door from mental anxiety and weeks in prison, one of the most discrete women in the world is prostrate. The hoary-headed hypocrites of Plymouth Church and happy husbands cuckold by Beecher in the name of the Lord smile as they contemplate the burial of a woman who prefers honest devils to sneaking fakes.' Amen to that, huh, Vic? We'll take them honest devils any day."

The *Pittsburgh Leader:* "'The world will soon be rid of one of the most remarkable, albeit terrible and dangerous women who ever lived.'"

"Is that a backhanded compliment?" Blood asks.

"Yeah," Tennie says. "Good thing they put that 'remarkable' in there." She reads from the *New York Sun* as Roxanna brings more mustard plaster. "If Mrs. Woodhull had been born and educated in a different sphere, if her surroundings had been refined and inspiring, she would have developed into a great and glorious character.'"

"*Ach!* So your boyfriend is putting down our family now!" Roxanna plops goop on Victoria's chest with a loud slap.

"Johnnie Green didn't write it, Mama. They wouldn't let him." She picks up the *Chicago Tribune*. "'Mrs. Woodhull's illness is a dodge to create sympathy. Our primary question is: What affect will this have on the Beecher-Tilton scandal?'" Tennie snorts. "My god, a woman is fighting for her life and all they can think of is their precious preacher."

By Sunday, Victoria's room is overrun with flowers. She is still unconscious, and Tennie and Blood continue their vigil, reading her the Sunday newspapers.

"Oh, I hope you're right about Victoria being able to hear us, Colonel. This is a good one," Tennie says, reading from the *Baltimore Sunday Telegram*. "'A woman called crazy by society is waging a war with death. We say she is crazy like Joan of Ark and Swedenborg were crazy and hope she wins the battle. It would be a great benefit to the world if more of our women, and our men, too, had half Victoria C. Woodhull's craziness.'"

Suddenly Victoria stirs and half opens her eyes. She pats Blood's hand.

"You are my loyal, true love," she mummers and then lapses back into unconsciousness. Blood's eyes tear up, but Tennie jumps into his lap, hugging him excitedly.

"If she woke once, she'll do it again! Oh, Colonel, she *is* gonna live!" Her smile fades. "Ain't she?"

Victoria remains unconsciousness on Monday, and Tennie fights to be cheerful as she sits by the bed with a stack of letters.

"My god, Sis, you gotta wake up. The ladies haven't forgotten you. Elizabeth Cady says that if her testimony to Beecher's Committee will rescue you and dethrone Beecher, she will make them call her, which apparently they haven't done yet. Her or Susan Anthony. Which tells you something about that farce of a Committee." Tennie hands a letter to

Zulu Maud, who hovers nearby. "Here, Zulu Maud, you can read this one from Paulina Davis."

"'I am too ill at present to withstand controversy, but after my death you may use this letter as you wish. The story you printed about the scandal is true in all its essential particulars.'" Zulu Maud reads with a crisp voice.

"See, Sis? They still love you!" Tennie touches Victoria's forehead. It is so hot she snatches her hand away and panics. "Zulu Maud, run get Granny quick! And bring ice! Lots of ice! Hurry!"

Finally, on Tuesday morning, Victoria opens her eyes and looks around. She sees Zulu Maud asleep in the armchair and Tennie dozing in the wooden rocker by the bed. Victoria touches Tennie's arm and she jumps awake.

"My god, Sis, you're alive!"

"He came to me, Tennie. Our Lord Jesus Christ laid his hand on my forehead and whispered in my ear, 'For many are called, but few are chosen.' He willed me better to fulfill my mission."

Tennie feels her sister's forehead. The fever is gone. Tennie's yell wakes Zulu Maud.

"Mama! Come quick! Victoria is healed!" She hugs her sister. "My god, Sis, you had us crazy with worry! But I knew you wouldn't leave me."

"Where is James?"

"Wouldn't you know it? He just finally dragged himself away to attend to urgent matters at the office. Zulu Maud, ask George to run for him. He's been an awful wreck, Vic."

"Don't be huggin' your sister back into the spirit world, Tennessee," Buck says, pulling up his suspenders as he walks to the bed and leans over. It's more of a brushing than a kiss, but it almost shocks Victoria back into unconsciousness. He steps back, immediately gruff. "Thank God you're back. Your mother's prayin's been keepin' me up nights, interferin' with my gamin'." He strolls out, leaving Victoria to touch the spot his lips have grazed. Tears of joy spill down her cheeks.

"He kissed me, Tennie," she says. "He honest to God kissed me like a father should!"

Chapter 42

On Wednesday, Victoria is weak but, with Tennie's help, she props herself up in bed.

"Are you sure you're up to this, Sis?" Tennie fusses with Victoria's curls. "I'd be happy to tell Mr. Bowen and his cronies to go hang themselves."

"No, I want to hear what they have to say."

"Are you ready?" Blood asks, poking his head into the room. Victoria nods and Blood disappears. He returns in moments with Henry Bowen and his Committee. Victoria's gaze is strong as Bowen walks to her bed and takes a seat. The others stand in a group behind him.

"Mrs. Woodhull, as you know, our Committee is investigating the matters you have written about," Bowen says. "We have a few questions, but let me know if you become too tired to go on."

"Thank you. I am fine."

"Do you know Theodore Tilton?" Bowen asks.

"Yes. Intimately. The same way I know Mr. Beecher."

"What is your proof of these allegations?"

"I have his love letters."

"Mr. Tilton's?"

"And Mr. Beecher's."

"Mr. Beecher wrote you love letters?!"

"After several weeks of intimacy it would be foolish to think our correspondence merely platonic."

"Mrs. Woodhull, it is best for all concerned for you to turn over the documents you have. It will allow the Committee to take the action we deem best."

"I am inclined to agree, but I have suffered much at the hands of you Christians. How can I trust you?"

"Mr. Beecher has maligned both Mr. Tilton and me as he has you. I am sure you have read about it in the newspapers."

"There are many things printed. I must have proof that you are not in league with Mr. Beecher."

"And I must have proof that you have the documents you allude to."

"Tennie, bring me the strongbox." Tennie hurries to the wardrobe and retrieves the box. Victoria opens it. "Most of my papers are either destroyed or entrusted to a third-party, but these should satisfy your curiosity." She removes two letters, folding them so that only Beecher's signature is visible. Bowen tries to grab them, but Victoria quickly returns the letters to the strongbox, closing and locking it.

"Gentlemen, in two days the obscenity charges against us will come to trial. If they are laid to rest, I might be persuaded to release these and other correspondences to you." Her look leaves no doubt as to her meaning.

Two days later, Victoria, Tennie, and Blood face the judge. The courtroom is hot and muggy, and Tennie and Blood keep an eye on the still-peaked Victoria, who fans herself nervously. Charley Brooks pats her hand, whispering reassurance. When the jury is in place, Comstock takes the witness stand and the District Attorney steps forward to question him.

"Mr. Comstock, in connection with the obscene article—"

"Objection! No obscenity has been proven. It is why we are in this courtroom."

"Sustained."

For the next few minutes, Charley Brooks objects to every question asked, and each is sustained. The DA scratches his head.

"Your Honor, since it appears that my witnesses are not to be allowed to say anything, the prosecution rests." He sits, and Charley Brooks walks confidently to the front of the courtroom.

"Your Honor, defense will be brief, and we can all have a splendid lunch. My clients have been arrested pursuant to laws dating to eighteen sixty-five and seventy-two. You will note the opinion from General Butler, author of those bills, that neither covers newspapers." He hands the judge Butler's published letter. "And while Congress passed a law earlier this year that does cover newspapers, my clients cannot be prosecuted under a law that came into existence after their arrest. Defense rests."

"Mr. Purdy, it appears that the prosecution cannot be maintained," the judge tells the DA, who throws up his hands. The judge bangs the gavel. "This criminal case is ended."

"Your Honor, the defendants are entitled to a verdict," Charley Brooks says.

"You have heard the man," the judge says to the jury. "What is your verdict?"

"Your Honor, we find all three defendants not guilty." The other jurors agree in unison with their foreman. The crowd goes wild.

"And they say Church and State are separate," Victoria murmurs.

A few days later, after Victoria has kept her part of the bargain with Henry Bowen, Henry Ward Beecher finally publishes a statement in the *Brooklyn Eagle*:

> **I have learned that Mrs. Victoria Woodhull claims to have letters of mine that contain information about certain infamous stories against me. Mrs. Woodhull has my consent to publish them. The rumors circulating about me are grossly untrue, and I stamp them as utterly false.**

"My god, now that you have given Mr. Bowen the most damaging letters— You should'a held a couple back. We could've printed them tomorrow and sold a ton of papers."

"Tennie, I don't want to fight anymore. I just want to give my speeches and enjoy a bit of God's sunshine and summer gardens before our fall tour. And if we make enough money, I'd like to see Paris before I die."

Two weeks later, Utica Claflin is found wandering the streets, drunk, drugged, and dazed. Her death from Bright's disease a few days later hits Victoria hard, and she sits on the floor by Utica's bed and sobs all night. When the dawning sun peeks through the window, she finally rises and walks wearily down the stairs. She stops outside the kitchen when she hears her mother ranting to Polly.

"Your sisters and that *schurke* Colonel poisoned Utie just like they poisoned Victoria's husband and yours!"

"Mother, the autopsies—"

"*Ach*! I don't care what no coroner says. It was them sisters of yours. Them, I tell you. How many more will they take from me? First your brother Maldon—"

"What?" Polly is shocked.

"Those girls flaunted their bodies and stirred up urges a teenaged boy cannot control. He had to run away. I never heard from my son again. Never saw him again!"

"Mother, Victoria was twelve when Maldon left, and she didn't have a sexual bone in her body. Maldon raped her. Just like he raped me."

Roxanna slaps Polly hard, but Victoria, already racing up the stairs, doesn't hear. She rushes into the bedroom where James dozes in a chair and shakes him frantically.

"James! James, wake up! You must go for the coroner. Mama and Polly are talking crazy again. We have to get an autopsy on Utie before they start spouting more lies about town."

~ ~ ~

Victoria cannot stop grieving her sister's death; she becomes thin and drawn as she pushes herself beyond endurance at the *Weekly*. Tennie gives her a worried look as her head nods drowsily after one particularly long day at the paper.

"Hey, Sis, it's late. Let's go. The Colonel will be worried."

"If he's so worried, why isn't he here?" Victoria snaps. "You know, Tennie, just once I'd like a man to take care of me instead of the other way around."

"My god, how can you say that? The Colonel's devoted his *life* to you. He's put up with Ma, sat in a stinking prison without one word of complaint—"

"I know. I know. I couldn't ask for more devotion. Maybe that's it. Maybe he's *too* devoted."

"My god, I wish I had someone who loved me that much."

"He's too modest for a man. Does he have no ambition other than *mine*? Is it our cause that binds us and not love?" Victoria walks to the window and stares out, deep in thought. Tennie doesn't know what to say. Neither of them notices Dr. Treat listening from the shadow outside the doorway as Victoria speaks without turning.

"I never really thought about dying, Tennie. Even in that terrible prison, even when I was most desolate, I was fueled by my anger to fight. But what was I fighting for? No one really cares about any of it, and just like that—" She snaps her fingers. "It's gone anyway."

"Hogwash! I care. The Colonel cares. A lot of people care."

"I wish I could count on James to run the newspaper and give the lectures. How can he be content to sequester his name in the shade when, with his intellect, he could be glittering in the sun?"

"Maybe the Colonel *will* lecture. Have you ever asked him? Maybe he hangs back because he thinks that's what you want."

"He could be man enough to ask me." Victoria stares out the window for a long moment. Then she sighs. "I'm tired, Tennie. So very, very tired."

"Well, my god, if you're so tired, let's go home. It's not going to make you less tired to stay here late every night." When Victoria doesn't respond, Tennie becomes impatient. "You know what? Feel sorry for yourself if you want, I'm outta here. I got problems of my own. I'm almost twenty-eight years old, and no man's ever really loved me. Johnnie Green's backing off lately. Maybe Buck's got a bottle of whiskey—"

"Don't you ever, ever say that! Don't ever even think about drinking!" Victoria whirls around. Her voice catches. "Promise me, Tennie! I couldn't stand to lose you."

"My god, Sis, I didn't mean it." Tennie rushes over and puts her arms around Victoria. "I just wanted to snap you out of this—this— You scare me when— If you give up, I got nobody to lean on! Nobody."

Tennie begins to cry. Victoria caresses her sister's hair and forces a tearful smile.

"Goodness, aren't we pathetic? If those who are so afraid of us could see us now, wouldn't they have a laugh?"

"My god, you're right," Tennie says, swiping at her tears.

"You go on home, honey. I'll finish this article and be right along." She gives her sister a long hug. "We'll be okay. We'll be fine." She kisses Tennie's lingering tears and shoos her out the door. After another moment of looking out the window, Victoria returns to her desk. An hour passes before she finally stretches and begins to gather her things. Movement at the door startles her, but she smiles when she sees Dr. Treat.

"Goodness, I thought I was the only one working late," she says.

"I've written a couple of extra articles. I thought maybe I could take on more around here. You carry so heavy a load. With your sister passing and all, you need a break."

"I certainly won't argue with that."

"Since I separated from my wife, I like to keep busy. I was thinking— Have you got a minute to discuss something?" Treat walks behind her and gently leans her back in her chair. "Let me work on those neck muscles while we talk. Seeing such knots goes against my doctor's grain." As he massages her neck, she tries to relax. "This is much too pretty a neck to be all knotted up." Victoria tenses. Treat quickly resumes his pitch. "Anyway, I think Channing might be ready to take on more of the writing, with a little guidance naturally. And I could do some extra writing myself. With Hume at the presses, we could pretty much run the paper. Take that burden off you."

"Unfortunately, I like to keep my finger on the pulse of things. The *Weekly* is my most important tool to make a difference in this world. We must keep it going."

"You could still pick the subjects and have final approval on what is printed."

"My neck feels better. Thank you." She pats his hand to stop the massage and stands. "I'll think about your proposal. It's quite tempting."

She is totally unprepared for the kiss he plants on her lips. She steps back. "Dr. Treat!"

"I-I'm sorry, Mrs. Woodhull. I meant to comfort you."

"You're forgiven," she relents, seeing him crestfallen.

"I admire you so much, Mrs. Woodhull."

"I admire you a great deal, too, Dr. Treat. Just not in the way that leads to kissing."

"I understand." He smiles, but his eyes darken with malice.

~ ~ ~

"I'm really worried about Sis," Tennie tells Blood as they wait for Victoria to return home. "She hasn't been the same since Utie died."

"I know, Tennie, but I am at a loss how to help her."

"We gotta think of something." Tennie brightens as if she has just had an idea. "Hey! Have you ever thought about doin' some of the lecturin'? Maybe that would help."

"Tennie, I am not a public speaker. The last time I was a frontline person was in the war and that was only because they sent worker bees like me in first to get shot at. I will give my life for you and your sister, but from behind the scenes. I have been faithful there, haven't I?"

"Sis couldn't ask for more."

"Besides, it's Victoria they pay to hear. No one can replace her on the platform."

"My god, what can we do? She's lost all her zest. Especially since little Bennie Tucker went back to Bedford."

"It's only been six weeks since Utie died," Blood reminds her. "That affected Victoria more deeply than she admits. On the heels of her own illness, for the first time she is facing her mortality. Believe me, that changes a person. The brave sometimes know their first fear. I think that is what has happened to Victoria. I've asked Bennie to come on the tour. Between him and being back on the platform, I think some of the old fire will return."

"My god, you're right. I just hope she don't have a breakdown before that happens."

Chapter 43

The "Brother Love" tour through New England and the Midwest is a whirlwind. After each lecture, it's back on the train, bouncing off the miles. In a couple of cities, Victoria, suffering from pleurisy, is unable to speak, so Tennie delivers the lecture. Crowds are sometimes small but always enthusiastic.

On Monday, September 15, 1873, Victoria appears at the American Association of Spiritualists' annual convention in Chicago. The highlight of the meeting is the vote, at Victoria's suggestion, to rename the organization. To symbolize their concern for global harmony, they elect to call themselves the Universal Association of Spiritualists.

Victoria has several detractors, however, who fear her political aspirations have degraded their organization's mission. While she manages to win over some of them, by the time she presents the keynote address on Thursday, the altercations have left her frazzled. Even the warm fall breeze does not temper her agitation.

Still, she steps bravely forward to present her speech "The Elixir of Life or Why Do We Die?"

"I speak tonight on a subject which ought to command the attention of the enlightened world but which receives the anathema of so-called Christians." She pauses and her voice is strident as she continues. "Are we not endowed by nature with the sexual passion? And is it not given to us for a purpose? A purpose that should be a blessing instead of the curse it is to most women." A collective gasp rises through the hall. Red-faced women buzz to their neighbors. Victoria ignores it and plunges ahead.

"Do you know that fully one-half of all women seldom or never experience pleasure in the sexual act? I've had hundreds of wives say to me, 'I would not endure these conditions were I not dependent on my husband for a home.' I say wives are sexual slaves! They may not think they are slaves, some may not be, but let the large majority attempt to assert their sexual freedom and they will quickly come to the realization!" Women applaud, although several stop when their husbands give them reproving looks. "So I am seeking the truth about sexual congress and will follow it if it leads me to heaven or hell.

"Some people think that Free-lovers will cohabit with anyone, but that is not true." Victoria glances pointedly at Dr. Treat, whose white linen suit makes him stand out in the audience. "On the other hand, I say it is better for a woman to bear twelve healthy children by twelve different men that she loved than to bear one child by a man she didn't love."

"Mrs. Woodhull, you will be a better advocate of the principles you champion if you detail your personal experience as a Free-lover!" The man beside Dr. Treat, goaded by the doctor, stands to question her.

"Yes! Speak! Divulge all!" the crowd agrees.

"Exactly what do you want me to explain, Sir?" Victoria gives him a syrupy smile, although her eyes glitter with anger.

"How many men have you prostituted yourself with to forward your cause?" Victoria hesitates. The crowd hushes, expectant. The heckler sneers and presses his point. "Oh, so you can tell on Mr. Beecher but not on yourself?"

"No. I was thinking about a man questioning my virtue. Have I any right as a woman to answer him?"

The convention chairman quickly steps to the podium and bangs his gavel.

"I hardly think this is necessary."

"I'm not worth the powder to shoot at," the man in the audience says, waving off his remark. "But I can detail the lady's private life if she chooses not to."

"Have you ever had sexual intercourse with me?" Victoria asks him, her voice harsh. Red spots of anger color her cheeks. Her eyes bore into his.

"No."

"Do you personally know details of any man who has?"

"No."

"Then what in the name of heaven can you prove? I have never had sexual intercourse with any man with whom I am ashamed to stand side-

293

by-side before the world! I am not ashamed of any act of my life. At the time it was the best I knew. Nor am I ashamed of any desire that has been gratified or any passion alluded to. Every one of them is part of my own soul's life, for which, thank God, I am not accountable to you!" Victoria turns her attention to the audience.

"This gentleman mentioned my cause. I was under the impression this was *our* cause. Why have you made me your president? Is it because I have shown cowardice during the past two years? No! It is because I have gone through the very depths of hell to give you freedom! All my might, all my strength, all my faculties are engaged in this labor. I prostituted my body by speaking to you last night when I was scarcely able to stand. I shall do the same tonight in order to advance a great truth to the world that shall prove its salvation."

The crowd is on its feet. The cheers and applause are tumultuous. Victoria motions for them to sit and continues in a more moderate tone.

"When I came out of prison, I came out a beggar. I asked the Spiritualists, the reformers, to send their money that I might provide you my paper. But you left me to starve in the streets. So I went to the bankers, presidents of railroads, gamblers, and prostitutes and got the money that has sent you the paper you have been reading. And I do not think you are the worst for handling it.

"I have done whatever was necessary to perform what I conceived to be my duty, and so long as I live I shall continue to do whatever is necessary, even to giving my life, to fulfill my heavenly obligation. And, if I devote my body to my work and my soul to God, that is my business and not yours! Are there any of you who would put *your* bodies into the gap? Who among you would pay a tithe of its cost to me? Driven from my former beautiful home, reduced from affluence to want, my business broken and destroyed, dragged from one jail to another, and in a short time I am again to stand trial for telling the truth. I have been smeared all over with the most opprobrious epithets and the vilest names." Her eyes land on her caustic critic. "So until you are ready to accept my notoriety, with its conditions, to suffer what I have suffered and am yet to suffer, do not dare to impugn my motives!"

~ ~ ~

As their train pulls out of Chicago, Tennie plops down beside Victoria.

"My god, that's the Victoria we've been missing!"

"I may never speak so boldly again, Tennie. What's the point really?" She smiles ruefully.

"My god, you're not a quitter!"

"No I'm not. But maybe Mama is right. Maybe I should seek the refuge I crave from God."

"Oh good grief."

Chapter 44

As Victoria reassesses her future, all hell breaks loose across the country. When Northern Pacific Railroad defaults on a million-dollar note and plummets the premier banking firm of Jay Cooke and Company into bankruptcy, it starts a chain reaction.

Before the sun goes down on September 18, forty more banks and brokerage firms have gone under and the country plunges into economic depression. Even the New York Stock Exchange is forced to close as the greed-driven Gilded Age of America teeters on the brink of destruction.

Cornelius Vanderbilt makes President Grant an offer: Unfreeze thirty million from the Treasury, and he will throw ten million dollars worth of railroad bonds into the economy to get it back on track. The President declines.

For ten days, as businesses fail and breadlines grow, the stock market remains closed. On the day it shakily reopens, the Commodore makes his final trip to Wall Street, calming nervous brokers and encouraging them to get back to work. Then he pumps money into the economy by expanding and improving his railroads, some say single-handedly saving the United States from bankruptcy. Still depression holds America in its grip.

While Anthony Comstock pursues vice with a vengeance and the suffragists hold a high-toned, high-minded Woman's Congress that accomplishes nothing, 4,000 impoverished citizens pay their money to hear Victoria publicly denounce the villains who have destroyed their livelihood. Her trials have aged her beyond her thirty-five years and she looks worn and ill in her black skirt and tailored jacket. As she addresses the packed house at Cooper Institute, her voice is raspy from a severe cold.

"A few years ago we witnessed devastation on Wall Street as this Administration aided robber barons Jim Fisk and Jay Gould in their plot to corner the gold market. On September twenty-fourth, eighteen sixty-nine, a day that will forever be known as Black Friday, we watched ruined men plummet from buildings or shoot themselves on the street. Following this debacle, a new system of robbery flourished: the insidious system of credit. 'Buy now, pay tomorrow' became our motto in this Gilded Age. Well, Ladies and Gentlemen, tomorrow has come. And the system has collapsed around us.

"I charge that this government is a failure because it did not foresee and forestall this catastrophe by putting safeguards in place. I charge it is a failure because it has not secured individual freedom, maintained equality, or administered economic justice to its citizens. The Wall Street crash is a warning. No longer will thousands of men, women, and children eke out a miserable life upon what a 'sport' would disdain to feed his dogs while the favored few wallow in superfluities!"

As millions of unemployed roam the countryside looking for any work they can find, and others stand in line for hours for a bowl of soup and chunk of bread, they are happy to see Boss Tweed finally convicted of embezzlement and sentenced to twelve years at Blackwell's Island Workhouse.

Victoria comments in the *Weekly*: "The fine the villain Boss Tweed was assessed is over fifty thousand less than what this humble editor was forced to pay, even though we were acquitted of any crime! Even more sadly, Mr. Tweed will undoubtedly pay the amount with some of the millions he took from poor citizens who could sorely use it now! I cannot call this justice."

January of 1874 sees no relief from the iron grip of the depression, so Stephen Pearl Andrews and other labor leaders gather thousands of homeless and unemployed at Tompkins Square for a protest march. Their banners and placards tell the story: "1 in 7 Americans Say Give Us Our Jobs" and "We Are Homeless, We Are Hungry." As the parade surges down the street, mounted police gallop into its midst, swinging clubs and trampling marchers.

"What are you doing? We have a permit!" Pearl shouts above the chaos, but the police don't care.

"You are banned! You are banned!" one says, galloping up to Andrews.

"No one told us! Stop the killing, and we will disband!"

The policeman swings and his club connects. Andrews is down. He crawls to protection from the stampeding crowd as the policeman gallops away. After what seems like hours, the Square is silent. The bruised Andrews pulls himself to his feet and wanders sadly among the bloody bodies looking for survivors. There are a few, but dozens are dead. Victoria, on tour in Delaware, reads the news and weeps.

"I should have been there for Pearl, Tennie. Is there no hope for any of us?"

"My god, Sis, something's gotta break open soon, or we'll be in the breadlines ourselves.

"I know, but I don't know what to do. The spirits who guided me for so long have deserted me. I feel powerless and yearn for a normal life: A husband to equally bear the responsibilities, nights at home with my family, and intimate mother-daughter conversations with Zulu Maud."

"My god, Sis, we'd both die of boredom with such a life, and you know it."

Despite the cries of the populous, President Grant continues to refuse to increase the available legal tender to help the economy. The depression drags on.

At their winter convention in D.C., the suffragists give speeches and spout resolutions, but the campaign has no spark. When the Chief Justice rules that suffrage is a state question, many of the women decamp to the temperance cause. Hordes of angry females invade saloons with hatchets. Some kneel and pray loudly for the patrons' salvation while others smash bars, tables, and windows.

As the first electric streetcars scoot through New York City, Victoria hails the formation of the New York Society for Prevention of Cruelty to Children.

"At last someone has taken formal steps to end the abuse of our children. I congratulate Mr. Bergh and Mr. Gerry for caring so greatly for our human offspring, although I think it ironic that this effort comes eight years after these same men founded the ASPCA for better treatment of animals. The charge has been leveled at me that my embracing of the philosophy of free-love will bring great harm to our children, but our present institution of marriage brings the greater harm. Unhappy people lash out in anger, and violence begets violence. I know from personal experience that bad treatment can leave lifelong scars on our children and that verbal abuse is as demoralizing as physical acts.

"Because women are still given no say over their own bodies and whether or not to hatch offspring, four-fifths of children born today are unwelcome and neglected. In New York City alone, ten thousand juvenile vagabonds are adrift on the streets. Children who should be playing with dolls and trucks are struggling to survive. Why are our metropolises filled with places like New York's Dutch Hill from which gangs terrorize our citizens? I'll tell you why. Because gangs give a sense of community these abandoned children have never known. And so our urchin boys prepare for the almshouse, prisons, and gallows, and our sweet, innocent girls enter the horrid halls of prostitution. Thank god Mr. Bergh and Mr. Gerry have addressed this tragedy."

Chapter 45

On March 5, 1874, the final libel case filed by the teenage-molesting broker Luther Challis brings Victoria, Tennie, and Blood back to court. Hundreds of spectators are turned away for lack of even standing space in the halls. Challis' attorney questions Victoria first, smiling patronizingly.

"In your opinion, should a woman desert her husband and live with another if prompted by such a desire?"

Attorney Charley Brooks, whose bold Irish confidence has not waned, sweeps his red hair from his freckled forehead and objects to the question as immaterial. He is overruled, but Victoria waves aside her attorney's protest.

"It's all right, Charley. I'm happy to answer. If her will takes her away from a man, a woman ought to go. Any man or woman, married or unmarried, who consorts for anything but love is a prostitute."

"Enough!" The judge bangs his gavel to quiet the hoots and cheers. "This court will not be subjected to immoral social theories! We are dismissed. Remove the prisoners to the Tombs."

"Your Honor, my clients are not a danger to society, and they have neither the means nor desire to flee their certain vindication! I request bail—" Charley Brooks is cut off as the judge bangs the gavel and hurries out. Zulu Maud begins to wail, and Victoria turns frantically to George.

"Please keep my children safe."

The next day Charley Brooks begins the case for the defense by presenting the legal definition of the libel as being a published statement that is false and has the malicious intent to defame a person's character or subject them to ridicule. To refute the first criteria, he presents an affidavit from Molly de Ford, madam of the house to which Mr. Challis and Mr. Maxwell took the young women. She attests to the truth of Victoria's report. The judge sneers as he skims the affidavit. He peers at Charley over the top of his wire-rimmed glasses.

"So we are now to take the word of a whore against an upstanding banker?" he asks.

Ignoring the slur, Charley Brooks next calls Mr. Maxwell, who also testifies to the truth of the article. And then another man, who asks to be known as Mr. Smith, corroborates Maxwell's testimony.

To address the "malicious" criteria for libel, Victoria takes the stand, and Charley Brooks asks her to tell the court why she published the article about Mr. Challis.

"Mr. Challis took two young schoolgirls from Baltimore, plied them with champagne, then dragged them to Madam de Ford's brothel and robbed them of their purity. One eventually took her life because of the shame. I wanted justice for those poor girls and wanted the world to realize that men who are guilty of immorality should be ostracized as much as women are."

"So there was no maliciousness in your intention?"

"Not at all, Sir. This was simply a matter of bringing social evils to the front for discussion and redress."

The judge, red-faced with anger over the enthusiastic applause, quickly adjourns.

After ten days of testimony, closing arguments end, and the judge instructs the jury that "nothing but a guilty verdict can be returned or even considered." The next morning, however, they return with a verdict of Not Guilty. The court erupts in wild cheering, but the judge is furious. Veins throb on his neck as he roars above the din.

"This is the most outrageous verdict ever recorded. I am ashamed of the jury who has rendered it!" He stalks out without even adjourning court.

With their legal challenges behind them, Victoria and Tennie rent one floor of a house on Eighteenth Street, between Union Square and Third Avenue. Bennie and Roxanna move in with them, and they once again live in Bohemian disorder.

After the Beecher-appointed Committee exonerates their pastor, the shaky truce between Tilton and Beecher flounders and at Tilton's behest, an independent Ecclesiastic Council is called to look into the scandal.

301

Victoria quickly arranges to be on the lecture circuit, glad they are destroying each other now instead of her.

These hearings, too, of course, are a total farce. The *Brooklyn Argus* says of it:

> **This is the most marvelous of human dramas, more intense than any work of fiction. It is greater in plot, development, and effect than Hawthorne's *The Scarlet Letter*, which it closely parallels, and more titillating than George Elliot's *Romala* or Shakespeare's *Othello*, perhaps having its only counterpart in Faust.**

Neither Victoria nor Elizabeth Cady are called to testify and Susan B. Anthony refuses to appear so there is no one to refute Lib when she denies the affair and blames Victoria for her false confession. She offers no explanation, however, as to why she now leaves her marriage forever.

Tilton blames everything on the suffragists. As does Beecher, who calls them human hyenas as he denies all wrong-doing. The media uses the testimony to discredit the woman's movement, with even the long-tolerant *Herald* writing: "As it now stands, let us hear no more of this 'reform' for at least a generation."

"Apparently truth is not something they are seeking," Victoria says, when questioned about the Council. "Mr. Beecher has weakened his manhood by labeling suffragists human hyenas and using Lib like a football. He has starred in the Gilded Age as a sentimental fool, long-winded buffoon, and hypocritical stuffed-shirt. But we see through his mask. We see in him culture's sin of hiding its sordid truths behind a decorous façade. This scandal is the richly deserved unveiling because it leads to the question: If it is proven that such men as Henry Ward Beecher and Theodore Tilton find the marriage laws too stringent, might it not be well to review such laws?"

~ ~ ~

Returning to New York, Victoria is stunned when her nephew Channing informs her Dr. Treat has deserted the *Weekly.*

"We had the articles you sent from the road and the news of the Council against Mr. Beecher so we got by. Subscriptions are off, with the depression and all, but we haven't missed an issue. Your brother George has been a tremendous help, Colonel. He even had Byron doing simple things like folding papers, which By loved doing." Victoria's praise is interrupted as Tennie dashes in, waving a pamphlet.

"My god, I'll write an article to lay this blackguard lower than Hades! Better yet, I'll shoot him dead!"

"Tennie, calm down. What is it?"

Tennie hands her the pamphlet. Victoria blanches when she reads the title: *Beecher, Tilton, Woodhull, the Creation of Society: All Four of Them Exposed, and if Possible Reformed and Forgiven, in Dr. Treat's Celebrated Letter to Victoria C. Woodhull.*

"My god, the maggot slime bucket blackens the names of our entire family!"

"I should have listened to you, Tennie," Victoria says, becoming more and more appalled as she leafs through the pamphlet. "You sensed it long ago. I thought I could at least trust a fellow Spiritualist with fair play. How could he believe in a divine spirit that connects us all and then betray us so? It is a treachery too great to imagine. He is a Judas and a bigger hypocrite than Mr. Beecher!" She spins toward Blood. "And I blame you, James, for bringing that man into our lives!"

"Victoria—"

"Don't say it. Let me be angry for awhile."

Blood looks at Victoria sadly for a moment, then walks away. The door closes behind him.

"A bit harsh with the Colonel, weren't you?"

"Drop it, Tennie. Right now we need to figure out how to respond to this trash."

"What if we swear out a warrant for libel?"

"I have neither the health, the funds, nor the energy to go into court again. No one will believe us anyway, and it will only call attention to the pamphlet."

"My god, it is so unfair!"

303

"Yes, it is." She draws Tennie into a hug, but freezes when she sees the bulky figure of "Tearful" Tommy Shearman heading toward the office. "Tennie, quick, be calm." She nods toward Shearman. Tennie has donned a look of contempt by the time Beecher's attorney reaches them.

"Mrs. Woodhull, Miss Claflin, I heard you had returned to the city. Your lecture tour was a success I hope?"

"What can we do for you, Mr. Shearman?"

"It has come to Dr. Beecher's attention that a nefarious pamphlet is being circulated about your family. He is in sympathy with the agony of false accusations, especially from a former friend. And on the heels of your unjust persecution by the courts . . ." Shearman lets the sentence dangle. Victoria and Tennie exchange a distrustful look and wait him out. He finally clears his throat and proceeds. "In any event, the Reverend thought an extended vacation in France might give you the opportunity to regain your health. He will make the funds available if you desire to go. And while you are gone, my partners and I will see what can be done to silence the talk Mr. Treat's pamphlet is inciting."

"And you want what in return?" Victoria asks.

"Nothing but your absence until the Council has disbanded. And your discretion, of course, concerning the source of your travel funds."

Victoria and Tennie accept the deal and pack for France.

"My god, Sis, you said you wanted to see Paris, but who would've guessed Beecher would pay for the trip."

"Since the Council won't call me, I am amazed that his supporters feel it necessary to get me out of the country. But who am I to refuse a much-needed rest without the expense of it? We will rejuvenate and return to fight the battle important."

"I know why you're taking Bennie with us, but I don't understand why you're taking Ma and not the Colonel. How much rest are we going to get with her carping at us every minute?"

"Mama's prayers have been a great comfort to me over the past weeks, and she deserves the reward. I'm sure the beauty of Paris will soothe her temper. James brought that-that awful Dr. Treat into our fold— I'm hoping a separation will renew my good feelings toward him."

"My god, me, too. Ain't no one loved anyone as much as the Colonel loves you!"

Birds sing and waves lap gently against the shore as Victoria and Tennie board the ship *Lafayette.* Reporters surround them, shouting questions:

"Is Mr. Beecher paying for your trip?"

"What are your comments about the accusations in Dr. Treat's pamphlet? Is what he claims true?"

"We have had a long and successful lecture tour," Victoria responds. "But my health has suffered, and my doctors think I will benefit from Paris sunshine."

"I have something to say about Treat!" Tennie adds. "He is a reprobate, blackguard, and rejected suitor! You gentlemen know that if my sister and I were prostitutes we would not be ashamed to tell you. And my sister Utica, God rest her soul, was too drunk to whore. Any messages of this kind you can send through your papers will be appreciated. Oh, and to accuse my saintly mother is too ridiculous to even address." She turns and flounces up the ramp and onto the boat.

~ ~ ~

The sisters are still in Paris when the Ecclesiastical Council finally announces its findings. They conclude that Lib had inordinate affection for her spiritual mentor; that Theodore Tilton and Frank Moulton maliciously and vengefully blackmailed Beecher; and that Henry Ward allowed his generosity and love to lead him to drop his guard with traitorous friends. In other words, you didn't do anything wrong, Reverend Beecher, but don't do it again. Reactions on the street are immediate and opposing, with Stephen Pearl Andrews summing it up perhaps the best.

"The major concern of society is not with Henry Ward Beecher's pompous hypocrisy but with his personality. His indulgence in socially destructive antics is titillating yet frightening. For the populace to admit him guilty is to admit that their own moral perspective on life might be wrong, and they are not willing to entertain this thought."

Theodore Tilton is not surprised by the verdict and immediately files a civil suit charging Beecher with alienation of Lib's affections. The lawsuit sets the country in an uproar.

~ ~ ~

The Beecher-Tilton drama is a world away from where Victoria enjoys the city of romance with Bennie Tucker. On the day the Council concludes, Victoria gazes out at the bustling city beyond the window of her suite in Paris' Grand Hotel. Bennie stands behind her, rubbing her shoulders. She moans in pleasure as he kisses her neck, but stiffens as a forlorn-looking Tennie wanders into view on the street.

"What's the matter, Victoria?"

"I cannot bear to see Tennie so downcast. It takes away whatever pleasure I might enjoy." She turns to face him and an idea lights her eyes. "I know! You can love her this afternoon. That will bring the youth back to her face!"

"I don't want to love thy sister!"

"Wouldn't you do it for me?"

"I can't believe thee would ask such a thing! I thought thee loved me!"

"I do, silly. But I love my sister, too. Your kind administrations are exactly what she needs."

"Mrs. Woodhull, I am not a toy to be handed off when thee tires of playing with it."

"I'm not saying you are, Bennie. We will love again. But how can I enjoy your attentions if my sister is despondent? Nobody can love me who doesn't also love Tennie."

"Are thou saying that if I do not sleep with thy sister, I do not sleep with thee?"

"You will find her most satisfying. She is more well-versed in the Kama Sutra than I am."

"I don't sleep with thee for the mechanics!"

"I'm not talking about mechanics! I am talking about spiritual comfort and release. Variety is essential to all of us. Seamstresses change thread colors when working their needles, writers change pens, taste is numbed if only one food is eaten. Even the sense of hearing is impaired by constant monotonous sound. Why are the sexual organs an exception? This is the very principle of Free-love that you profess to believe in as much as I do. Sampling another's love will enflame our own passions."

"My passion for thee does not need enflaming! I love thee with all my heart, Victoria." He stares at her sadly for a moment, makes a decision. "I am leaving."

"Leaving?"

"Yes. And I shall never darken thy door again."

"Then *Mizpah*. May you go with God." She turns away to hide a tear as Bennie gives her a last pleading, puppy-dog look. When she doesn't relent, he throws his clothes into a bag and storms out—just as Tennie enters.

"My god, what got into his shorts?"

"Bennie has left us for good, Tennie."

"You're kidding."

"Ah that I were. I will miss him greatly, but he is too young to understand unconditional love." She walks to the window and watches Bennie stride from the hotel. "Men can be so frustrating! On the one hand I have James, who grants me so much freedom I wonder if he truly cares about me at all. On the other is Bennie, whose love wants to chain me to him alone. There is a balance neither seems to see."

"My god, forget about men. Let's have some fun! With Ma and Zulu Maud off shopping, we are on our own to do what we like."

"I'd like to walk in Paris' beautiful parks and drink the aroma of flowers. Later we can find an outdoor café for some delectable *vin, le fromage*, and *les bonbons*."

"Huh? Don't be going all Prof Perlo on me here. This is a fine city, except I can't understand a bit of the language."

307

"Wine and cheese and candy, Tennie! And we can try the famous French pastries. Even some crepes and crème brulée, if you like." The thought brightens Victoria, and Tennie grins in relief.

"My god, Sis, lead away."

By October, Victoria is back from Paris, refreshed, renewed and ready to fight on for truth, justice and the American way. She takes to the lecture circuit with her new speech "Tried As By Fire." The day before they leave, she and Blood walk in a wooded area of Central Park, relishing the vivid fall hues.

"James, I have decided to take Mama with me tomorrow. Her presence and prayers have become a great comfort to me."

"When have you needed someone else's prayers? You speak directly to your Spirit Guides!"

"Not so much anymore. They have mostly deserted me. Even Demosthenes appears only rarely."

"Maybe you just haven't been listening."

"I do not want to argue."

"Nor do I." He catches a red leaf as it floats to the ground and twirls it morosely between his finger and thumb. "I've lost your love, Victoria. It dismantles me because my devotion has never faltered. Tell me what I can do to regain your heart and I will do it."

"I need time. I want you to stay in New York to help Channing on the paper."

"Are we estranged then?" he asks, his voice husky with sadness.

"It's not punishment. It's just . . . with mama coming— I can't have both of you with me. The animosity will drain me."

Unshed tears glisten in Blood's eyes. He lets the leaf fall to the ground and takes her hand. They walk in silence, scaring a rabbit that looks at them with doe eyes. As it wiggles its nose and hops away, Blood turns Victoria to face him. Passion mingles with the wetness in his eyes.

"My love will never slake, Victoria, even if you cast me aside."

"That I have never doubted."

"It is the conundrum of free love that, believing in it as I do, I must let you follow your heart."

"I'm sorry. I'm truly sorry." She rises on her toes and kisses him.

With a low groan, he hugs her desperately.

~ ~ ~

Despite her inner turmoil, Victoria speaks for 150 consecutive nights to record crowds. In a testament to her celebrity, her lecture fees soar to three hundred dollars a lecture, an unbelievable sum given the persisting economic depression. It is, in fact, the highest for any woman and most men even in good times. Crowds respond enthusiastically as she again talks of sex.

"Don't tell me I cannot discuss the sexual question. I would like to see the law that can prevent me. You remember that little game was tried in New York and failed. When I published the biography of the American Pope, the authorities, urged on by the minions of the Church and Comstock's Y. M. C. Assassination, swooped down and carried me off to jail. I remained there for weeks. Apparently Mr. Beecher is bigger than the free press and of more consequence than free speech."

~ ~ ~

"I advocate complete freedom for sexuality the same as for religion," she tells a predominantly Mormon audience in Salt Lake City. "I advocate freedom for the monogamist to practice monogamy, for the promiscuous to remain promiscuous, even for the celibate to refrain from sex altogether. Am I, therefore, a proponent of promiscuity or monogamy or celibacy? No. To advocate freedom for individuals to choose their personal sexual practice is by no means synonymous with the advocacy of whatever practice they choose.

"I will make this clearer, lest some not understand. As I said, I advocate religious freedom. Every individual has the right to be Catholic, Jew, Mormon, or even Presbyterian like certain famous personages in Brooklyn." She pauses to let the audience have a laugh, and then continues. "They can even be Pagan, if they so desire. This freedom of religion is a right guaranteed by our nation's Constitution. If an attempt were made to subvert this right, every hand would rise against it. Nobody would think of calling me a Romanist because I say that everybody has the right to be a Catholic if they so choose, or a Mormon because I say

309

that everybody has the right to practice Mormonism. But transfer the question from religion to sexuality, and I am denounced as an advocate of promiscuity. Do you get my point about the whole matter of free-love now?"

Chapter 46

On January 11, 1875, four years to the day after Victoria pointed out to the Judiciary Committee that women already had the Constitutional right to vote, the alienation of affections trial of Tilton versus Beecher begins. With the public's fascination with celebrity, the entire world focuses on Brooklyn. Such global attention is even more amazing since word of mouth and newspapers alone spread the news.

Overflowing ferries cross in a steady stream beneath the construction of the bridge to Brooklyn, and the streets surrounding the City Courthouse have a carnival atmosphere. There are refreshment and souvenir booths, and people as far as the eye can see. Neighborhood saloons do a rousing business as politicians and aristocrats fight with common folk for seats distributed by lottery. Tickets fetch outrageous sums on the black market.

Inside the courtroom, an overabundance of floral arrangements fills the air with the cloying odor of violets, lilies, camellias, and roses. Vendors stroll the aisles, selling opera glasses, sandwiches, and soft drinks to those who refuse to move lest they forfeit their seats. Reporters crowd the press galley. Channing Miles, representing the *Weekly,* is among them. A few spectators recognize him and point and whisper as they look around for Victoria and Tennie, both conspicuously absent.

There are 500 people crammed into the 300-seat room by the time the judge calls the session to order. The clerk drones out the long, declamatory charge that calls for damages of one hundred thousand dollars. Tilton leaps to his feet, announcing he will give all monies to charity should he win. Suddenly a lad rushes into the courtroom.

"Mr. Beecher has arrived! Beecher is here!" the boy yells. Loud cheers rise from the balcony, which looks like a Plymouth Church prayer meeting. The parishioners, mostly female, lean over the railing and strain to see their hero.

Outside, guards escort Henry Ward through the throngs that part like the Red Sea. He jokes, waves, shakes hands, and signs autographs like a politician on parade. At one point, he drops his handkerchief, and it is immediately torn to shreds as people fight to claim it as a souvenir. White lilies are strewn in his path. One pretty young lady hands him a bouquet of violets, and he kisses her cheek. As he walks on, he sniffs the flowers and laughs at children who jump rope, chanting:

> *Beecher, Beecher is my name*
> *Beecher till I die*
> *I never kissed Miz Tilton*
> *I never told a lie.*

Loud applause greets his appearance in the courtroom, until the judge threatens to banish all onlookers. With a bang of the gavel, the trial begins.

As the days flip past, and the Beecher-Tilton trial drags on, the public expects the *Weekly* to be the inside source for every word uttered and every move made by the participants. Instead, Victoria sticks to social commentary, writing such things as:

> **The drama in Brooklyn began with an exposé intended to address the social issues of our time. It has now turned into a carnival of sensation. Our goal is not to advance the circus, but to wring as much social good from it as we can.**

Other newspapers are filled cover-to-cover with trial news so only the *Weekly* seems to notice national and world events like the groundbreaking Civil Rights Act, co-authored by Benjamin Butler, that is signed into law on March third. The Act bans all public accommodations from discriminating on the grounds of race, thereby abolishing segregated restaurants, theaters, and railroad cars. Having spent years exercising passive resistance by staging sit-ins in whites-only railroad cars, Frederick Douglass sends Victoria a telegram thanking her for covering the historic event. His note brings her to tears, and she dashes off a reply:

> **Dear Mr. Douglass,**
> **You have waited a long time for just treatment. We women have, too, and as we continue to fight for *our* inalienable rights, we thrill at yours. Society has attempted to pound both of us to the ground, but like Harriet Tubman, we will 'keep on going' until every man, woman, and child enjoys the freedom to live up to their God-given potential. *Mizpah.***
>
> **Victoria C. Woodhull**

After Frank Moulton, as the go-between, has consulted copious notes to lay out the facts of the scandal for the court, and Emma Moulton has supplied the most damning testimony against Beecher because of her patent honesty and sincere distress over Beecher falling off his moral throne, Theodore Tilton takes the stand. Beecher's lawyers immediately bring up his relationship with Victoria.

"There was no affair," he lies. "It was solely Mr. Beecher who was responsible for my connection with Mrs. Woodhull. Otherwise I wouldn't dream of associating with a woman of her type. It was foolish and wrong."

"Victoria has done a work for women that none of us could have done," Elizabeth Cady rants to her husband when she reads of Tilton's testimony. "She has dared men to call her names that make women shudder and chucked principle, like medicine, down their throats. I ought to go pull that reporter off our front steps and tell him everything I know."

"Now, Lizzie Lee, we have agreed not to interfere."

"Well, it's wrong. Just wrong."

"Be that as it may, I forbid you—"

"Excuse me?"

"Lizzie, Lizzie, can we not just enjoy our breakfast together? We have so few of them."

"As you wish, Venerable Sire."

Accustomed to her sarcasm, her husband returns to reading his paper.

~ ~ ~

As her name is bandied about the Brooklyn courtroom, Victoria speaks to a full house in Chicago, her subject not the scandal on everyone's minds but on temperance.

"The temperance movement's call to sign a pledge to 'just say no' to hard drink does not work," she asserts. "The fight against alcoholism must begin at the root, with the proper influences for our children. Nothing else will cure the world of drunkenness."

As she leaves the lecture hall, reporters bombard her for comments on Tilton's testimony.

"Mr. Tilton acts like a sniveling little schoolboy," she says, and then mimics him. "Beecher made me do it. If it hadn't been for Mr. Beecher. I was wrong and foolish." Victoria shakes her head, disgusted. "Theodore will make quite a man if he ever grows up."

"What about Mr. Beecher? Were you lovers with him as well?" a reporter asks.

"No comment. He has too many resources to use against me."

A few nights later, Victoria and troop bounce across Indiana by train. Zulu Maud is curled up beside Tennie, who flips through the *Indianapolis Herald.* Victoria and Roxanna doze across the aisle.

Tennie's hoot wakes Victoria.

"Tennie, shush!" she scolds. "Mama is exhausted."

"My god, I'm sorry. But the Bates' hotel in Indianapolis—ain't that where Byron fell?"

"Yes," Victoria whispers. "Why?"

"The lady who ran that hotel. The Reverend had his way with her, too. Listen to this headline: 'Mr. Beecher's history of affairs from Betty Bates in Indiana to Mrs. Henry Bowen and others in New York.' They say Betty Bates was his first— My god, she was just a teenager."

Victoria doesn't respond. Her mind drifts back to the fateful day her son's life had changed forever.

Twenty-one-year-old Victoria strolls along an Indianapolis sidewalk, enjoying the beautiful summer day. Approaching the Bates Hotel, she hears her four-year-old son jabbering from a second-story window. Watching him nervously, she picks up her pace.

Suddenly her worst fears are realized as Byron plummets from the window! Victoria screams and catapults forward. Just in time. Byron lands in her outstretched arms, and they hit the street with a loud thud. Victoria rushes inside, Byron hanging off her arms, screaming for pretty Betty Bates, who is at the front desk, to call a doctor. Betty sends a porter running as a hysterical Victoria dashes up the stairs.

A short time later, the doctor examines the toddler and shakes his head. Victoria grabs the boy, keening inconsolably. The doctor turns his attention to Canning Woodhull, who is out cold on the floor, an empty bottle of liquor still pressed to his lips. The doctor nudges him with a toe, and Canning's head flops backwards with a loud snort. His jaw twitches.

Betty and the doctor give Victoria pitying looks as they leave. She isn't even aware. She is in a trance, blouse ripped open, toddler pressed against her breast.

It is almost dawn when Victoria returns to reality, still holding her son tightly against her. She looks down at Canning, snoring loudly, his head heavy against her leg. Flicking off her husband's weight, Victoria puts an ear to Byron's mouth. Feeling his breath, she leaps to her feet, shouting with joy, "He's alive! Oh, thank you, Great Spirits, he's alive!"

"My god, small world, huh? Want me to read you the article?" Tennie's voice snaps Victoria back to the present.

"What?"

"The article about the preacher's dalliances. Want me to read it to you?"

"Oh. No, Tennie, I have no interest. Investigators can uncover hundreds of affairs the man has had, and no one's going to care. He's been placed on a great white throne and nothing can topple him."

Chapter 47

Spring is budding in Brooklyn as, on April 4, 1875, four months into the trial, Stephen Pearl Andrews is called to testify. Everyone is on alert for Victoria to sneak in under disguise to hear him, but she stays miles away as Tilton's attorney steps forward.

"Professor Andrews, Mr. Beecher and Mr. Tilton have both been disdainful of Mrs. Woodhull, citing her low associations. Can you tell the court who some of those associations are?"

"Certainly. Her salons were regularly attended by several people in this courtroom." He gestures toward Ohio's James Garfield, leading Republican in the House. "Representative Garfield, there, and several reporters in the galley, including *Tribune* editor Whitelaw Reid." He ignores Reid's glare and continues. "Other frequent guests were Albert Bisbaine and Henry Clews, among other bankers; several members of the Stock Exchange, including its President; business owners like Western Union President William Orton, as well as Mr. Rockefeller and George Westinghouse. Grant's former Chief of Staff William Hillyer came often; as did P.T. Barnum; Jim Fisk, God rest his soul, and Mr. Gould; other guests included the Reverend Octavius Brook Farthingham; the renowned Dr. Josiah Cummings, as well as a number of governors, senators, generals, General Benjamin Butler being one, and—"

"I think that will do," the judge says.

"I have a shorter list of ladies."

"I think we will omit the ladies," the judge says.

"We ought to have the names of the ladies," the attorney counters.

"Very well, then, the ladies."

"Besides Queen Jadgiva of Poland, ladies in attendance included Mrs. Elizabeth Cady Stanton, Miss Susan B. Anthony, Mrs. Beecher Hooker, Mrs. Phelps, Mrs. Bullard. Even Lucretia Mott came by one time when she was in the city. And all the ladies of the Sorosis club, columnists Jennie June and Fanny Fern—"

"Enough," the judge says.

Spectators murmur in surprise at the impressive list as the gavel bangs.

By mid-April, it is time for Beecher's defense. Their strategy is to persuade the jury that Theodore alienated his wife's affections himself by having an affair with Victoria. After questioning three of Victoria's former servants in rapid succession, all of whom testify to seeing Victoria and Theodore in half-dress or compromising poses, Henry Beecher is called. He again milks his celebrity as he arrives late and is ushered through the boisterous crowd, directly to the stand.

Over nine days of questioning, Beecher plays with gems, sniffs flowers, and frequently acts out his responses with great theatrics. "Tearful" Tommy Shearman adds his own histrionics as they establish that Theodore Tilton was Beecher's favored son at Plymouth Church and that Lib Tilton was loved like his own daughter before they both betrayed him. It's more a performance than courtroom testimony.

When the Reverend is cross-examined, he maintains his bravado, but both he and his flowers are wilted as, after fifteen days and 894 answers of "I can't recollect," "I don't know," or some similarly evasive reply, including many outright lies, he leaves the stand.

As Beecher immediately flees to his summer home in upstate New York, Mark Twain expresses the common sentiment: "That man's faith is as pulpy as a banana. His conscience must have leaked out his pores as a child."

Victoria talks about Beecher's testimony as she addresses Spiritualists in New Jersey.

"The Andover Review today, in their account of his time on the stand, called Mr. Beecher our Demosthenes. I have communicated regularly with the great Greek orator since I was three years old, and let me tell you, Henry Ward Beecher is no Demosthenes!" She has to wait for the laughter to subside. "But I am more concerned about the significance of this trial to our society than I am about Mr. Beecher's performance. Throughout this past decade—this Gilded Age—money, power, and standing in the community have created false reputations that hide all kinds of sin and corruption.

"Christianity will survive, as it always has, with or without Henry Ward Beecher. The real question is whether the wealth and influence of the great political machine called Plymouth Church and the power of the Beecher name will overcome the force of proof, lessons of law, and instincts of justice! It is tragic that the Great Pope now claims to have been victimized by a saint, burned by a woman's charms like Samson was by Delilah's. This has been man's excuse for failure ever since Adam ate the apple. 'The woman tempted me and I did eat,' Adam said, and Mr. Beecher follows the same justification. 'The woman tempted me, but I did *not* eat.' In both cases, she gets the blame.

"And God help the woman who finally has had enough of such servitude to man and demands a divorce. Did you know that eighty percent of men seeking divorce cite their wife's failure to be a submissive helpmate as their reason? But if a woman asks for a divorce, generally because of physical cruelty, society whispers it is she who is somehow to blame for the marriage's failure. This double standard must end."

As Victoria leaves New Jersey, she is surprised and pleased to encounter Elizabeth Cady on the train. After a brief, awkward silence, they are soon chatting away. The topic, of course, is the trial.

"I am beside myself over this abominable mixture of deceit. Both male players are ready to sacrifice Lib to save their own skins," Elizabeth tells her. "Not to mention what they are doing to you!"

"That is the ploy of the ages. Unfortunately, woman herself allows it by selling herself too cheaply."

"How can she help it? She has been taught to do so from an early age. The Bible itself fosters belief in woman's inferiority. Someday I am going to write a Woman's Bible. It will reinterpret the Bible's derogatory references to women in the light of nonsexist passages, reason, and common sense."

"I will buy the first copy!"

~ ~ ~

In May, new scandal rocks the Grant Administration in the form of a "Whiskey Ring" that has misappropriated three million dollars from

318

liquor taxes. Warrants are issued for the two ringleaders and 238 others, including the President's personal secretary and his Secretary of War. Luckily for Grant, except for in the *Weekly*, the news is buried as Beecher's defense team continues to slog through witnesses. With such stimulating details as Tilton's abuse of his wife and his affair with "the corrupt Mrs. Woodhull" being offered in court, who can be interested in a small matter of tax fraud reaching all the way to the White House? Besides, word is out that Victoria has been subpoenaed and will appear in court. It's what everyone has been waiting for.

On the morning of May 12, 1875, the mob at Brooklyn City Courthouse almost riots when court is delayed. Dozens of policemen struggle to maintain order. When the doors finally open, a group of Scottish tourists is almost trampled as their guide leads them inside. They are too excited to care.

The gavel can't stop the buzzing and hissing when Victoria and Tennie enter. Victoria wears a tailored, navy blue suit with pleated skirt, black straw hat, and a white tea rose at her throat. Spectators stand and gape as she walks to the front, returning Frank Moulton's nod and Tilton's hard stare. Her eyes flick to Eunice Beecher, who sits like a sphinx behind the lawyers, long, black shawl clutched in black-gloved hands. A black bonnet tied in a bow under Eunice's pointed chin leaves only a narrow ribbon of brittle gray hair to soften her deeply lined forehead. Her eyes are tiny slits of hatred fixed on Victoria. When Victoria returns the stare, Eunice pointedly leaves the room. Victoria reaches the front and starts toward the witness stand, but "Tearful" Tommy Shearman stops her.

"You don't have to take the stand," he tells her. "We just want your letters."

"I will produce them only upon direct order from the judge, and I request that I be allowed to explain them."

"Your Honor, I object to entering anything Mrs. Woodhull has into evidence unless she is sworn in as a witness," Tilton's attorney, Mr. Beach, says. Everyone in the room strains to listen as Victoria speaks to him in a low voice, warning him that if she is put on the stand she will tell truths Tilton does not want told.   "Never mind," Beach says, throwing up his hands in resignation as Victoria addresses the judge.

"Your Honor, I have only a few unimportant letters written by Mr. Tilton to myself that are not in the least discreditable," Victoria says. "I have reason to believe other letters of mine, from both Mr. Tilton and Mr. Beecher, are in the hands of the defense, as well as the prosecution. As you know, I have been imprisoned several times, with most of my private correspondence being carried off."

"Well, turn over what you have," the judge says.

Victoria opens her leather briefcase and extracts six letters. She hands them to Shearman and waits while the attorneys look them over. They are disappointed.

"This is the worst," Shearman tells his cohorts. "'Put this under your pillow, dream of the writer, and peace be with you. Affectionately, Theodore Tilton.'" He hands the letters back to Victoria. "These won't do, Mrs. Woodhull."

"Well, I am not the judge of that. But you were anxious to have them." She turns to the judge. "If that is all, Your Honor, I would like to leave."

The judge raises a questioning eyebrow to the attorneys. Both sides shrug and nod. He turns back to Victoria. "You are dismissed, Mrs. Woodhull. Thank you for your cooperation."

Tilton expels a sigh of relief, but a large uproar rises from the crowd.

"We are cheated!"

"I paid twenty dollars for this?"

Even the Scottish tourists are disappointed, although just getting a glimpse of the infamous woman has fulfilled a dream.

The trial drags on, eating up columns of print and dwarfing such news as earthquakes in Venezuela and Columbia that kill 16,000, Mary Todd Lincoln's commitment to the Bellevue Place insane asylum by her sole surviving son Robert, and the first Kentucky Derby, won by the three-year-old chestnut Aristides.

The constant pummeling of her character in court begins to eat at Victoria and her health suffers. Continuing to be plagued with pleurisy, she cancels two weeks of lectures to rest. As Eunice Beecher testifies and stands by her man, Victoria sits up in bed and pens an editorial for the *Weekly*.

"My god, Sis, you should be sleeping," says Tennie as she pokes her head into the room. "How're ya ever gonna get better?"

"I must get this written." Victoria's words are halting as she struggles to breathe. She keeps her hand on her chest to hold back her coughs. "Will you read what I have so far? Tell me what you think?" Victoria leans back and closes her eyes as Tennie perches on the bed and reads.

"The eyes of the world are on Brooklyn and the infamous trial that drags on month after month. The exposures in court rattle our views about personal life and religious faith and reflect the metamorphosis of our opinions about marriage and divorce, intimacy and sexuality. The public's rapt focus on the salacious revelations is understandable. We all wrangle with the same passions and perplexities as do the actors in this drama, and the trial gives us something on which to hang our confusions and disappointments. It provides a bird's eye view of our anxieties about sex, power, race, wealth, guilt versus innocence, and villainy versus victimization. With our fears and foibles played out before us, we hope to find a safe route over the rocky road to our spiritual growth.

"This scandal is not the first of our era. The last decade alone has been rife with them. And like with the others, the newspapers' feeding frenzy draws upon and deepens Americans' infatuation with celebrity gossip as a means of feeling better about ourselves. It is somehow comforting to find that persons of stature are not blameless idols, but mere humans after all."

"It's not done yet, but what do you think?" Victoria asks, opening her eyes.

"I think no other paper cares about the significance of this thing. All they want is the dirt, which unfortunately will sell more papers."

"True, but we exposed the scandal for the betterment of society and we will continue on that course." The effort of speaking incites her coughing. She grabs her chest, choking out her words. "I feel like I'm being strangled, Tennie."

"Don't the preacher wish."

~ ~ ~

When Lib is not allowed to read a statement in court because she is a woman, Elizabeth Cady Stanton has had enough and grants an interview to the reporter who has been camped out on her doorstep.

"For nearly four years this nauseating secret has rotted and crawled beneath the surface of the hymn-singing, tear-shedding, sermon-shouting, smug religiosity that gave Brooklyn its proud title of the City of Churches," she tells him. "Now the velvet curtain has been stripped from the Gilded Age bourgeoisie, and a culture of tough-minded realism, free from illusions about human nature, has been erected. I will tell you all I know of this affair as told to me by Mr. Tilton himself."

Susan B. Anthony is furious when she hears Elizabeth has spoken and rushes to Tenafly to confront her. Elizabeth offers tea, which Susan spurns.

"I am on a schedule and not here to stay," Susan says. "But I had to deliver my opinion in person so you can know how you have hurt me. You and I have loved the Tiltons as our own family. To violate their confidences is treachery unparalleled. Nonetheless, if you insisted on doing it, you had no right to bring my name into it!"

"Offended Susan, pull my ears! I shall not attempt a defense. But the whole odium of this scandalum magnatum has been rolled cunningly over our suffrage movement. It is unjust, and we must not let the cause of woman, as innocent as Lib Tilton is innocent, go down in the smash."

"This trial is ending, and the cause of women will go on. But if our friendship is to continue, do not ever speak for me again!" She spins around and stalks away.

It is June by the time Beecher's team calls the last of their ninety-five witnesses and summations begin. Over several weeks, attorneys spout lofty eruditions designed to show off their forté with words. They quote Byron, Shakespeare, Carlyle, Saint Paul, Walt Whitman, and Jesus himself. They read portions of *The Scarlet Letter* and *Griffith Gaunt,* earning applause like actors on stage. The trial is a spectacular spectacle, lasting longer than any in history. Over one hundred witnesses utter more than two million words. But it is finally left in the hands of the jury, who are sequestered in the courthouse after having all food, clothing, and toilet articles inspected. Reporters climb on rooftops, trees, and lampposts and use field glasses and telescopes to watch the jurors take turns sleeping on a pair of old mattresses.

On the second day of deliberations, a summer heat wave hits the city, and several jury members faint. They are all moved to a cooler end of the courthouse, and reporters vie for new perches from which to watch every move. Sitting in trees and on window ledges, they see jury members, half-naked in the heat, sprawl across the tables and cast yet another ballot.

Victoria, meanwhile, interviews Samuel Clemens, better known by his pseudonym Mark Twain. Having heard Victoria is an avid and able billiards player, he suggests they talk over a game at Pfaff's Beer Cellar. She readily agrees, grinning at the raised eyebrows and sizzling whispers when they enter. Sam orders himself a whiskey and Victoria a red wine. He fires up his pipe and racks the balls.

"Before we begin, I'd like to acknowledge your incredible gift," Victoria tells Clemens. "My son's poor mind can't grasp much, but your jumping frog story has him jumping about like he's a frog himself. It is pure joy."

"Then let me return the admiration. I heard you speak in Hartford and was extremely impressed. Most women orators, and quite a few men, get their audiences wrought up and ready to explode with enthusiasm, but fail to spring the grand climax at the precious instant. You sprang at the precise moment for maximum effect."

"My goodness, I am honored by such praise."

"Of course I wouldn't want my wife Livy to hear you."

"Then I shall send her a personal invitation to my next lecture in your area," she teases. They both laugh and then Victoria gets down to business as she breaks and sinks a solid-colored ball. "I am focusing my reports of the trial on the calcification of social morals brought about by the opulence of our Gilded Age. And specifically how this set the stage for the fascination that has kept the Beecher-Tilton scandal page-one news for a year. I am in need of your unique insight."

"Do you mind a little history lesson to set my comments in context?"

"Not at all," Victoria says, taking her shot and missing.

"After the war between the States, reconstruction of our cities, industrialization of our economy, and rapid expansion to the West brought prosperity to America. It also created a society glittering on the surface but corrupt underneath. It seemed that those with money and a good name could get away with anything, rather like a thin plating of gold makes an object look like the real thing. Hence, when Charlie Warner and I wrote about the era, we dubbed it The Gilded Age." He sinks a ball and misses the next. "In any event, another offshoot of the time was the dream that every man had the potential to be a Cornelius Vanderbilt. The theory became that anyone who worked hard could become wealthy and those who did not were morally deficient."

"Ergo the worship of the almighty dollar."

"And ergo the excitement caused by exposing corrupt federal officials, morally bankrupt elite—and now, an amorous holy man—as no more moral than anyone else. When the gilding of a popular, respected man is tarnished, there is mass entertainment as well as mass trauma. Those educated by Mr. Beecher take it personally and care very deeply about the attacks against him. Others cheer at his downfall. Many more huddle by their hearths for solace. And this scandal is the worst of all because it invaded the home. When industrialization moved commerce out into the community, home became a sacred space to be preserved— romantic, idealized, where children and morality could flourish without the influence of rapid change. This affair shattered that sanctity."

"So it is not the struggle between two men and a woman that commands the attention," Victoria says, lining up her shot. "It is because the players represent a new kind of trinity. A spiritual ménage a trios, so to speak."

"That shot was as good as that comment!" Clemens says as Victoria sinks two balls with one stroke.

"I am afraid the main players of the drama don't even know the truth anymore, so long have they spent their energies engaging in lies to cover up deeds that now burn like acid over their tarnished reputations."

"Now there's some truth," Clemens complements. Victoria is winning, so he concentrates on the game as he tries to catch up. When his ball finds a pocket, he finally speaks. "I remember the first time I saw Henry preach. His pulpit pyrotechnics left me dazzled with an overwhelming impulse to applaud."

"Walt Whitman once told me he saw Beecher as a combination of St. Paul and P.T. Barnum," Victoria says.

"To Walt, that is undoubtedly a compliment," Clemens says with a chuckle. "The problem is, all his life two compelling, dynamic forces have seethed in the Reverend: his hunger for love and his hunger for power. Both were greater than any honor he might have had. When he became a slave to his own reputation, a group of wealthy men, loving truth and justice less and their own pockets more, stepped in to insulate him from assault."

"None of them have any more principles than a blue jay and will protect their leader though he be a religious mountebank, morale ulcer, and hypocrite!"

"Now tell me how you really feel." Clemen's eyes twinkle.

"I'm sorry to be so blunt. I understand this must be hard for you because of your relationship with the family and with Harriet and Isabella being your neighbors."

"I always have my cats."

"Oh, yes. I hear you have several."

"Abner, Motley, Freudian, Buffalo Bill, Soapy Sue, Cleveland, Pertinence, Famine, and Sour Mash. How many does that make? I should get more. They make better companions than most people I know."

"Perhaps I will get one as well," Victoria says, sinking the eight ball and winning the game. "In any event, now we wait for twelve men on a jury to make up our minds for us as to what kind of man Mr. Beecher is."

"They will hang themselves and not decide. They'll want to bring in a verdict for Beecher, but they won't be able to do it. He couldn't shake off the wild animals, but to give the decision to Tilton destroys their protection from the liberal religion they see taking us down a slippery slope to moral degradation."

"So we are judging between two devils," Victoria concludes. "With the woman, as usual, caught between and buffeted by both."

"Sometimes it's a pity Noah and his party didn't miss the boat, isn't it?"

On July 2, 1875, after a long, hot week with no resolution, the judge reconvenes court. Samuel Clemens prediction proves correct as the jury foreman reports that they are hopelessly deadlocked at nine-three in favor of Beecher. The courtroom explodes with both cheers and sobs. Clemens watches, puffing on his pipe, amused and sad at the same time.

"Once again the gold-plated article has passed for pure," he mutters.

When Victoria gets word of the verdict, she has an even more pointed comment.

"This horrendous non-verdict of the courts proves but one thing: Justice has not triumphed. It has risen and strangled us!"

Epilogue

Mark Twain said: "It is impossible for the historian, with even the best intentions, to control events or compel the persons of his narrative to act wisely or to be successful. It is easy to see how things might have been better managed: a little change here or there would have made a very different history."

And so it is with this story.

The Gilded Age, the era where reputation and celebrity forgave sins, protected Henry Ward Beecher from the consequences of his folly. Oh, his paper and publisher both went bankrupt, but Eunice stood by her man, as did his church. He continued in the pulpit until just prior to his death, arrogance intact, redeemed in his own eyes.

Theodore Tilton retired to Paris where he wrote bad poetry, pined for his family, and died alone.

Lib Tilton disappeared from the public attention until 1878, when she confessed in newspapers that Victoria's exposé was true. By then, no one cared.

As July 4, 1876 approached, the United States went into high gear for its hundredth birthday. The day of the Centennial dawned warm and sunny, and thousands came to celebrate at Independence Square in Philadelphia. After helping to organize and sponsor the event, the suffragists were banned from participating. So, following a public protest, they held their own celebration with Lucretia Mott, now eighty-four, presiding. With music by the popular Hutchinson Singers and speeches from the movement's luminaries, the women renewed their hope that the next Centennial would find them welcomed on the political stage.

Victoria, meanwhile, was again running for President as the Equal Rights Party candidate. Having permanently closed *Woodhull & Claflin's Weekly*, she didn't expect to win, but she campaigned to force candidates to speak out about the issues and to pave the way for future generations of women to have an equal opportunity to attain the highest office in our land.

Colonel Blood, in a desperate attempt to save his marriage, filed a libel suit against Dr. Treat, but it wasn't enough. In September of 1876, Victoria divorced him. Devastated, he drifted from a Coney Island sideshow to a carnival, and finally to the African gold fields where he succumbed to a fever. His love for Victoria never diminished, and his final words were of her: "The grandest woman in the world went back on me."

As 1876 drew to a close, Susan B. Anthony and Elizabeth Cady Stanton began writing the first volume of an exhaustive history of the woman's movement. When Elizabeth brought up Victoria's argument to Congress, Susan refused to include it or anything about Victoria. Because of this exclusion, many later historians never even knew about her.

Belva Lockwood, after becoming the first woman to argue before the Supreme Court in 1879, ran for President in 1884. Only Victoria, also a candidate, cheered her on. Ignored by the suffragists, both candidacies were forgotten by history.

In January of 1877, at the age of eighty-two, Cornelius Vanderbilt's time had come to an end. Tennie was not allowed to see him and mourned for weeks. The Commodore's estate was valued at over a hundred million dollars, five million more than the entire U.S. Treasury. Never known for his philanthropy, he surprised the nation by leaving a million dollars for the founding of Vanderbilt University in Nashville, Tennessee. Most of the remaining estate went to his son William, setting off a bitter legal battle among the heirs. William, to ensure his triumph in court, decided it was best to have Victoria and Tennie out of the country. So, in his death, the Commodore inadvertently became their benefactor once again. The sisters headed to England and a whole new life.

In London, Victoria quickly regained her health and continued her fight for women and equality. She married John Martin, a bearded, distinguished-looking gentleman, at thirty-seven three years her junior. He was an Oxford graduate, very athletic, and heir to Britain's oldest bank. He was madly in love with her, and she burst into tears when he proposed. At last she had found the protector she had always craved.

Tennie C. wed as well. Francis Cook, a man thirty years her senior, was tall, intelligent, and known for his philandering. As Great Britain's largest manufacturer and distributor of fabrics, he was also, as Tennie said, "richer than God." He moved Tennie into a palatial London home on the Thames River that featured his world-famous art collection and an equally impressive collection of ancient rings. A month after their wedding, Cook, who also owned a large estate in Portugal, was named Viscount de Montserrat by Portugal's king, and wild-child Tennie became Lady Cook, the Viscountess of Montserrat.

Unfortunately, Viscount Cook had no tolerance for Tennie's free-spirited ways, and when she refused to fight back, Victoria became so upset the sisters rarely saw each other for the next 15 years.

In 1886, a Sixteenth Amendment for woman's suffrage in the U.S. was defeated by a vote of 34-16. No other amendment was offered until after the turn of the century. Few of the original crusaders ever saw women cast a ballot. When Susan B. Anthony's NWSA and Lucy Stone's AWSA finally joined forces in 1890, they were a group of middle-class women who had lost the energy Victoria had brought to the movement. Most of the new members weren't even aware of her contribution.

No one in the organization even acknowledged Victoria's return to New York in 1892 to launch her fourth and final campaign to become President. Although she received the endorsement of the National Equal Rights Party, who selected Mary L. Stowe of California was her running mate, she wasn't surprised when incumbent Grover Cleveland, despite being saddled with a sexual scandal, won the election.

"To be perfectly frank, I am too many years ahead of this age," Victoria admitted to Ashley Cole and Johnnie Green over tea. "Still, I at least put some cracks in that giant glass ceiling erected above women."

In 1901, Tennie lost her husband and regained her childlike innocence and joy. She gave lavishly to charity, set up seven progressive elementary schools in Cintra, a small town in the Lisbon district of

Portugal, and sponsored a dozen novices at a convent in London. She tried to open a home for wayward girls, but the city voted it down, so she organized a free, traveling art show of Cook's extensive collection.

Victoria became a widow at age 58 when John Martin died of pneumonia way too young. She grieved for her "Johnnie" the rest of her life. In a eulogy at his funeral, Zulu Maud said that the Martins' marriage was a perfect union, marred only by persecution.

His death made Victoria the largest shareholder of Martin's bank and owner of his vast holdings. She took up residence at Norton Park, in its lovely, sixteenth century manor house. The pastoral estate was situated a little over 100 miles from London on the lower part of Bredon Hill, overlooking the Avon and Severn Rivers. Its 1100 acres contained dozens of villages. Demosthenes' prophecy had finally come true: She lived in a mansion in a city surrounded by ships and ruled her people.

And what a ruler she was.

She repaired cottages and improved village life by paving the roads and installing running water, electricity, telephones, and streetlights. She set up a post office and a library in each hamlet and turned an old tithe barn into a Village Hall where she threw elaborate parties for her "subjects."

She established avant-garde schools that stressed practical training and development of individual character. The schools taught art, cooking, sewing, carpentry, and gardening in addition to the standard studies. They also provided nature walks, hot meals, fresh fruit snacks, and bi-monthly visits from Victoria's personal physician.

She gave land to women and set up a residential college to teach them how to farm, and how to can and preserve their produce. Her love for flowers turned a small floral show into an annual fair, and her astute management of her lands brought accolades from peers and joy to her heart.

It was the advent of the automobile, however, that brought Victoria the most pleasure. She collected a stable of cars, and when she got too old to drive, she hired young chauffeurs and made them speed through the countryside with the top down, while she stood in the back seat, facing into the wind and shouting, 'Faster! Faster!'

After the turn of the century, Victoria was thrilled to see a brash young woman named Alice Paul arouse women's passion for suffrage once again. She cried over their struggle and persecution, and rejoiced when, on August 25, 1920, the Nineteenth Amendment finally gave U.S. women the vote. Eighty-two-year-old Victoria invited Tennie for a celebration, and with Zulu Maud and Byron, they laughed and danced and clapped until dawn. It was one of the last times the sisters saw each other.

Tennie died on January 18, 1923, at the age of 78. Not having a will, her inheritance from Cook went to Victoria, who overcame her grief by using the money to tirelessly improve the lives of others.

She earned the title of Lady Bountiful for her work in fostering relations between Great Britain and the United States. During World War I she turned her efforts to the Red Cross, raising money, providing material for clothes for the troops, sending food to hospitals, and entertaining the wounded.

Finally, on June 10, 1927, just months shy of her ninetieth birthday, Victoria Claflin Woodhull-Martin died in her sleep, sitting upright in her rocking chair. She left everything to Zulu Maud, who took care of Byron until his death of old age.

Victoria's only request was to be cremated and have her ashes strewn between her two very dear homes. So, sixty-six-year-old Zulu Maud and seventy-two-year-old Byron chartered a small plane and flew over the Atlantic, letting their mother's ashes float to the sea before turning to face the future without the brightest star they had ever known.

Prior to her death, Victoria tried several times to write an autobiography, believing, as Immanuel Kant did, that "you cannot understand a man's life by what he has accomplished but by what he has overcome accomplishing it." She had overcome great sorrow to become "full of love and rich with joy," but the telling of her story eluded her. The most she could ever put to paper was:

I am thinking, with all the bitterness of my woman's nature, how my life has been warped and twisted out of shape. But, I retain not one ill recollection. I gave America my youth. It was sweet and gallant and fruitful. Its memories are buoyant. The higher I reach for light, the more I am convinced that our greatest mission is to respond to our hungry heart's desire for truth. The outline of truth lies on the retina of our brain, and I feel assured that whatever the misrepresentations to which I may be subject, time will unravel all distortions and right all wrongs. Whoever I am, whatever I have done, belongs to the Spirits.—Mizpah

ABOUT THE AUTHOR

Karen Hicks is retired and lives in Henderson, Nevada. This is her second book. Her first book was a self-help book titled *The Tao of a Uncluttered Life*. Karen served as in-house editor for author Steve Allen and has written several screenplays, as well as poetry, short stories, and essays.